Bei

C000088946

The Loving Son

Ralph Alcock

Ralph

Published in 2011 by Paperbooks Publishing

First Edition

Chapter 1
A Son is Born

"That's it, just one more big push," exhorted the staff nurse, as Susan's contractions fought to expel the glistening baby into the bright lights of the delivery room. Gentle encouragement had given way to crisp commands and quick, knowing glances between the nurses. Forceps had been clamped to the baby's head. Susan could feel the cold of the metal arms as they brushed against her sweating thighs. She lifted her head off the pillow; she wanted to see herself giving birth. Her urge was to push but the sight of the forceps being manipulated by the nurse's strong forearms caused her to hold back, as if not wanting to release her baby to this crude instrument. She had a flashing image of her baby being torn in two as it battled with the mechanical manipulator.

She gave one huge, screaming push as she felt her perineum stretch, and then relief as the baby finally slithered into the world. Her baby dangled from the midwife's arms - wet, limp and blue - as a second nurse worked quickly to unwind the umbilical cord from the baby's neck. The midwife administered a smack, then a second, to the tiny rump. Susan looked quickly for any signs of concern from the nurses but her baby interrupted with a loud and prolonged shriek - the most wonderful sound she thought she'd ever heard.

She would never forget this date, the fifth of October, 1970. She lay back on the damp pillow, her

3

sweat-matted hair clinging to her neck and forehead, framing her pale English complexion. In the euphoria of the moment she almost forgot that she had just given birth – to a boy. She had a son!

A lonely, empty, feeling suddenly washed through her brain like a black tide. Gerald, her husband - there were times when she wished she'd never met him, and now he was the father of their child. Did she hate him? Perhaps, but now she had a child to consider. She had thought that her pregnancy would somehow change things, but how wrong she had been. It was as if he'd decided that ignoring her situation allowed him to dismiss the imminent arrival of their child! The very thought of his involvement in rearing her child caused her to gasp. She gritted her teeth, fighting back the urge to weep. The lump in her throat ached; she felt alone and vulnerable.

The piercing cry from her red-faced baby in the cot next to her bed startled her. Its needy plea erased any thoughts of Gerald. She soothed herself and her child as she lifted him to her breast, splashing his face with milk from her leaking nipple. She would call him William. He looked like a 'William'. The name seemed to suit him. *William*; she loved the sound of it. She began repeating it over and over. She was sure he reacted when she whispered his name – yes, he did it again.

She knew Gerald would have no objections to the name; this child might as well have been someone else's for all he seemed to care. He already had two children from his first marriage, and he had been less than enthusiastic about her pregnancy. It was Susan's first and would be her only child. She was thirty-five years old when William was born.

*

4

That seemed a long time ago, if you took the trouble to count the years. Even longer if you trawled back through the memories - the twists and turns that led to this. Today was William's nineteenth birthday.

Susan was led towards the visiting room by a prison guard, a large collection of keys dangling from his belt. The keys jangled as the guard unlocked the entrance gate into an antechamber fitted with heavy steel bars. It had two padlocked gates, one leading into the chamber from the corridor and a second leading out of the chamber and directly into the visiting room. Susan felt claustrophobic and had a momentary fear of becoming trapped in this cage-like cell. The guard struggled with the lock on the gate leading to the room, cursing loudly at its reluctance to open. She caught the musky whiff from his sweat-stained armpits. He belched, unapologetically, staining the air with a reflux from deep within his gurgling stomach and then turned to grin at Susan, as if pleased with his efforts. Susan stepped quickly through and into the visiting room, relieved to enter, despite its drab and unwelcoming appearance. It had smooth plain walls painted a dull green, no windows, and a second door on the opposite side of the room through which the prisoners would be led. Four prison guards were already in the room, chatting and laughing as if they were in a bar. Their demeanour changed as she entered and one of them nodded in the direction of one of the carefully spaced tables.

She sat waiting patiently at the heavy table to which she had been assigned. They had steel frames, painted grey, and thick wooden tops which had been repeatedly sanded and re-varnished in vain attempts to remove the graffiti and explicit artwork that tattooed the edges. Susan recoiled when her fingers inadvertently touched something sticky on the underside of the table. She had been told not to put her hands underneath the table and now she knew why. There were remnants of previous visits - wads of chewing gum and saliva-filled pouches of chewing tobacco attached like rows of limpets, some of whose shells had yet to harden.

There were fifteen prisoners on Death Row, including William. They were led into the room one by one in faded orange jumpsuits, each manacled to a prison guard who shepherded them to their respective tables and clipped the manacle to an eyelet on the side of the table frame before releasing the other end from their own wrist. They all appeared mean and frightening to Susan, as if they'd been irredeemably scarred. Most looked manic: wide-eyed, twisted smirks, poisoned lives. Scum left after the holy water had drained from the font. Some walked with a swagger as if displaying their bravado. Most shuffled in, uninterested in life. A couple stared hard at Susan, looking as if they'd rape her if given half a chance. William looked completely out of place in this collection of hardened criminals and violent psychopaths. All killers - killers of men, women and children - children just like poor William, poor defenceless William. In her eyes, he was still a child. He'd never really grown up – not since...

She stopped herself from going any further. It was another painful memory. She hid her hands as if wanting to reveal as little of herself as possible and concentrated on looking only at the door through which William would come. She glanced again at the prisoners in the room – these were the men who were William's neighbours in the lonely line of cells that constituted Death Row. He had been at the prison for just a few days and it was her first visit, but it felt as if

William had been here for much longer. Time seemed stretched, moving slowly and inevitably to a fateful end. William would not be permitted the normal luxury of being allowed to experiment with the time available in a usual life. His 'time', such as it was, would from now on be for others to control. He was a 'lifer', someone with no life at all. She shuddered at the thought. But it was barely a week since the jury had been unanimous in finding him guilty and the judge had inflicted the harshest possible penalty – the death penalty. How many times would she be making these visits? How long could he survive in this jail?

The door hinges creaked again, signalling the arrival of the last of the prisoners. Susan recoiled at the sight of the biggest and ugliest of the collection. He filled the doorway and stood for several seconds, surveying the scene. There was a hush as he moved forward. The guards and the other prisoners moved slightly back and lowered their gaze in deference to the entrance of this big man. This was Louis Allain and William had been placed in the next cell. Shuffling slowly and hesitantly forward in Louis' wake was William, clad in bright new orange overalls, steel manacles dangling on his thin wrists. He crept into the room, his eyes fixed firmly on the floor, not daring to look at anyone, not even her. He finally looked up when he reached her table. His pale blue eyes suddenly flashed as if they'd caught a ray of morning sunshine splicing through the kitchen window blinds. This was a rare treat. William had always found it difficult to look directly at people. He glanced at two of the other prisoners at nearby tables who hadn't received any visitors and had taken to staring menacingly at Susan and William. His eyes suddenly lost their intense lustre and he retreated, as he often did, behind their opaque, empty gaze. He looked again at her, as she willed him to blinker himself against the other inmates. His eyes were still dull. *Why me?* she thought, staring intently at his face. *It's me, William, your mother.*

At first he didn't say a word. He just sat staring, staring past her at the wall. His cheeks quivered and he was obviously biting into his lower lip. She reached towards him and he gave a tiny smile when she quickly touched his hand.

"Hello, Ma ... nice of you ..." It was as much as she'd hoped for.

"No touching!" shouted one of the guards. The reprimand made William shudder.

*

Driving home, she felt gnawingly empty knowing that William was an inmate on Death Row. Images of him flashed into her head, disturbing images: William as a toddler screaming for attention, William facing a furious Gerald, a sullen teenager slamming doors as he stormed into his room. Then other images. William tugging contentedly at her breast; William playful and happy, splashing in the waves on the shoreline; William playing the piano; William giving one of his rare warm smiles; and William in an orange suit, chained to a prison guard.

Susan was startled by the blaring horn of an oncoming car. She swerved hard, and instinctively stamped on the brake, slinging her car back onto her side of the road and into a waltzing spin that flung gravel high into the air as her car came to a screeching halt on the hard shoulder. Susan gasped and felt the blood drain from her face. She slumped forward, her head resting on the wheel, and wept, uncontrollably.

Chapter 2
Invitation

Susan Buckley was a Professor of Political History at the State University of Ohio. Her small features had become sharper and more pinched with age and she wore her dark hair cut short in a pageboy style, which gave her a pixie-like appearance. Her high cheek bones stretched her pale skin, making it appear taut and delicate set against her thick black hair. It was only when she had been pregnant that her face had assumed the soft fleshy look of her youth. She had become a little round-shouldered, as if her frame had given up the fight after years of sagging over a desk. She could still become rigid and straight-backed when required – it usually signalled that her infamous temper was about to boil over.

Her husband, Gerald Martin, was an Associate Professor of Education at the same institution. Susan had kept her maiden name. Gerald wasn't bothered, but she didn't want to be a 'Martin' - it sounded like a frightened bird, and Susan Buckley was no frightened bird. She was also proud of her Irish heritage and her name gave her a tangible link with family roots. Gerald had filled out considerably in recent years. The rangy, gaunt look of his youth had gone. His face was now large and plump and a paunch hung from his frame, obscuring his belt buckle. He liked to wear an old and well-worn tweed jacket that hung limply from his shoulders. It was patched at the elbows, frayed around the misshapen pockets, and the lining was sagged and torn. Susan had given up urging him to get a new one. He seemed to take perverse pride in looking scruffy, as if it conveyed the image of someone clever and too engrossed in being intellectual to bother with his appearance.

Gerald was six years older than Susan and it was clear that he was unlikely now to rise above the rank of associate professor. It had created a difficult situation, since Susan had risen quickly through the ranks and was now a full professor. Gerald blamed his Dean of School, Professor Roberts. His disdain for the Dean had initially bothered Susan, but she'd given up trying to discuss the matter. Gerald had decided the Dean had it in for him and nothing was going to persuade him otherwise.

Dean John Roberts had little time for Gerald. His appointment, an appointment he had personally sanctioned - even pursued - had been disappointing from the start. He had encouraged Gerald to come from England on the expectation that it might lead to collaborative international work to raise the reputation of the School and, more importantly, Professor Roberts' own standing and prestige. In Professor Roberts' view, and the view of many of his colleagues, Gerald had failed to deliver. His lectures were criticised by students, fellow staff complained that he didn't teach to the syllabus, and worst of all, as far as the Dean was concerned, he failed to make any international contacts of note. It had also come to his attention that Gerald was known to revel in criticising and mocking his position as Dean to other staff members.

10

*

Susan and Gerald met at Manchester University when he was a junior lecturer in educational philosophy, and she was completing her doctorate. She had a feeling of unease even before they married. She'd felt pressured; Gerald wanted them to take up academic posts in the USA and even in the sixties marriage was still the expected option for a long-term relationship. It was just pre-wedding nerves, she told herself.

"It's normal," her mother had said. "I had no idea what I was letting myself into when I married your father."

That's what concerned Susan. What was she getting herself into? Gerald had recently been through an acrimonious divorce and her relationship with a post-doc had ended abruptly. He'd simply sent her a note saying he needed to move on – not even a chance to meet up. She felt as if she'd been punched in the stomach. It hurt. It was a conspiracy of fate. Gerald appeared confident and commanding and she'd loved the way he pursued her: leaving messages, sending lines of poetry, meeting her for lunch, buying theatre tickets, taking her for dinner and arranging to meet in the bar. She was also attracted by his almost child-like enthusiasm. He was petulant and demanding but Susan found this appealing, as if it confirmed Gerald's affections for her.

But there were things about him that had given her whiffs of concern. He could be cynical and arrogant. He was often unreasonably dogmatic and she began to get annoyed at his frequent and repetitive outbursts. If he wasn't mocking, even deriding, his students and colleagues, he was complaining bitterly about the failure of his work to be recognised. He wanted it all. Praise from his colleagues, admiration from his

11

students and even adulation from her. She'd chosen to ignore her anxieties. They were just facets of his character. *We all have quirks,* she told herself. *He'll change, I know he will.*

How naive she had been.

*

Gerald was ecstatic to learn that he'd been asked to give a keynote paper to a conference at Ohio State University. His head of department, Professor Willoughby, had originally been asked but at the last minute had to cancel. He'd recommended Gerald.

"Susan," he shouted as he flung open their front door. "I've been asked to give a keynote address at the University of Ohio!"

"Where?" replied Susan, as if she'd never heard of the place.

"The University of Ohio," he replied, breathless with enthusiasm.

The conference, organised by the American Education Association, was to be held at Ohio State University at their main campus in Columbus. The title they'd suggested was *'Planning for Education – An Art or a Science?'* Gerald had submitted an article critical of educational planning to the *Times Educational Supplement.* The title, *'Education - A Thinking Man's Philosophy',* was as cynical as the content of his article. To his surprise, it was published in full, including the title. It caused a storm. Education correspondents from the major newspapers praised him for his forthright views and the *Times Education Supplement* wanted him to submit more articles.

Gerald had been delighted with the response, which he felt was no more than was deserved. He couldn't understand Professor Willoughby's annoyance that Gerald hadn't informed him prior to submitting the article. Professor Willoughby had to field a number of questions from the press and was embarrassed that he hadn't seen a copy of the article, let alone sanctioned its release.

"It was typical of Gerald," he told a colleague. "Very bright, but it's always on his terms."

*

The audience of academics listened intently to Gerald as he delivered his address in his clipped, slightly aristocratic, English accent; something he had cultivated for effect. His speech received sustained applause. The Dean was quick to offer his congratulations and invited him to share a table over lunch.

"Gerald, let me again thank you for coming all this way to the conference. It was an excellent keynote speech."

"Thank you Dean, I found it thoroughly enjoyable, even inspiring." Dean John Roberts had a deep gravelly voice, the type that is associated with the life of a serious smoker. His tar-coated larynx produced a tone that was deep and resonant, like that of an actor. His nicotine stained fingers twitched intermittently as if missing their customary cigarette. He wore an expensive looking grey suit which hung neatly on his tall lean frame. Gerald noticed that the Dean occasionally raised his yellowed fingers to his lips, discreetly sniffing the remnants of nicotine etched into his skin and exhaling, as if pushing out the last whiffs of cigarette smoke from his lungs.

Dean Roberts enjoyed the authority and prestige that went with his position. He had a reputation for being a conservative at a time when liberal ideals were very much in vogue. His views were much appreciated by politicians and the elders of the State. As a

13

consequence, he had a wide circle of friends and what he liked to refer to as 'friendly associates'. They were members of the State Legislature, State senators, members of the University's Board of Regents, and local politicians. Although he was well known and well liked by the politicians, this was not a view shared by the senior staff at the University. They were wary of his political connections and begrudged his influence with State leaders. The University President was an old fashioned academic who was no match for the articulate, urbane and well-connected Dean Roberts. It was a commonly held view that members of the University's Board of Regents consulted first with Dean Roberts before making any decisions about the future of the University. It was also the commonly held view that his School got far more favourable allocations than any of the other academic centres.

The leaders of the University were frustrated by his political nous and envious of his suave style. There were, however, divided opinions within the School's faculty. Many of the staff felt intimidated by his abrupt and sometimes impatient way of exercising authority. Others in the School were in awe of his skills in securing the best funding and resources. Those in his favour were particularly well rewarded. It was a system that produced envy in some and intense loyalty in others. Overall, there was a palpable frisson among the staff that gave the Dean a sense of raw power. He had the skill of being able to spot those who might be of benefit. He was also forthright, blunt and rude to those he felt were no longer being effective in enhancing the School's reputation. He viewed Gerald as someone who might improve the School's international reputation, something he felt was lacking.

14

It soon became obvious to Gerald that the Dean had another agenda on his mind. After probing him with questions on his views on teaching, on educational philosophy and on educational research, he got round to the main purpose of asking him to lunch.

"Look Gerald, I like what you said in your speech this morning and I have thoroughly enjoyed our discussions over lunch." He paused and blew delicately over his fingers. "I'd like to offer you a position on the faculty. We have a vacancy which we are currently trying to fill and I'd like to put your name forward. What about it?"

"It's a fantastic opportunity," replied Gerald. "I'd be a fool not to consider it, at least."

"Tell me about your other commitments - your family, for example." It was an area the Dean explored at length.

"I'll expect a reply by the end of the week," said the Dean, finally, as he rose from his chair. He slapped Gerald on the back, more as a gesture to encourage him to remain where he was. "Finish your coffee, and enjoy the rest of the conference." Dean Roberts felt pleased with himself. He liked to vet all appointments if at all possible. And he enjoyed leaving with more than just a hint of his status.

*

"What you really mean is, you want to take up the offer," said Susan.

"I suppose I do," replied Gerald. "I'm stuck in a rut here and I'm not getting any younger – I doubt if I'll get many opportunities as good as this. It's a decent salary, lower cost of living, and a prestigious institution."

"Sounds like your mind's made up," replied Susan. "What about us? Is this it? Do we simply say farewell

15

or had you some sort of distant arrangement in mind? But I suspect you've not given 'us' any consideration." There was a hint of resignation in Susan's voice.

Gerald beamed. "Don't look so pleased about it," said Susan, crossly.

"Well, it so happens that the Dean asked about family arrangements. I told him about you. I said we were married – I don't know why – I felt a bit pressured."

"I'm flattered – I think," replied Susan. "Although I suspect you thought midwestern conservatism might not like the idea of a divorced man having a younger partner – they might see it as *living in sin*."

"Something like that did flash through my mind, I admit. But it wouldn't be a bad idea, would it?"

"Do I take it you are proposing we get married? A marriage of convenience? It's not what I had in mind and I certainly have no intention of playing the dutiful wife for the benefit of your Dean."

"Ah, but there's more," answered Gerald with a sly grin. "The Dean made enquiries about a post in the Department of History. They have a vacancy for a research associate – something to do with the influence of the Irish diaspora on political thinking in the US. There'd be some teaching as well. Right up your street." Gerald fumbled in his briefcase. "Look, I've got a copy of the position." Susan scanned the job description, and then gave it a careful read. She gave a gasp.

"What is it?" asked Gerald, fearing a fierce rejection.

"The project leader. It's Professor McGrath."

"Is that important?"

"Just that he's one of the top academics in his field. I can hardly believe it! This would be an amazing opportunity." Susan turned to look directly at Gerald. "Gerald...is this serious?"

"Well yes, the Dean thinks you'd be a very strong candidate. He's a pal - a 'buddy' - of the Dean of the School of History and Political Science."

Chapter 3
Columbus, Ohio

The house they rented was in an older suburb of Columbus about six miles from the campus. The street was lined with large elms whose summer leaves twitched in the wind, creating dappled pinholes of colour. In the fall, leaves gathered on the lawn in a crisp carpet of rich autumnal colours; and in the winter months, the denuded trees were the colour of charcoal, their dark, twisted silhouettes standing starkly against the snow covered pavements. Susan enjoyed the winter. The streets were blanketed in glistening snow and ice, the windows were glazed with frost, and the light from the early morning sun glittered on the powdery snow. Even when the old wooden house they had rented was buffeted by winter storms and the draughty sash windows shook in their frames, and snow blew across the porch and crept under the front door, Susan was unperturbed; secure in the knowledge that this old house with its groaning timbers had weathered many severe storms in the past.

Susan was delighted at the position she had secured. Although initially concerned that her appointment had been orchestrated, she was flattered by the enthusiastic welcome given by the Dean of History and Political Science, Professor Steve Mullins. She was assigned to a project with one of the senior members of the Faculty; a foppish silver haired professor with bright blue eyes and a lined face that creased easily as he spoke. She had referenced a number of Dr Mark McGrath's papers on Irish history in her dissertation and now found herself working under his guidance. It was this opportunity, as much as anything else, that had encouraged her to come to Ohio State University.

Dr McGrath was impressed by his newest member of the team. She was bright, quick to learn, and had a sound grasp of the subject. She had an instinct for research and an ability to interpret the dialectic elements of an issue that he found particularly impressive. He enjoyed watching her. She moved quickly as if hurrying to get some thought down on paper. She held her head high with her eyes fixed on something distant, something virtual; isolating herself from anything that might be a distraction from what she was intent on doing. She reminded him of his late wife, Mary. Her full bottom flexed rhythmically as she walked and her neat breasts, slightly smaller than those of Mary's, he reckoned, jutted forward, shaping her taut thin sweater.

Gerald, however, was soon complaining to Susan about Dean Roberts' reluctance to give him a more serious academic role. Roberts had expected an almost immediate benefit in securing Gerald's appointment. He had, after all, gone to considerable trouble to get Gerald and to persuade Steve Mullins to offer Susan a post. He was annoyed that Gerald seemed incapable of using his obvious intellect to the School's benefit. He had been a major disappointment. Professor Roberts had quickly grown tired of the comments from the other Deans and from the University President in particular.

19

"How's that English fella, Gerald Martin, doing? It's about time he produced something of note," commented the President. He liked to rub it in whenever he could. "I didn't think you, Dean Roberts, of all people, would make such an error of judgement."

Dean Roberts found himself in an impossible position. He couldn't admit that his appointment of Gerald had been an absolute disaster, but he couldn't ignore his poor performance either. And then there was Steve Mullins, Dean of the School of History and Political Science. Professor Mullins took great delight in making a show of thanking Roberts, especially when they all met with the University President at their weekly briefing.

"Whatever you may think of Gerald Martin, his wife, Susan Buckley, is a real gem. Prof. McGrath can't speak more highly of her. The old dog nearly salivates every time we discuss her work, and it's not just her work he's drooling over. She's just received a research grant funded by the Irish American Society – one of many to come, reckons McGrath. Then there's her publication record. Two refereed articles this year."

"Okay, I'm pleased she's been a hit – I just wish she'd persuade her husband to be as effective," commented Dean Roberts.

"Thing is," interjected the President, "I've been discussing this with Steve and I agree with him. We've got to do everything we can to keep her here – she's already seen as one of our top academics and she's attracting a lot of interest from other universities..."

"And ...?" interjected Roberts.

The President smiled – he was enjoying this. "Unless you can persuade her to divorce her husband – which I think would be a little unethical, even for you, Dean Roberts - I need you to hang on to your appointment, so please, don't upset the apple cart. You look after Gerald Martin and both Steve Mullins and I will be extremely grateful. Of course it wouldn't help your image ... your reputation, if Gerald Martin had to leave with the University's star in tow."

John Roberts was furious. The University President and the other Deans, Steve Mullins in particular, were enjoying this. He'd make damn sure that Gerald Martin wouldn't advance any further under his administration. He decided that if Gerald had to remain as a member of his faculty, he'd be shoved in with one of the teaching departments and be stripped of any responsibility for international work. He wanted Gerald as far away from his table as was practically possible. He'd instruct one of his department heads to give the news to Gerald under the label of 'restructuring'.

It was Professor Steele who was given the task of informing him. Professor Steele did most of the dirty work on Dean Roberts' behalf – and conveying this 'news' to Gerald was something he would relish. Professor Steele had complained frequently to Dean Roberts in recent weeks about difficulties he was having with Gerald.

"The Dean has taken the decision, very reluctantly, to reassign you to a teaching role. He would have liked to have continued supporting your work on international projects; however, given the funding cuts announced by the Board of Regents, he feels he has no other option. He knows you will find this disappointing but he has asked me to assure you that you have a valuable role to play in the School."

Gerald was genuinely shocked. He knew, of course, that he hadn't quite lived up to the Dean's expectations, or his own, for that matter. But this – it was something he hadn't anticipated. Professor Steele delivered his

21

message and then abruptly left. Gerald had been too shocked to respond.

He tried to get an appointment to see Professor Roberts. The Dean's PA, Lillian Gustafson, was a formidable woman. She wore rimmed glasses with frames matching the colour of her hair - big hair - that was brushed and lacquered into a bouffant style that never seemed to change no matter what the season or time of day. She had sharp angular features and her jaw was square and masculine. Lillian was a lover of authority. She worked for Dean Roberts 'and nobody else', as she was fond of repeating to the other women in her circle. Many were in awe of Lillian – they admired her efficiency and her unquestioning loyalty, and her bigotry. It made more than a few of them smile when she held forth about blacks, Jews, Native Americans and the unemployed, groups she lumped together as if they were similar in almost every respect. They were happy to hide their own bigotry behind that of Lillian's. Others loathed her for her crass views, her blatant ignorance and her intolerance. Most were wary of her. She was renowned for her caustic remarks, her unbending loyalties, her loathing of those who had offended her in some way – and they never quite knew when, or if, they might have given offence. She bent her head forward ever so slightly and looked at Gerald over her rimmed glasses as he entered her office.

"Yes, Professor Martin, how can I help?"

"I'd like an appointment to see Dean Roberts," replied Gerald in as firm a tone as he could muster. Lillian seemed to be prepared for Gerald's request.

"I'm afraid he's very busy this week and is likely to be for some time. I'll have a look in his calendar." She feigned a scrutiny of her desk diary, flipping over the weekly pages with a swipe of her well-manicured forefinger. "He won't have any time this month. I suggest you write to him, or better still, talk to Professor Steele - he has regular meetings with the Dean."

"I bet he does," replied Gerald, making no pretence at hiding his annoyance. Lillian didn't rise to the bait; she just ignored him as if she hadn't heard his remark.

"Will that be all, Professor Martin?" Gerald felt his face redden in anger and embarrassment. He grabbed at the door handle, his sweaty hand slipping on the knob, and tugged violently to open the door. He bounced off the door frame and into the hallway, leaving the office door swinging on its hinges as he scurried off to his own office, muttering and cursing to himself. He glared at a couple of colleagues coming in the opposite direction and nudged into one of them in his haste. They turned to watch him disappear through the fire-doors at the end of the corridor.

"Looks a bit upset," one commented, "Must have had an encounter with Lillian." The other gave a nervous laugh, hoping that Lillian hadn't overheard them.

Gerald rounded on Susan as soon as she entered through the front door.

"Do you know what that bastard Roberts has done? He's taken me off international projects." Gerald threw his briefcase across the room in vexation.

Susan paused for a moment. She was trying to remain calm. "Don't take it out on me. This is between you and Professor Roberts. If you were honest with yourself, Gerald, you'd admit that things haven't gone as planned – no international conferences, no international projects..."

"Oh – thanks! Nothing like a bit of support from my loyal wife!"

23

"Gerald, calm down. I'm only trying to look at this from both sides – I want to help, but it's impossible if you won't be realistic about what's gone on."

*

Dean Steve Mullins knocked on Susan's office door just as she was about to sort a pile of papers that had gathered on her desk. "Dean Mullins, come in. I must apologise for the mess, I've been editing a paper this week – I have a deadline and..." Steve Mullins held up his hand.

"It shows how busy you are – you should see mine, paper everywhere." Susan knew this wasn't true. Dean Mullins was renowned for being exceptionally well organised. It always appeared to Susan to be sterile and unloved. She needed a romance with her office; a workbook to scribble on, reminders pinned on the wall, bunches of pens visible from the half-open right hand drawer, a stapler where she could grab it, relevant papers and research notes spread out for her to flick through. Dean Mullins, on the other hand, took pride in only having a clean yellow pad and three pens neatly arranged on a glass tray that appeared designed for the purpose and a wooden in-tray that contained a minimum of pending items.

"I'd like to have a word about your work."

"Oh," gasped Susan, not knowing what to expect.

Steve Mullins gave a broad smile. "It's nothing to worry about – quite the opposite. I want to let you know that we are extremely impressed with your work. Professor McGrath regards you as an indispensible member of his team." Susan blushed, not knowing if she was expected to reply.

Dean Mullins continued: "We want you to know just how much we value your contributions. We are very keen to keep you at this University. I want you to

24

know that I'm putting your name forward for the Research Prize. It carries a stipend of $10,000, and your photograph will hang on the honours wall in the library." Dean Mullins paused; he wanted to gauge Susan's reaction.

"I'm flabbergasted! I'm extremely grateful for giving me the opportunity to work with Professor McGrath and for your very kind words. It is nice to know my work doesn't go unnoticed!" added Susan.

The Dean laughed. "Quite the contrary - your contribution to the reputation of this School and to the University is recognised at very senior levels." He hesitated for a moment. "There is one more thing I need to discuss with you."

"Oh," replied Susan, looking slightly disconcerted.

"Your husband, Gerald..." Susan tilted her head and thrust out her pointed chin in a defiant manner.

"What about Gerald?"

"Well, as you know, things haven't gone too well for him and his relationship with Dean Roberts has become - how can I put it - strained."

"It's no secret. Gerald is upset about the role he's been assigned and, quite frankly, I don't blame him."

Dean Mullins gave a rueful smile. "Dean Roberts does have his concerns about Gerald's work, but he is willing to give further consideration to Gerald's position."

"That's quite a turn around," replied Susan. "Does Gerald know anything about this?"

"No, not as yet," replied the Dean. "I was keen to have a conversation with you about your invaluable work, before Dean Roberts made any suggestion to Gerald about a new role – back in international projects."

"I'm sure Gerald will be thrilled," replied Susan. "Wait a minute...what you're really saying is that if I continue working at the University, then Gerald's position will be looked at more favourably?"

Steve Mullins paused. "You could make that interpretation. Let me put it bluntly; we are very keen for you to continue your work at the University. We are concerned that Gerald might look elsewhere for a position, and that would result in you feeling obligated to leave with him."

"Possibly," replied Susan, immediately wishing she hadn't added this remark.

Dean Mullins continued. "I just want you to know how important you are to the University and if that means providing Gerald with a more important role, it's something we are willing to do."

"And Professor Roberts is willing to go along with this?" asked Susan.

"Let's just say that Dean Roberts has seen the value of enhancing the reputation of the University – and if that means a role for Gerald, it's something he's willing to support."

"Very magnanimous of him," commented Susan.

*

Gerald bounded through the door like a schoolboy who'd just received a prize from the Head.

"You'll never guess what happened today," he gushed. "That greasy slimeball Steele called me into his office. He wants me to work on international projects again! I'll be reporting to him – but at least I'll be back on projects. That's what I enjoy, that's what I'm good at. That's why I came here in the first place. Apparently Roberts decided this was a priority area and, despite the cutbacks, he wanted to support this important work. I can't say that Steele looked particularly enthused about

26

me reporting to him. He'll just have to do his best, I suppose." Gerald could hardly contain his enthusiasm. It was almost childlike, as if his tantrum had been assuaged by a gift he'd always wanted. Susan felt suddenly nauseous, partly at Gerald's juvenile response and partly because she felt complicit in the deception that had been perpetrated.

"That's wonderful, Gerald. You must be pleased." Gerald grunted an acknowledgement, as if he felt Susan was stating the obvious. "Of course I am," he added quickly, having caught Susan's chiding glare.

Chapter 4
William

It was a year later when Susan suspected she was pregnant. The testing kit she got from the pharmacy gave a positive result, as did her doctor. She couldn't quite believe it, despite the evidence and the obvious symptoms. There was her age - she was 35 years old - and then there was her relationship with Gerald. But part of her was delighted. She felt she'd been cheated of some fundamental experience by not having a child. It was a feeling that had grown in intensity as she approached an age when pregnancy was less likely, and on occasions she had felt a despairing resignation that she would remain childless.

She waited for a couple of weeks before telling Gerald.

"You – pregnant! It's not as if we've been trying." Susan burst into tears.

"Is that all you can say! Good God, Gerald, you are going to be a father. Can't you think of anything nice to say?"

"Sorry," mumbled Gerald. "It's such a shock, that's all. You know I didn't want to have any kids..."

"Perhaps you should have thought about that every time you sulked because we hadn't had sex for a while!"

28

"I thought you'd have been more careful," retorted Gerald.

"Oh, it's my fault, is it? What do you want me to do, have an abortion?"

"No, of course not. I'm sorry Susan, it's just the shock ... I'm sure I'll get used to it."

"Used to it! What do you think I'm having, a bloody alien?"

Gerald cowered under the onslaught. "Look, Susan, if you're happy to have a baby, then I'm sure we'll work it out – we'll do our best..." Susan headed for the bedroom, slammed the door, and flung herself on the bed.

*

Gerald collected Susan and William from the hospital a week after the birth. It had alarmed her that William had been kept in an incubator for the first two days. The young doctor, who'd been called in by the delivery nurse, said it was just a precaution.

"It was a difficult birth," he said. "I think it best that we watch him closely for a couple of days – nothing to worry about."

Susan fretted. In her mind, 'nothing to worry about' meant there was everything to worry about. She couldn't sleep and kept peering into William's little glass chamber, looking for anything that might be unusual. She watched his little chest as it rose ever so slightly as he slept. It was hypnotic and comforting. But every little twitch and spasm caused her alarm. The nurse assured her this was normal. "All babies do it - they're just dreaming." Susan wondered what an earth babies would dream about.

The next morning, the senior paediatrician, a gruff man with a distant manner, peered in at William. He pulled and prodded at his tiny arms and legs in a way that caused Susan to gasp.

"I'm just checking his reflexes." He clipped his stethoscope to his ears, warmed the end and pushed it up and down on William's tiny chest. "He's perfectly fine – a strong little fella. You can both go home tomorrow." Susan felt an overwhelming sense of relief.

Gerald arrived to collect them carrying a bouquet of flowers. It was so unlike Gerald, that Susan was overcome with emotion. Her lower lip trembled in a way she hadn't experienced since she was in puberty. Gerald looked dismayed. "I thought you'd be pleased..."

Before she could reply, he turned abruptly and peered in at the cot. "Is he alright now?" he asked.

"He's perfect!" replied Susan. "We've both been given a clean bill of health. I can't wait to get home. I've packed everything and we're ready to go. I'll carry William." With that she scooped up William and headed for the exit, leaving Gerald to collect Susan's clothes, her toiletries, the baby's items and the carry cot. He left the bouquet of flowers on the bed.

*

William wasn't an easy baby. He always seemed restless as if expecting something that Susan couldn't provide. He wouldn't suckle from her breast, preferring milk powder formula through an artificial teat. He wriggled furiously whenever Gerald picked him up, often howling loudly until Susan comforted him. But it was his head movement that gave her the most concern. He wouldn't look directly at her for more than a few seconds before stretching his neck to look over her shoulder. At first, Susan thought he was attracted by the light from the window or from the table lamp but she realised that more often than not he was simply looking away, staring at objects, inanimate objects that didn't offer any warmth or carry inflections that looked for his attention.

Susan agonised about any decision to return to work. William was at his worst when she attempted to leave him with anyone else. A neighbour had offered to help out so Susan could go shopping, but it was obvious William had given her a difficult time. Gerald was hopeless. William appeared to shriek the loudest for Gerald's benefit - so much so, that he told Susan it was impossible for him to be left alone with 'that child'. Susan became depressed. She had visions of being forced to look after William for the rest of his childhood, unable to leave him and certainly unable to contemplate returning to work. Worst of all, she felt guilty. Guilty at despairing for her sanity, guilty at wishing William would leave her alone, guilty at feeling William had intruded on her career and, alarmingly, guilty for not loving William unreservedly. It was Gerald who persuaded her to put an advert in the local paper.

"What have you got to lose? If there is someone who's willing to look after William, then you can think about returning to work. God knows we could use the money."

"It's not about money, Gerald," retorted Susan angrily. "It's about William!"

"And it's about you," replied Gerald softly. "You can't go on like this. You need to find some way of getting out and about."

"I know, I know. But I can't bear the thought of William screaming all day waiting for me to return."

"Well, give it go, anyway."

*

31

Three days after Susan's advert in the local paper was published, Mrs. Miller phoned. "I saw your ad in the paper – wanting a nanny?"

"Oh, yes," replied Susan, surprised by the call. She'd almost given up hope of anyone responding. Mrs. Miller explained that she had three children of her own. They were all in their twenties and the last one, Alec, had recently left home to go to college. "I love kids, especially babies so this seemed right up my street. Would you like me to come over to your house – it's on Jefferson Avenue, isn't it?"

"Yes, number five," replied Susan. "Can you come tomorrow morning, about ten?"

It had been a difficult morning. William had refused the bottle of milk formula she had prepared and continued a loud and demanding wail, leaving her feeling inadequate and useless. He'd wriggled so much when she changed his diaper that most of the contents had spilled onto the floor, and he'd cried almost incessantly since she'd attempted to get him to sleep in his cot. Mrs. Miller arrived to a scene of abandoned toys, the smell of dirty diapers, scatterings of baby biscuits, a crying child and a distraught mother.

She was a strong-looking woman, with a large frame which was exaggerated by the small brown handbag that dangled from her arm. She wore a chocolate-brown dress with short sleeves that stretched over her plump upper arms. She had dark permed hair that was beginning to grey at the edges and a round face that was bright and shiny. Mrs. Miller stood and waited on the porch, as if aware that Susan was making her first assessment.

"Mrs. Miller?" asked Susan. Mrs. Miller peered over Susan's shoulders as she entered the door. "Brings back memories," she said, with a smile that signalled understanding.

"Come in, please," said Susan, rather redundantly. "I'm sorry about the mess..."

Mrs. Miller gave another of her broad, warm smiles. "There's nothing for you to apologise about," she said, moving over to William's cot and peering in.

"May I ...?" She gestured to pick up William. Susan stood back, allowing Mrs. Miller to scoop up William effortlessly in her large plump hands. She popped him against her shoulder, rubbed his back and smiled again as William let out a loud burp and dribbled sick on her shoulder.

"He's been a bit sick, sorry about..." Susan stopped. William was no longer crying. He looked content and almost serene, with his head resting quietly on Mrs. Miller's damp shoulder. She gently carried him back to the cot, placed one of her large hands over his eyes, and slowly withdrew her caress as William's breathing slowed.

"That's amazing!" whispered Susan, handing a paper towel to Mrs. Miller.

"Let's leave him to sleep," said Mrs. Miller. "How about a cup of coffee in the kitchen?"

*

Susan could hardly wait to tell Gerald.

"She's incredible..."

"This Mrs. Miller?"

"Yes. William was shrieking in his cot and she just picked him up, got his wind up with a couple of back rubs – he was sick down her shoulder – and popped him in his cot, soothed him with her hand and within minutes, he was fast asleep."

"What did she do, cast a few spells?" replied Gerald, continuing to read his newspaper.

33

"Gerald, be serious. This woman is remarkable. She brought three references as well. They all said much the same thing – couldn't praise her enough – a marvel with babies and young children. One said she wouldn't have gone back to work had it not been for Mrs. Miller."

"Sounds familiar," retorted Gerald. "Does this mean you'll be going back to the University?"

"Yes, I think so. I'll need to give it a try first – see if it works out with William."

Mrs. Miller was every bit as capable as she'd first appeared. Indeed, William seemed much more content in her company than he'd ever been for Susan. She felt a touch envious.

Why can't I cope as well as Mrs. Miller? she thought, but Susan scolded herself. This was not the time to feel jealous. Everyone seemed pleased at her return to work. Dean Mullins was pleased to see his much-prized academic back at her desk, as enthusiastic as ever, and as for Professor McGrath, he was just pleased to see her. He'd resisted the urge to visit her when she was on maternity leave. Instead, he'd sent a steady supply of handwritten cards with snippets of news, mainly about the School of History and Political Science. Gerald was also pleased that she was now able to return to work. He regarded it as having some sense of normality returned to their disrupted household. Mrs. Miller became a permanent fixture; the constant that gave Susan the opportunity to enjoy her work and her child.

*

From a very early age, William loved to organise his toys. He would arrange his building bricks in neat rows, smashing at them in frustration if he couldn't get them lined up exactly as he wished. Later, it was his toy cars.

They had to be arranged in pairs, and always the same cars in each pair. Gerald took some interest in this stage of William's development.

"It's just the sort of thing I did when I was a child," he told Susan. "I can remember being obsessed with getting my toy cars in the right order..."

"The 'right order'?" teased Susan.

"Well, it was important that they should be arranged properly," replied Gerald, defensively. "And that's what William tries to do. I admire him for that."

"Well, that's something, at least!" Susan replied.

William was an attractive child; tall for his age with hazy blue eyes, like sea mist, which gave him a faraway look that Susan found endearing. His fair hair was thick and spiky, like Gerald's, but he had her pale porcelain-like complexion. He had big hands that were delicate-looking, with long thin fingers and shiny pink nails. But he was restless, just like he'd been as a baby. He was rarely quiet, rarely still and seemed to have difficulty concentrating, except when there was music playing and when he was engrossed in organising his cars and other toys. He was then in a world of his own, isolating himself from the others, especially Gerald, who'd given up being interested in William's obsessions. William had taken to swiping his neatly arranged lines of toy cars across the room as soon as Gerald made any attempt to get involved.

"Gerald, leave his things alone," implored Susan, exasperated at her husband's insistence on rearranging William's layout.

"But he hasn't got it quite right, there are two cars not lined up..."

"Gerald, for God's sake – they are his toys. Stop interfering, let him play and arrange them how he likes. I'll get you a set if it bothers you that much!"

35

*

Mrs. Miller's relationship with William was special from the start. When he heard her voice he would turn to look in her direction, waiting for her to pick him up in those large, comforting arms, and hug him to her breast. Susan looked forward to Mrs. Miller's punctual arrival before she set off to work, despite her initial jealousy about the bond developing between them. It was obvious that William thought the world of Mrs. Miller. He trotted after her, clutching his toy cars and holding them out to show her, as if looking for her approval.

Mrs. Miller liked to listen to classical music and it quickly became apparent that William also loved music. This was no surprise to Mrs. Miller. "I've never known a child who doesn't like music," she told Susan. She said it was soothing, both for her and for William. Gerald, however, claimed he needed peace and quiet and was determined to exercise his authority over William. He flicked off the music as soon as he walked in, which invariably caused William to shriek in protest, as if he was being denied something he craved.

"That bloody kid," Gerald would mutter under his breath. "How on earth can I be expected to concentrate with him wailing like that?"

"He was fine before you came in," was Susan's retort. Gerald would grab his newspaper and hide his head behind the pages, erecting a wall between himself, his wife and William.

Susan was delighted when Mrs. Miller first told her that William had begun to look directly at her.

"Not all the time – but he has begun to turn his head towards me when I call his name." She gave one of her conspiratorial smiles. Susan knew what she meant. William shared his world with only them. He ignored

Gerald. *Maybe we all exclude Gerald in some way,* thought Susan.

When William was five, his behaviour changed. He became aggressive and hyperactive, especially when he was bored with arranging his toys. He took to running from room to room, careering into the sofa, and bouncing off the furniture like a pinball in a bagatelle machine. When he became tired of crashing around the house, he would bang his head on the floor in a rhythmical intensity that caused the normally unflappable Mrs. Miller to become quite concerned. Susan tried to talk to Gerald about it, but he dismissed it as 'typical boy behaviour'. He tried to reassure her that it would pass. Susan wasn't so sure.

His kindergarten school teacher told Susan he was disruptive in class, so much so that other parents had complained. The one thing that calmed him down was music, especially classical music, and the piano in particular. His behaviour did become more normal after a few months, although he still had the occasional outburst. He was at his worst in shops and supermarkets and would run up and down the aisles, shouting at the top of his voice, knocking into people, trolleys and carefully-stacked shelves. Susan dreaded these excursions and avoided taking him into shops whenever possible.

William moved from the nursery to the primary school the following September. It was a day that Susan would never forget. There were tears and tantrums before they set off in Susan's Oldsmobile, and he clung to her in the school corridor like a limpet. And, like a limpet, she had to prize him from her coat – no amount of encouragement was going to persuade William to let go. The teacher led William away, grasping him firmly by the arm.

"He'll be fine when you've gone," the teacher tried to reassure her. "Won't you, William?" He let out another piercing scream, bit the teacher's hand and rushed back to Susan, locking his strong fingers around the folds of her coat. Feeling embarrassed and inadequate, and resisting an impulsive urge to simply lift William in her arms and take him away from this place and these people that were causing him so much grief, Susan coaxed William into the classroom, eased his fingers from her coat and quickly left him in the room, not daring to look back. Tears streamed down her cheeks as she rushed to her car, fumbled with her keys and climbed quickly into the driver's seat.

Susan drove to collect him at four in the afternoon. She'd found it difficult to do any work. Her mind was on William and the feeling of abject failure that had engulfed her ever since she arrived back in the house after dropping William off at his school. It was obvious he'd been crying. His face was smeared wet where he'd repeatedly wiped his hand and arms across his red cheeks.

Mrs. Miller was pragmatic. "He gets frightened when his routine isn't the same and when he has to meet new people. It's as if his mind is in overload and he can't cope. Why don't you give yourself a break – let me take him in for the rest of the week."

"I'm not sure how that would help," replied Susan, defensively.

"He's been used to you going off to work after I've arrived. Suddenly it's all changed. You're leaving him with someone else – and I think that it's been too difficult for him to cope. He'll need a bit of time to get used to the new routine – and you could collect him," she added quickly, seeing Susan struggling with any suggestion that she needed someone else to tell her how to look after her own child. Susan stared at her hands; they were trembling.

"I suppose it's worth a try..." she said.

A year or so later, his behaviour took another dramatic turn. He became quiet and withdrawn, almost sullen, especially with Gerald. At first, Susan was pleased. His behaviour had improved and was much more predictable, but there was something – still something - not quite right.

Susan dreaded William's move to middle school. She'd heard the reports about bullying and was concerned that he would be a target, especially if he was perceived as being 'different'. The first week was dreadful.

"I hate that place. I'm not going to school!" William told her on the third day. His new lunch box was scuffed on all sides. "They took it off me and kicked it round the yard – said it was for football."

"Who's 'they'?" Susan asked, hoping somehow that he would accept her support. "Can't say," replied William. His head turned away from her. "They punched me in the stomach. They said they'd hit me harder if I told." Susan pulled William towards her and hugged him hard. He squirmed in her arms and struggled to be freed. Susan's tongue went dry, her throat ached and tears welled in her eyes.

"Oh, William ..." she said, trying to hug him again. He pulled away and let out a big sigh, as if resigned to his plight. Perhaps Gerald was right, she thought. Maybe William has just got to find a way of coping. "I'm afraid that's life!" Gerald had remarked.

To Susan's surprise, a week later, William came home from school swinging his bag as if he hadn't a care in the world. He even smiled at her as he came through the front door.

39

"Hi, William, how was school?" It was the same question she'd asked every day. But instead of the sullen look and inarticulate response she'd come to expect, William gushed enthusiastically about his day.

"It was brilliant," he replied, beaming in a way Susan had rarely encountered. She was taken aback.

"William, that's wonderful. What was it that was so brilliant?" she asked.

"Music - we had music today." Susan had been pleased to learn that the school provided some alternatives for those preferring not to join the sports clubs on Wednesday afternoons.

"That's the music group..."

"Yeah ... it was great. We got to try out some instruments. Mr. Waite..."

"He's the music teacher?" added Susan, suddenly enthused at what she was hearing.

"Yeah," replied William, in a tone suggesting he was annoyed at her interruption.

"Sorry," Susan replied, quickly. "Go on, please."

"There are ten of us in the class. Mr. Waite said we were all special because we all like music. We listened to lots of different music. Then we got to try out instruments and say which ones we liked – which ones we'd love to be able to play. I liked the piano. I didn't try any of the other instruments, just the piano. Mr. Waite showed me how to hold my hands and play three chords – that's when you push some keys down at the same time. I played them over and over. At the end of the lesson, Mr. Waite said I was a natural. He got me to demonstrate to the rest of the class – and do you know what? They all clapped, including Mr. Waite." Susan was staggered. She had never seen William so animated. She had never seen him so enthused. She'd never known him talk so lucidly about anything. She felt a lump gather in her throat.

"That's wonderful, William!" Her words felt inadequate and tears rolled down her cheeks. "It's...wonderful!"

About three weeks later, Mr. Waite called Susan.

"It's about William," he said. Susan had a sudden dread of what might come next. "He's got a real gift." A feeling of utter relief swept through her. "I think he could be very good at the piano. He's mastered some rudimentary chords very quickly and he's got a great sense of timing. If it's alright with you, I'd like to arrange for him to have a few piano lessons over the next month or so, just to see how he gets on."

"That would be wonderful, Mr. Waite. William is loving his music class. He talks of little else. It's the highlight of his week." Susan was delighted. The last few weeks had seen William grow in confidence. He'd even found a couple of friends in the music group. "I can't thank you enough for what you've done for William, Mr. Waite. He's been a different boy since he started your class. I'm so grateful."

"He's a pleasure to have in the class," replied Mr. Waite. It was the first time Susan had heard any of his teachers express such a positive opinion of William. She had become used to his teachers telling her of his disruptive behaviour, his lack of concentration and his poor social skills. "I could arrange for him to have a lesson from Mrs. Fisher - Angela Fisher. It would have to be after school, a Wednesday or a Thursday," continued Mr. Waite.

"Angela Fisher - isn't she the wife of the police sergeant...?"

Mr. Waite interjected, as if reading her mind, "Yes, but don't let his reputation put you off. He'll have nothing to do with the piano lessons – Angela always arranges to have them when her husband is on duty. She's an accomplished pianist and a gifted teacher. I wouldn't suggest her if I didn't think she'd be right for William."

"But her husband - he's got such a reputation..."

"He's a brute," added Mr. Waite. "But believe me, Angela Fisher is different - she's something special. She was in my music class about ten years ago and went on to study music at college. She got a full scholarship. I thought she was destined for a career as a pianist. But then she married Jake Fisher. She'd known him at high school. He was a thug then. Angela's sensitive – a bit like William. She'll be just right for him; I know she will. And besides, I recommend William gives it a try for a month. We'll know by then if it's working. I'll keep a close eye, just to make sure he's making the progress I'd expect."

"I'd love to see William make a go of this," replied Susan. "I think I'm just a bit scared that he won't be able to cope."

"I've seen a lot of kids in my time and believe me; William has the potential to be very good. It's not just a fascination with the piano; it's as if he's developing a relationship with it. It's a talent that I think should be nurtured." Mr. Waite made it perfectly clear that he was in no doubt that William would benefit from these lessons. Susan tingled with excitement. Mr. Waite had agreed to discuss it with William before he came home. She knew that William would listen to Mr. Waite's proposal. Mr. Waite had achieved an almost God-like status in William's mind.

She heard William's steps on the porch just before he flung open the door. An excited, breathless, William bounced into the room. She knew, before he spoke, that he was delighted at Mr. Waite's suggestion. "Mum, Mr. Waite - he wants me to go to piano lessons!" Susan felt giddy with pride. Perhaps William felt it to. He beamed at his mother.

Chapter 5
William's Lessons

"William, will you stop playing that bloody piano, it's giving me a headache!" Gerald boomed, as he tried to raise his voice over the loud fortissimo style that William adopted for nearly all his music pieces. William appeared not to hear him and continued his monotonous practice with an exaggerated and deliberate striking of the keys. He'd been having piano lessons for over ten months and his development was exceeding even Mr. Waite's positive assessment. Susan had bought a second-hand piano for him after the first trial month. Mr. Waite had helpfully found a Yamaha that he said would be ideal.

Gerald shouted again, louder this time. "William, please stop that infernal din. You've been playing that piece for over half-an-hour!" William stopped abruptly, slammed the lid down and sat staring at his hands resting on the curved and polished veneer. Susan rushed in from the kitchen and saw the look of subjugation on William's face.

"Gerald, what an earth is your problem! You should be delighted for him. William has found something he really enjoys, something he's really good at!" She glared at Gerald.

"Good for him!" he retorted staring back at her as if raising the ante. "What about me? I've got this report to write, in case you've forgotten."

44

William sat impassively on the piano stool, his fingers tapping the lid on imaginary piano keys. Susan glanced briefly at her son. She hissed at Gerald, her words sending projectiles of venomous spit in Gerald's direction.

"Gerald, don't you dare! You selfish, childish bastard!"

She caught Gerald's eye glancing over her shoulder. William had crept towards the hallway and was quietly closing the door. She felt a shudder course through her body. Gerald tried to make light of the incident.

"Susan, I didn't mean to upset him. I just wanted him to know that there are others in the house. We need to toughen him up. How's he going to cope if he can't give and take a bit?"

"And that's your way of doing it? I suppose you think you're helping him! Look Gerald, Angela is delighted with his progress. It's been nearly a year since he started going to piano lessons with her, and he's never yet missed a lesson. It was the best thing we ever did for William – I'm so grateful to Mr. Waite, and Angela. They've made such a difference to William. Even you, Gerald, have to admit that. You know he loves his music; adores it, in fact."

"Adores her, you mean. He blushes every time we mention her name."

"That's only because you started teasing him about her, telling him to watch out, and those remarks about her being attractive – *every boy's dream*, you said. That's not helpful, Gerald. You may think it's funny but it will only upset William – and the last thing I want is for him to give up his music." Gerald couldn't resist a further comment. It was if he was jealous of William's success, jealous that his son's star might be brighter than his.

45

"Twice a week, and over an hour at each session - seems a bit excessive to me. His other school work will suffer. But do you know what also concerns me?"

"Tell me, Gerald, what is it that's really bothering you?"

"It's little Miss Angela. She's from the wrong side of the tracks – grew up in that trailer park, the one near Lincoln Street, the one with those dilapidated trailers. And from what I hear from some of the staff at the University, she was a right little bombshell – had quite a reputation."

"I can't believe I'm hearing this!" replied Susan. "These music lessons have been the best thing. He's even putting more effort into his school work - you'd know if you took the time to look."

"I've hardly got time to do my own work without having to supervise William as well."

Susan threw up her hands. "And I don't have time for you, Gerald! Quite why I'm still in this awful marriage I don't know. If it wasn't for the fact that I feel William needs a father, I'd have walked out long ago. And what's laughable is that he doesn't have a father - not in the real sense."

*

William's transition to high school was a lot easier than she had feared. William had grown in confidence, and his reputation as a gifted pianist gave him an elevated status. He could play anything – from boogie to classical, from jazz to rock-and-roll. He started giving impromptu performances with some encouragement from other students who'd heard him play.

"Go on, William; give us a Jerry Lee Lewis." William took delight in pleasing the crowd. He was becoming a focus of attention, especially with the girls.

There were jealousies, especially from the jocks, but the admiration of others, the girls in particular, gave him a kind of protection – at least in school. But he'd begun to acquire a few 'friends' who used him. With their encouragement, almost insistence, the impromptu performances grew a bit wilder, with rock-and-roll performances in the hall on several lunch breaks. The sessions eventually descended into chaos as the numbers swelled and some of the hard jocks took it as an opportunity to do some damage, smashing chairs and heaping tables into the corners.

The Head took a very dim view. The jocks blamed William, but several girls spoke in his defence, and Mr. Waite intervened. Fortunately for William, he also took music at the high school and the Head was loath to cross swords with Mr. Waite. His skills in putting on concerts were legendary, and as for the marching band - he had transformed them into a team of performers with their complex criss-crossing manoeuvres, stick twirling drummers and a resonant chorus of woodwind instruments that blended with a gusto that brought the football crowd to its feet at the halftime displays, no matter what the score was. People started to come to the games just to see the marching band, people who had absolutely no interest in football. At first the coach had been delighted at the increased attendances, but now he wasn't so sure.

*

"Mum, it's Billy and Josh," shouted William to Susan, who was upstairs sorting out some papers for Monday's meeting with her research team. "They want me to go with them to the mall – that okay?"

Susan was caught off guard. She wasn't too keen on either of them. Josh had been in trouble for shoplifting and Billy, who was all charm and guile, seemed to be at the back of most acts of petty vandalism in the area. Before she had time to marshal her thoughts, she heard Gerald's voice from the living room.

"That's fine, William. Be back before six – and don't do anything too foolish," he added light-heartedly, waving at Billy and Josh through the window onto the porch. Josh sneered at Gerald before he had time to discontinue his wave.

"Thanks," called William, as he rushed out to join them.

Susan rushed downstairs just as the door closed. "Gerald, I'm not too happy with William tagging along with those two. They're much too streetwise for him."

"Nonsense," replied Gerald. "It'll do him good. He needs to get involved with others besides those very serious friends of his."

"The music group, you mean? I much prefer him to be with them. Billy and Josh are always in some sort of trouble. That Billy in particular – he's the ringleader."

"You've been listening to too many of the gossips," interjected Gerald. "They're both on the football team, aren't they? Billy's a bit of a star from what I hear."

"Oh, I suppose that makes them alright then!" replied Susan, her voice rising in frustration.

"They're just high spirited – no different from most boisterous teenagers. He'll enjoy being with them. It'll boost his confidence. I never thought I'd see the day when two of the stars from the football team would call round for William. I think it's great."

"I wish I could share your enthusiasm, Gerald. I hope he's okay."

*

Susan answered the knock at the door. It was nearly seven and she was beginning to fret that William wasn't home yet. Her heart thumped in her chest when

48

she saw the two uniformed police officers standing on the porch.

"Is it William?" she blurted, her eyes wide as if straining to absorb any signal, any hint that could warn her of what was to come.

"William's okay," replied the police officer who'd rapped on the door. The other officer was standing a few paces away, one foot on the porch the other on the steps, nonchalant, as if he was too bored to bother. "He's down at the station." Susan stood, transfixed, waiting for the officer to provide her with all his information. He seemed to take some perverse delight in having her stand looking upset and uncomfortable.

Gerald saw the police car parked in their driveway from the bedroom window. He bounded down the stairs, still fastening the shirt he'd been changing in to. He thrust his head past Susan's as if taking over from her.

"What is it officer, what's happened?"

"It's your son, William; he's been arrested for shoplifting at the mall." Susan let out a gasp.

"But he went with two others, Josh and Billy," said Gerald. "They're at his school - they're on the football team, for Christ's sake!"

Susan found her voice: "I don't see what being on the football team has to do with it, but I'm sure they were involved somehow," she offered, wanting the police officer to confirm her suspicions.

"Billy Mansell and Josh Divine you mean?"

"Yes," replied Susan. "I couldn't remember their surnames."

"Nice boys they are," stated the police officer, sending a tremor through Susan. "Good footballers too." *Oh, fuck you*, thought Susan straining to stop herself from screaming at the officer. "They spotted

49

William helping himself to tapes in the Music Store," continued the officer.

"But they were with him," Susan explained, incredulously.

"Yes," replied the officer. "But they left him in the store when he said he wanted a few minutes more. They waited outside and then saw him pushing tapes into his jacket."

"I don't believe this," said Gerald, as forcefully as he dared. "What tapes did he steal?"

"There were six, all heavy metal stuff ..."

"But that's not music he likes," insisted Susan. "I bet it's the type of stuff Billy and Josh like, though."

"Careful what you're saying," replied the police officer, suddenly looking very threatening. "I wouldn't want any false accusations." His buddy moved forward as if to reinforce the point.

William was released into their custody. He'd been charged with theft and would have to attend the court offices the following Monday. Gerald and Susan went down to the holding cells at the police station to collect William, accompanied by the two officers. Gerald took it as an opportunity to berate the two officers who'd arrested William and protest his son's innocence. Susan was pleased with Gerald. He'd insisted it was all a big misunderstanding and that Billy and Josh must either have been mistaken, or must have been involved themselves. "After all, they were the ones who've been in trouble before," he'd argued. The deputy didn't like Gerald's insinuations.

"I don't like your tone, and I don't like your funny accent. If you'll take my advice, you'll put your foot down with that son of yours. We don't like hoodlums on our patch."

"Hoodlum – who the hell are you calling a hoodlum!" shrieked Gerald. For once Susan felt proud of Gerald. He was creating quite a fuss. She wasn't sure how this would help William, but it was a venting of anger that she shared. She gave Gerald a nod of appreciation. Then Sheriff Jake Fisher appeared, striding along the corridor towards them, hitching up his belt as he did so.

"I can hear this racket from my office!" he boomed. "If you raise your voice to one of my officers again I'll have you on a charge for disturbing the peace!" he shouted, looking directly at Gerald.

Susan nudged Gerald when they saw William being brought towards them. It seemed to take an eternity for him to be released. His belongings were tipped from a plastic bag onto a table. William was asked to state that these were his, confirm that nothing was missing, and then sign his release forms. Gerald had to sign a document agreeing to accompany him to court the following Monday.

William didn't say a word as they drove back to their house. Once inside, Susan tried to hug him, but he pulled away.

"Look, William," said Gerald, as if he was defending William in the court, "we know you didn't steal those tapes – and we also know that Billy and Josh are the ones the police should be talking to. We just want you to know that you have our full support."

"Yes," added Susan, in a considerably softer tone, "we love you and we know that you would never be involved in shoplifting. You've been set up by people you thought were your friends. It's a hard lesson, but you have to realise that not everyone is an honest as you are." William fidgeted with his hands and stared out of the window. He looked pale and frightened.

51

Susan tried to move towards him, but he took a step towards the window. She felt powerless and impotent, incapable of helping her son, incapable of absorbing any of his pain. William was now staring at his shoes.

"I did it," he mumbled, so softly that Susan barely heard him. She hoped it wasn't what she thought he said.

"Sorry William - did you say that you did it?" she asked. Gerald looked at William as if his entire defence strategy had suddenly been undermined.

"I did it," said William in a louder voice. "I stole those tapes." Susan glanced at Gerald. He looked ready to blow.

"You did what!" exclaimed Gerald. Susan jumped in before Gerald had chance to berate William any further.

"William, please be sure you are not mistaken," she said, hoping ... "Are you absolutely sure you were the one who stole the tapes – no one else?"

"Billy said they wanted some tapes – they'd shown them to me in the Music Store. I said I'd get them. Billy said it would be easy – especially for me, because I was always in there, looking at music."

"But why, William?" asked Susan. "You've never been in trouble before..."

"Not been caught, you mean," interrupted Gerald. Susan gave him one of her icy glares. William twisted his hands as if wringing out a wet rag.

"I took four tapes and stuffed them into my jacket. Then I went outside to give them to Billy and Josh. They were waiting for me by the coke machine. The manager must have seen me. He ran towards me, shouting. I just stood there, I couldn't move. My legs were like jelly. A police officer arrived. He must have heard the shouting. I saw him talking to Billy and Josh, they were pointing at me. Then the police officer asked me if I'd stolen some tapes." He took a deep breath. "I said I had. I told them I took the tapes," stammered William.

"And did you, William? Is that true?" asked Susan.

"Yes, but only because Billy said I had to. He put handcuffs on me and we waited until another police officer came. Everyone was looking at me. Then they took me to their patrol car." Gerald had heard enough. He stormed out of the room, slamming the kitchen door. Susan slipped her arm around William's shoulder. This time he didn't move away. He stood, impassively, letting her hug him as if it was a punishment he had to endure. Susan started to cry. She mumbled to William that she needed a tissue and ran upstairs to the bathroom. In her haste, she knocked the box of tissues behind the toilet bowl. As she reached down to retrieve them, she heard Gerald storm into the front room. He was shouting at William.

"How could you? How could you disgrace me like this! I'll be a laughing stock – they'll be sniggering behind my back – why couldn't I have a normal son, someone with the guts to stand up to shits like Billy Mansell and fucking Josh Devine? They're scum – and you are no better!"

Susan hurtled out of the bathroom and down the stairs. She flung the door open just as Gerald hit William across the face with the flat of his hand. The room snapped with the sound of the smack. It sent William backwards and he half stumbled, before sinking to his knees. He looked up at Susan like a frightened animal. He sprang up and shouted at Gerald.

"I'm sorry – isn't that enough for you? I'm sorry!" He slipped out of the room, leaving Susan and Gerald to flounder in the dense silence.

53

Sensing an opportunity – a fissure in the gloom that engulfed them - Gerald tried to speak. "I'm sorry Susan, I . . ."

"Don't you *dare* try and apologise. I'll never accept any apology for what you've just done! Never! What on earth were you trying to do – teach him a lesson? You're as big a brute as Josh Divine and Billy Mansell. Worse - they're kids; you're an adult, a father!"

Susan slammed the door, intent on comforting William and protecting him from Gerald. Gerald sank onto one of the chairs at the dining table and buried his head in his hands. "Oh, God," he muttered to himself. Images of losing control flitted into his mind. *William deserved it*, he told himself. But a part of him rejected the argument. A part of him was stricken with sick grief that twisted his stomach into a tight aching knot, squeezing bile into his throat. He grabbed his handkerchief and retched – a cold, dry retch that rubbed like a coarse, scratching file.

*

Susan ignored Gerald as much as she could over the next few days. She made it perfectly clear that she wanted as little to do with him as possible. She moved into the spare bedroom, which she also began to use as an office instead of the table in the living room. William hid away in corners of the house. He rehearsed pieces at the piano over and over again as if this also provided sanctuary from the tension in the home. They ate what meals they shared in complete silence. Gerald was doing as much as he could – as much as he dared – to demonstrate his remorse. Susan had expected Gerald to flee in a fit of pique. Instead, he tried to ingratiate himself by doing domestic chores. He washed dishes, laid the table at meal times, washed the kitchen floor, vacuumed all the carpets and cleaned all the windows –

things that Gerald had done only at Susan's insistence. Susan would never forgive Gerald, but she couldn't help but feel a tinge of sadness for Gerald's inability to support William rather than react so aggressively. She'd been pleased at the way Gerald had argued so strongly with the police officers – but perhaps that was for his own pride rather than for William. She also knew William would need Gerald's support in court. This was not the time to appear to be a fractured family; she would deal with Gerald in her own good time.

The following morning, she persuaded William to have breakfast at the table with them and allowed Gerald to utter a stumbling attempt at reconciliation.

"I can't undo what I've done, but I'll do whatever I can to make it up to you both - I promise," he said, slowly and quietly. He paused, searching for something else appropriate to say. Susan interjected before it became unbearably tense for all of them.

"Gerald, all I need is for you to support William in court, nothing more. I'll speak to Mr. Waite, and perhaps he'll agree to be a character witness."

"Good idea," added Gerald. "Perhaps I could ..." He stopped when Susan glared at him.

William left the table as soon as he could and went up to his room. Susan relaxed a little when she heard music coming from his tape player; it gave the suggestion of life returning to some degree of normality. Only the bruise on William's cheek gave any indication to the outside world of what had occurred.

*

Gerald spoke well in the courtroom the following Monday. The judge for the Franklin County Juvenile Court nodded as Gerald spoke up for his son.

55

"William's never been in trouble, not at school, and certainly not with the police. He's a sensitive boy and can be easily led. He's making no attempt to hide from what has happened – he admits the theft – and although he won't say so, we feel he was coerced into this by others."

"Have you any evidence of this?" asked the Juvenile Court judge.

"No, nothing that would pinpoint those we suspect."

"Then I must insist that you don't attempt to assign blame to anyone other than William."

"No, we wouldn't want to do that either," replied Gerald.

"I'm glad to hear it," said the judge. "We've heard from the police, from the store manager and from William, who admits stealing the tapes. Is there anything else that I should take into consideration?"

"Just to say that Susan and I are naturally very disappointed at what has happened and having talked to William, we know that he is deeply ashamed at what he did. We would also like you to hear from two people who are prepared to act as character witnesses."

". . . and they are Mr. Waite, the school's music teacher, and Mrs. Fisher, who provides piano lessons for William?" said the judge.

"That's correct, Sir," replied Gerald.

Both Mr. Waite and Angela Fisher testified how surprised they had been to learn of William's arrest. Mr. Waite reinforced Gerald's comments about William's sensitive nature and both Mr. Waite and Angela pointed out just how engrossed in music William was. They had been shocked to hear of his being accused of theft from the Music Store – 'so out of character,' they both insisted. They also stated they felt William could have a career as a musician. Angela

56

Fisher informed the judge that William was a gifted pianist - the best she'd ever encountered. The police officers who'd given evidence sat, staring at Angela, as she delivered her statement. She only faltered when she turned briefly in their direction and saw their eyes fixed on her.

The judge asked William to stand.

"William, you've freely admitted stealing music tapes from the Music Store and you are therefore guilty of the crime with which you are charged. I have listened to the statements given by your father, and by your character witnesses, Mr. Waite and Mrs. Fisher, and I am persuaded that this is not something you have done in the past, nor is it likely you will engage in such crimes in the future. I have therefore decided to issue you with a caution and to place you on three-month probation. You are free to leave this court, but you must contact the probation officer before the end of this week. I would also suggest you thank your father, Mr. Waite and Mrs. Fisher for speaking so persuasively on your behalf. I don't expect to see you in my courtroom ever again, William. But if I do, I won't be so lenient."

The judge then banged his gavel and left the courtroom.

Chapter 6
Angela Fisher

Angela Fisher's father now looked a frail old man. He lived in the nursing home, just a few miles from Angela's house. He was only in his early sixties but could easily have been mistaken for a man nearer eighty. He'd been a smoker since he was twelve and proudly boasted on many occasions that he was a 'sixty-a-day' man. He was now racked with emphysema and crippled and bent with arthritis. His skin looked like thin brittle parchment, yellowed and stained by layers of nicotine and blotched with large, dark-brown age spots. It was hard to imagine that he'd once been a large, skulking, brawling, hell-raiser who liked to hone his vicious skills on his wife and daughter. He still had the meanness in his eyes, but his vicious temper had been blunted and dulled. Only his large hands, ironically tattooed with letters spelling 'L.O.V.E' across his knuckles, gave any indication of his former self. Angela rarely went to see him. It was only a sense of duty that compelled her to make the occasional visit. And Angela's mother, who lived in a small apartment on the edge of the town, had never been to the nursing home – never visited her husband. She'd often wished he was dead, and now, in a sense, he was.

*

Angela married Jake a few months after finishing her degree. She hadn't been able to get a job, despite her excellent grades. She'd found herself back in the trailer living with her battle-weary mother and her menacing father. She hated the trailer park, with its shanty-like stamp of poverty. She hated their trailer in particular: the orange crate that propped up the rotten steps, the dull white cladding that was warped and stained brown where pieces of broken guttering hung limply from the eaves, and the old car tyres that had been fixed round the bottom rim of the trailer, each holding a stagnant pool of rain water that became a breeding ground for flies and mosquitoes in the hot summer months. The living room interior had a rust-coloured shag carpet stained by remnants of two permanently swollen ashtrays that sat on a coffee table in front of a large free-standing TV. A gas heater was fixed to the wall and a white Formica table stood next to the opening that led to a small kitchenette, which had a gas cooker, and a gas-fired water heater fixed above a sink unit. A garbage bin stood at the far end of the kitchenette. Its lid had been discarded so that Angela's father could pitch his spent beer cans from his chair in front of the TV.

In winter, the trailer filled with lingering smells from cooked food, cigarette smoke, spilt beer and the faintly intoxicating noxious fumes from the gas appliances. The bathroom had a shower cubicle with a small corner sink, and a toilet with a broken wooden seat. The door to the bathroom didn't have a lock and the door catch was unreliable. Her father often walked in when he heard her in the shower, mumbling an apology but remaining there until she screamed at him to get out. Two adjacent bedrooms were separated by a thin partition. She heard him talking loudly at her

59

mother, occasionally shouting and uttering a string of expletives. She could almost feel her mother's quiet acquiescence. This was a woman who had learnt when to be silent and submissive. Her mother had felt his anger and his violence and Angela had seen him weep with remorse at her mother's bruises, asking for her forgiveness and getting angry again if she hesitated. Worst of all was the creaking of the bed when he forced her mother to have sex. She hated her father. She was depressingly ashamed of her inability to face up to him, and she was disturbingly numb to the plight of her mother. Why didn't her mother leave him?

"Where would I go?" was her mother's stock reply whenever Angela raised the subject.

She had to get away from this.

*

Despite being rather plain and round-faced in her early teens, her progression through puberty resulted in a shapely figure and an attractive face framed by her mop of thick black hair. Her long legs, that once appeared too long for her body, were now a considerable asset giving her a grace of movement that complimented her quiet demeanour. Angela hadn't realised how attractive she had become and was, at first, flattered by the attentions of Jake Fisher in her last year of high school. When she went to university, she tried to put her old life behind her, and that included people like Jake Fisher.

She soon had admirers at college and a boyfriend who was also studying music. But he dropped her when he found out where she grew up. "I don't want to be seen with trailer-court trash," he'd said. She then had a succession of casual relationships – it was better than risking humiliation, she reasoned. It resulted in her getting talked about, at least in the music school, where reputations were made and broken by relationships and jealousies.

She worried about following in her mother's footsteps - marrying some work-shy local and ending up where she had started, living in a trailer court. But it was never her default option. She would do anything to get away from the life her parents had led.

Jake Fisher called as soon as he heard she was back living with her parents. He was now a man with a career. He'd followed his father and become a police officer. Her need to escape from the trailer court and all it symbolised overcame any reservations she had about Jake. He had been a loud-mouth and a bully at high school. *But people change*, she had told herself. He was reasonably good looking, despite his developing beer-belly. He was tall - well over six feet - stood very erect, and, although he had thinning blonde hair it was cut short, revealing widow's peaks that suggested someone of maturity, someone older.

It was only a couple of months later when Jake suggested they should get married. Angela saw him as her way out, her means of escape from the life her parents led. He wasn't her ideal choice - far from it - but she reckoned she didn't have the luxury of being choosy. Jake wanted to marry her – the bright, good-looking girl from his class – and she was delighted he did.

Her mother had been less than thrilled. "You're not going to marry Jake Fisher? He's a thug, just like his father, a thug in a uniform. They're the worst kind. They can get away with anything – and they know it. You'll regret this Angela. All that training, all that success at college ... are you just going to throw that away?"

61

"Leave her alone, let her marry Jake. It'll be good to have him in the family," retorted her father from his armchair. "I'd like him as a son-in-law. I used to get along okay with his dad."

"I can't believe what I'm hearing," shouted Angela's mother across the blare of the television. "He was a bastard – used to beat the crap out of his wife, and knocked Jake about a bit too."

"Didn't do him any harm," replied Angela's father. "Look where he is today." He turned up the volume on the TV, signalling an end to the conversation.

Bob Waite was dismayed, and told her as much.

"He'll destroy that talent you have. He's just not right for you. You can do better, Angela. You deserve better, considering ..."

"Considering where I've come from," added Angela, finishing his sentence for him. "I can look after myself, Bob. I've been doing it all my life."

"I know," he replied, "but can you handle Jake Fisher?"

Angela had convinced herself that she had no option other than to marry Jake, but she was disturbed by what Bob Waite had said. She knew in her heart that he was right.

Angela hadn't realised that Jake took his bullying so seriously. He liked to tell her about his day, and a good day for Jake was one that involved him hitting somebody. It was usually for what Jake referred to as 'resisting an officer'. Angela knew that it took very little provocation for Jake and his buddies to give a beating to some unfortunate who'd happened to cross their path at the wrong time. Of course, there were many good citizens who admired Jake, just as they'd admired his father. The bar owners could rely on Jake and his crew to make sure a fight didn't get out of hand, or to take care of some drunk who wouldn't go home. The mayor wanted 'tough policing' – something Jake interpreted quite literally. Shop keepers wanted to know that their stores wouldn't be vandalised, and parents wanted Jake and the other officers to keep an eye out for gangs, drugs and individuals that had a criminal record, or looked likely to get one. The more Angela showed any hint of dislike for Jake's accounts of his day the more graphic they became, with every blood-spilling punch and body-bruising blow of his truncheon given in graphic detail. She was glad, at least, that she had her music pupils.

*

Bob Waite had been as good as his word and had provided her with ten enthusiastic piano students. William was the pick of the crop. She smiled to herself when she thought of William.

He'd been a shy shuffling teenager that first day when his mother brought him round to her house to introduce him. He had let his mother do all the talking while he stood staring at the piano. And when she first saw him sit on the piano stool, slowly lift the lid and then stretch his fingers so they hovered over the keys, she sensed his love of the piano was every bit as acute as hers.

Angela quickly realised that William had a special talent. She had been reluctant to take on another of Bob Waite's pupils. They were all reasonably accomplished, but lacked some form of innate ability. They were too mechanical, too well-trained, too well-schooled. They were Bob Waite's stock-in-trade. He wanted musicians who, quite literally, 'knew the score', and played as such. She had decided that this was her lot in life: to provide further lessons for Mr. Waite's better piano students.

And then along came William. He played in a free-flowing way, his arms and hands skimming over the keys, searching for a sound that was implied by the music sheet and not just something to be copied. He wasn't as technically accomplished as some of the others, but that would come with practise. What he had was a quality and style of playing that carried a signature – his signature – to the music. She had found in William someone who was likely to be at least her equal as a pianist. It renewed an excitement for her music that she'd assumed was virtually lost to the repetitious tedium of providing weekly lessons, and listening to the discordant sounds that her piano emitted at the hands of many of her pupils. She'd also given up practising since marrying Jake. He made it clear he didn't like the 'stuff' she played. He flicked on the radio to one of the many country music stations as soon as he walked in. Tammy Wynette singing *'Stand by Your Man'* was one of his favourites. It had a poignancy that Angela found disturbing.

She looked forward to William's weekly lessons. He responded, with an enthusiasm for his music that was infectious. It reminded her of the enthusiasm and effortless commitment she once had. She knew the feeling – an overpowering urge to rehearse and refine a piece over and over again, until it produced a tingling thrill, and sometimes a shiver of sheer delight. Then, she couldn't wait to perform. She could see the same proud excitement in William when he came for his lessons, pleading with his eyes to play the piece he had been given for the week. And then the palpable relief when he had finished, staring for a few moments at the keys before shyly looking round for her approval. She knew that they shared a talent that provided them with something special – refuge, a temporary absence, an

64

excuse for ignoring the hurt they encountered. For Angela, it was immunity from the influence of her parents, and it enabled her to distance herself from some of Jake's intimidating ways. What, she wondered, would William secretly stow in his musical fortress?

*

She thought she heard the metallic pinging of the fly-screen rebounding against the weatherboarding. She definitely heard the front door slam. Wood, smacking loudly against wood. An aggressive, unwelcome sound that was still filling the still air in the hallway as Jake strode into their house.

Angela jumped. "What's the matter, Jake? I didn't expect you home so early ...?" He cut her off before she had time to say any more.

"What the hell were you doing in the courtroom this morning – defending that little shit?" bellowed Jake.

"I just wanted to help him, Jake. He's a good kid, I know he is. Bob Waite asked if I would speak up for him, that's all."

"That's all! You are a dumb fucking bitch! You've made me look like an idiot. My buddies made an arrest, he's as guilty as sin, and then you come along telling the judge what a great kid he is and the judge gives him just a telling off because of what you said! They think I've gone soft!" Jake moved towards her, thrusting his big head into her face. She could see the veins in his neck pumping furiously as if trying to catch up with Jake's rising anger.

"Well I'm not soft, am I, Angela?" Jake lunged forward and grabbed her shoulders. "Am I, Angela?" He shook her hard. She could feel his blunt fingers digging into her shoulders. He looked angrier than she'd ever seen him. He relaxed his grip and pushed her back against the couch. She stumbled and tried to

65

prevent herself falling. She reached out, grabbing at Jake's arm. Her fingernails slipped against his hand, raking his skin. He flinched and for an instant they both stared at the red scratches.

"Sorry, Jake, I didn't mean ..."

"You fucking bitch!" Jake swung at her face with the flat of his hand, hitting her hard across the side of her head. She gasped as the blow spun her around, banging her head onto the edge of the door. She staggered as an intense pain pierced her skull and a sudden blackness threatened to fill her head. She fell against the back of one of the soft, mock-leather arm chairs and pulled herself upright. Her hand moved instinctively to the pain where the side of her head had cracked into the door. A thin slick of blood stained her hand.

"Oh my God," exclaimed Jake, suddenly filled with remorse. "I'm sorry, Angela – I didn't mean to hit you like that. Please forgive me – I just lost it!" He tried to reach out to her but she held up her hand, signalling him not to come any closer.

"Don't touch me, Jake! Get out of here – go and see your buddies – go and tell them what a big man you are!"

Jake sank his head into his hands. "I love you, Angela – I'd never do anything to ..."

"You just did! And if you ever touch me again, or if I hear you or your buddies are bullying William, I'll leave you Jake - I swear I will."

"Never, Angela, never again, I promise." He looked pathetic in his pleading. For an instant, Angela wanted to reach out and hold him. "I'll ... I'll get something for that cut..."

66

"No, Jake – I'll look after myself." Angela stumbled past him and went upstairs to the bathroom. Jake stood and watched her go, floundering in his own silence.

Chapter 7
The Pupil

Angela had no intention of leaving her home and returning to live in the trailer court with her parents. She couldn't stand the thought of giving anyone the satisfaction of seeing that she'd made a mistake in marrying Jake. Outwardly, at least, she gave the impression that nothing had changed between her and Jake.

"I tripped on the carpet and fell against the door," she told her friends. Most were sceptical of her account, and her mother wasn't convinced in the slightest.

"You should leave him, Angela. He's no good. It'll happen again – mark my words." Angela tried to feign surprise at her mother's assumptions.

"I fell. That's all. Poor Jake, he was so concerned."

"Poor Jake, my ass. It's poor you I'm worried about." Angela felt distinctly uncomfortable at having to evade her mother's inquisition.

"I'm okay, honest."

For the next few weeks, Jake began paying her the kind of care and attention he had shown when she'd first returned from university to live with her parents. He even asked after William, and made no comment when she took to occasionally playing her piano in the evenings. She wasn't fooled though. She knew Jake was making an effort that was out of keeping with his normal behaviour, and this last week he'd shown a few signs of returning to his old ways.

*

The week following his court appearance, William didn't show up for his scheduled lesson. One part of her was relieved. She didn't want him to see her bruised face. But she also knew it was important for William to get back to his regular schedule as quickly as possible. She decided to call his mother.

"Hello, Susan? It's Angela. I'm calling about William. He didn't come for his lesson on Tuesday. I guess he's worried about coming over."

"Oh Angela, thanks for calling. William's been a bit upset. He had a row with Gerald, which hasn't helped. He's been practising on the piano; in fact he's been doing little else." Angela smiled to herself. She knew that William would immerse himself in his music. It's what she tried to do when she needed to escape.

"Can I speak to him? I'd like to see if I can persuade him to come on Thursday."

"I'll see if he'll come to the phone. I'd be delighted if he'd agree – would you believe he hasn't been out of the house since the court case?" Angela didn't comment. She wasn't surprised that William had become reclusive. She could hear Susan calling to William.

"William – it's Angela. She'd like a quick word ... William, please!" Angela's heart was pounding when she heard William's voice. She knew it was a small victory.

"Hello." His voice was barely audible.

"William," said Angela, breathlessly, "I know you're upset." She paused. She could feel William's pain in his raspy breathing.

69

"I want you to come to your lesson on Thursday." She took a deep breath and continued. "You've a special gift, William. It's what makes you ..." Angela paused again. "It's what makes you different. It's not easy being different – I know that. It can make you feel very lonely at times, and I know that too. That's why I want you to come. I need you to come, William." She suddenly stopped. She'd said too much. She scolded herself for attempting to be analytical - for attempting to get him to understand the penalties of being sensitive, talented and insecure. She'd talked to him as if he was an adult – someone mature enough to understand. She waited for what seemed an eternity. All she could hear was William's breathing. And then she heard the clunk of the receiver being placed on a table. It was Susan who picked up the phone.

"How did it go?" asked Susan.

"I don't know. He didn't say a word. I hope I haven't made things worse."

*

Angela had virtually given up on William coming for his lesson. He was supposed to come at four o'clock and it was now nearer five. She had poured her third cup of coffee, waiting for William, and was reaching for a biscuit from the top shelf in the kitchen when she heard the door bell. She cursed to herself. She really didn't want to talk to anyone right now.

It struck her as strange there'd only been one ring. That wasn't one of her friends - they leant on the bell until the chimes reverberated through the house. She suddenly realised it might be William's hesitant ring. She ran to the door, hoping he hadn't left. He had just walked to the end of the drive and was about to cross the street. Angela waved her arms and shouted.

"William ...William!" He slowly turned, almost reluctantly; perhaps now hoping no one was home. He was wearing a cap and a scarf, despite the mild weather. He lifted his arm in acknowledgement. It was a stunted movement as if embarrassed at the thought of signalling any form of recognition. She saw the reason for the hat and scarf as soon as he entered her house. They partly hid a large ugly mark on the side of his face. He hadn't turned to look at her; he seemed intent on hiding his own bruises.

"William, what happened?" She suddenly realised. "You had a row with your father, didn't you? Did he do this?" He nodded, still looking at his feet. He shuffled into the lounge and strode over to the piano. His confidence seemed to soar at the prospect of playing his music pieces. Susan breathed an almost audible sigh of relief, and followed him over to the piano. William's eyes were fixed on the keys; he hadn't once turned to look at her. That wasn't unusual and, in one sense, she was relieved he hadn't noticed her face. She'd done her best to cover up most of the bruising, but she still had some swelling and, no matter how liberally she applied her make-up, it wasn't going to hide the worst of the discolouration on her face.

William adjusted his seat and began to practise his scales. It was something Angela had encouraged him to do as a means of stretching his hands and getting the feel of the piano. His hands fluttered gracefully over the keys, and his fingers stretched to find the correct note. He went through his scales and arpeggios, varying the speed and controlling the tone. William liked practising in this way. It gave him license to improvise, gradually altering the repetition and developing an impromptu composition that touched the various pieces he had previously played. Angela moved closer, standing next to him to get a better view of his technique. He suddenly stopped playing and turned and stared at the marks on the side of Angela's head, as if he'd just realised that there was something different about her, something he hadn't expected. She instinctively raised her hand to the source of his gaze. William reached up as if wanting to touch her bruises. There was a questioning look on William's face that caused Angela to respond.

"I banged my head on the door, William," she said, quietly. He appeared uninterested in her reply, as if he knew it had nothing to do with the cause of her bruising.

"Which door?" asked William, accusingly.

"That one," she replied, nodding in the direction of the door to the hallway. "I slipped on the carpet." Angela stroked her hand along William's bruised face. "Thanks for asking - we're a bit alike," she said softly. William turned and stared intently at the piano keys.

"I don't think it was a slip." His voice sounded firm, almost angry. Angela felt an urge to hug him, hold him close and caress his puffed, purple cheek. She took a half step away from the piano as if sensing a danger in this feeling of intimacy.

"Let's hear your piece – the Schubert you've been practicing." William's gaze moved slowly from her bruises to her eyes. It was one of the few times William had looked directly at her, and the first time he had held her gaze for any period of time. And, for a moment, his soft blue eyes suggested a desire that she found disturbing.

*

Over the next couple of weeks, William's playing became even more inspired, especially with the romantic pieces he was now practising. He mastered a difficult piece from Schubert's *Piano Concerto in A Minor*. In parts, his head bent forward, almost touching the keys with his lips as he caressed them with his long fingers producing a feathering of the tone that gave his performances - for they were now more than just practice pieces - a passion. And at times, he appeared to be in an exalted state as he threw himself into a crescendo and created a peal of sound that reverberated throughout the room.

When he played the slow, soft movements he would occasionally lift his head to glimpse at Angela as he stroked the keys. She could almost feel his gossamer-like caresses brushing her skin, and then the tingle as his fingers plunged into a rich sharp staccato that almost made her gasp; and the deeper base notes, resonant and dominant, only really yielding to the higher, lighter keys when their sound had given its full effect. It was all consuming, a flood of tones that she found erotic and thrilling. This was, after all, in part her creation. She threw her head back, revelling in the skills of her pupil.

William never tired of practising. Quite the contrary, he was never keen to move on from his current piece, as if he wasn't quite satisfied - as if he knew he had more to offer. He seemed to sense that there were improvements to make and improvisations he could try at every playing, and with every hint of encouragement from Angela. She revelled in the willingness of her pupil to attempt to master the pieces he played. She wanted him to feel the music as if it was a part of his soul.

Angela suggested he should move on to a short piece by Debussy – *Claire De Lune*. It was a gentle, swaying piece that she thought would allow him to further explore his technical capabilities. And because it was short, it required William to consider every note, every pause, and every stop and half-stop. William loved the piece. He laboured just as much over the pauses and half stops as the sound his playing created. She watched his hands as they lifted ever so slightly; stilling the sound, punctuating the music like a poet polishing his prose.

"I'd like you to try something from Rachmaninov," said Angela. "His *Rhapsody on a Theme. Rhapsody on a Theme of Paganini*, to give it its full title."

"I think I've heard it," replied William.

"I'm sure you have," said Angela. "The opening bars are used in commercials, even film scores. It's magnificent! I played it as one of my pieces for my exams at College. Move over, I'll play a bit for you."

William shuffled along the piano stool and Angela squeezed in beside him, her leg pushing against his as she instinctively reached for the pedals. She could feel the warmth of his body as she shuffled into position. She reached across him as her hands flitted along the keys, producing the unmistakable opening bars. She felt William's body sway into hers, almost pushing against her, in a shared intimacy that was swelled by the flowing ripples of music. Angela didn't stop; she didn't want to stop. She played the entire piece as well as she had done at any time. William sat, enthralled at her playing, excited at her closeness and the warmth of her body, hoping this wouldn't end. At that moment, he knew he was in love with Angela.

A week or so later, Angela suggested they try a piano duet, Rachmaninov's *Italian Polka.*

"It'll give you a bit of a break from the *Rhapsody* piece. And it'll be fun to do a duet. What do you think?"

74

"I don't know," replied William. "I've never tried a duet."

"It's a different technique – it can take a while to get used to each other's playing. We'll take it in easy stages," persisted Angela.

Although William struggled at first, he loved sitting so close to Angela. They bumped into one another with their arms and hands and there were times their heads moved so close that William could feel her hair brush against his cheek. And when she helped place his hands and arms to improve his playing, he felt his skin tingle at her touch. He could smell her perfume, he could feel her breast against his arm as she stretched across to play her notes, and he could feel her thigh rubbing against his as they both positioned themselves to use the pedals. He was sure Angela must have noticed his excitement, but she just kept practising and playing, nudging him to catch up whenever he slowed and praising him with a swift tilt of her head when his rhythm blended with hers.

*

"I'm going over to Angela's," called William from the hallway.

"Okay, see you later," replied Susan, glad to see her son so happy.

"Is that three times this week?" asked Gerald. "I'm not sure this is healthy."

"Oh, Gerald, what's your problem?" retorted Susan, angrily. "William has never been happier. He loves to play his piano and Angela has been wonderful. He can't wait to get over there and Angela says that his musical talent is beyond question. She thinks it might be a career for him."

"Bit early to make that kind of judgement, I would have thought. Anyway, I think she's leading him on.

75

William is obsessed with her - and he seems to be over there whenever Jake Fisher is out cruising in his patrol car."

"Just what are you suggesting, Gerald?"

"Surely I don't have to spell it out. He fancies her!"

"He goes to Angela for piano lessons..." replied Susan, in an exasperated tone. "She's his teacher, for God's sake!"

"I'm telling you – he fancies her. I can't blame him, she's a cracker. I blame her."

Susan retorted in an instant. "For what Gerald - giving you fantasies that have nothing to do with William?"

"Let's hope you're right, for William's sake," snorted Gerald. "If Jake Fisher ever suspected his good-looking wife was having an affair with our son, there'd be hell to pay."

Gerald wished it was him visiting Angela each week. He'd seen her in the supermarket reaching up for a tin on the top shelf. It was an image he mentally captured and stored. It was one he liked to manipulate when he was lying wide awake, while Susan slept in a protective curl on her side of the bed.

*

Shortly after William's eighteenth birthday, Angela suggested to Gerald they should get him a small second-hand car.

"Look Gerald, he's rushing home from school and then on to Angela's house three times a week now. It's quite a walk and I don't like the idea of him having to trail that distance in the winter. When it's lashing with rain, Angela has to run him home. I know that big anorak he likes to wear keeps him reasonably dry, at least his top half. Sometimes his trousers are soaked by the time he gets home."

"He can always take them off to dry at Angela's," said Gerald with a sneer. Susan glared at him.

"All he needs to do is call, he knows that," added Gerald, before Susan had a chance to speak.

"And how many times has that happened, Gerald? There's nothing more embarrassing for someone William's age than to have a parent sitting at the school gates, and besides, we're never easy to get hold of. No one at the University is going to chase around to find you or me, unless it's an emergency. We could get him driving lessons – and he can drive himself on 'P-plates'."

"But he's only a kid," protested Gerald.

"No he isn't," replied Susan, emphatically. "He's a young man. He may not look it, but he's a year older than most of his classmates."

"Oh, yes," replied Gerald, cuttingly, "you decided he should repeat a year. Not that it's done any good."

"Oh, come on," Susan replied. "It was the right thing. He just needed a bit of extra time. It's not that unusual anymore." She quickly switched back to the car. "Many of the high school students have their own transport. We can set clear rules – he'd only be able to use it to get to Angela's."

"And if it's pouring with rain, what then? He'll not want to walk with his car sitting there."

"Okay", replied Susan, "there are going to be occasions when it makes sense for him to use the car – but only if we agree first."

"Sounds like your mind's already made up," replied Gerald in a dismissive tone. "On your head be it."

William was delighted when Angela gave him the news.

"You mean it, Mum - a car?"

77

"There will be rules. The car will be mainly to allow you to get to Angela's. You'll need some lessons of course and I don't want you using the car without telling me first – is that agreed?"

"Yes, yes, of course," replied William, excitedly. "It'll be great. When can we get it?"

"Well, I've made enquiries at Foster's Motors. They have a second hand Ford Pinto. It's about 8 years old – a 1980 – but it's in the right price range, and Mr. Foster says it's in good condition."

"What colour is it?" asked William, as if that mattered.

"Blue, I think," replied Susan, smiling at William's apparent concern.

"That's great," replied William.

William could hardly wait to show the car to Angela. "What do you think?" he asked, beaming with pride as he gestured in the direction of his small Ford car, parked on the street.

Angela laughed. "That's brilliant, William. No excuses for being late." William looked perplexed.

"But I'm never late," replied William, his face suddenly expressing concern.

"Oh William, I'm just teasing," replied Angela, briefly draping a comforting arm around his shoulder. "You can park it in the drive, if you'd like. I'd hate to see it get scratched."

"It's got a few, already," replied William. He took pleasure in parking in Angela's drive from then on. It made him feel more of a friend – not just her pupil.

*

Gerald couldn't get the thought of William and Angela out of his head. The more he thought about it, and the more often William went over to see her, the more convinced he was that they were having an affair

- or, as he saw it – that Angela was seducing William. He thought about it a lot. He guessed how it might have started. William trying to play the piano with an erection pushing hard against his jeans; Angela noticing his predicament, her hand brushing against it, as if by accident, and then beginning to caress his erection around the damp patch that was staining the outside of his jeans. And then Angela tugging at his belt and slowly lowering his zip. "You'll feel better," she'd murmur, gently fondling him. He'd turn to kiss her clumsily on the lips. "Open your mouth ... that's it," she'd whisper, her tongue tracing his upper lip. And then there were tongues, hers exploring his, her hands on his erection, his quick climax - Gerald felt his own erection growing hard.

Gerald's fantasies never went any further. It was if he couldn't quite imagine William and Angela having sex. William was too young, too immature. What Angela needed was a mature man, a real man - *someone like me*, he thought. Angela would want him, and besides, she'd have no option - not if she didn't want that thug of a husband to find out about her and William.

Gerald followed William over to Angela's house on a couple of occasions. He parked a few blocks away and then lurked around outside, moving just close enough to hear the piano's muffled chords seeping through the thinly clad walls of the wood sided house. A small window was open the second time he watched. He could see them, sitting very close, playing a duet by the sound of it. It gave added credence to his fantasies.

Chapter 8
The Visit

Gerald parked his Oldsmobile in a small car park at the back of a 7-Eleven store. It was about four blocks from Angela's house. He'd done this before, checking to make sure Jake left at about the same time for his late shift. He walked round and waited until he saw Jake leave, slowly pulling out of the driveway, his arm resting on the open window on the driver's side. It was just three o'clock and the streets were relatively quiet. In an hour or so, mothers would be collecting their kids from nursery school and straggly gangs of teenagers would be out from the high school, sauntering down to the fast-food strip where McDonalds and Burger King now took preference over the once-iconic diners that looked like garishly decorated trailers.

His heart was pounding as he approached the house. He looked furtively around to see if he had been recognised, before making his way quickly to the front door. There was a large pine tree in the front garden which had, over the years, grown to provide the small porch with protection from winter winds, as well as hiding the view from much of the street. Gerald stepped quickly under this cover and rang the doorbell.

Angela was surprised to see Gerald when she opened the door. She'd barely spoken to him before, other than a quick 'hello' when she'd dropped off some sheet music she had forgotten to give to William, and a nod of recognition when he had caught her eye in the supermarket. It took her a couple of seconds to realise who it was. Gerald smiled, noticing the brief look of surprise.

"Hi, I'm William's father..."

"Of course. Gerald, isn't it? I hadn't expected to find you at the door. Is it about William?"

"Yes," replied Gerald. "Look, it's a bit personal. Is it okay if I come in?" Angela was concerned. He sounded breathless, as if he'd been jogging down the street, and she thought he looked a little furtive. She clung to the edge of the door, trying to assess the situation.

"Where's Susan?" she asked, as casually as she could.

"Oh, she's gone to a meeting she couldn't afford to miss. She asked me to drop round. Is that okay?" Gerald was getting alarmed. This wasn't going as smoothly as he had expected.

"I suppose you'd better come in," said Angela, somewhat reluctantly. "Coffee?" she asked. It was her usual invitation whenever anyone came round. She made the offer out of social habit – a reaction - and not as any form of encouragement for Gerald to stay longer than was absolutely necessary. Gerald seized the opportunity and followed her through to the small kitchen at the rear of the house, flinging his wind jacket onto one of the chairs. He didn't particularly enjoy the weak, lukewarm coffee that homes and restaurants in the midwest served – he much preferred his coffee thick and black - but this was an invitation, of sorts.

"Thanks. No milk," he replied, seeing her gesture towards the fridge. He noticed she hadn't poured a cup for herself. She stood by the sink, waiting while he took a sip of his coffee.

"We are very pleased at the progress William has made with you, Angela - delighted, in fact. I know he's doing well, musically, but he's also coming on in other areas as well. It's these 'other areas' I'd like to have a chat about."

"I'm not sure I know what you mean," exclaimed Angela, now feeling distinctly uncomfortable.

"He's behaving more like a teenage boy should," replied Gerald. "You know... combing his hair, checking himself whenever he passes a mirror, stealing my aftershave, spending ages in the bathroom, and even being secretive in his bedroom." He let out a low snigger and looked directly at Angela. She took a step backwards, pushing her hips against the kitchen worktop. She was becoming increasingly alarmed. She wanted this conversation to stop. She wanted Gerald to leave.

"I think he's got a girlfriend, or thinks he has," he added.

"Perhaps I could come round and discuss it with you and Susan? I think I'd be more comfortable talking about this with both of you," Angela suggested, in what she hoped was a forceful tone.

"I think it would be best if we chatted about things first. You see, I know you and William are having what I might call *fun*."

"What!" exclaimed Angela. "You'd better go – now! Jake will be back any minute."

"Oh, I don't think so - he's just started his shift, hasn't he? I know about you and William – I've seen you together, through the window."

"You've been spying on me!"

"I've been watching you and William - that's all. And I like what I saw. I promise not to tell anyone, especially not Jake – I know how upset he can get." Gerald paused; she looked frightened. He liked that ... it made her seem more vulnerable. There was no turning

82

back now. This was his big chance, and he was excited beyond control.

"I just want a bit of fun, that's all. I reckon you'd enjoy some real fun – more satisfying than just playing with a young lad like William." He took a step towards her, aiming his arms and body at hers. Angela gasped in horror. She felt numb, unable to move. *This isn't real*, she told herself. *It isn't really happening!*

"You're sick," she suddenly shouted, as loud as she could. Her voice felt weak and pathetic. "Get out of my house ..."

Gerald lunged at her, grabbing her head with both hands and pushing his open mouth onto hers. She tried to wriggle free and move her head, but he was too strong. He pinned her against the counter, grinding into her thin skirt and shoving his wet mouth against hers. She gagged as he forced his tongue to the back of her throat and then bit down hard, clamping her teeth on the side of his tongue. Gerald yelped in pain and jerked back.

"Bitch!" he shouted, and then leered at her. "Like to play rough, eh?" He grabbed a fistful of her hair in his left hand, forcing her head to one side and exposing her long slim neck. He pulled her loose sweater and her thin black bra-strap off her shoulder. He released her hair as he plunged his face against her breast and grabbed her, pulling her hard against him. She tried to wriggle free and succeeded in moving her leg enough to knee him in the groin. He grunted at her attempt, grabbed her leg and lifted it in the crook of his arm, pushing her skirt high above her waist. He shoved hard against her. He was panting loudly, grunting and getting even more forceful. His fingernails cut into her back. She had to do something.

Angela's mind raced, her brain screamed. *This bastard is going to rape me, hurt me, maybe kill me! The bread-bin! I have to get to the bread-bin!*

Jake kept a gun hidden on a shelf behind the bread-bin. She needed to get over to the other side of the kitchen. Angela leaned towards him.

"Steady, steady... I don't want my clothes ripped," she whispered, hoping she sounded convincingly compliant. Gerald relaxed his hold, but kept her pinned against the counter.

"That's more like it," said Gerald, lessening his grip. Angela knew she had to make this convincing.

Be strong, she told herself. *Be strong. You've got to beat this bastard!* She managed to smile into his leering face and pushed him firmly backwards, and then slowly lifted her sweater over her head, throwing it onto the floor in an act of bravado, like a matador teasing a bull. It gave her courage. She backed slowly towards the other counter, beckoning him to move towards her as she continued to move backwards to the other side of the kitchen.

"Come here," he said, reaching out to grab her. She hadn't quite reached the counter. Angela felt a surge of panic.

"Wait ..." she said, trying to sound breathless and excited. He stood transfixed, as she quickly unzipped her skirt. She swung it like a cape, flashing and then hiding from him, as if playing a game. She pretended to stumble slightly to get herself against the counter, just in front of the red and white enamelled bread bin. She delivered the final taunt. "Come here, if you want me." She hoped the fear in her voice wouldn't betray her.

Gerald only heard her words; he was beyond assessing any intonation in her voice. An image of him on top of her pushing into her suddenly flashed through her mind like a toxic message. She had to do this. It was him or her, the matador or the bull. And she was far tougher than he might suspect. A girl from the trailer court has a lot of experiences to draw on.

She leant against the counter, her back almost touching the red and white enamelled bread bin as he moved towards her, ripping at her bra and sinking his face into her breasts like a slobbering dog. She leaned back against the bread bin and moaned as if responding to his touch, holding herself with one elbow on the edge of the counter while she reached behind the bin with her free arm. Nothing! Her fingers frantically explored the hidden recess. She'd seen it sitting there just yesterday, like a black ugly slug hiding in her kitchen. She managed to push herself further back and turned her head so she could just see the shelf, as Gerald became ever more aggressive. She lifted herself further onto the counter and lifted her legs as if helping Gerald. Angela had just one thought: *Where was the fucking gun!?*

Then she saw it; it was in the back corner of the shelf. It looked solid, heavy and dangerous. She reached back, and grabbed it. It was heavier than she'd expected and she almost dropped it. Was it loaded? She'd no idea. She couldn't risk it. She slowly raised the gun, and then brought it crashing down on his head. She wanted to smash his skull, she wanted to feel bone crack, she wanted to see his blood spraying round her clean kitchen. She wanted to kill the bastard!

The instant Angela aimed the gun at his head, Gerald sensed her movement. In that split-second, he caught sight of the butt of the gun flashing towards his head. He flinched instinctively. The gun glanced off the base of Gerald's skull and thudded into his neck, causing an intense searing pain, like sharp needles piercing the base of his skull. He slumped to his knees, grasping the back of his head.

The impact twisted the heavy gun out of Angela's hand, sending it flying across the room. Gerald saw it skating past; Angela launched herself off the counter and flung herself across the floor, reaching for the gun. She grabbed it and tried to adjust it so that she was holding it properly. It seemed to wriggle in her hands. She had it!

Gerald recovered, and was reaching for her. She turned and aimed the gun at him just as he sprang forward, knocking her to the floor. She felt the gun twist in her hands as his body fell across hers, trapping the gun against her body. She jerked hard to free her hand. Her finger slipped against the trigger. The sharp crack of the revolver echoed off the kitchen walls. Angela gasped and stared wide-eyed, trying to grab Gerald as he rolled away. She could feel blood oozing through her fingers. *Her* blood!

She gasped again and then fell back. She felt her lungs spasm trying to expel blood that now filled her throat like choking red velvet. A hot, poker-like piercing pain speared from her chest down to her abdomen. Her fingers curled across the tiled floor, trying to hold against the spinning room. A thick blackness slowly engulfed the vortex of light that whirled in her head. She sank into the floor, motionless.

Gerald stared at Angela's body stretched out on the floor. The neat hole in her side was oozing thick, deep-red blood. It had pooled in the depression around her navel and was spilling over her hips and onto the floor. The gun lay on the floor, placed neatly between them. The barrel sat like the hand of a clock, pointing in his direction.

His head throbbed intensely. He felt numb. This wasn't real! His skull thudded, his mouth felt dry and sweat beaded on his forehead, dripping down his nose. He pulled himself slowly upright and peered out of the kitchen window at the small garden. It looked so different from the carnage that surrounded him. He stared at the flowers, the neatly-edged lawn and the path leading to a gate in the low wire fence. The first golden leaves from the elm tree in the neighbour's yard were blowing gently across the lawn, glittering in the low afternoon sun.

"Thank Christ," he whispered to himself, but he knew he had to act quickly. Blood was splattered on the front of his shirt, and his suede shoes had dark spots where drops of blood had soaked into the leather. The back of his hand had a smear of blood, but then he realised it was *his* blood. She'd scratched his hand and two of her fingernails had gouged through his skin. They were deep and painful.

He wrapped his hand in his handkerchief and began scanning the room. He needed to get out of the house as quickly and quietly as possible. Maybe he wouldn't be spotted. He was sure no one had seen him go in. He grabbed his wind jacket, zipped it up to his neck and turned up the collar. He had to get out quickly and maybe, just maybe, he'd get away with this.

"Why didn't she just go along with it?" he growled to himself in frustration. "The stupid bitch!"

Chapter 9
Fugitive

Gerald peered again out of the kitchen window, and breathed a sigh of relief. There didn't appear to be anyone in view. Were the neighbours out? Maybe he was in luck. He slipped out of the back door and hurried down the concrete path to the gate. The gate's metal frame screeched and shuddered against the concrete, as Gerald dragged it wide enough for him to slip through. The sound alarmed him, setting his nerves on edge. The gate led to a path linking the back of the houses. Several overhanging branches from a line of large elm trees along the edge of the path provided a reasonable amount of cover. He smiled at his good fortune.

So far, so good, he told himself. A youth on a BMX bike flashed by, almost knocking into Gerald. His heart raced at the unexpected encounter. He realised that the high school must have ended for the day. He checked his watch, it was just four. In a few minutes the streets, and especially secluded areas like this pathway, would have pods of high school students sharing smokes, laughing at boasts of boyish bravado, exploring incipient loves, and agonising over the traumas and fickleness of teenage relationships. He needed to get further away before he was recognised. If he went back to pick up his car, he might be spotted. He would leave it there and pick it up later.

The path led into the town park and across the park was one of the older shopping malls, which had still managed to survive despite the emergence of larger new ones with their ample parking areas, wide tiled floors and glassed atriums. Gerald moved quickly through the park. He didn't see anyone he recognised. There were a few young mothers. Some were pushing their babies in prams, and others were escorting toddlers on their first hesitant steps across the manicured lawns. The normality and tranquillity of the park briefly comforted Gerald's fevered brain. He turned, nervously, when an angry mother shrieked at a youth riding his bike near to her toddler.

"No riding!" she shouted as the biker veered away, pedalling hard and laughing as he did so. He flashed his middle finger over his shoulder at the mother who'd bent down to sweep up her child. She looked angrily around and waved an arm in Gerald's direction.

"Did you see that idiot?" She turned to address a couple of other mothers nearby. "Some example he is!" Gerald was relieved he hadn't become embroiled in her protest.

It seemed to take him an age to reach the park gates. He had to resist the urge to run, telling himself to stay calm. The last thing he wanted to do was to draw attention to himself. He quickly crossed the road and entered the shopping mall. He felt tense and jittery. His head throbbed, he was breathing heavily and for a few seconds his vision was distorted - everything appeared to be abnormally coloured in a wash of fused, pale hues. He steadied himself against the arm of a bench seat in the mall's main aisle, and wondered if he should sit down until he felt better. For a bizarre moment he felt that he should sink onto his knees and pray for forgiveness. The moment passed. He spotted the toilets further down the mall's main corridor. Once inside one of the cubicles, he slipped off his jacket, hung it on a peg on the door and sat heavily on the seat. His hand was surprisingly painful where Angela had scratched him. He looked at the red welts and replaced the handkerchief – he'd get some gauze dressing from the pharmacy.

He forced himself to breathe calmly and then looked closely at his shirt and tie. They were badly stained with her blood, and his shoes had several dark spots where splatters of blood had been absorbed by the suede. He dunked a handful of toilet paper into the bowl and rubbed at his shoes until the paper disintegrated into clumps of soggy tissue, stained with ingrained dirt and pink from the bloody patches. They looked a bit better where the water had wetted his shoes. He looked again at his shirt - it was a mess. He'd buy a new one, ditch the tie, and get changed in the toilet cubicle. It was all so simple. He felt pleased with himself and distinctly better. He zipped up his jacket, washed his face and hands in the sink and dried himself with the coarse paper towels.

When he next emerged from the toilet, feeling calmer and somewhat refreshed in a pale-yellow shirt he'd purchased from Coles Store in the mall, he heard someone calling his name. Heading towards the toilets was Mrs. Miller, her ever-present handbag dangling from the crook of her arm. He pretended not to notice her, but she called after him again.

"Gerald ... hello, Gerald, it's me!" *Stating the bloody obvious*, thought Gerald.

"I haven't seen you shopping here before," she said, pointing at the green plastic bag with the shop's name and logo which now contained his blood-stained shirt and tie. "You've hurt your hand," she said, motioning towards his stained handkerchief.

"Oh, it's nothing," replied Gerald, trying to regain his composure. "I caught it on a wire fence walking over here. I just popped in to look for a magazine," he blurted, pointing to the shop opposite and immediately regretting this attempt at trying to deflect Mrs. Miller's focus on his blood stained handkerchief. The shop specialised in magazines for handymen and model enthusiasts, such as *The American Woodcutter*, *Meccano*, *Classic Toy Trains*, as well as various home improvement magazines and many others with titles and topics only an enthusiast could love.

"I'd no idea you were a craft person," said Mrs. Miller, suggesting they were a special and quirky breed. "My husband, Ron, builds model trains. He's always in there. I sometimes think he likes to read the magazine from cover to cover before he buys it! I don't mind; it lets me get on with my shopping in peace."

Good God, thought Gerald, *I've got to get away from this woman.*

"Got to go," he said, abruptly. "In a bit of a rush." She pointed at his hand, just as he turned to go.

"You'd better get something for that hand, Gerald. It looks nasty."

He strode off in the direction of the magazine shop and bought a copy of *Popular Mechanics*. It was the only title he recognised.

*

William drove carefully home from the high school, wishing he had the confidence to go faster. Three other students overtook him in their cars, speeding past with horns blaring. He wanted to get home quickly; it would soon be time to go round to Angela's for his lesson. He parked on the kerb side and ran up the steps leading to the porch, glancing back to admire his car. He ran through into the kitchen, glugged milk from the bottle in the fridge, and snatched up the sandwich Susan had left for him. A couple of big mouthfuls, a final slurp of milk, and he was on the move. He grabbed his jacket – the leather one Angela had said looked cool – pocketed a chocolate bar, bolted out onto the porch, and bounced down the steps as the front door slammed shut behind him. He paused to take stock of his car, climbed in behind the wheel, turned the key and pulled the shift lever into 'Drive'. He knew he'd be a bit early for his lesson. It was supposed to be a four-thirty pm start but he invariably arrived earlier, especially now that he had his car.

Angela seemed not to mind. It had become an in-joke. 'You're early, William,' she'd say, with feigned surprise. William would counter by looking at his watch and informing her just how many minutes early he was. Today was likely to be a record. He'd got out of high school a few minutes early, and although he'd had a frustrating wait in the school car-park, he'd made good time to his house and had encountered little traffic on his drive to Angela's. He reversed into her driveway, something he'd learnt to do expertly by practising over and over on the driveway of his own house. He hopped out of the car, half-hoping that Angela had seen him reverse so precisely.

William knocked a couple of times and then pushed the door open. Angela usually left it off the latch when he was due to have one of his lessons.

"Angela," he called, "it's me." He stepped through to the living room and flung his jacket over one of the lounge chairs.

"Angela," he called again, guessing she must be in the kitchen. The door leading to the kitchen was ajar. He pushed it open, and gasped.

Angela was lying in a pool of crimson blood. Her breasts – those breasts he'd dreamt of – were bare and exposed. Her skirt lay on the ground in front of him, spread out like a bathroom mat. Her long, smooth legs were splayed and angled as if posing for a glamour photographer. Her torso was covered in blood and just next to her outstretched fingers was a gun. The gurgling sound from her throat startled him. It was if she'd saved up her last breath for his arrival. He rushed over and knelt next to her, cradling her head in his arms. She groaned again and her eyes suddenly opened and looked at him. He felt he was sharing his soul with hers. Her eyes flickered in recognition and then fixed on him with a blank, unblinking stare. William knew she was dead. He hugged her and kissed her cheek. His shoulders shuddered and he sobbed uncontrollably. He attempted to wipe the stinging tears from his eyes, smearing her blood onto his cheek.

He slowly lowered her head to the kitchen floor and picked up the gun, examining it as if trying to find out how this little weapon had damaged her in this way. He pushed himself upright and lurched over to the sink, dry-heaving over the enamel bowl and almost knocking over a half-filled cup of coffee on the counter top. He watched the remains of the coffee slosh around, glad that it hadn't spilled over the sides. He carefully picked up the cup, stretching his thumb and finger across the rim, as if it was dirty and contaminated, and moved it away from the sink. He liked things to be neat and tidy and it was even more of a compulsion whenever he felt stressed.

A sense of terror suddenly engulfed him. The gun was still dangling from his hand like a memento of his horrific encounter. He looked again at the gun. What was it doing in his hand? Why was Angela lying on the kitchen floor, half naked and covered in blood? He'd thought of her lying naked in front of him many, many times - but covered in blood? What had gone wrong? What had he done? *Nothing*, he told himself. He'd come for his lesson, he'd come to see her, to be with her. His dreams, his guilty dreams, were always about Jake being killed in a car crash and Angela being comforted by him. Not this!

He had to get help. Confused and dazed, he stood motionless, looking at her as if in a trance. He felt disconnected from his body, disconnected from reality, disconnected from time. He gazed slowly around the kitchen, trying to focus on what he needed to do. He wandered slowly into the living room, the gun still hanging at his side. Had he killed her? The last thing he could remember was reversing into Angela's driveway. *I must get home - I need to tell Mum*, he told himself. He could see his car though the front window. He ran outside, flung open the door and threw the gun onto the passenger seat.

Chapter 10
Suspect

Jake Fisher had just parked his police car outside the house and stepped onto the driveway, as William was easing the Pinto forward. He glanced at William and then fixed on his smeared bloody face. He peered in at the car and saw the gun - his gun - lying on the front seat. He tried to grab the passenger side door handle. William panicked. He hit the accelerator pedal and screeched out onto the street, glancing off a car parked on the opposite side of the road.

Jake ran into the house, through the living room and into the kitchen. The first thing he saw was the blood shouting at him from the white kitchen tiles. He gasped at what he saw. He'd seen a number of dead and battered bodies; murder victims clubbed, shot, strangled, car crashes with mangled bodies and crushed skulls, and victims of violence bearing the scars from fights, muggings, and domestic abuse. But this - his wife lying nearly naked, her clothes strewn across the kitchen floor, blood seeping from the corner of her mouth, a red sheet of blood gathered near her side - this was grotesque.

"Angela!" he shrieked, rushing forward. He bent down and slid his hand under her head, hoping. He felt for a pulse by her carotid artery: nothing. He gasped. "Angela ...what the hell's happened?"

Acting on instinct and a rush of adrenalin, he shouted loudly:

"William Martin! William Martin! You fucking murdering bastard!" He released his wife's head; it clunked against the tiles.

"Sorry," he whispered, as if she was still alive. He bounded out of the house and ran to his car. He grabbed his police phone and tapped impatiently on the emergency buzzer.

"Go ahead, Jake, what's the problem?" It was the Duty Sergeant, Brian Witney.

"Murder – been a murder, Brian. It's Angela ..."

"Jake – are you telling me Angela's been murdered?" Jake was on automatic pilot now.

"She's dead, Brian ..."

"Jake, where are you?"

"My place – that's where I found her."

"Hell, Jake...I'm sorry..."

"Not now Brian, we've got to get the little fucker!"

"Who Jake? Who're you talking about?"

"William Martin, that's who - lives on Jefferson Street. He's just fled the scene driving a blue Ford Pinto heading west, towards Randolph Road."

A flicker of recognition flitted into Brian Witney's brain. "Isn't that the kid arrested for theft, got off when Angela ...?"

"That's him," snapped Jake, angrily. He sped off in a squeal of rubber. He was mad now; raging mad. He slapped the dashboard with the palm of his hand. This wasn't the time to start weeping and grieving. He hit the siren as he sped in the direction William had taken. The flashing blue and red lights and the Doppler-like screams of the car's siren numbed any thoughts of Angela. He had a killer to catch.

Brian Witney's voice barked instructions on the car radios. He was one of the very best - Jake was relieved

96

Brian was still on duty. He heard him shout at someone to get an ambulance to Malthouse Drive, number ten. *That's my house*, thought Jake, briefly taken aback as if he wasn't aware of where he was. He shook his head and gritted his teeth.

Brian's gravelly voice crackled in the static from the radio. "All cars, all cars – this is a code red. I repeat – a code red." It was the signal for all cars to drop whatever they were doing and follow orders. It usually meant another officer had been killed or, at the very least, was in serious trouble.

"Murder suspect fleeing in a blue Ford Pinto. Ohio plates. William Martin, about 18 years old. White, Caucasian male. Murder victim is Angela Fisher - shot, presumed dead." There was a pause; a clear, static-free pause. "It's Jake's wife," he added in a tone so deep it echoed in the receivers. There was a brief silence, something approaching a mark of respect, before Brian Witney started issuing specific instructions.

"Jake, we've got five cars, you make six. You up for this?"

"Damn right I am," replied Jake. It's just what Brian Witney expected, and feared.

"Okay," he replied. "But do it by the book – and that goes for all of you. I want an arrest, not a lynching, is that clear?"

"I hear you, Brian," replied Jake, cutting into the silence. Brian Witney hoped he meant it. He'd seen too many good cops sacrifice their careers because things got too personal - a local vendetta, an ex-wife's boyfriend, a reporter that asked too many questions. But this, the murder of a cop's wife – it was going to get personal, no matter what. It had started now, and all he could do was make sure he did his damnedest to see that they operated by the book. He had an image of Jake losing it and beating this kid to death while the

97

other officers stood and watched, not daring to interfere. At best, Jake was a thug in a police uniform. And a raging Jake would be virtually uncontrollable. *Hell,* he thought. *I just hope this kid's found and in custody before Jake gets anywhere near him.*

"Sarge, it's him!" Gene Ryman's whining voice screeched over the radio. He was the thinnest cop on the force. He had a face that was all sharp angles - a long pointed chin, an angled jawline, a sharp ridged nose and small pointed teeth. He reminded Brian Witney of a Rottweiler when he revealed them with his grimacing sneer. He rarely smiled. *Just one more psycho cop*, thought Brian Witney. "That's all we need," he said out loud.

"He's heading east on Morse Road," added Ryman. "He's just jumped the lights at the intersection with Kart Street."

Jake heard Ryman's call and immediately turned next right, heading for the intersection. Ryman and his partner, Bill Duke, were about ten minutes ahead. Bill was driving fast and aggressively. It made even the normally phlegmatic Ryman twitchy as they sped past the traffic; siren wailing, lights flashing, beams on and Bill Duke pounding on the horn at slower vehicles.

"Hell, Bill," Ryman exclaimed as they weaved in front of a Greyhound bus, scraping past an oncoming car. "My breakfast aint too comfortable." Bill Duke's face briefly creased into a half-smile. He continued to gun the patrol car, pleased he'd given tough guy Ryman a bit of a scare. Ryman tugged at his seat belt, hoping it wouldn't fail him, and concentrated on scouting for the Pinto.

"That's him!" he suddenly shouted. "Got to be. He's just turned off." Bill Duke had already seen the blue Pinto take a sharp left turn.

William heard the police sirens as he approached Morse Road. He'd thought briefly about driving home. He desperately wanted to see his Mum; to bury himself in her arms. He sobbed as he drove. His eyes stung with tears and he had to blink to clear his vision. He struggled to control the car. He'd never driven this fast before and everything seemed a blur. He saw the patrol car in his rear view mirror, gaining on him by the second. He swerved left onto a minor road, hoping they hadn't seen him. Jake heard Ryman's voice, updating Brian Witney back at the station.

"He's just turned off Morse Road, opposite the Catholic Church."

"Okay," replied Witney. "Let me know as soon as you get him."

"I'm about five minutes away," called Jake. "I'll get him." Brian Witney jumped in.

"Leave it, Jake. Ryman and Duke can handle this."

Jake pretended not to hear him.

"Okay, I'm on my way," he said. Brian Witney was becoming increasingly alarmed.

"Come in, Jake - that's an order!" Ryman and Duke heard the exchange on their radio.

"'Ain't no way he's going in," commented Ryman. "He won't want to miss this."

"Yeah," grunted Duke. "Hope he doesn't do anything stupid."

*

Gerald heard the wailing of the police sirens. *Perhaps I was seen*, he thought. He realised they were heading towards the mall, and he was gripped by a sudden wave of panic. He could feel his heart beating wildly and he felt hot and flushed. His head pounded and an aching pressure gathered at the back of his eyes. He felt claustrophobic; he needed to get outside.

He headed for the exit, almost dropping the bag containing his stained shirt. He had a smaller plastic bag that had a box of band-aid plasters, a strip of gauze and his newly acquired copy of *Popular Mechanics.* Two police cars flashed by, heading out on Morse road. Relief spread through every nerve of his body like a main line of heroin. He felt euphoric. It wasn't him they were after. He headed back towards his car, avoiding the park and skirting well away from Angela's house. He tried to think as he walked. The first thing to do was get back to his office at the University. It wasn't an issue. He was often away from his desk attending meetings, hiding in the library or having a coffee in one of the cafes on campus.

*

William braked hard as he approached a four-way stop sign. A truck was passing across the road in front of him, blocking his path. He pulled hard on the steering wheel, slewing his Pinto across the road. The front wheel hit the kerb and the steering wheel spun violently. William tried to grab hold of the wheel, and pushed his foot hard down on the accelerator. The car lurched across the road and plunged into a muddy road ditch. William was flung sideways onto the passenger seat, just as the car crumpled. The steering wheel had pierced the driver's seat, grazing William's arm, and the doors were flung open, cracking their hinges. The passenger door had wedged open against the grassy bank of the ditch. The engine shuddered and died. For a moment, perhaps just a second, William experienced a sensation of absolute calm and a silent, almost serene, image of his car hitting the ditch.

The blare of the siren from the patrol car made him jump. A blind panic engulfed his brain. He could feel the gun wedged against his hip. He picked it up and began sliding out of the passenger seat and onto the bank. His legs felt rubbery and weak. He felt bruised and he had a throbbing pain on the side of his head where he'd cracked his skull on the door frame. The gun dangled from his hand. He wanted to fling it into the mud before he was surrounded by police. The screech of the patrol car as it slid to a stop deflected his attention. He curled in a ball by the car and buried his head between his knees. Ryman jumped out and aimed his gun at William's Pinto car.

"Don't move!" he barked.

Duke sprinted towards his partner, catching sight of William crouching behind the passenger door.

"He's behind the door – I think he's got a gun!" Ryman steeled himself. This was only a kid - but the kid was armed and scared. Anything could happen. He called out to William:

"William, I want you to come over to me. Throw out the gun ... I don't want anyone to get hurt." He was sure he could hear William sobbing. "Look William, I know you're upset, but I want you to come out – we need to know what happened."

"I didn't do it!" shrieked William. He sounded hysterical, struggling to control himself. "It wasn't me," he shrieked again, weaker this time. "I wouldn't ..."

The squeal of breaks from Jake's patrol car interrupted William's pleas. Ryman and Duke turned as Jake leapt out of his car, gun in hand. "Steady, Jake, kid's got a gun," called Duke. "Gene is talking to him. It'll be all over ..."

"You bet it will," exclaimed Jake, pushing past Bill Duke. Gene Ryman still had his eyes fixed on the car door as Jake strode up to him.

"That him, behind the door?" barked Jake.

"Yeah ... but leave it, Jake. I can talk him out." Jake ignored Ryman, and shouted at William.

"Come out now," he bellowed. "You fuckin' little shit – I'm goin' to skin you alive!"

Gene Ryman tried again. This was getting out of control, he knew that. He turned and signalled to Bill Duke to call in to the Station. Bill slipped quickly into the car and called Brian Witney.

"Got a problem, Sarge. Jake's just shown up – mad as hell. The kid crashed the Pinto. He's behind the passenger door – and he's got a gun. Gene was talking to him – but now Jake's ... oh fuck ..."

"What's happening, Bill? Bill, Bill ..."

"Jake's just pushed past Gene – aiming his gun ..."

"I'll get back-up there soon as I can," called Witney. He banged his fist on the counter and signalled for full back-up services.

Jake was strutting towards the Pinto. His face was flushed with anger. But he didn't rush. He wanted to savour the moment – to scare William as much as possible.

"Bet you're shitting yourself aren't you, William?" he taunted. "I'm goin' to shoot your balls off and then blast your head away."

Ryman tried again. "Jake, stop it now, Jake. This isn't right. You kill the kid and it's all over." Jake ignored Ryman's plea. William could hear Jake's boots crunching over the bits of dirt and grit on the tarmac road. He crouched as low as he could and hugged the grassy bank. He could smell dog shit and clippings of wet grass. He suddenly shouted out.

"It wasn't me ... it wasn't me!" he shrieked, his voice stifled by huge, stomach-wrenching sobs.

"You little murdering fuck! I'm going to blast your brains and send your balls in a bag to that stuck-up mother of yours."

William lay on his back, his head resting against the inside panel of the door. He wanted it all to end. He

102

pointed the gun at his head. Then he heard Jake rushing towards him. He rolled instinctively toward the car. The gun jerked in his hand and the piercing bang numbed his ears. He heard Jake crash into the car and then saw his leering face staring down at him over the top of the door. Jake's eyes were wide and staring. Blood dripped from his head and splashed onto William's face. The bullet from William's gun had ripped through the top of Jake's skull. William couldn't move - he just lay on his back staring at Jake's cold eyes. Jake's head lolled over the frame of the door as if waiting to be guillotined.

Ryman walked carefully forward, with his arms outstretched and his gun supported in both hands. He glanced at the gaping hole in Jake's head, signalled quickly to Bill Duke, and then peered around the door frame. William was lying flat on his back, staring up at the head of the dead police officer. The gun was lying against his open palm. Ryman bent forward and quickly picked it out of William's hand.

Bill Duke radioed in to the station officer.

"Brian, Jake's been hit ..."

"What?" snapped Witney. "I knew it. I just knew it. How bad?"

"He's been shot in the head. The kid did it – blew half his brains across the road."

"Oh Jesus," replied Witney. "Where's the kid now?"

"He's just lying next to the car, still as a board. Ryman's taken the gun off him."

"There's an ambulance and two other patrol cars on their way now. I'll get another ambulance out there as quickly as I can. You make sure the area is cordoned off. I don't want anyone anywhere near. Tell Ryman to stay with William Martin. Detectives Sparrow and Murphy are also on their way."

Minutes later, the two ambulances arrived, accompanied by two patrol cars. The two detectives pulled up just as the other officers were climbing cautiously out of their cars. Detective Sparrow walked slowly over to the Pinto car with Jake's body still hanging over the passenger side door.

"Did the kid do it?" Sparrow asked Ryman. Ryman nodded. "You and your partner saw it happen?"

"Yeah, we saw it alright. Jake was moving towards the car. The kid was crouching behind the car door. Jake called out, telling the kid to throw out the gun. Next thing the kid fired. Jake was only a few feet away. It blew a hole in the top of his head. I reckon it killed him almost instantly. He stood still for a second or two, like he was trying to get his balance, and then fell forward across the door."

Chapter 11
In Custody

The interview room was furnished only with a steel table and six straight-backed wooden chairs. A bright neon strip illuminated the room and there was a desk-light next to a voice recorder at the end of the table. The small window would have provided a glimpse of the outside world, but it was covered by a thick black roller blind. Detective Sparrow led William into the room and motioned for him to sit on one of the chairs, so that his back was facing the door.

Detective Murphy and Police officers Ryman and Duke followed them into the room. Detective Sparrow reached to switch on the voice recorder and sat opposite William, who sat staring at Sparrow's belt buckle as if he'd determined to focus on this object for the duration of the interview. Ryman and Duke each pulled up a chair and sat on either side of Sparrow. The four police officers sat looking directly at William. No one spoke. William fidgeted in the oppressive silence, rubbing his palms against the edge of the table. Sparrow broke the silence in a loud, strident tone that reverberated off the bare walls.

"William Martin ..." William's body twitched in an involuntary spasm that caused his knees to hit the underside of the table.

"Listen carefully," added Sparrow, his voice now at a softer level. "I want you to give me your full attention." William didn't look up. Sparrow hit the top of the steel table with the flat of his hand. William jumped again and his head shot up, his eyes flicked across Sparrow's face and fixed on a crack on the far wall.

"That's better, son," said Sparrow in a voice that was again soft - softer still. "I want you to answer my questions out loud." He nodded in the direction of the tape recorder. "Now, let's get started. Bill, read him his rights," he said, without taking his eyes off William. Bill Duke went through the *Miranda* speaking quickly in a quiet monotone voice.

"You have the right to remain silent ..." William heard the blur of words like background noise. The door to the interview room creaked open and William tried to glance over his shoulder towards the sound. Sparrow placed his finger on the pause button and barked at him in his loud aggressive voice.

"Keep your eyes facing this way," he shouted. His soft tone returned. "I wouldn't want you to make any sudden movements that we might mistake as an assault." Ryman sneered. "Ryman here enjoys dealing with anyone who gets aggressive."

He slid his finger off the pause button and spoke directly to the recorder. "Police Officer Johnson has just entered the interview room. Officer Johnson is an observer for the course of this interview. He's not directly involved in this case." Police Officer Johnson winked at Ryman and nodded to Bill Duke, before taking a seat at the end of the table. He leant on his elbows and sat, staring at William.

"Okay," said Sparrow, speaking directly to William. "Let's start with the shooting of Police Officer Jake

Fisher. Tell me what happened after you'd crashed your car."

"The wheel spun in my hand – I think I hit the kerb. The car skidded across the road and ended up in the ditch. I slid out of the passenger door – it was flung open when I crashed."

"What about the gun?" quizzed Detective Sparrow. William looked uncertain.

"It must have been in my hand when I slid out. I think it was on the passenger seat."

"And then what happened?" pressed Sparrow.

"I crouched behind the door. One of the police officers started talking to me. He wanted me to come out."

"Did he ask you to throw out the gun?" asked Sparrow.

"He might have done," replied William.

"And then what?"

"I heard Mr. Fisher calling me. He sounded pretty mad. I was really scared - I wanted it all to stop. I had the gun in my hand. I...I wanted to shoot myself. Then I heard Mr. Fisher walking towards me. I panicked and the gun went off."

"You shot him – you shot Police Officer Fisher?"

"Yes – but I didn't mean to shoot him. The gun just went off."

"You shot him, didn't you?" repeated Detective Sparrow. "You blew his brains out, didn't you?"

"Yes." William sat impassively, staring at the wall. The crack seemed larger, like a spreading fissure. He felt a sense of relief, a purging that freed him from the crushing accusations. Detective Sparrow sat back, grim-faced, hiding his self satisfaction at eliciting such a straight forward confession.

"Now, tell me what happened earlier. Why did you go to see Angela Fisher?"

"I had a piano lesson."

"What time was that?" asked Detective Sparrow.

"The lesson was supposed to start at four-thirty. I got there early, at about four, I think," William replied.

"Was Angela Fisher surprised to see you?"

"She didn't come to the door. It wasn't locked so I went in and called out her name. And then I found her. She was lying on the kitchen floor, and there was blood everywhere."

"She'd been shot?" asked Sparrow.

"I knew she had - there was a gun near her and blood on her body."

"What was she wearing?" Sparrow leaned in. William could smell his stale breath.

"She was nearly naked." Sparrow paused. He wanted the tape recorder to capture William's words without any interruption from him.

"What did you do next?" he continued.

"I remember lifting her head. She opened her eyes and looked at me, and then ..."

"And then what?"

"I knew she was dead. I wanted to get help. I ran out of the house. I saw Mr. Fisher pulling up across the street."

"Wait a minute – you had the gun with you, didn't you?"

"I must have picked it up. I remember throwing it onto the passenger seat of my car. Then I drove off."

"You shot her - that's why you ran off."

"No – I'd never hurt Angela. I love ... I mean, I liked her."

"You fancied her, didn't you William?"

"No ... yes ... I think I loved her," he mumbled.

"You wanted her. You got there early and tried to rape her." His voice grew angry and loud. Spittle flew into William's face. "All those fantasies you were

108

storing up – you thought she'd want you too, didn't you William? I reckon you knew where Jake's gun was – you'd been there often enough. I bet she told you about it. So, when she wouldn't play ball you got a bit over-excited – a bit angry. You made her take her clothes off. She told you to get out. Maybe she called you names, maybe she said you disgusted her, maybe she said she never wanted to see you again."

William was wide eyed with fear. He suddenly became agitated and more animated than he'd been at any time since his arrest.

"No, it wasn't like that ..." His voice trailed off, stifled by the constriction he felt in his throat.

"Oh, have I missed out some detail? What was it like, William?" William felt himself shudder as he recalled what he saw.

"She was on the floor. There was blood – lots of blood."

"Did she look nice, William – lying there, naked? I bet you'd thought about her naked many times." William didn't answer. He felt confused. Was this what happened? He'd longed to see her naked. Did he do this? Did he make her take her clothes off? Did he shoot her? She'd looked more beautiful than he'd imagined.

"You shot her, didn't you William?" persisted Sparrow. William couldn't think. Images of Angela's naked body flashed into his mind. His cradling of her head seemed somehow erotic. It was a dream that had been realised. Sparrow's voice penetrated his drifting thoughts.

"William...William! Wake up – don't pretend you can't hear me – you killed her, didn't you William?"

"I ... I must have." He shuddered and slumped forward into his folded arms. For a moment he felt relieved. It was over. And then he wept, uncontrollably.

Susan heard the wail of police sirens as she drove home from the University. She had a meeting that night and she wanted to get home early to see William after his piano lesson, and have something to eat before setting off to her meeting.

She caught sight of their flashing lights as she approached Morse Road – two, maybe three police cars and an ambulance, its noisy klaxon squeezed by the intense pulsing screech from the police cars. *Must have been a bad accident*, she thought. It always gave her twinge of discomfort whenever she encountered an ambulance heading at full speed to the hospital, especially when it was accompanied by police cars. She turned into her street and was shocked to see two other police cars parked outside her house. One police officer was peering through the windows on the front porch. Two other officers got out of one of the cars.

"Oh my God!" gasped Susan. She stopped in the middle of the street and ran over to the officers.

"Is it William – is he alright? Has there been an accident?" Their impassive stance caused her even more concern. "What's wrong? Is he injured?" She stumbled towards the nearest officer and grabbed at his jacket. "I saw the ambulance ... I've got to know, how is he, what happened?"

"That wasn't William," he said, tersely. "That was Jake Fisher, Police Officer Jake Fisher. William's in police custody – he's been arrested. He crashed his car – but he's not hurt. He's giving a statement at the county jail." Susan felt relieved that it wasn't William in the ambulance. He wasn't dead, he wasn't badly injured. She felt as if a clamp around her head had been released, at least by a couple of notches.

"Did he cause the accident? Has he injured someone?" The officer on the porch had re-joined the

110

others. They gathered in an arc in front of her, all looking very serious and very solemn.

The senior officer stepped forward from the group and stood directly in front of her. She could smell the tobacco on his breath and from the nicotine-stained edges of his white moustache. "William has been arrested on murder charges."

"Murder!" exclaimed Susan. "Murder charges! It can't be! It's a mistake! William wouldn't hurt anyone. This just isn't true!"

She looked wildly at the other officers, her eyes pleading for one of them to give a hint of doubt to the accusation. They stood, stoic and still, as if attending a funeral.

"He's been charged with the murders of Police Officer Jake Fisher and his wife, Angela Fisher," continued the police officer. Susan gasped.

"But Angela ... she's William's music teacher. He loves his music more than anything else." She regretted the remark as soon as it left her lips.

"*Was*," corrected the police officer, glaring at Susan. She felt the blood drain from her face. She felt weak and light-headed. She focussed on the police officer's dirty moustache. She wanted to catch every word he uttered.

"Police Officer Fisher was one of our colleagues," he said, in a slow and deliberate tone. The other officers leaned forward in a show of support. There was nothing soft in their demeanour. They had an aura of vigilantism; of a posse intent on revenge. Susan felt very scared.

"You'd better follow me down to the station," said the police officer, motioning to her car.

"What about Gerald, my husband?" asked Susan, suddenly aware that his name had not been mentioned.

"We're trying to contact him at the University. A patrol car has been despatched to his office. We'll leave an officer here in case we miss him."

*

Gerald was at his desk when Lillian Gustafson, the Dean's PA, poked her head around the door. She never bothered to knock.

"Two police detectives are here to see you, Dr. Martin." She could hardly contain her inquisitiveness. "I hope it's nothing serious," she added. Before Gerald had time to compose himself, the two men brushed past her and showed their badges. He was so shocked that he hardly looked at their IDs. They were stern and grim-faced. *Oh shit,* thought Gerald, trying to remain composed. *I must have been seen.*

Lillian Gustafson hung onto the door frame. She was reluctant to leave this source of intrigue. The thin detective, wearing clothes that appeared at least one size too big for him, ushered her from the door.

"Thank you, Mrs. Gustafson. We'll be in touch if we need you." His partner, a man of medium build who might have fitted in any office setting, stood looking directly at Gerald, while the other detective quietly closed the door.

"I'm Detective Sergeant Sparrow. This is my partner, Detective Murphy. We're from Homicide." His voice had the deep tone of a heavy smoker.

"How can I help you?" Gerald squeaked; his voice sounded thin and reedy. He felt breathless and clammy. He rubbed his hands vigorously on his knees underneath the desk, causing his shoulders to rock as he did so. He felt dangerously weak and out of control.

Detective Sparrow took out a small tape recorder from his pocket and placed it on the desk in front of Gerald. "Okay if I use this?" he asked, switching on the

112

recorder. Gerald didn't say a word. He just nodded in the detective's direction.

"We're investigating two murders that were committed this afternoon."

"Two murders?" said Gerald. This wasn't what he'd expected. "Were they connected?" he asked.

"Oh yes, they most certainly were," replied Detective Sergeant Sparrow. "One was Police Officer Jake Fisher and the other was his wife, Angela." Gerald sat in shock. Jake murdered as well; could this be just a coincidence? Surely they weren't here to arrest him for a double murder?

Before he could marshal his thoughts, the detective sergeant continued. "The prime suspect is your son, William."

"For both murders?" asked Gerald, seeking clarification.

The two detectives exchanged glances.

"Yes, for both murders."

Thank God, thought Gerald. *It isn't me they're after. They think William did it.* A feeling of utter and exquisite relief swept through him. He relaxed in his seat and exhaled; a long, slow release that had been binding his chest since the knock on his door. Detective Sparrow's gravelly voice interrupted his thoughts.

"He's been charged with the murders of Police Officer Jake Fisher and his wife, Angela Fisher." Gerald had to fight a bizarre urge to break into a broad smile. He caught the detectives looking at him curiously. They were expecting something different - a different reaction to the news that his son had been charged with committing a double homicide.

I think this guy is in shock, thought Detective Sparrow. Gerald suddenly appeared to break down.

"I can't believe it! William - not William!" He thrust his face in his hands, willing himself to express remorse. "Surely this is an enormous mistake. He wouldn't hurt a fly – and he couldn't possibly commit murder. What happened – can you tell me?"

"He's been charged with the murder of Angela Fisher in her home and with the subsequent shooting of Police Officer Fisher when he resisted arrest. That's as much as I can tell you at this stage."

"This is incredible. Where is he now?"

"He's being held in custody in the county jail. Your wife is on her way there. You'll probably want to join her."

"Yes, yes. I need to see them."

"I suggest you get a lawyer for your son – a good defence lawyer."

"Yes, of course – thank you. I'll get down there straight away."

"Just a couple of routine questions before you we leave," said Sparrow. Gerald's constricted breathing returned. "I need to know your whereabouts this afternoon. Where you went, who you met, that sort of thing."

Gerald hadn't anticipated that he would be expected to provide an account of his movements. He mentally scolded himself for being so lax. *Got to be careful*, he told himself.

"Let me see ... I ate in the university main cafe. I had two cheese rolls, a coffee and a cookie."

"Did you speak to anyone, meet with anyone?"

"I said hello to a couple of people - I didn't really engage in any conversation until I was joined at my table by John Timmings and Walt Prendergast. We're all in the same faculty. Their offices are on the ground floor of this block.

"When was that?"

"I'd been in the library. I left there shortly after 12. I remember looking at my watch. I wanted an early lunch."

"Why was that?"

"Why was what?"

"Why did you go for an early lunch?"

"Oh, I had lots to do in the afternoon, and I needed to get a new shirt." He gave himself a self congratulatory pat. This would tie in nicely with having met Mrs. Miller.

"I left about half-an-hour later. Must have been around twelve-thirty. I came back to my office and then left later in the afternoon. There was a sale on at the mall on Morse Road."

"What time was that?"

"I can't give you the exact time – it was towards the end of the afternoon – I'd guess it was about four-thirty."

"Did anyone see you leave?"

"No, I don't think so. It was pretty quiet here that afternoon and I left by the side door." Gerald moved on quickly. He was anxious to skip as much of his account of the afternoon as he could, especially the time around Angela Fisher's murder. "I went to the mall and bought a shirt in Coles – they had a good sale on casual shirts. I bumped into Mrs. Miller just after I'd bought my shirt. She sometimes helps Susan, my wife, out at the house – been with us for years. She was originally employed to look after William when he was a baby."

Detective Murphy gestured towards Gerald's hand. "I see you've hurt your hand - how did that happen?"

"I caught it on a wire fence; just a scratch. I bought some band-aids and gauze dressing at the pharmacy in the mall."

"And then you came back to your office?"

"Yes, I heard the police sirens when I was leaving the mall. I thought there must have been an accident. I guess they must have had something to do with the murder?"

"Murders," corrected Detective Sparrow. "Okay, Mr. Martin. We won't take up any more of your time. I'm sure you're anxious to see your son. We may need to talk to you again."

Detective Sergeant Sparrow closed Gerald's door. The two detectives walked out of the building towards their car.

"He's a bit odd," commented Detective Murphy. "He was as nervous as hell when we first met him. His reaction when we told him about his son being on a murder charge was ..."

"A bit delayed?" interjected Detective Sergeant Sparrow. "Yeah – he was nervous, all right. I put it down to shock. Some people act in ways you wouldn't expect. They can't believe it's real. But he was odd, I'll grant you that. We'll have a chat to this Mrs. Miller – and you'd better have a word with staff in the mall."

*

Gerald signed in at the county jail desk and was escorted to an interview room. Susan and William were huddled together, their foreheads touching and tears streaming down their faces. William gave a shuddering sob. Susan turned when she heard the door close.

"Oh Gerald, thank goodness. William..."

"I know," interjected Gerald. "I've just been informed by two detectives at my office. We need to get a lawyer, and quickly." He could barely bring himself to look at William. "What happened?" he asked William. "What did you do?"

"Gerald," hissed Susan, barely containing her anger. "This isn't the time." She hugged William tightly to her. His body shook as his grief poured out. He

116

suddenly pushed her away, stopped sobbing and flopped forward, his head resting on the cold metal table. Susan looked up at Gerald. She fought to compose herself and resist the urge to scream; to scream at the young police officer who looked not much older than William, and scream at Gerald who she hated for his insensitivity. She knew, at that instant, that she alone would have to fight for William.

"Gerald," she said, in a commanding tone, "go and 'phone Brindley and Schultz, the lawyers. I want Mr. Schultz to represent William."

"Brindley and Schultz?" replied Gerald. "But they're the most expensive firm in the City, and Schultz – he'll cost a fortune."

"I don't care if it takes every dollar we've got," snapped Susan. "I want Mark Schultz to represent William – and no one else!"

Chapter 12
Evidence

Mark Schultz had a reputation as one of the best defence lawyers in the Midwest. He often represented well-known celebrities on cases ranging from alleged assault to drug use, and even murder. 'Murder' was his speciality. He'd taken on a number of high-profile murder cases and had a reputation for sowing seeds of doubt in the minds of jury members when it appeared to be an open-and-shut case. He was a master at identifying those jury members who were likely to be swayed by his arguments.

Schultz wasn't available. He was in California representing one of his celebrity clients. Susan was stricken by the news. Everything seemed to be conspiring against her and against William; the police, legal representation, and even Gerald.

"Yes," she mumbled to herself, "even Gerald."

Gerald came back into the interview room looking pleased with himself. "I've managed to engage one of Brindley's other lawyers, David Singleton. He used to be a senior partner and he still takes on a few cases. Mr. Brindley assures me that Singleton is a very capable defence lawyer. He's Brindley's brother-in-law." Susan felt somewhat reassured. At least he'd be represented by one of Brindley's lawyers. Their reputation alone was worth something, she told herself.

It was the next morning before David Singleton was able to meet with William. He insisted that both Susan and Gerald should be present. Susan had no intention of being anywhere else. William looked pale and tired following his night in the county jail. He had a copy of William's signed statement. He went through it, line by line, asking William to tell him if everything written down was accurate and factual as he remembered it. William was patently very tired and depressed. David Singleton struggled to hold William's attention. Gerald gave occasional sighs of frustration at William's inability or unwillingness to give his full cooperation. Susan was alarmed at the content of the statement and tried her best to help David Singleton.

"William, please. This is very important. Mr. Singleton can only help if you answer all his questions." William stirred himself after each of Susan's exhortations for him to cooperate. But it was a long slow process and the longer it took the more tired and uncooperative William became. His eyes appeared to look beyond them all, as if their presence was pointless. David Singleton finally got to the end of the statement, having done his best to get William to confirm or refute the content. It was clear that William either accepted that the statement was accurate, or was unwilling to offer any other explanations. He turned towards Susan and Gerald, and gave a slight shrug of his shoulders.

"I need to talk to you outside," said David Singleton, nodding to the door.

"Thank you, William. I'll be back again tomorrow. If you remember anything else, please..." He wasn't sure William was listening. His words seemed

119

redundant. Susan gave William another long hug, and kissed his cheek several times.

"I didn't do it; I didn't kill Angela," he murmured, almost inaudibly.

"I believe you," replied Susan, whispering in his ear.

"It doesn't look good," David Singleton told Susan and Gerald in the corridor outside the interview room. "Two police officers witnessed the shooting of Jake Fisher – and William admits that he shot him. He was probably very scared. But shooting and killing a police officer in front of witnesses means it's virtually certain a jury will find him guilty. And then there's his admission, of sorts - that he may have killed Angela Fisher." Susan felt black with grief. Her head swam and she grabbed Gerald's arm to stop herself from falling.

"What happens now?" asked Gerald. "Is there nothing we can do?" Susan was relieved that Gerald had finally spoken. He'd said very little in the interview room, except to get angry at William's long silences.

"There'll be an arraignment hearing before a judge," replied David Singleton. "The prosecution will state the charges and I will be asked to enter a plea on William's behalf. The district attorney is going for a charge of aggravated murder in the case of Jake Fisher. It's possible the judge could refuse bail, in which case we need to get things moving – for William's sake. There will then be a preliminary hearing to consider the evidence in more detail and the judge will suggest dates for the trial. I'll push for it to be held as soon as possible, unless of course there is any evidence that comes to light that might help William's case."

"Such as?" asked Gerald.

"Well, if there is evidence that someone else was seen entering or leaving Angela's house, for example, then we'd request more time for such a lead to be thoroughly investigated." Gerald became a bit agitated.

"Has someone come forward?"

"No, not that I'm aware of," replied David Singleton. "I'm speaking hypothetically. However, it's important to sow that seed in the judge's mind. I'll request at the arraignment, and again at the prelim, that the police keep investigating this possibility. It's a scenario that the judge, and the jury, needs to accept as plausible."

"But surely the judge will allow bail?" It hadn't entered Susan's head that William wouldn't be allowed bail.

"It's not unusual for bail to be refused, especially when the victim is a police officer. If the judge accepts that the DA's charge of aggravated first-degree murder is reasonable, it's possible he will refuse bail. I just want you to be prepared for such an outcome. I'll ask for bail based on his age and low risk of flight. The DA will fight it. He'll argue that anyone who's admitted killing a police officer shouldn't be given bail – and the judge will find it hard to disagree."

"Oh my God – this is it – he'll never be free again! He'll be locked up for the rest of his life!" Susan felt destroyed by what was happening. Her son, her only son, was going to be incarcerated for God knows how long. How would she cope? How would he cope?

"He's not been to trial yet," said Gerald. "Let's not give up hope." He put an arm round her shoulders and hugged her tightly to him.

Gerald knew he had to give every impression that he was doing his best to help William. At the same time, the last thing Gerald wanted was a protracted investigation, or the assumption there may be another suspect. He leant closer to Susan. "It all seems so hopeless," he said, rubbing his forehead. "I can't understand why he's done this. Why would he want to kill Angela? He was infatuated with her!"

"It's a good question," replied David Singleton, "and one the jury will want an answer to. Let's take the shooting of Jake Fisher. William was fleeing from the scene of Angela's murder. It seems likely that he shot her, and that's the view that the police have. But he may have witnessed the killing, or perhaps arrived after the murder took place."

"But what about his admission?" asked Gerald.

"That doesn't help, I agree – but let me go on. Jake Fisher is convinced William is the killer. I want to suggest to the jury that he's got only one thing on his mind – to get William. And by the time he gets to William's crashed car, he's raging mad. He threatens William, scares him to such an extent that William shoots in self-defence, or perhaps fires a warning shot. The jury might then buy the argument that William was under significant duress and had not meant to kill Police Officer Fisher."

"And what about Angela?" asked Susan.

"The only chance is to give the jury the idea that it might not have been William - that the evidence is not sufficient to establish beyond reasonable doubt that he killed her."

"Except for his statement," Gerald commented.

"Except for his statement," repeated David Singleton. "And the gun that killed Angela and his clothes covered in her blood. It's a long shot – and I'm not convinced the police will look very hard for another suspect. This is not going to be easy. You must prepare yourselves for the worst."

"Which is?" asked Susan.

"The shooting of a policeman and his wife is a capital offence. He could be looking at ..." he paused "... at the death penalty." Gerald gasped. He hadn't expected this. He'd only wanted a bit of fun with Angela, and now his son had killed Jake Fisher and was the only suspect for Angela's murder. He twisted his hands in genuine grief. He was responsible for Angela's death and might also be responsible for the execution of his own son. He looked up at the ceiling and let out an anguished cry. Susan rushed towards him and cradled his head against hers.

"Oh, Gerald ..." He pushed her away. Tears were streaming down his face. He felt he was being punished for failing to love his son unconditionally. He'd been intolerant of William's needs, and judgemental of his difficulties in socialising. He'd seen similarities with aspects of his own behaviour and it left him unable to respond to William in anything other than a critical way. He could end this right now. He could explain what happened, that he hadn't intended to shoot Angela – it was an accident. Which did he want to face: the prospect of his son being charged with a double homicide, or the likelihood of his being accused of Angela's murder? Nobody would believe that it was an accident. They'd assume he shot her deliberately. He'd be locked away, maybe even face the death penalty. A wave of terror pulsed through him at the thought. He could live with the shame of having a son a murderer, but he couldn't face the shame and utter devastation that being labelled a murderer would bring, let alone facing the death penalty. And even if he wasn't found guilty of her murder, there would be the revelation that he went looking for sex with Angela. His life would be over.

William and Angela had brought this on themselves. He couldn't help that, and he wasn't prepared to help William now. He had no choice – he had to save himself, even if he had to watch his son condemned for a murder he didn't commit. He wanted someone to berate him for being such a pitiful wretch of a man. He wanted to feel the lashes that would tear his flesh and release his pain. He wanted to be physically punished for being a tragic, pathetic worm - one capable of condemning his son to death. He wanted to see the pity in people's eyes that a physical beating might bring.

"Are you alright, Gerald? You look awful." Gerald flinched at hearing Susan's voice. He had the thought that she could read his mind; see the twisted images in his head.

"I'm okay," he mumbled. "Just upset, that's all."

"I know, Gerald. This is the worst nightmare." She steeled herself with an aching resolve against the wall of tears that threatened to reduce her to an incoherent wreck. *You've got to deal with this, for William's sake,* she told herself.

David Singleton gave a slight, polite cough.

"I think our only hope is for William to plead guilty to shooting Jake Fisher, but not guilty to murder in the first degree. We will need to convince the jury that William had no intention of shooting Police Officer Fisher. And that's something only William can make clear. We need him to help himself, but I'm not sure he's willing to do that. He seems resigned to his fate. He's given an admission of sorts that he may have also killed Angela. I'm not sure he knows if he killed Angela Fisher or not, but I doubt if a jury will see it that way. 'A confession is a confession' is likely to be their assessment."

"But he says he didn't kill Angela, and I believe him – he adored her, she was such a special person ..." Susan stopped, realising she was repeating the suggestions in the statement as to why William had murdered Angela. David Singleton understood her train of thought.

124

"Exactly," he said, quietly. "And there are no other suspects. The police are convinced that William murdered Angela and as I understand it, they aren't going to be doing much more, not now they have William's confession - or should I say acceptance - that he shot Angela."

*

The Offices of Brindley, Schultz and Associates were in a small brick building in the older section of Columbus, just off Rich Street. David Singleton was waiting for them in the lobby.

"Come through," he said, holding the door open. The far corner of his snug office displayed memorabilia associated with his long career as a lawyer. There were framed diplomas, a signed baseball bat, and several family photographs. Pride of place was a large photograph of President Johnson standing with three men, one of whom was recognisable as a much younger David Singleton. A large Jackson Pollock painting adorned another wall. Its spiral splashes of colours added a touch of modernity to what would otherwise have been a typical lawyer's office, with the rows of law texts and reference journals that filled the shelves on the other walls. Susan felt immediately at ease in this warm environment. It suggested someone who had interests beyond those usually associated with a city lawyer. Gerald pointed to the photograph with the former President.

"That's you, isn't it?" David Singleton smiled.

"Yes, that was in 1965, nearly 25 years ago. I was a junior lawyer in the Legal Affairs Division at the White House."

"Sounds very impressive," commented Gerald.

"Coffee?" David Singleton asked as he raised one of the mugs from the salver on the small conference table in the centre of the room. He was pleased that both

125

Susan and Gerald seemed more relaxed. This was going to be difficult for them all and he needed Gerald and Susan to be comfortable in discussing the case and any family issues that might be relevant.

"I've picked up a copy of the police report. I got it late last night from the District Attorney's Office. The statements from the two police officers who witnessed the shooting of Jake Fisher corroborate the statement given by William. One of them claims he saw William fire the gun. The other had his view of William partially blocked by the door, but he's in no doubt that William fired the fatal shot. He was standing closest to Officer Fisher and described the effect of the bullet passing through Fisher's head in graphic detail."

Susan glanced at Gerald. He was leaning on the table with his forearms, gripping his coffee mug with his outstretched hands.

"Do we have to hear this?" His voice sounded unusually weak.

"I know this isn't easy, but I want you to be prepared for what you're likely to hear in court. The jury will also find the officer's testimony very shocking. It could set the jury firmly against William. He could be the prosecution's most powerful witness. It might give the jury an excuse for viewing William as a killer – and that word is dangerous. It makes it easier for the jury to see William as Angela's murderer." David Singleton paused, anticipating some reaction from Susan and Gerald. Instead, there was just the creaking of chairs in the uncomfortable silence. David Singleton eased the discussion forward.

"There will be a ballistics report to confirm that Angela and Jake were shot with the same gun. The police are confident that this will be the case, which leads us to Angela's murder. The forensics report states that the bloodstains on William's shirt are the same type as Angela's. She's a rare blood type - *AB negative.*"

"What's the importance of that?" asked Gerald.

"Only about five percent of the population are *AB negative,*" replied David Singleton. "William is type *O* which means that the blood found on William and on his clothes is Angela's. That virtually rules out the suggestion that someone else might have killed her."

"So that's it then," said Gerald, giving a resigned sigh. Susan felt helpless.

"I just can't accept this," she said, the frustration evident from her exasperated tone. "I know William is innocent. He didn't kill Angela!" David Singleton glanced at Gerald. His expression and quick shrug of his shoulders suggested he wasn't as convinced as Susan.

"The evidence against him is compelling, I'm afraid. Ask yourselves, if William didn't kill her, who did – a passing stranger?" Gerald felt his pulse race. He could smell the guilt oozing from his pores. He could feel the warm dampness in his armpits and on the palms of his hands, despite the cold shiver that trickled down his back. He glanced at his hands. They were clenched into tight fists. He slowly released his grip and stretched his trembling fingers. The scratches on the back of his hand throbbed under the gauze patches. Blood was seeping through as if the dressing was unable to hide the stigmata, the mark of guilt with which he was scarred. He was suddenly aware that Susan and David Singleton were staring at him. Susan put a hand on his shoulder:

"Are you alright, Gerald? You look awful." David Singleton poured a glass of water and handed it to Gerald. He almost dropped the slippery tumbler in his damp shaking hands.

"I'm fine ... it's just a lot to deal with." Susan felt a yank of compassion. Gerald was struggling with this more than she had realised.

"I know," she replied. "But we've got to be strong – for William's sake." Gerald wasn't sure he could cope with this. He knew he was casting off his son in order to save himself. He had to fight the compulsion to reveal everything and free himself from this torture. *You've come this far,* he told himself. *There is no turning back.*

"Yes, I'm okay, thanks." David Singleton flicked through to the police report. He'd studied it in detail and highlighted various sections.

"William's fingerprints were on the gun – which is no surprise. It merely confirms the statements given by the other officers. They also found William's fingerprints in the kitchen, on the door handle and in the lounge. Some other fingerprints have simply been photographed and catalogued. They don't seem to have been very thorough. They're convinced they have the perpetrator, given the sequence of events and William's statement." Gerald squirmed in his seat.

"I suppose we must prepare for the worst. I'd hope that at least he'll avoid the death penalty."

"Gerald, we can't just accept that he'll be found guilty!" replied Susan. "He didn't shoot Angela. He couldn't – he wouldn't!"

"I'm afraid Gerald is right, Susan. William must decide how he wants to plead. I'll recommend he pleads guilty to the murder of Jake Fisher." Susan wrapped her arms tightly around herself and rocked back and forth. The wicker seat squeaked in rhythm to her movements.

"What about Angela?"

"My recommendation is that he pleads not guilty," said David Singleton. He knew that's what they wanted

128

to hear, but he had real concerns about this strategy. It might go against him if the jury found him guilty and he was also concerned about William and the statement he had given. Getting him to state clearly that he was innocent would be difficult, and getting the jury to accept this wouldn't be easy.

"Are you sure that's the right thing to do?" asked Gerald. "Might that go against William if some form of plea bargain is necessary?"

"I can't believe what I'm hearing!" exclaimed Susan turning to glare at Gerald. "We've got to get him off. I don't want you, Gerald, to accept that he killed Angela. It's just not true!" Her lips quivered and she had to dig her fingernails into the table to stop herself from bursting into tears. David Singleton attempted to ease the tension.

"I'm not here to take sides, Susan. My role is to give you the best legal advice that I can. Pleading not guilty does have some risks – and it also means we must have William's full cooperation. He needs to be convinced he didn't shoot Angela, and then he needs to convince the jury that he didn't commit this murder. It's not going to be easy. And Gerald is right; it could go against him if the jury are of the view that he's guilty. I will also need background on William that might help the jury see him as a normal person."

"Normal? He's not a freak!" Angela yelled.

"He's killed a police officer and may have killed the police officer's wife. I'm afraid the jury will not view that as normal behaviour."

"I'm sorry," said Susan. She breathed slowly and forced herself to remain calm. "What sort of information do you need?" David Singleton took a gulp of his coffee and reached for a yellow legal pad from the neat stack on an adjacent work table.

"I want to be able to tell the jury about William. I want them to see William as a person – a young man – and not someone they could assume was capable of murder. I want to explain his characteristics; his strengths and weaknesses, and what in your eyes makes him a special person. I want them to understand that William has a soul, just like them."

*

The more David Singleton heard about William, the less he liked it. Here was a loner, someone who didn't fit in with his peer group, someone who could be described as socially inept. His school reports made depressing reading. His early years in a classroom had been disruptive and it was clear, even from the sanitised statements from his primary school teachers, that William's behaviour had been 'challenging'. Some teachers had advised that William be put into a programme of 'special education' so that he could be taught in a more structured environment, with teachers who were trained to deal with disruptive behaviour. Susan had met with his teachers on a number of occasions and somehow managed to convince them to let him stay with the mainstream group. But she'd had to agree that he should repeat a grade. William would always be a year older than others in his grade, although he looked several years younger than most.

And then his behaviour pattern had changed. From being a hyperactive child, virtually incapable of going through the school day without at least one temper tantrum or some other form of disruptive behaviour, he became quiet, solemn and withdrawn. But the real change came when he discovered his gift for music. His reports from his music teacher, Mr. Waite, were glowing, and his other schoolwork improved. His school reports now told of a shy and sensitive pupil who had a special talent and who had markedly improved in all aspects of his academic work. Mr. Waite had persuaded Angela Fisher to take him on as one of her pupils, and he'd lived up to his billing. According to Susan, he'd developed his skills and repertoire to such an extent that there was a genuine hope that he'd be good enough to get a scholarship to study music, perhaps even to the Julliard Music Academy.

"I think he was infatuated with her," said Gerald, wanting to steer the discussion to William's relationship with Angela.

"I wouldn't say infatuated," said Susan, suspecting that Gerald's comment wasn't helpful. "His music meant so much to him and he developed so quickly with Angela."

"He talked of little else," added Gerald. "I think they had a close relationship."

"Musically, you mean?" commented David Singleton.

"Of course 'musically'. What else?" replied Susan, quickly. David Singleton decided to move on.

"From what I have gathered, he became quite popular."

"Yes," replied Susan, pleased that the conversation had moved away from William's relationship with Angela. "He started giving impromptu concerts at lunch times. They got so popular, especially with the girls, that the Head had to put a stop to them. I think some of the boys were getting a bit jealous of all the attention he was getting and started making a mess – even breaking chairs, so Mr. Waite told me."

"What about girlfriends?" asked David Singleton. "You said he became popular, but did he have any girlfriends?"

"No," replied Susan, "none that I know of."

"I think that he was content to meet Angela a few times a week. I often wondered if he might have seen having a girlfriend as some form of betrayal," added Gerald. Susan was shocked.

"Gerald, how can you say such a thing? I don't think he was ever confident enough to ask a girl out – but I'm sure that will change soon. He's a lot more confident now." She spoke as if William hadn't done anything other than been grounded for staying out late, and Gerald gave David Singleton a knowing look. David Singleton paused, and picked up several sheets of paper from his file that were clipped together. He looked at the report and spoke while he scanned the first page.

"Tell me about this trouble he got into for stealing tapes from the Music Store."

"I was furious," said Gerald. "He'd gone off with two of the most popular students at the high school. He'd never had many friends and I felt that this would be the making of William – get him to mix with his peers – that sort of thing." Susan was itching to get a word in. She ignored David Singleton and spoke directly to Gerald.

"They were jocks," she said, rather indignantly. "They weren't William's type. I was very nervous at him going off with the two of them. I just felt there might be trouble."

"And William was foolish enough to find it," replied Gerald, speaking towards David Singleton. Susan's temper got the better of her.

"You didn't help, encouraging him to go with them - and then hitting him when you learned about him being arrested!" She glared at Gerald, who looked taken aback. He hadn't expected that she would tell this to David Singleton. He turned quickly to face Susan.

"I was angry, very angry. He'd let me down. He needed to know just how angry and upset I was. All I could think of was how much he'd let us down – and how embarrassing it was going to be."

"Oh, and you thought hitting your son was the right thing to do," exclaimed Susan. David Singleton raised his hand. "This isn't the time to get angry with one another," he said, quietly but firmly. "It isn't helpful."

"Sorry," mumbled Susan. Gerald glared at Susan for a brief moment and then stared at the floor.

"Okay," said David Singleton. "I'd like to quickly go over what happened when William went to court. His music teacher, Mr. Waite, spoke for him as did Angela Fisher. I understand that she spoke quite passionately on his behalf, despite the fact that she was the wife of a police officer, her husband Jake. I'm sure that can't have been easy for her." Susan regained her composure.

"Yes, she helped to persuade the judge to treat him leniently. I know it was very difficult for her; I could see the looks she was getting from the arresting officers."

"And William continued with his lessons?"

"Yes," replied Susan. "He wouldn't go back at first – he was too embarrassed. It was Angela who spoke to him on the phone and appealed for him to return. I think he was delighted she asked. So was I. She was the only one who could have got him back to his music." David Singleton rubbed his hand over his thinning grey hair.

"He obviously thought a lot of her."

"She was an inspiration," added Susan.

"And she must have been fond of him as well. She'd been willing to speak up for him in court and persuade him to return to his lessons with her."

"Yes," replied Susan. "He was just as enthusiastic about his music, perhaps even more so. He seemed to be delighted with the pieces she was giving him to play. He was developing into a confident, competent musician."

"Was there anything in his behaviour that suggested his attitude to her was changing in any way?" asked David Singleton. Susan paused and glanced at Gerald. He leaned forward to speak. Susan knew what was coming but felt powerless to deflect anything he might say.

"I think he was besotted with her. I even think she led him on a bit." Susan felt her face become flushed.

"Gerald, would you please stop implying that there was something going on between William and Angela. You know perfectly well that isn't true. He adored her as a very gifted music teacher – not in the way you are implying." David Singleton intervened. He turned to Gerald.

"Have you any basis for suggesting there might be anything more to their relationship?" Gerald became quite defensive.

"Look, I'm not saying there was anything going on between them, but it was obvious that William had a crush on her. Maybe that's something in his favour?"

"Maybe, maybe not," replied David Singleton. "What I will say is that this isn't going to be easy." Susan let out a groan. She tried to speak but her tongue floundered in the back of her mouth. The best she could manage were short gasps of breath that refused to be made into any discernible sound. She felt a desire to strangle Gerald, to squeeze the breath from his body so that he was incapable of uttering any more statements that might implicate William in Angela's murder.

*

David Singleton was glad when they had gone. The tension in his office during the last twenty minutes or so had been oppressive, almost unbearable. Gerald had appeared quite reasonable and seemed to fully accept that William was in a difficult situation. He also appeared to be more honest about the relationship that was developing between William and Angela. Susan, on the other hand, was determined to defend William and appeared quick to give Gerald a stern look of disapproval whenever he made any comment that suggested William might have had ideas about a relationship with Angela, other than those of teacher and pupil.

It seemed obvious to David Singleton that William was infatuated with Angela. The prosecution would make the same assumption and would in all likelihood suggest to the jury that William's infatuation got out of control. That's exactly what he would do if he was the prosecuting attorney. And then there was William's background. He was socially inept, but he'd found a talent in music that had become his passion. The prosecution would suggest to the jury that this passion for his music led to an infatuation with Angela. It was a lethal combination, which resulted in William believing Angela was in love with him. It also resulted in an intense jealousy, even a hatred, of Jake Fisher. The prosecution might well attempt to suggest the murders were connected. Angela Fisher, because she had spurned his advances; and Jake Fisher, because circumstances gave William the opportunity to shoot him.

He felt exhausted. He knew what the prosecution lawyers would do; he'd been in the game long enough to have been witness to most of the tricks that lawyers play. In the end, it always comes down to what the jury finds believable. A good prosecutor would have little difficulty in convincing a jury that William had firstly murdered Angela Fisher, and then shot Police Officer Jake Fisher when he was confronted by him. And then what? The prosecution would be certain to ask for the death penalty, even for someone as young as William. This, after all, was a double homicide of a police officer and his wife. In the opinion of the police and of the jury, it would be seen as the worst double homicide anyone could commit.

*

The arraignment hearing went as David Singleton had expected. The district attorney announced that William would be charged with the aggravated murder of Police Officer Fisher, and the second-degree murder of Angela Fisher. The accused would be charged with the double homicide of a police officer and his wife. The DA's office would be asking for the death penalty. The DA also made reference to bail. He requested that William remain in custody, given the seriousness of the crimes with which he had been charged. He wanted him placed on a 24-hour watch, considering his probable state of confusion and depression. David Singleton told the judge that his client would plead not guilty to the charge of first-degree murder of Police Officer Fisher, but would plead guilty to the lesser charge of second-degree murder. He then told the judge that William would plead not guilty to the murder of Angela Fisher.

The judge was not willing to allow bail, despite David Singleton's pleas.

"This is his first offence, judge ..."

"Correction," snapped the DA. "He was guilty of shop-lifting – he has a record ..."

"Enough point-scoring. You can save that for a jury," said the judge. "I think what Mr. Singleton was going to add is that it's his first offence, apart from the misdemeanour you referred to."

Chapter 13
Support

The trial was scheduled to commence on the second of November, just ten days after the preliminary hearing. Susan visited William every day, and stayed as long as she was allowed. She was concerned at William's demeanour. He was very quiet and expressionless and clammed up completely at any mention of Angela or Jake Fisher. The station officer was sympathetic and promised to do what he could to make William comfortable. His cell was adjacent to the room occupied by the duty officer, and well away from the other cells. There was a small television and a few books that the station officer had provided. He agreed that Susan could bring in William's stereo system, a set of headphones, and a few of his favourite tapes. Susan was delighted at William's reaction. He looked brighter and was obviously pleased with these unexpected luxuries.

Gerald came along the first three days, and then announced he was finding it all too difficult. He'd 'try' and come with her every other day. Susan was past arguing with him. Her duty was to her son. Professor McGrath had called her as soon as he heard about William's arrest. He told her to take as much time as she needed. Susan wondered to herself just what that would really mean. She did at least take some comfort from Prof. McGrath's support and his urging for her not to be concerned about her work at the University. Dean Roberts had written to Gerald authorising six months paid leave. The University President had also written a letter to Susan and Gerald expressing his regret at what they were going through. There was no mention of William, she noted. Gerald told her she was being hypersensitive.

Gerald was depressed, she knew that. He rarely ventured outside the house except to collect the newspapers. He seemed obsessed with articles about the murders that were now appearing in the national as well as the local press. He took to clipping out every reference to the murders he could find. But he rarely wanted to talk about what was happening. Susan, on the other hand, desperately wanted to talk about the murders. She wanted to tease out every morsel of information she possessed. She wanted to cogitate about what she knew; she wanted to speculate about what may have happened but most of all, she wanted to talk – to talk about what was happening. She needed to hear her words pouring from her mouth, draining the pus that filled her head and sickened her stomach. She needed someone to help her sift through the thoughts that flittered in her brain and teased her with fruitless possibilities, remonstrating with her for daring to have hope.

*

The phone rang just as Susan got back from visiting William. Gerald picked up the receiver and then held it towards her.

"It's Mrs. Miller, again!" he said, not attempting to shield his voice. Mrs. Miller had called every evening since William was first arrested. Susan hadn't wanted to talk to anyone at first. Now she desperately wanted the chance to pore over the events of the last few days. Mrs. Miller seemed to sense what was needed. Her phone calls had been brief.

"Hello Susan. I'm just calling again to say if you need me ..."

"Thanks, Mrs. Miller." As soon as she paused, Mrs. Miller took it as her cue to sign off.

"I'll call again ... if that's okay."And then she'd replace the receiver.

The phone rang again the following day at almost the same time. Susan grabbed the phone. This time, Susan was relieved to hear Mrs. Miller's voice.

"I'm sorry I've been ..."

"You've nothing to apologise for," interrupted Mrs. Miller. "I can only imagine what you are going through and my heart bleeds for you both, you and William. I'm so fond of that boy. He's special, we know that."

"Thanks, Mrs. Miller. I feel I need to talk to someone now. And I'd like to talk to you if that's alright. Could we meet?"

"Of course," replied Mrs. Miller in her calm, measured tones. Susan felt a sense of relief as if she'd taken a positive step. "How about coming round here?" suggested Mrs. Miller. Susan took a deep breath before answering. She needed a moment to marshal her thoughts.

"I'd prefer if we could meet at my house. Gerald has taken to hiding himself in the spare bedroom; in fact, he virtually lives in there. Could you come round tomorrow morning, about ten? We won't be disturbed, Gerald doesn't surface until lunchtime. He's become a night owl."

"Yes, that's okay," she replied. "I bet you haven't had much chance to do anything in the house and a spruce-up can't do any harm. If Gerald makes a sudden

140

appearance it will just look like my normal weekly visit." Susan couldn't help giving a low chuckle.

"See you tomorrow, then," she said, feeling distinctly brighter.

The sight of Mrs. Miller at the door gave her a similar sense of relief to that she'd felt when Mrs. Miller had first picked up and calmed a shrieking William. It seemed like just yesterday. She wore similar clothes, her hair was permed and dyed in exactly the same style and, as always, she had a large handbag dangling from her forearm. Mrs. Miller had changed very little except that her appearance was now more in keeping with her age. She was one of those people who seemed to have always been the same age. There were a few signs of her status as a senior citizen. She had become a little round shouldered and her face was not as plump and round as it had been. In recent years, Susan had insisted she only come for half a day each week. It was a token gesture by both of them that signalled a continuing friendship, and her fondness for William in particular. It was a bond that Susan was reluctant to break.

Mrs. Miller stepped into the hallway, allowed her handbag to slip to the floor, and opened her arms towards Susan. Susan stepped forward into their warmth and felt the reassuring comfort of Mrs. Miller's plump frame and the smell of face powder that reminded Susan of her own mother, hugging her close when she'd had a fall.

"Thanks for coming," said Susan as Mrs. Miller released her from their affectionate embrace. In all the years of their association, Susan had only ever referred to her as 'Mrs. Miller'. Susan liked it. It gave a detachment that elevated Mrs. Miller's status in her mind - and probably William's too, she thought.

Mrs. Miller quickly busied herself tidying, polishing, cleaning the kitchen and rearranging the furniture in their front room. It gave the room a fresh look and made Susan feel alive again. She made a fresh brew of coffee and signalled to Mrs. Miller. They sat at the kitchen table, sipping their coffee and sending crumbs bouncing off the inadequately small plates as they each nibbled on a biscuit. The two women, who had each invested so much in William, allowed the calm silence to hang like a snug blanket over the intimate setting they had created. Mrs. Miller reached across the table and rested her large hand on Susan's arm.

"He didn't do it. He didn't kill Angela," she said. Susan felt tears running down her cheeks.

"I know he didn't," replied Susan in a determined tone. "But what can we do? He's condemned himself – I think he's overwhelmed by it all. At times I think he's given up. And, God forgive me, there are times I think it's all pointless. He's going to be convicted ... I just know he is."

"He's innocent," repeated Mrs. Miller, with a hint of admonishment. Susan immediately felt guilty and inadequate.

"Thanks," she said. "You're the first person who's said that."

Chapter 14
The Trial

The jury foreman was Alan Nicholson. He'd been intent on being the spokesperson from the minute he was selected to be the first juror by the prosecuting attorney. It gave him the feeling of being part of their team and his role would be to make sure the jury understood the prosecution's case. Alan Nicholson's view was that this boy was probably guilty – unless the defence could convince him otherwise.

Alan Nicholson was the owner of a local insurance company, Nicholson's Insurance. He was small and dapper, always immaculately dressed and rarely without a black leather briefcase that his wife, Carol, had given him when they moved the business from a room in their house to the present office suite. Carol Nicholson was meticulous in keeping the records of every contract and ensured that their customers were invited to have an 'insurance health check' every six months. She was also very strict and made sure the two young girls who worked for Nicholson's were gainfully employed from the minute they were open for business through to closing time at five-thirty. She was equally dapper, and her weekly hair appointment at the same hairdresser she had used for the past ten years or so ensured she rarely had a hair out of place. They had no children and put all their efforts into their business. Perhaps as a consequence, they were rather intolerant of youngsters, except those that excelled at sport. Alan Nicholson had been a reasonably good baseball player when he was at high school and enjoyed mixing with the coaches and the jocks.

Most people were impressed with Alan's willingness to put himself forward and with his effectiveness in getting things done. It helped his business. Others thought him too pushy and overbearing. Alan didn't care. For every person that took their business elsewhere, there were ten who responded positively to his sales pitch. He was a warden at a local church. It was one he had deliberately targeted because of the size of its congregation. His position in the church gave him credibility with the congregation and access to the parishioners. He would make a point of visiting new families who joined the church and would give them a mix of token items - badges, pens and notebooks, a calendar with his name on it and a cake bought from the local bakery. His second visit – there was always a follow-up – was about business. He provided leaflets explaining the need for all responsible families to have life insurance, health insurance and any of the numerous other forms of insurance that he could persuade them to buy. Most did. It was a formula he had developed with considerable success.

The Nicholsons provided funds towards several of the score boards at local high schools, including the one William attended. Alan Nicholson usually went to three or four of the 'home' games and gave a prize to the best footballer. This year it had been Billy Mansell, one of those that had befriended William and persuaded him to steal from the Music Store in the mall.

Jury selection didn't take long. The judge asked Alan Nicolson if he knew of Jake Fisher. "Yes, I knew who Jake Fisher was. No, I didn't know him personally."

"And you didn't sell him any insurance?"

"No, I missed that one." There was a ripple of hesitant laughter; even the judge's blank expression creased into a quick smile. The judge asked all the potential jurors if they knew Jake Fisher, Angela Fisher or the defendant. Most of the jurors gave similar answers. You could hardly live in the community without having at least heard of Jake Fisher or seen his photograph in the local paper. One admitted he sometimes had a few beers with Jake Fisher, and was dismissed. Three other potential jurors knew William's parents and as a consequence were also dismissed from jury duty. None of them admitted to knowing Angela Fisher.

Judge Webb had a reputation for being tough but fair. He held a pre-trial meeting with both sets of attorneys advising them how they were to behave in his courtroom. He was all too familiar with most of the tactics that attorneys used in trying to convince a jury.

"This is not a theatre," he told them. "It's a court of law, and I am the presiding officer. I expect you to be nothing but professional. As you well know, this has become a high profile case and I don't want any attempt to play to the media or to the gallery. Please restrict your performances to addressing the legal issues pertaining to the case. Do I make myself clear?" There were discreet nods of agreement.

*

The jury were ushered into the small courtroom, led in procession by the clerk to the court, and took their places on the tiered seats set along the wall to the left of the judge's bench. The witness box was also on the

145

judge's left, between his bench and the jury. The court stenographer sat at a small desk immediately in front of the judge, feeding a paper scroll into her archaic looking machine. Lawyers for the prosecution, and for the defence, sat at separate tables, an aisles width apart, just in front of the public gallery.

William sat next to David Singleton, his head bowed. Susan and Gerald sat in the public gallery, immediately behind their son. At the instruction from the clerk to the court, everyone in the courtroom rose to their feet. Judge James Webb, wearing a black robe, walked quickly in from a side door to the right of his bench, stepped onto the raised dais, took his seat in front of a large photograph of President Ronald Reagan and waved his hand for everyone to be seated.

Judge Webb turned to address the members of the jury.

"Members of the jury, you will hear evidence from the prosecution that alleges the defendant, William Martin, shot and killed Police Officer Jake Fisher shortly after murdering Angela Fisher, Jake Fisher's wife. She was also William Martin's piano teacher. William Martin has pleaded guilty to murder in the second degree of Police Officer Fisher and not guilty to the murder of Angela Fisher." The judge paused and scanned the members of the jury. He wanted to be sure that they each understood the allegations they must consider.

"It is important that you understand the distinction between first and second-degree murder. In the state of Ohio, first-degree murder is the killing of an individual without lawful justification, where the person either intends to kill the individual or knows that his act creates a strong probability of death." He peered at the jury over the rim of his glasses.

146

"First-degree murder is the most serious of crimes. Punishment is either imprisonment for life without the prospect of parole, or the death penalty." His delivery was deliberately pedantic and his tone was deep and expressionless. There was an audible gasp from the public gallery. Even a few of the jury members hung their heads, as if not realising that this was something they might have to decide. Susan glanced at Gerald. He sat staring at the judge. He was as white as a sheet.

"Gerald, are you alright?" she whispered. He nodded, but didn't take his eyes off the judge. Susan hoped he was capable of getting through this, for William's sake.

"In the case of a second-degree murder," continued the judge, "the defendant must convince you he was under intense pressure resulting from serious provocation from the person he killed. The defence contends that the defendant, William Martin, felt threatened and discharged the gun accidentally."

The judge paused for a moment to relieve the tension that was obvious in the faces of the members of the jury. Some of them exhaled and took the opportunity to breathe more normally.

The lead attorney for the prosecution, and David Singleton, William's attorney, had both completed their respective summations of the evidence the jury had heard. Judge Web thanked them both for the professional way in which they had handled the witnesses and the evidence in what he referred to as an intriguing and unusual case. The stenographer took the opportunity to reset her machine and adjust her small seat near to the standing flags of the United States and the State of Ohio.

Judge Webb poured himself a glass of water, took a couple of sips, and then leaned towards the jury box. "Members of the jury, I will summarise the evidence you have heard, starting with the death of Angela Fisher."

The court officer slid a thin sheaf of papers in front of the judge. He slowly leafed through the papers, arranging them in front of him. "The defendant has pleaded not guilty to her murder. The defence has asked you to accept that William Martin arrived early for his lesson and that he'd found Angela Fisher lying on the floor, virtually naked and covered in blood. The defendant has testified that he heard Angela Fisher attempt to speak and that he'd tried to revive her. The defence argues that this explains the significant amount of her blood found on his clothes, and on his face and hands. He then picked up a gun from the kitchen floor and took it with him - apparently intent on getting help - when he saw Police Officer Fisher returning to the house. He panicked, jumped into his car, with the gun, and sped off." The judge paused and turned deliberately and directly to the jury.

"You must ask yourselves: why did the defendant fail to stop when he saw Police Officer Fisher? The defence asks you to accept that he was so disturbed at finding Angela Fisher's body that he reacted on instinct and wanted to get help as quickly as possible. Encountering Police Officer Fisher only added to his state of intense shock and confusion. He wanted to get as far away from the scene as quickly as possible. In his statement to the police, the defendant, William Martin, admitted that he may have killed Angela Fisher. The defence have argued that William was upset and uncertain. They have also pointed out that his statement was made without legal representation being present and allege that his statement was given under duress."

The judge paused and took another sip of water. A few of the jurors were taking notes. Most were staring intently at the judge, trying to absorb every word. A

148

couple of jurors seemed determined to fix their gaze on William, watching for any reaction he might display to the judges summing up. William sat fidgeting constantly, squirming in his seat at every reference to Angela.

"Members of the jury," continued the judge, "you have heard the prosecution allege that William Martin is guilty of the murder of Angela Fisher. You've seen the graphic and disturbing photographs of the victim. She was lying on the kitchen tiles in a pool of blood. She was virtually naked – her clothes were strewn around the floor. She had been fatally wounded by a single shot from the same gun that killed Police Officer Jake Fisher. You have heard expert testimony stating that the blood found on William and on his clothes matched that of Angela Fisher. Her blood type was type *AB negative* which, according to the expert testimony, is only found in a small percentage of the population. The defendant's blood type is the common type *O*. You also heard that the defendant's fingerprints were found in the kitchen, the hallway and the lounge. The defendant's fingerprints were also on the gun that shot both Angela Fisher and Police Officer Jake Fisher. Police despatch records confirm that Police Officer Fisher made an emergency call to say that his wife had been shot, and that he'd seen the defendant fleeing the crime scene."

The judge paused to rearrange the papers on his bench.

"The prosecution alleges that William Martin was besotted with Angela Fisher. The prosecution maintains that William Martin convinced himself that Angela had sexual feelings for him. The prosecution suggested to the defendant that he made sexual advances, which she tried to rebuff. They outlined a possible scenario. A struggle - perhaps she tried to calm him down by pretending to play along. She thought that if she could get hold of her husband's gun she could hold him off. But William Martin got it first. He got mad that she wasn't cooperating. He made her strip. Maybe she taunted him. He was out of control. He couldn't get what he wanted. If he couldn't have her, nobody else could – so he shot her, shot her at close range."

The judge looked up from his notes and peered in the direction of the jury box as if checking they were all paying attention, and then continued.

"Members of the jury, you may accept that this is a likely portrayal of what occurred, in which case you must conclude that the defendant is guilty, guilty of murder in the second degree. If you are not persuaded by this, or have some doubt as to the likelihood that the defendant killed Angela Fisher, then you must return a verdict of not guilty."

The judge signalled to the court officer who placed a second folder in front of the judge. He replaced the papers pertaining to Angela Fisher's death and carefully and deliberately spread out several pages of notes he had made regarding the shooting of Police Officer Fisher.

"In the case of the killing of Police Officer Fisher, the defendant has admitted that he shot the officer, but that this was unintentional. You have heard important testimony from the two police officers who gave chase to the car the defendant was driving. They have testified that they waited for the more senior officer to arrive – Police Officer Fisher, in this case – before trying to do anything other than contain the situation. You also heard them testify that Police Officer Fisher showed great courage in volunteering to step forward to try and persuade the defendant to give up the gun he had in his possession."

For an instant, David Singleton wondered if he should lodge an objection to the judge quoting what amounted to speculation by the police officers. He thought better of it. He'd already tried to object on the same point when it was first introduced by the prosecution, and it had been firmly denied by the judge. Before David Singleton had time to marshal his thoughts, the judge started speaking to the jury again.

"The defence accepts that William Martin shot Jake Fisher, but they allege that he had not intended to kill him. They have argued that the defendant, William Martin, was extremely frightened by the police chase and felt threatened by Jake Fisher in particular. If you decide Jake Fisher's actions in trying to persuade William to throw down his weapon were a normal part of his role as a police officer, and that the defendant chose instead to shoot the police officer as he approached – then you must conclude that the second-degree murder defendant is guilty of murder in the first degree. If, however, you are persuaded that Police Officer Jake Fisher acted unreasonably or recklessly, and that the defendant was unaware that his actions could result in the fatal shooting of Police Officer Fisher, as the defence allege, then you must bring in a verdict of murder in the second degree."

*

Alan Nicholson led the jurors into the jury room. He poured himself a cup of black coffee and helped himself to one of the doughnuts that had been laid out on a side table. He positioned himself at the head of the long rectangular table and waited impatiently for the others to take a seat.

"Is everyone aware of what we have to do?" he asked. There was a nod from most of the jurors. "Good." He then continued. "I think you'll agree, the murder of Jake Fisher is straightforward – William

Martin has admitted he killed him." Frank Divine raised his hand. Frank was employed in a bank and it was in his nature to be thorough in all aspects of his work.

"We've got to listen carefully to what the defence tells the court. I'm not sure if it *is* first-degree murder."

"And anyway, maybe the gun went off by mistake," added a thin, nervous-looking woman. Julie Taylor was a primary school teacher. Her heart pounded as she spoke and she hung her head when Alan Nicholson gave her a dismissive look and continued as if he hadn't heard her.

"We must make sure our decisions are factually based. There is no room for conjecture," he said as he looked at each of them in turn. Julie Taylor sank even lower into her seat. "The decision regarding Jake Fisher's murder is simple enough. We know he's guilty. There's his admission, the eyewitness accounts, and the ballistics report on the gun. We have to decide if he's guilty of first-degree murder. My opinion is yes – it's first-degree murder. We all heard the testimony of the other police officers. They were full of praise for Jake Fisher's bravery. He tried to persuade William Martin to give up the weapon, and was shot and killed in the process. It shows that this kid had nothing but contempt for Jake Fisher. He shot him when there was absolutely no need for him to do so. He should have thrown out the gun and surrendered. Jake Fisher was a very brave man. He didn't deserve to be gunned down by this young punk." Most of the other jurors nodded in agreement as Alan Nicholson spoke. Frank Devine raised his concerns:

"I'd like to discuss the issue of first-degree murder. We could be condemning this boy to a death sentence."

"He's very young," added a stout middle-aged woman who occasionally met Mrs. Miller in the coffee shop. She'd heard from Mrs. Miller say just how shocked and upset she was. Mrs. Miller had said she'd never believe that William could kill anyone. She wondered if she should say that to the rest of the jury, but decided it wasn't right for someone else's views to be heard at this stage.

"That's really not relevant," snorted Nicholson. "He's old enough to be tried for murder. Our job is to decide if he's guilty of first-degree murder, not feel sorry for him because of his age."

"Surely the first issue is his guilt or innocence of murder," said Frank Divine, lifting his hand hesitantly like a schoolboy in a classroom. Alan Nicholson gave him a blank look.

"He's admitted murder," exclaimed Alan Nicholson. "But just to make sure that we are all able to proceed on the basis that he's guilty of the murder of Jake Fisher," he said, dismissively, "I'll ask the question. Raise your hand if you agree the defendant is guilty. Please bear in mind he's made a full confession, the shooting was witnessed by two fellow police officers, and he's pleaded guilty." It was if he was lecturing a group of schoolchildren. He could hardly believe he was having to do this. At least it would get them comfortable with the voting procedure, he told himself.

He raised his own arm and then looked around the table. A few glanced round to see how others were voting, before slowly lifting their hands. Arms followed raised arms, until all the jurors signalled their agreement that William Martin was guilty of murder.

"Thank you," said a smiling Alan Nicholson, as if he'd just received a vote of confidence. "That's unanimous – good." Several of the jurors shifted nervously in their seats. "And now to the issue of murder in the first degree." He paused to pick up some typed notes the judge had provided for his benefit.

"Here it is – first-degree murder." He spoke as if he was selling the benefits of one of his life insurance policies.

"I'll read from the information sheet provided by the court. *First-degree murder is the killing of an individual without lawful justification, where the person either intends to kill the individual or knows that his act creates a strong probability of death.* I'm going to go through this in stages," said Alan Nicholson. It was a tactic he used when getting clients to agree to a key clause in one of his policies. There was always the danger they'd reject the entire clause, but it was less likely if he steered them through bit by bit.

"*Killing an individual without lawful justification.* I take it we all accept that is what the defendant did – that's what he's guilty of?" He looked round the room. Everyone nodded.

"I'll move to the next bit - *where the person either intends to kill or knows the act will create a strong probability of death.*" It was familiar wording. Alan Nicholson revelled in the confusion that officially-worded phrases could bring in their need to be legally accurate. "He's guilty of first-degree murder if he intends to kill – and he's also guilty if he knows that firing the gun will have a strong probability of death."

A silence had stolen over them as Alan Nicholson went through the issues to consider. The ticking of the wall mounted pendulum clock seemed to get louder in the stillness of the room. It was Frank Devine who spoke first. Alan Nicholson felt his neck redden with irritation.

"I'm not sure about *intent to kill*," he remarked. A couple of the jury members nodded. "I'm sure I speak for a number of the others," added Frank Devine, feeling emboldened by the murmurings of support from those on either side of him.

"But you're not here to speak for the others," said Alan Nicholson, in his best authoritarian voice. "If others wish to make a point, they must do so on their own behalf."

"I must agree with Frank," said the lady seated on Frank Devine's left. "I'm not absolutely convinced that he intended to kill the police officer."

Don Slater spoke up.

"But he shot him at point-blank range. If that's not intent to kill, I don't know what is!" Don was a clerk in the personnel section of haulage firm on the outskirts of the City. He had his final professional exams coming up in a couple of weeks and had been quite annoyed at being called for jury duty. He wanted this over as quickly as possible. Alan Nicholson was pleased at his intervention. Most of the jurors were now nodding in agreement with Don Slater.

"And as for committing an act that has the strong probability of death, that's a no brainer." He suddenly realised what he had said.

"Sorry," he mumbled.

"That's alright Don, we know what you meant," said Alan Nicholson, not wanting to dilute the potency of Don Slater's comments. "Does anyone else wish to speak?" They all peered round the room. One, maybe two, would have liked to continue the discussion, but Don Slater's remarks had taken the wind out of their sails.

Alan Nicholson sensed the discussion had reached a conclusion of sorts. "I'd like to put this to the vote. If you now agree with that the defendant is guilty of murder in the first degree, please raise your hand." It was several seconds before anyone stirred. Alan Nicholson thought for a moment that no one was going to participate. Don Slater slowly raised his arm. "Thank you, Don," said Alan Nicholson. It was the catalyst need to spur the others into signalling their view. With painfully slow reluctance all the jurors raised their hands, with exception of the school teacher, Julie Taylor.

"I'm sorry; I can't send anyone to their death. It's not something I can support." Alan Nicholson jumped in before others had the chance to voice similar concerns.

"Let me ask you this. You agree that he's guilty of murder? We've already voted on that." Julie Taylor nodded. "And do you agree that the defendant committed a murder that fits the definition of first-degree murder?"

"Yes, I suppose so, but ..." Alan Nicholson cut her off.

"It's our role to give the court a verdict, not to impose the penalty - that's the judge's job. He decides if he will receive the death penalty, not us."

"But it gives him the option," suggested Julie Taylor, feeling on distinctly weaker ground. "I suppose I have to agree," she added, hesitantly. She gingerly raised her hand and quickly pulled it down when she realised the others no longer had their arms in the air.

"Thank you, Ms. Taylor. That's unanimous." He felt it was a tenuous decision and to avoid any chance of further reflection, he moved on quickly to the issue of Angela's murder. There was an obvious sense of relief from the jury members. They had dealt with the difficult issue of first-degree murder. The verdict for the murder of Angela Fisher would be much more palatable, irrespective of the guilt or otherwise of the defendant.

"The murder of Angela Fisher is the next case or us to consider." Alan Nicholson had decided not to attempt to force the jury to take a particular decision. He'd already achieved what he wanted - the defendant would be charged with first-degree murder. "The defendant is charged with second-degree murder." He reached for his notes. "This is a lesser charge and doesn't carry the death penalty. The defendant has said he's not guilty. We need to be convinced that he did murder Angela Fisher but that there was no planned intent. I'll summarise the evidence as best I can – please stop me at any time if you'd like to add something, or correct my interpretation." It was a much more conciliatory tone.

"The gun was the same one that shot Jake Fisher. The gun was recovered after Police Officer Fisher was shot, and the ballistics report confirmed that the same gun was used. And then there's Angela Fisher's blood type. She's a rare blood category and her blood was found on the gun and on William Martin, and he had a lot of her blood on his clothes and some on his hands and face. He was seen leaving the house by Jake Fisher – this was confirmed by the police despatch reports. His fingerprints were all over the place – the doors, the living room, the kitchen, as well as some older prints on the piano and other items of furniture. And then there's his confession." He paused to allow the other jury members to have their say.

"Yes," said Don Slater. "It's a strong case. But the defence says that she'd been shot before he arrived and that he tried to help her as she was dying. That explained the large amount of blood on his clothes." Don Slater felt he needed to redress the comments he'd made earlier. *Perhaps I'd spoken too forcefully,* he thought. *I'm the one who's condemned him.* "The police did find other fingerprints in the kitchen," he added.

"But they couldn't match them to anything on the gun," replied Alan Nicholson. He couldn't resist making a comment, even though he'd resolved to take a back seat.

"But that's because the gun had been smeared with Angela Fisher's blood," said Don Slater. "They had difficulty picking out any prints, even those of the defendant. What was it they said? The prints on the gun were smeared and couldn't be relied upon."

"The confession he gave gives me some concern," said Julie Taylor, finding her voice and determined to make a contribution, no matter how Alan Nicholson might try to dismiss her. "I can believe that he was very frightened and confused when he made his confession to the police."

"Thank you for your input," said Alan Nicholson. He felt it was time to move this along, aware that the jury might not be able to agree a decision if they continued to reinforce views that William Martin might be telling the truth. "Is anyone prepared to support the argument that the defendant is innocent of the murder of Angela Fisher?" Don Slater raised his arm.

"I think there is a chance that someone else may have committed the murder. But I'm not prepared to say he's innocent. All the evidence points to him being guilty, but there's just a chance he might be innocent."

A large man sitting next to Frank Devine decided to speak. John Templeton was not used to sitting in a hot, stuffy room and even less comfortable with voicing an opinion to a group of people. Frank was a gardener with a local nursery. He enjoyed working outside and even liked the oppressive heat of the glasshouse. It was different when the heat was helping his plants germinate and grow, unlike the stale air of the jury room. He liked telling people how to look after plants. They were often impressed with the way this man, who appeared slow, even simple, had such a sound practical knowledge of horticulture. It was the only thing he was really interested in. He spoke in a slow, hesitant voice.

"He did it," he said, staring at his big hands. There was a stunned silence. None of the other members of the jury knew how to respond. "No one else could have done it. I believe that it happened as the prosecutor said." Alan Nicholson waited until it was clear that John Templeton had said all he wanted to.

"Do you think that anyone else might have been involved?" asked Don Slater.

"No," replied John Templeton. "He was seen coming out of the house just before she was found." John Templeton knew he could be confused by the different scenarios expressed by the other jury members. He liked things to be clear and straightforward. "He had the gun, and he was covered in her blood." John Templeton was encouraged to see many of the jurors nodding in agreement. "It's not complicated," he added, pleased at his own contribution.

Alan Nicholson wasn't sure if the nods were in support of the opinion of John Templeton or an expression of empathy with the way this plain man had managed to put forward his views. He hoped it might signal a willingness of the jury members to reach a decision.

"I'd like us to take a vote," he said. "Please raise your hand if you think the defendant is guilty of the charge of murder." A huddle of three jurors at the far end of the table did not raise their hands.

"We don't think he intended to kill her," said the thin lady in the centre of the trio. "We've been looking though the notes we were provided. I think he's guilty of shooting her, but it should be a charge of manslaughter, not murder."

The other two spoke almost in unison. "We ... I agree."

Jane Edwards, the apparent spokesperson for the trio, continued. "From what I've read, it's not murder if there was no intention to kill. It seems to me that William Martin killed her in some sort of rage and I, for one, am of the view that he hadn't set out with the intention of killing her. I think he probably killed her in a fit of passion, as the prosecution has suggested. But I don't think that's murder, I think it's manslaughter." Most of the other jurors were now nodding vigorously at Jane Edward's assessment. Alan Nicholson tried to clarify the situation.

"We can recommend to the judge that we find the defendant guilty, but only guilty of the lesser charge of manslaughter - is that the view?" Heads nodded once again. "Can I have a vote on that?"

Chapter 15
The Outcome

Alan Nicholson led the jurors back into the courtroom.
The judge asked him if they'd reached a decision in the
case of the murder of Police Officer Jake Fisher. Alan
Nicholson stood, and addressed the judge.

"We have," he replied. "We find the defendant
guilty of the charge of first-degree murder."

Murmuring voices swept through the courtroom.
Reporters scribbled furiously on their pads, and the
prosecutor's bench nodded to each other in a self-
congratulatory manner. The jurors sat in silence staring
straight ahead, determined to avoid any eye contact
with William.

The judge waited for silence to crawl through the
courtroom. Angela's father suddenly sprang to his feet.
He pointed his finger at William.

"You murdering little bastard!" He was silenced by
two police officers who had been deliberately posted
close to Angela's parents. They escorted him from his
seat and out through large swing doors at the back of
the courtroom.

Susan gripped the edge of her seat. The outburst
from Angela's father had startled her. She looked
across at William. He was visibly shaken and appeared
to have cowered under his wagging finger. David
Singleton had primed them to expect a guilty verdict. It
was a foregone conclusion, he'd said, given William's

confession and the testimony of the police witnesses. But it was an artificial preparation. This was reality. Her son had been found guilty of murder. They'd pressed David Singleton for his view of the outcome. Manslaughter, he'd said, was the best they could hope for.

She forced herself to look at the jury members. Most were looking down at their hands. A few were now looking at William and a couple were looking directly at her, as if expecting her to burst into tears at any moment. The judge banged his gavel on the table.

"And have you reached a verdict in the case of the murder of Angela Fisher?"

"Yes, sir," replied the foreman, still standing. "We find the defendant guilty." There were gasps from the gallery. Susan couldn't contain herself any longer. She buried her face in her hands. She could taste her salty tears and feel the splatter from her stifled sobs. The judge glanced in Susan's direction, and then continued:

"Guilty of murder?" he asked.

"Guilty of manslaughter," replied Alan Nicholson. The judge nodded, sagely. He re-arranged papers on the bench, before turning to speak directly to William.

"William Martin, you have been found guilty of the first-degree murder of Police Officer Jake Fisher. In the State of Ohio, first-degree murder of a police officer is classified as aggravated murder. It is a capital offence and carries with it the harshest penalty. You have been found guilty of the gravest of crimes, and this court must send out a message to the public that the murder of a police officer will always result in the strictest penalty. You have also been found guilty of the manslaughter of Angela Fisher, someone who lost her life in a bloody and horrific way. I have therefore decided to use the ultimate power of this court and impose the death penalty for the first-degree murder of

Police Officer Jake Fisher, and the manslaughter of Angela Fisher."

Gerald leapt to his feet. He screamed at the judge. "You've got it all wrong – he's innocent! Please, I beg you, not the death penalty!"

The judge banged his gavel and looked sternly at Gerald. "Any more outbursts and I'll have you evicted from the court."

Gerald's legs gave way and he slumped down onto his seat. Susan gripped his arm, and sat staring at William. She suddenly felt exhausted and drained. She heard the judge speaking once again. His voice seemed weak and distant. She'd heard all she ever wanted to hear from the lips of this man.

"William Martin, you have the right of appeal to the Supreme Court. Have you anything you want to say to the court?" Everyone in the courtroom fixed intently on William and leaned in his direction to catch anything he might say. He sat in silence, looking like someone who was barely old enough to understand what was happening. Eventually he spoke in a barely audible whisper. There was a tremor in his voice.

"I didn't do it – I didn't kill Angela."

*

Susan eventually got back from the Southern Ohio Correction Facility where William was held. It was the only prison in the State that had prisoners on Death Row. The term 'correctional facility' had little meaning for anyone waiting to be executed. She remembered little about the drive. Her face was stained with black mascara, smudged into clown-like tears clinging to her cheeks. She knew it was a trip she would have to make several times a week. The strip search had been intimate and brutal. Two female prison guards had stood watching as she stripped off every item of clothing. She was made to lie face down on a couch and then she heard the snap of surgical gloves. She winced at the forced exploration.

"It's routine for a first visit," said one of the prison guards. She slapped Susan's backside. "Nice arse."

Susan grabbed her clothes and dressed as quickly as she could while they watched.

She wondered if Gerald would share the burden. She could understand his grief, but it was a grief he refused to share, as if his pain was more acute than hers. His behaviour was bizarre. He refused to talk about what had happened and he looked as though he wasn't sleeping – not that she'd really know. He'd moved into the spare bedroom and had moved his clothes and some of his books. She desperately wanted him to get help, but he dismissed the suggestion with a derisive angry snort whenever she attempted to raise the subject.

Gerald knew he would have to tread very carefully. The sentence William had received had shaken him and his outburst in court had been completely spontaneous. But now was the time to be mentally tough, he told himself. He would capitalise on the grief he felt and the injustice of the court's decision. Having people feeling sorry for him would, he thought, make it easier to remain in the role of the grieving father. He was, after all, genuinely aggrieved at the sentence William had received.

Mrs. Miller annoyed him. She looked at him with what he took to be an air of mistrust. Apart from Susan, she was the one person who was absolutely convinced that William was innocent of Angela's murder. She was suspicious to the point of being zealous in her commitment to finding the real murderer. She'd given Susan the confidence to believe that William was innocent and that something would turn up. She worried Gerald.

Gerald was scanning through his pile of papers, doing his best to ignore Mrs. Miller. They ate the meal Mrs. Miller had prepared in almost total silence. Susan could hardly wait for Gerald to skulk off to the spare room. Susan poured them both another cup of coffee.

"I'm glad you've come," she told Mrs. Miller. "I can't talk to Gerald. He's disappeared into his shell, quite literally." She pointed in the direction of the bedrooms.

"I'm glad to help in any way I can – you know that. I don't believe for one minute that William is guilty of shooting Angela." Susan gave a sigh.

"I'm glad to hear you say that," replied Susan. "I've felt that I am the only one who believes he's innocent."

"As for the shooting of Jake Fisher," said Mrs. Miller, "William wouldn't deliberately shoot anyone. I believe he was scared out of his wits. That Jake Fisher was a brute. If he thought William had killed Angela, he would have gone after William like a mad bull. I reckon that the gun went off accidentally. It certainly wouldn't have been a deliberate killing."

"That's the sort of reasoning that's been going round in my head," replied Susan. "The trouble is he admits firing the gun – and then there's the testimony from the two police officers. The way they tell what happened doesn't sound good for William."

Mrs. Miller gave a quick snort. "Jake Fisher's fellow officers are going to make sure it looks bad for William with a brave Jake Fisher doing his duty. William needs to go over what happened in infinite detail. You need to get him to recall every second of what happened."

"I don't think he wants to do anything like that. He seems resigned to the fact that he shot Jake Fisher, and unwilling to discuss the circumstances."

"You've got to convince him."

"I know," replied Susan. "To be honest, I'd just about given up. I couldn't see any way forward."

"We've never given up on William before," said Mrs. Miller. "And now he needs us more than ever."

Susan smiled. She felt part of a team, a duo determined to do whatever was necessary to get to the bottom of these murders. They would start from the assumption that William was innocent.

Neither of them had touched their coffee. It was now cold and unappealing. Mrs. Miller went over to the worktop in the kitchen and put on a fresh brew.

"I think we'll need this," she commented. Mrs. Miller returned to the table and turned to Susan. "We'll go over Angela's murder first. After all, that's what started the events that led to William accidentally shooting Jake Fisher."

"Accidentally?" queried Susan.

"Yes," replied Mrs. Miller. "We need to approach this from the assumption that William didn't shoot Angela and that he accidentally shot Jake Fisher. If we don't, we have no chance."

"Thanks," replied Susan, "you are right. I've needed wise counsel. Okay...where do we start?" The coffee percolator started to gurgle.

"Coffee, I think," replied Mrs. Miller. She was pouring two fresh cups before Susan had chance to move. "We need a notebook," she continued, as she brought the coffee to the table. Susan rifled through the desk drawer in the small office adjoining the kitchen and produced a spiral notebook. Susan began to feel excited at the task they were undertaking. If nothing else, it gave her a sense of purpose.

"Let's start with Angela's murder," she said, testing her ballpoint with a scribble on the corner of the first page. "It was a Wednesday. William's lesson was due to start at four-thirty, but I know he often got there a bit earlier. Maybe four, or quarter past," she said, recording this on the first page of the notebook.

"Maybe Gerald could help," offered Mrs. Miller. "I bumped into him at the mall not far from the Fisher's house. Maybe he saw something."

"Gerald!" exclaimed Susan. "In the mall? That's not like him. And anyway, he would go to the newer one - close to the University."

"He'd bought a new shirt from Coles. I remember - he was carrying one of their bags. He told me they had a sale on."

"Anything else?" asked Susan.

"Oh, yes, I've just remembered. He said he was going over to that shop that sells craft items and model magazines."

"I've never known Gerald show any interest in crafts of any sort and I can't imagine him buying one of those magazines – are you sure?"

"Yes. I told him about Ron, my husband. He's a real enthusiast and loves spending time in the shop. When we go shopping, I just leave him browsing and leafing through the magazines. He says it's the best shop for model and craft kits in the entire city."

"But Gerald has never expressed any interest whatsoever in crafts, models or anything similar. I don't think he's ever owned a screwdriver, let alone built something from a kit."

"There may be a very logical explanation," commented Mrs. Miller. Susan sighed.

"I'm so confused. This doesn't make any sense. Anything else you can recall?" she asked.

"Gerald had a handkerchief wrapped round his hand," replied Mrs. Miller. "I noticed the bloodstains. I told him he should get it seen to. He told me he'd caught it on a fence."

"Yes, he told me that's what happened. It must have been sore. He was changing the dressing at least twice a day at first. I offered to help when I saw him struggling to re-apply a gauze bandage but he claimed he could manage. Typical Gerald!"

Susan scribbled in her notebook and then paused and looked at Mrs. Miller. "I think we need to get acquainted with the area around Angela's house. It's not an area I know. I dropped William off a couple of times, but I just kept to the main road."

"That's a good idea," replied Mrs. Miller. "I know the area reasonably well. My sister lives in the next street."

The following day, Susan and Mrs. Miller walked along Malthouse Drive and past the house that Angela and Jake Fisher had lived in. Black and yellow striped police tape was still draped across the driveway. Behind the tape was a large sign saying 'Police Crime Scene – No Access'.

"The park is just behind their house," said Mrs. Miller. "You can see the large beech trees behind that row of elms." It was a bright morning, and Susan could see the copper tones of the remaining leaves glinting in the sun. "There's also a walk-way at the back of these houses. It's a favourite with teenagers from the high school."

"I hadn't realised just how close these houses are to the park," commented Susan, as they walked along the tree-lined alleyway. They walked slowly past the rear of Angela's house. It was also festooned with black and yellow police tape and had an identical sign warning that this was still a crime scene. Susan could see people in white overalls through the kitchen widow. They appeared to be cleaning the floor. There were bottles of bleach on the windowsill. A woman wearing yellow rubber gloves and a white overall reached for one of the

168

bottles. She caught Susan's stare, and turned to call out to someone else. Mrs. Miller tugged at Susan's arm, nudging her forward and away from the house. They walked quickly along to the end of the alleyway and stopped at the small gate that led to the rear of the park.

"I reckon whoever murdered Angela would have come this way. It's the quickest exit from the kitchen and these trees would have provided a reasonably good cover." There wasn't the remotest suggestion that she thought William may have been guilty. Mrs. Miller was absolutely sure of his innocence. In her view, whoever murdered Angela had, in all probability, left by the back door. Susan nodded in agreement. She was encouraged by Mrs. Miller's conviction that William was innocent, and with her determination to find the killer. Susan pointed towards the other side of the park.

"Isn't that the shopping mall, the one where you bumped into Gerald?" asked Susan.

"Oh, yes," replied Mrs. Miller. "The entrance is on the other side, away from the main road."

"Of course," replied Susan. "I didn't realise it was this close to the park."

"You wouldn't see it from the main entrance," commented Mrs. Miller. "I sometimes take a stroll through here with my sister. It's a nice walk. There are nearly always mums pushing prams and toddlers running around. It might be worth asking if anyone had seen a man walking in the park at the time of the murder." Susan reflected on what Mrs. Miller had said.

"I'm not sure," replied Susan. "It sounds a long shot and besides, the police aren't going to be very happy if they hear we've been asking questions."

Mrs. Miller wasn't going to be put off by Susan's reluctance. "I'm sure you're right. But we don't have any other ideas and we may get lucky. There aren't usually many men in the park at that time of the day and mothers usually have a routine. They will often take their children out on the same day of the week and at similar times. And then there are the high-school students using the alleyway. It will be the same groups coming along at similar times on any given day." Susan was becoming a bit more encouraged.

"You're suggesting we assume that whoever killed Angela would have come out of the backdoor, probably bumped into few high school students, given what we know about the time the murder was committed, and then walked across the park?"

"Exactly," replied Mrs. Miller.

"But he might not have gone anywhere near the park. He might have gone to the end of the alleyway and back onto one of the streets."

"You could well be right," replied Mrs. Miller. "But if I were in the murder's shoes, I think I'd want to get away from the area as quickly as possible. A walk across the park would be my choice."

"And into the mall?" suggested Susan.

"Probably," replied Mrs. Miller.

"And we are sure it's a man we're looking for?"

"I've absolutely no doubt it was a man," replied Mrs. Miller. They'd inadvertently wandered into the park as they talked. They sat on one of the wooden bench seats attached to a picnic table. Two mothers ambled slowly by, chatting to each other as they walked. They appeared to hardly notice Susan and Mrs. Miller.

"I don't think they'd notice anything out of the ordinary," commented Susan.

"Oh, yes they would," replied Mrs. Miller. "You know what it's like - mothers have a sixth sense. Their antenna would immediately be alert to anything that wasn't what they normally encountered. They might not remember who the other mothers were – they'd expect to see them anyway. But something a bit unusual ... I think they might remember that." Susan smiled; she was dealing with an expert in the rearing of children.

"So you think we should attempt some sort of reconstruction?" asked Susan.

"Yes," replied Mrs. Miller. "We know what day it was and we know that it was sometime in the late afternoon – just before William arrived for his lesson."

"His lesson started at four-thirty," said Susan. "But he liked to get there early if he could. And that fits in with the police reports. I reckon the murderer would have been leaving the house sometime between three-thirty and four. Probably nearer four, given that William said Angela was still alive when he found her."

"Good," replied Mrs Miller. "I'll come down here tomorrow at around three-thirty, and just ask any mother I see if they always come to the Park on a Wednesday and if they were here on the day the murder was committed. If they were, I'll try and find out if they noticed a man walking towards the main gate."

"Okay," replied Susan. "I'll come with you – but I'll talk to some of the high-school students who use the alleyway, and see if any of them remember anything that might help."

*

Mrs. Miller strolled towards a few of the mothers in the park. She had decided to try and gain their confidence before probing them with questions about anything unusual they might have seen. An opportunity came when a little boy fell as he ran along the footpath. She turned and scooped up the child, who stopped crying almost as soon as Mrs. Miller held him in her arms. The mother of the toddler was struggling with a crying baby she had lifted from its pram. Mrs. Miller

171

walked towards her, carrying the now-calm little boy in her arms.

"Thank you, thank you!" said the young mother. "He's just reaching that age ..."

"The terrible twos," replied Mrs. Miller. "He's a very nice young man, aren't you?"

"Darren - his name's Darren." It wasn't really a name Mrs. Miller cared for, but she was grateful to young Darren for his timely fall. She placed him gently on the ground. He looked as if he was ready for another chance to run off. Mrs. Miller reached down and held his hand in her large soft palm.

"Darren, you stay here and look after your little sister. It's a girl, isn't it?" she said as she turned to address the young mother.

"Yes - Louise."

"That's a pretty name," said Mrs. Miller, pleased to learn the baby girl had a more sensible name. The baby continued to wail and Darren looked as if he might run off again.

"Here, let me," said Mrs. Miller. "I think Darren is looking for a hug." Louise stopped crying almost as soon as she felt the reassuring warmth of Mrs. Miller's ample bosom.

"That's amazing," exclaimed the mother, as she picked up Darren and gave him a comforting hug. "I've never seen anything like it. You have a real gift!" Mrs. Miller placed the purring Louise into her pram and covered the baby with its pink blanket.

"Is this your usual route?" asked Mrs. Miller.

"Yes. I come here nearly every Wednesday. Louise usually sleeps and it gives a chance for Darren to run off some energy. That murder has scared me, though. I was a bit nervous about walking somewhere so close to where it happened."

"Were you here on that Wednesday?" asked Mrs. Miller.

"Yes. I heard the police cars, and then an ambulance. I thought there must have been a bad accident. There were police sirens blaring all over the place."

Mrs. Miller looked round at the others in the park. "I suppose it was all other mothers and children?"

"Yes, it's pretty quiet in the early afternoon. I usually see the same faces. Sometimes we stop for a chat, especially if the kids start playing." Mrs. Miller nodded.

"Did you see anything unusual before you heard the police sirens?" pressed Mrs. Miller.

"No, not really. There were a couple of teenagers who must have skipped school smooching on that bench over there." She pointed to one of the other benches. "There was this kid riding his bike across the grass – he nearly ran into one of the toddlers. It startled me. I wasn't that far away, and for an awful moment I'd lost sight of Darren. The toddler's mother shouted after him, but he just gave her a mouthful and sped off. I remember her shouting something to a man walking past."

"There was a man in the park? A grandparent, I suppose?"

"Don't think so. I didn't get much of a look at him. I didn't really see him until the toddler's mother called out to him. He wasn't that old, and he had a dark jacket with the collar turned up. He just kept walking. I don't think he wanted to get mixed up with an irate mum," she said, smiling. "I was more concerned with looking after Darren."

"I suppose he left the park over there," said Mrs. Miller, pointing to the gates across the park.

"Guess so," said the young mother. "Why all the interest?"

"Oh, no reason," replied Mrs Miller. "It just amazing you were all so close to what happened."

"Makes me shudder just to think about it," replied the young mother.

*

"How did you get on?" asked Susan.

"One of the mothers was very helpful. There definitely a man on his own walking through the park at about four. She said he wasn't old, and that he was walking quickly in the direction of the main gate, just across from the mall."

Susan was stunned. "You mean there might have been someone else?"

"Well, we now know there was a man crossing the park coming from the direction of the alleyway and going towards the main gate at about the time the killer must have left Angela's house."

"Did you get any more details?" asked Susan.

"She was getting a bit suspicious," replied Mrs. Miller. "The last thing we want right now is for the police to hear that we've been asking questions. How about the alleyway – any luck?"

"Not as good as you – but I did speak to a few of them. I made the excuse that my husband had been walking down here and that he thinks he lost his watch – the strap broke. I asked them if they'd seen the watch or seen him in the alleyway. It would have been the Wednesday two weeks ago, about four, I said."

"Good thinking," said Mrs. Miller.

"Most said there were usually a few people walking their dog. I got a bit of information from a kid riding a bike – he nearly ran into me. He stopped to ask if I was alright – nice kid, really. Anyway, I gave him the same tale. He remembered nearly hitting a man ... it was

174

close, he said. Gave him a fright and he nearly fell off his bike. He had a dark jacket with a collar pulled up. But none of the others I spoke to seemed to recall anything. One of the girls stopped to listen. *He's always racing down here – he's going to kill someone,* she said." Mrs. Miller grinned. "Well, for once, I'm grateful that he was racing down the alleyway. I think we've got a suspect."

"Do you think we should go to the police?" asked Susan.

"And tell them what – that we think someone else murdered Angela because a young mother saw a man in the park and a kid on a bike nearly ran someone over? Besides, they've got their conviction. They won't want to waste police time on this – and they'll be sure to warn us off."

"I suppose you're right," replied Susan. "But now what?"

Chapter 16
Suspicions

Susan and Mrs. Miller sat at the kitchen table to review the information they now had.

"So, we know there was a man in the vicinity at the time the murder was committed. We also know he was wearing a jacket with his collar turned up."

"He didn't want to be recognised," said Mrs. Miller.

"It's possible," replied Susan, "but lots of men wear jackets and turn up the collar – Gerald often does." There was a brief pause.

"Okay," said Mrs. Miller, "but we do know he walked fairly quickly from the alleyway to the main gate opposite the shopping mall."

"And we're presuming this is the same man that the bike rider almost ran into?" asked Susan, cautiously.

"Yes," replied Mrs. Miller, firmly. "I have no doubt that it's the same man. The timing is right, and he was next to the park."

"Okay... I'm convinced. Now what?"

"We need to think what he might have done next," replied Mrs. Miller.

"He could have gone anywhere..."

"I don't think so," interjected Mrs. Miller. "He would have heard the police sirens. I reckon he would have wanted to stay out of the way for a while – go somewhere where he wouldn't be noticed."

"He might have left his car at the mall and driven off."

"It's possible," replied Mrs. Miller. "But I think the police sirens might have scared him. He wouldn't have wanted to be stopped and questioned – it would be too risky. I think he may have ducked into the mall."

"That's a bit of a long shot," replied Susan. "But I suppose we have to speculate, otherwise we'll just come to a halt."

"Exactly," replied Mrs. Miller, glad that Susan was willing to follow her instincts.

"So, what are we looking for? A man, not old, wearing a dark jacket. He could be in his twenties; he could be in his fifties. It's not much to go on. It would describe most of the men in the shopping mall."

Mrs. Miller ignored Susan's shrug of despair. "Let's think. If he'd just murdered someone and walked quickly across the park, he'd be hot and sweaty, especially wearing a jacket."

"And he might have blood splatters on his clothes," added Susan.

"That depends how close he was when he shot her – but it's a strong possibility," replied Mrs. Miller. "What's the first thing he'd try and do?"

"Check he doesn't look too dishevelled – get cleaned up a bit," suggested Susan.

"That's just what I was thinking," added Mrs. Miller.

There was a long pause in the conversation. It was obvious that Mrs. Miller was struggling with something she wanted to say. Were her instincts pointing her in entirely the wrong direction? Could she dare raise her concerns with Susan? That...no, this was just her misguided attempt at placing the blame with someone other than William for Angela's murder- wasn't it? Her gut instinct savaged her again. She could destroy any attempt at finding Angela's murder with just one misguided comment. She could make assumptions that Susan wouldn't dare to contemplate. Susan's nerves were raw; she simply wanted William back. The question of there being someone else involved was secondary. And the suggestion that it might be Gerald could be too much. It could end any attempt at finding the killer. It might end their friendship and any association with William. She might be viewed as a vindictive, meddling old crone. This wasn't the time.

"Spit it out – you've got something you want to say," said Susan. Mrs. Miller looked very uncomfortable and plainly did not want to reveal what was on her mind. Susan had never seen her like this. There was something intensely sad in her face, as if she was on the edge of making a painful sacrifice. She turned away from Susan as she spoke.

"You'll agree we've got to consider any possibility, no matter how implausible it might seem?"

"Of course," replied Susan, wondering where this was going. Mrs. Miller again paused. She took a deep breath and then turned to face Susan.

"It's Gerald..."

"What!" said Susan. "You can't possibly think he had anything to do with this – it's absurd." She did have a few questions that had been gnawing at her brain. What was Gerald doing in the shopping mall?

"Hear me out," replied Mrs. Miller. "We agreed we'd consider any possibility."

"Well, yes," replied Susan. "But Gerald! I've never seen him so upset over what's happened. He's as convinced as anyone that William is innocent ... I know he is."

"Look, Susan. I've got some concerns that I'd like answers to. Maybe they are easily explained – in which case I'll be relieved."

"Okay," said Susan. "I'm listening." This was something she wasn't going to enjoy, and her defences were already in place. Mrs. Miller fidgeted in her handbag and took out a tissue and blew her nose.

"I told you that I met Gerald in the shopping mall. It was about four-fifteen; I remember glancing at the clock. I'd arranged to meet Inez Knight in the coffee shop. You know Inez, she works in one of the labs at the University – retires next year."

"Yes, of course," replied Susan, irritated by Mrs. Miller's unnecessary diversion. "Let's get back to Gerald."

"I saw him coming out of the toilets – I needed a quick pee before seeing Inez."

Susan felt herself getting angry at these little asides. "Go on – please."

"Sorry," replied Mrs. Miller. "I don't think Gerald was pleased to see me. I had to call over to him a couple of times. Remember, I said he was carrying a bag from Coles – one of those green ones with their logo on the side? He told me he'd popped in to buy a shirt."

"Yes, I did think it was very unusual. I've never known him buy a shirt in Coles – if he goes anywhere, it's always to the new mall," said Susan in a hushed voice.

"Oh, he did mention there was a sale on," said Mrs. Miller in response to Susan's comment. "Then he said he was going over to The Model Store. I could hardly believe my ears – Gerald, in a craft shop! I told him about Ron, my husband, he's always in there thumbing through magazines and buying bits and pieces." *He was probably just saying that to get away from you,* mused Susan to herself. She knew Mrs. Miller irritated Gerald intensely. She let Mrs. Miller continue:

179

"I noticed Gerald's hand as soon as I saw him. He had it wrapped in his handkerchief and it was obviously bleeding. I told him it looked nasty and that he should get it looked at. He told me he intended going into the pharmacy to get a dressing. He said he'd caught it on a fence."

"But this sounds plausible, don't you think?" said Susan. "It's unusual, I grant you. And the story about the craft shop – well, it may have been an excuse to get away, if you know what I mean."

"From me, you mean," replied Mrs. Miller. "I'm sure it was. But he went to such elaborate lengths to explain what he was doing in the mall. I'm used to Gerald's ways. He usually glares at me or dismisses me with one of his trademark snorts. But this wasn't the usual Gerald. He was acting very strangely. He looked hot and uncomfortable. I think ..."

"You think ...?"

"I think this was so unusual, so unlike Gerald, that we should try and find out more," added Mrs. Miller, in a determined voice.

Susan teased things over in her mind. Mrs. Miller was right about Gerald's behaviour. It was odd. But that didn't mean he had anything to do with Angela's death. She felt very frightened. She was on the brink of considering that Gerald was a suspect! Gerald – he wasn't easy to live with; he could be difficult, demanding and at times almost juvenile in his behaviour - but a murderer? She knew he wasn't a murderer. There had to be some other explanation. They were silly to even think that Gerald might ...

Mrs. Miller interrupted her train of thought. "We have to know," she said, quietly. "We have to know why Gerald was in the mall at that time."

Was it just a coincidence? Susan felt taut and on edge. Her skin tingled.

"There are a number of questions we need answers to – and he was wearing a dark jacket with his collar up," continued Mrs. Miller, adding a forceful emphasis, an exclamation, to her comments. Susan felt even more alarmed. She knew Mrs. Miller was right. They had to find out as much as they could. She wanted the proof that would convince them that Gerald had nothing to do with Angela's murder. Her stomach growled. She felt a wave of nausea at the prospect.

"Okay," said Susan, picking up her pen. "Let's list some of the things we need answers to. I'll start with: why was he in the mall at that time? Had he gone there deliberately to buy a shirt from Coles?"

"And why the interest in The Model Store?" added Mrs Miller. "And how did he get there - walk, drive? Where did he park?"

"I suppose we also need to know if anyone else knew he was going to the mall," said Susan.

"Maybe he told someone at work, "commented Mrs. Miller. "And what about those scratches on his hand?" Susan added them to the list.

"Anything else?" asked Susan.

"Can you remember what he was wearing?" asked Mrs. Miller.

"Yes, I think so," Susan replied. "We all had breakfast together. Gerald looked fairly smart for a change. I remember commenting on his appearance – I asked him if he was going somewhere. He had a blue Oxford shirt that he liked, a tie that nearly matched, dark pants and his old suedes. They were his favourite pair; he wore them nearly every day. I told him they didn't go with his pants, but he was halfway out of the door at that stage. He grabbed his jacket, shouted he was off and gave the door his usual slam."

"That's interesting," commented Mrs. Miller.

"Why?" asked Susan.

"When I met him he wasn't wearing a blue shirt – it was a pale shade of yellow. I remember it because it stood out against his dark jacket. And I don't think he was wearing a tie."

Susan's mind was racing. One part of her wanted to stop trying to find out anything else that might implicate Gerald. If Gerald had seen something or been close to the house when Angela was murdered, then she needed to know. Had he seen someone he knew? Was he trying to be secretive – or was that just the conclusion they had jumped to? The other part of her wanted answers. What on earth had Gerald been up to? Why the pretence at being interested in the craft shop? Was it simply to get away from Mrs. Miller? And the shirt – why would he deliberately take time away from his desk to go and buy a shirt in a mall he rarely went near?

And then she remembered. He'd been wearing a pale-yellow shirt when they met at the police station after William had been arrested. She'd been too distracted to bother about it then. But if he bought it in Coles he must have got changed somewhere – removed his blue Oxford and replaced it with the pale-yellow shirt from Coles. But why? Gerald hardly ever bothered buying a new shirt for himself. Susan sometimes made him buy one when they went to the shops – but it was more usual for her to bring a couple home for Gerald to try. Gerald – shopping in Coles for a new shirt! It was so unlike Gerald.

"He was wearing a pale-yellow shirt later that day when we met at the police station. He must have decided to change," suggested Susan, unconvincingly. Mrs. Miller wasn't convinced either.

"It's possible he could have torn his shirt when he scratched his hand."

"That's it," replied Susan. "That explains it! I knew there must be a logical explanation."

"Logical yes, but believable?" Susan felt the firm ground on which she stood for just a moment suddenly slip from under her. "There is the unthinkable," offered Mrs. Miller. "He might have had another reason for changing his shirt."

"You think he did it, don't you?" said Susan.

"I think it's a possibility we must consider – for William's sake," replied Mrs. Miller. They sat very still and in silence for several minutes. Mrs. Miller knew instinctively that this was a fragile silence that might shatter into an outburst from Susan and signal an abrupt end to these assertions - and possibly an end to their friendship. Susan hated this. She was disgusted at herself for contemplating that Gerald was involved – and yet, it was an assumption that might prove William's innocence. She straightened up and turned to Mrs. Miller.

"We should go to the police," she suddenly announced.

"I don't think we can," replied Mrs. Miller. "What would we say? That we suspect Gerald because his behaviour was a bit odd? We have nothing to go on other than a chance meeting at the mall. As far as they are concerned, the case is closed and unless we come up with some concrete evidence, there is no point in going to the police."

"We can't just leave it!" said Susan, suddenly alarmed that they might have reached an impasse. Any thoughts of reproach for contemplating Gerald as a suspect left her in an instant. "We've got to do something!" Mrs. Miller pulled in her chair and leant forward on her outstretched forearms.

"We should start with Gerald's clothes. We need to try and find his blue Oxford shirt, his tie, his dark jacket – oh, and the shoes he was wearing. We should also check out the new shirt he bought – and then see if we can find out who sold it to him. It's new, so you can claim it doesn't fit."

Susan smiled at Mrs. Miller's organised approach. "You should have been a company director – or a detective!"

Mrs. Miller grinned at Susan. She was pleased that Susan appeared to have got over her initial reservation about considering Gerald as a suspect – at least for now. The real test would come if they found any evidence to support their suspicions.

Susan found the new pale-yellow shirt in the bottom of the laundry basket. Gerald had only worn it once.

"Best not to wash it," said Mrs. Miller. I'll starch and iron it. It'll look as if it's never been worn." And indeed it did. They couldn't find the wrapping or the receipt, but Mrs. Miller had recently bought her husband a shirt from Coles and still had the bag and tissue in which the shirt had been wrapped. She was a natural hoarder and saved bags, tissue linings, cardboard boxes, string and decorations – just in case.

The shop manageress knew Mrs. Miller; it was where she usually shopped for any clothes they needed. She was always on the look-out for a bargain and Coles often had sales, so much so that their 'sale' sign was rarely out of the store window.

"I don't know why they bother," she'd commented to her friend, Inez, the last time they saw the large sign being carefully peeled from the glass.

"I'd like to return this shirt. It's for a friend of mine," she told the manageress. "Her husband popped in a couple of weeks ago – Wednesday afternoon - and she doesn't like it at all. You know what these men are like. They shouldn't be allowed out on their own." It brought a smile from the normally phlegmatic

184

manageress. She motioned over to one of the shop assistants.

"Julie was on the men's section all that week. I'll let her handle it." Julie was a thin whippet of a woman, quick and nervous with an infectious smile and a ready laugh that bordered on being vulgar. With a bit more flesh she might have been regarded as attractive. She had a brazen approach that men seemed to find appealing and her sales figures were testament to her effectiveness.

"Stuck-up bitch," said Julie, as soon as the manageress was out of earshot. Mrs. Miller nodded as if agreeing wholeheartedly. She handed over the Cole's bag and Julie slipped the tissue-covered shirt onto the counter.

"You want a credit voucher or an exchange?" she asked. "We don't do refunds I'm afraid – not without a receipt. It's store policy." She waved an arm in the direction of a customer information sheet taped to the underside of the glass counter top.

"A credit voucher would be fine," replied Mrs. Miller. "I think he'll be getting help next time."

Julie snorted. "They never learn, do they? Always in a blinding rush. I expect this one was just the same."

Mrs. Miller laughed. "You might remember him?" she said, hoping she sounded only casually interested. "It was the Wednesday before last, late in the afternoon – about four, I think."

"We were pretty quiet later in the afternoon." replied Julie. "Most of the sale items had gone by then."

"He's late fifties, medium build, wiry hair, bit of a paunch and usually wears a dark wind jacket at this time of year. He likes to turn the collar up – fancies he's Elvis, I shouldn't wonder," continued Mrs. Miller.

"Hey, I remember him!" replied Julie. "He had that thing zipped up under his chin. He was really anxious to get out. He just grabbed the first shirt in his size and left without getting his change – ten bucks. I shouted after him, but he'd gone. I treated the girls to coffee and doughnuts."

Mrs. Miller laughed. "Typical! That's men for you. They just don't know how to shop."

*

"I suppose it just confirms that he bought a shirt in Coles," said Susan after hearing Mrs. Miller's account of her chat with Julie.

"It does that alright," replied Mrs. Miller. "And he was in quite a rush to get out of there."

"It's not like Gerald to forget his change ..." said Susan, her voice trailing off in quiet disbelief.

"Defeats the point of buying in the sale," added Mrs. Miller. "We need to try and find the other shirt and tie he was wearing, and it wouldn't hurt to look at his shoes."

"The shirt and tie should be easy enough. The shirt will be in the washbasket and his tie will be hanging in the wardrobe. Why the shoes?"

"We've got to check everything. Including his jacket," said Mrs. Miller.

"He took his jacket to the cleaners," replied Susan. "He took it with him this morning. He said he'd got a bit of blood on the sleeve when he cut his hand." Mrs. Miller gave Susan quizzical look. "It sounds plausible," said Susan, defensively.

Susan was surprised that they couldn't find Gerald's blue Oxford shirt, or his tie. He hadn't worn them that morning; she'd made a point of checking. They searched the usual places – laundry basket, the ironing pile, bedroom floor, the wardrobe - and the unlikely places - the bathroom floor, under the beds, even in the washing machine. Mrs. Miller found his shoes. They were in the spare room in an old shoebox under the bed.

"Why on earth would Gerald hide them under the bed?" asked Susan.

"He's been giving then a good clean," said Mrs. Miller. "Look at the way they've been scrubbed. I think he's been trying to remove some stains."

"And you think they could be bloodstains?" said Susan.

"I think they could be Angela's bloodstains," replied Mrs. Miller, emphatically. Susan tried once more to offer a degree of scepticism.

"We don't know if it was bloodstains and even if they were, it could have been from Gerald's scratches to his hand." Mrs. Miller gave a snort, not unlike the sound that Gerald used so dismissively. For an instant, Mrs. Miller felt tempted to apologise, but she could see that it hadn't been picked up by Susan.

"Those scratches are having to account for an awful lot," she commented.

*

David Singleton provided Susan with a copy of the police report. He sensed there must be some reason other than just curiosity, but he decided to not enquire too deeply. Besides, the report was mainly about the police investigation at the scene of the crime and the shooting of Police Officer Fisher. The DA's office was sure they had their perpetrator and, as a result, the investigation was not especially thorough. This was something he intended using at the appeal. Mrs. Miller encouraged Susan to sit with her and go through it line by line.

"I don't even know what we're looking for," exclaimed Susan. She was sickened by the graphic descriptions and the unimagined horror of the murder scene. She slammed her hand down on the table in anger and frustration.

"I can't do this. This has become an obsession – trying to prove Gerald is involved. We're assuming he's guilty by virtue of a series of weak assumptions and coincidences. This can't be right – there must be another way." Mrs. Miller was quick to reply.

"This isn't a lynching of Gerald. It's about William's innocence. If our suspicions about Gerald don't lead anywhere, I think we'll both be relieved - in which case it will have been someone else who murdered Angela." Susan began to nod her head. There was clarity of thought in Mrs. Miller's rationale that she found comforting.

"We are looking for a murderer and if it helps to use the police jargon, 'we are trying to eliminate Gerald from our enquiries'," added Mrs. Miller. Susan felt her facial muscles reaching for a smile - it was almost worth a smile.

"Okay," replied Susan. "Thanks for the pep talk."

"This is a bit easier for me," replied Mrs. Miller. "My only concerns are for you and William." Susan returned to reading the police report.

"I nearly missed this," she said, stabbing her finger at the page. "William's fingerprints were found on a cup in the sink. It was partly filled with black coffee." Mrs. Miller realised immediately the significance of what Susan had found.

"William doesn't drink black coffee."

"He hardly drinks coffee at all. It has to be half milk and plenty of sugar before he'll touch it," remarked Susan.

"Gerald takes his black," said Mrs. Miller, in a slow, deliberate voice.

"I know..." replied Susan, softly. "He did it, didn't he? Gerald murdered Angela."

"I'm sorry to say it, but yes," replied Mrs. Miller, "I'm certain he did."

"But why?" said Susan. "Gerald wouldn't plan to murder anyone."

"Maybe he didn't," replied Mrs. Miller. "But he went to see her – she let him into the house and gave him a cup of coffee. You don't think they were having an affair?" asked Mrs. Miller, bluntly. Susan was beyond being shocked.

"I don't think so," she replied in a measured tone. It was as if Gerald was no longer someone she knew. She accepted now that he might have murdered Angela. "Gerald always claimed she had too much influence over William. He said that William was besotted with her. Maybe he was, but I think Gerald was also." Her eyes pleaded for help. "What do we do now?"

Chapter 17
Inez Knight

Gerald found himself virtually ostracised in his own home. Was it his imagination, or was Mrs. Miller treating him with even more disdain than usual? Despite all the years Mrs. Miller had been coming to their house, they rarely had a conversation. It had soon become apparent that Mrs. Miller had quite different views on what was best for William. When she'd first come to help with William, Gerald had been delighted with the confidence that Susan had in Mrs. Miller. It was, after all, his suggestion that Susan advertise for someone to help look after William – and God knows, it required someone pretty extraordinary to cope with him. William was not an easy child.

Gerald blamed Mrs. Miller for much of the problems in their marriage. It seemed to Gerald that Susan and Mrs. Miller conspired to virtually exclude him from anything involving William's behaviour. And any time he attempted to exert some fatherly discipline, Susan and Mrs. Miller would consult one another with subtle frowns and signals that resulted in Gerald being sidelined. His opinions on what was best for William counted for little. Susan soon relied exclusively on Mrs. Miller's advice as far as William was concerned. She became the sage on issues such as behaviour problems, nurturing and support, appropriate foods, stimulating toys and various activities that she opined would be beneficial for William. Gerald thought it was all too much. He felt these two women would only further damage William with their pseudo child psychiatry and assumed knowledge of all appropriate methods for nurturing a child who struggled with relationships. Gerald had formed the view that William was incapable of learning and reasoning like a normal child. Was William backward? Gerald often thought so, and he was convinced that Susan's approach would be detrimental to William in the long run. He'd wanted William to run with the pack. He wanted him to learn the art of adaptation – the subtle skills of learning to conform, of acquiring the instinct to develop allegiances and of developing a character that his peers would respect.

He'd been amazed when William showed an aptitude for music, even more so when it was obvious that William had real talent. But it was William's improvement academically, and even socially, that he appreciated. He viewed the music as just a useful mechanism for giving William confidence so that he was better able to cope. In truth, Gerald was jealous of William's musical talent. The more skilled William became, the more impotent Gerald felt. Susan no longer consulted on anything relating to William's upbringing and they no longer shared interests of any kind. Susan refused to listen when he tried to say that William wouldn't have a career in music; that he simply wouldn't be good enough to compete with the best. It would inevitably lead to disaster, he said on many occasions. Susan simply glared at him with one of her icy stares every time he expressed his opinion on the matter. As for Angela, Gerald's expressed view was she was just a tart - a very good looking tart - but a tart nonetheless. "She was trailer court trash," he said, "and always will be."

*

Gerald couldn't stop thinking about what had happened. He was sure of one thing – it wasn't his fault and he'd do his damnedest to make sure he wasn't implicated. Why hadn't she just gone along with him? She'd egged him on. She'd brazenly posed for him. She'd removed her clothes and let him move in close. God, how beautiful she was. The mere thought of her excited him. And then what – she'd suddenly changed her mind. She'd smashed that gun on his head and would have shot him if he hadn't tried to grab it. She'd shot herself, it wasn't his fault. He'd gotten clean away. Everything would have worked out if William hadn't shown up and found her. *If Jake Fisher had found her, I bet he'd be the one on a murder charge,* Gerald told himself. But then William shot Jake Fisher. In a way, that was a bit of luck, thought Gerald. There was no one else to look for. He wished it wasn't William. It was gnawing at his brain. He was having weird dreams:

He was walking with William and Susan along the edge of a cliff. Angela was lying on the beach below them, completely naked. William was waving excitedly at her. She looked up and waved back, beckoning William down to her. 'Doesn't she look beautiful?' said Susan. William stepped closer to the edge. Gerald stepped behind him, sending him hurtling onto the rocks below. Angela kept waving. She was waving at him now. 'What happened?' screamed Susan, pointing at him accusingly. She wouldn't stop screaming.

The dream was always the same. It always ended with Susan screaming and pointing a dagger-like finger in his face. He woke up, sweating and disorientated. It seemed real – too real. And once he'd woken from his nightmare, there was no going back to sleep. It gave Gerald time to think and to repeatedly go back over the things that he'd done and the steps he'd taken, just in

192

case he'd missed something. The more he went through the events since Angela's death, the more confident he was that he'd never be implicated.

He recalled in detail what he did on leaving the mall, reliving the events in his mind. That chance encounter with Mrs. Miller in the shopping mall had unnerved him. He walked quickly to the Seven-Eleven store where he'd left his car. The coolness of the fresh air helped him think as he walked. He knew Mrs. Miller would be sure to tell someone at some stage that they'd met in the mall. He'd need to be prepared for that. The calamity of police sirens gradually abated. There was just the noise of one police car, buzzing around like an annoying gnat, unsure of where it should be heading. He stuffed the bag containing his blood spattered Oxford shirt and smeared tie into an old hessian sack in the trunk of his car, and drove over to the University. He parked in his usual spot and slipped into his office block by the back entrance. There was a 'Men's Room' off the small entrance lobby. The figure staring back at him from the mirror was virtually unrecognisable. It had a wide-eyed stare, as if frightened by oncoming headlights. His face was flushed and his hair was even more dishevelled than usual. He turned on the cold tap and gingerly washed the scratches on the back of his hand. They were deeper than he had realised. He splashed some water on his face, dried his sore hand on a paper towel, and carefully fixed the dressing in place. He inspected his jacket and decided it looked clean enough. There were a couple of stains on the lining and one on the sleeve – but nothing obvious. He'd get the jacket cleaned later. He smoothed out his new shirt and folded his jacket over his arm. He made one final inspection in the mirror. He looked good, all things considered. He'd cleaned up well. He walked to his office and sat at his desk. He ventured a smile. *I'm in the clear,* he thought.

He nearly gave everything away when the two detectives told him William had been arrested. He knew he'd have to be even more careful now. He'd expected to learn of Angela's death on the radio news bulletin – that she had been murdered. His first reaction when he'd learned William had been arrested was one of relief. *It's not me,* he thought. But then he realised that it might bring him under closer scrutiny. He'd have to be careful. And how was he going to react when he met William? And Susan!

*

Getting rid of the shirt and tie was a priority. He'd thought about dumping the bag into one of the trash cans that lined the streets every Monday waiting for collection, but decided it was too risky. A dog or a cat might smell the blood and rip open the bag. It was a risk he couldn't take. He decided instead to add a brick to the sack and drop it into the river. He parked the car close to the bridge, took out the weighted sack, and walked as quickly as he could along the walkway over the bridge. It was dark, about eleven pm, and there was no-one around. He could see the dark river slipping and rippling along, illuminated in flickering strips from the street lamps along the bridge. He could see the lights of an approaching car as he lifted the sack over the rail and released the sack just before the beams caught him. The bright light blinded him for a moment and when he looked back at the river, it appeared black and still.

He'd have to think of some good excuse for Susan. She was sure to ask what had happened to his blue Oxford and his tie. She'd bought them for his birthday last year and it was a shirt he particularly liked. The tie wasn't any great loss. He dithered over the shoes. They were his favourite pair; comfortable and on the dandyish side of being trendy. Coming up with a logical explanation for his missing shirt and tie would be tough enough, but having to explain the whereabouts of his favourite pair of shoes – that would be very difficult. He decided to keep them. He'd clean them thoroughly – wear them for a day or so – and then clean them again. He'd repeat this several times, just to make sure.

*

The question hovered over them. Gerald had prepared the script, he'd rehearsed his answers, he wanted Susan to get on with it and ask him. Was she toying with him? Was there a game of bluff and counter-bluff being played out that he was not yet understanding? Gerald was beginning to think he should raise it first – *Susan, about my shirt and tie ...*

Susan was waiting for the right moment. She hadn't intended to keep this dangling, but it was obvious that Gerald was itching to get something off his chest and she suspected it might have something to do with the missing items. When Susan finally asked, just as Gerald was leaving the kitchen, she could see his discomfort. Gerald suddenly felt ill-prepared. He hadn't expected it to go like this.

"Gerald, I haven't seen your blue Oxford shirt – the one I bought you last year. You were wearing it the day William was arrested, I think." It was soft speak for saying she knew Gerald was wearing the shirt on the day Angela was murdered. "You must have got changed into that awful pale-yellow shirt you bought at Coles. I took it back, by the way – it's just not your colour." Gerald's draw dropped. This wasn't exactly the lead-in he'd expected. She'd ad-libbed.

"Oh ... thanks." It was clear that Gerald wasn't interested in his new shirt.

195

"And your nice blue Oxford?" persisted Susan. Gerald felt a tinge of relief. At least they were back on script.

"I got blood on it when I caught my hand on the fence. It was bleeding quite badly and I somehow managed to wipe it all over the front of my shirt. You know how clumsy I am. I even got a few drops on my jacket - I've put it into the cleaners." Gerald felt pleased. He couldn't have delivered his lines any better. But he paused, and before he had time to complete his explanation, Susan drilled down just a little bit further:

"Why don't you let me have a go at cleaning it? I've got some stain remover – and cold water sometimes works for bloodstains."

"It was too badly stained. I threw it in the bin – the tie as well." Gerald felt very uncomfortable. "Got to go," he added. "I'm going to pop into my office for an hour or two. I think it would help if I had other things to concentrate on."

"Besides the murder of Angela Fisher? William didn't do it ..." Gerald was shuffling out towards the door.

"That's not what the jury have decided. You are going to have to accept it, Susan. We'll both have to accept it, even though it's painful." Susan stared at him.

"You'd better go, Gerald," she said, quietly.

*

"He did it!" said Susan as soon as Mrs. Miller stepped foot inside the door. "The bastard!"

"I presume you've quizzed him about the shirt?" Susan didn't answer; she didn't need to.

*

Inez Knight had lived next door to Sally and Ron Miller for over twenty years. Inez was ten years younger than Sally Miller and was one of a few people who called Mrs. Miller by her first name. To her they

196

were Sally and Ron. Sally Miller had the appearance and demeanour of someone older and more mature, even when her children were quite young. She was also very intelligent and self-confident, despite having left school with only a high school diploma. Ron was her teenage sweetheart and they were in no doubt that they would be getting married as soon as their parents would allow. Ron got a job at the local timber yard and Sally found a job as a filing clerk in the mayor's office. They married six months later and their parents clubbed together to get the deposit for the comfortable timber-framed house in which they still lived.

Sally Miller's skills were spotted within a few months of starting work. She was efficient, reliable and well-respected by both her peers and her bosses. She was somehow able to get the most out of those with whom she worked, often showing those struggling how to be more effective. She'd recognised that all too often those labelled as slow or difficult had simply not had enough support when they were first employed. She was soon in charge of an office group and her status was signalled by most of the employees, and especially the newer ones, in referring to her as 'Mrs. Miller'. It was a mark of respect and Sally Miller quickly realised the benefits of maintaining a degree of authority that the use of her surname gave. As the years clicked by, only a small number of people outside her immediate family knew her by her first name.

One of the select few was Inez Knight. Inez and her husband, Mickey Knight, had bought the house next door over twenty years ago when they'd moved to Columbus for Inez to take up a post as a technical specialist in immunology at the University. Mickey was employed in the postal service. His passion was building scale models, an interest shared by Ron Miller. They quickly became good friends, spending most evenings in Mickey's garage working on new models, or shooting pool on the table at the other side of the garage.

"They hardly ever speak," commented Inez, cupping an ear towards the garage.

Sally laughed. "Maybe more people should take up model building."

Inez nodded, and smiled. Sally and Inez had a profoundly different form of friendship. Unlike their respective husbands, they didn't share any hobbies. What they did have in common could best be described as an aura of self-confidence. It gave them both a certain calm detachment; some would say aloofness, which many found daunting. But in their own spheres they had a perceived wisdom which gave them an authority that was rarely questioned. They both smiled, knowingly, at the deference they were accorded in shops, the cafe they regularly visited, at the church they attended and in the various charities they helped organise and run. It was a personal power they were well aware of, and yet they both tried to ensure they didn't misuse it.

This strong bond was cemented by an event that occurred about two years after the Knights had moved in next door to the Millers. Sally and Inez had already become good friends, as had Ron and Mickey. There had been a spate of burglaries in the area. They always took place in the late morning when there was either no one at home, or someone on their own – usually a young mother or an elderly person. The burglar pulled a mask over his face just as the door was opened, and forced his way in armed with a knife and a piece of lead pipe. He always demanded money and jewellery and on several occasions had resorted to a burst of violence when the terrified victim had been slow to cooperate. The police had been unable to catch the burglar, despite increased patrols. Sally Miller decided to take the initiative. She, and Inez, organised a petition demanding the police chief meet with their spokesperson, Mrs. Miller. She wanted the police chief to issue a leaflet advising all vulnerable households in the area to have a marked hundred dollar bill to give to the burglar. The police chief refused. He thought it was a weak response that wouldn't help his career. Mrs. Miller anticipated as much and had a second strategy. She'd noticed that the police cars patrolled at the same time along the same streets. She simply suggested that it should be a random patrol. With Inez's help, she'd drawn up a schedule for the patrols that was pseudo-random with no discernible pattern.

Sally had popped home early that day to grab a quick bite – a brunch. She'd been in the office since eight am helping complete a report on jobs vacancies. She'd promised a copy for the local paper before lunch so they could put out some information in the evening edition. Since their office was fairly close to her home, she decided to combine her errand with a quick stop to have an early lunch. She peered lazily out of her front window and across their small strip of lawn that was bordered by the pavement. It needed cutting. She'd remind Ron to get it trimmed.

It was warm in the house and she reached to open one of the sash windows. She heard the noise almost as soon as she'd raised the lower frame. She thought it was a child screaming in vexation – or fear.

It was Inez. It was unmistakably Inez. She was screaming with every breath in her body. And then silence. Sally knew what it was. She grabbed her son's baseball bat from the hat stand, flew out of the door, ran across the adjoining front lawns and burst through the front porch door.

The burglar turned in shock at the speed at which she'd flung open the door. He was bending over the prostrate Inez. Sally caught sight of the blood where he'd slashed Inez's shoulder with a knife in his left hand. He'd just clubbed her to the ground with a heavy lead pipe in his right hand. As he turned to confront Sally Miller, she let out a samurai-like scream and swung the baseball bat, Babe Ruth-style, catching the attacker on the elbow of his left arm. He shrieked in pain and dropped the knife. Sally was already delivering her next blow - it bounced off his left shoulder and caught the side of his head. He reeled backwards clutching his left arm and cowering down, trying to defend himself.

Sally Miller hadn't finished. Her next swing was aimed at his leg. It cracked into his kneecap, causing the defenceless burglar to writhe in agony on the floor. He was shouting, "No, No!" as Sally Miller delivered her next blow to his ankle. He let out a shriek of terror and his useless body jerked in pain as Sally reigned in with more blows to his shins. Sally Miller left him gasping for relief, incapable of moving with the agony in his bruised and broken limbs. She turned to Inez, who had attempted to shuffle out of the way. Inez managed the faintest of smiles.

"You're a brute," she whispered. "Thanks." Her head was swimming and she slumped against the wall. Sally ran to the dining room and grabbed pillows from the couch. She made Inez as comfortable as she could and then grabbed the phone and dialled the emergency services.

"They're on their way," she said to Inez.

The blow from the lead pipe had smashed into Inez's ear and damaged her eardrum. It left her dazed and dizzy with severe vertigo that caused her to feel nauseous as soon as she attempted any movement of her head.

"She's lucky to be alive," the doctor told Sally. "That blow could have killed her."

She also had a deep knife wound to her left shoulder that reached to the bone of her upper arm. "It hasn't done any permanent damage," confirmed the nurse, "but it will to take several weeks to heal. Don't tire her out," she added, as Sally went into the room to sit with Mickey. "She needs plenty of rest."

Inez heard the nurse. She was propped up in bed with a saline drip in her left hand. Her shoulder was heavily strapped and she had a large wad of gauze bandaged against her ear.

"Sally – this is the second time I'm glad to see you." Her eyes had regained their alert sparkle. "No baseball bat!" she quipped.

"You saved her life," said Mickey. The room fell silent for a few seconds.

"I had to do something," replied Sally. "When I saw that animal, I just saw red." Inez was on the brink of tears.

"I'll leave you now," said Sally. "You need to rest. Oh, and you're not to worry about little Josh. I'm going to look after him for a while." Josh was Inez and Mickey's only child. He was five years old and in his first year at primary school. "I'll let Mickey explain." Sally quietly closed the door behind her, pleased that her friend had not suffered any permanent physical damage.

"She's arranged to take some time off work to look after Josh. She's insistent – says it's the least she can do," Mickey told Inez.

"She saved my life ..." It was all Inez could manage. She fought back the tears and fell back against the pillows.

"Are you alright?" asked Mickey, anxiously.

"I've just realised what a lucky person I am," she said, squeezing his hand.

Inez was discharged from hospital ten days later. Mickey and young Josh had fetched her home. Mickey was concerned that Josh's obvious enthusiasm at having his mother home would be too much for her, but Inez was delighted to see him. She picked him up and hugged him hard, ignoring the soreness she still felt around her ear. She winced when he flung his arms around her neck, catching her bruised shoulder.

"Not too tight, Josh," said Mickey, seeing the expression of pain on her face.

"Nonsense," exclaimed Inez. "I'm on the mend. No kid-gloves, please." Mickey laughed. He knew it wouldn't take long for Inez to show her indomitable spirit.

Inez was delighted to see Sally when she popped round the following day. The two women hugged as if greeting a son or daughter who'd returned safely from the theatre of war.

"I can't thank you enough," said Inez. "I'll never be able to repay you for what you've done – but if ever there is a time don't hesitate to ask – no matter what."

"All I want is my friend back, fit and well," replied Sally. They smiled at one another.

Chapter 18
A Crime

Sally Miller sat down with Susan at the breakfast table. Susan looked drawn and tired.

"Gerald thinks he's got away with it," she said, in a slow, bitter tone. "He went off to work this morning, but he won't visit William. He says it would make him too upset. He wouldn't even sit and talk about the appeal. He said it would be pointless, until David Singleton explained that all capital sentences must have an appeal. I thought I caught a look of disappointment on his face when he learnt that." Susan paused for a moment. "I think we should go to the police."

"If that's what you think is best, then you must," replied Mrs. Miller.

"But you don't think I should, do you?"

"No," replied Sally Miller in a quiet voice that conveyed sympathy for Susan and empathy with her predicament. "I'm afraid I still hold the same views – perhaps even more strongly. I don't think the police will take us seriously. We still don't have a hard piece of evidence to link him to Angela's murder. Plenty of well-founded suspicions and strange behaviour that point to Gerald's guilt. But it won't be enough to have him arrested, let alone found guilty at a trial. That wouldn't do William any good. It would let Gerald off the hook. It would alert Gerald, so that he'd be even more careful and the police would simply decide that you are not to be taken seriously – ever." Susan felt disappointed and let down. It wasn't what she wanted to hear. There was nothing but logic in what Mrs. Miller had said, but it signalled an end that she couldn't bear.

"I don't have any option, do I?" she pleaded. She caught the steely look of determination in Sally Miller's eyes.

"What is it – tell me, please! Is there any hope?"

"There could be a way," replied Sally Miller, "but it's dangerous and risky...very risky."

She looked directly into Susan's eyes. They were crazed red like a Martian surface and underscored with dark puffy crescents. She had the frightened look of a deer caught in the headlights of a four-by-four, sensing it was in danger. Susan stretched out her fingers on the table and stared at them, as if checking they were still all there.

"I'll do anything, anything!"

It seemed an eternity before Sally Miller spoke. "We need to implicate him in Angela's murder."

"You don't mean we should fabricate evidence to frame him?"

"That's exactly what I mean," replied Sally Miller.

"But that's illegal!" exclaimed Susan. "We'd be guilty of convicting him ..."

"For a murder he committed," interjected Sally Miller. "And he's prepared to let William pay for his crime. Gerald is guilty of murdering Angela, and is responsible for the murder of Jake Fisher. If William hadn't discovered her dying in the kitchen, he wouldn't have shot Jake Fisher." She paused, letting Susan absorb her accusations. Then she spoke softly. "If William is executed, he'll be responsible for his death too - another crime to add to the deaths of Angela and

Jake Fisher." Susan twisted a damp handkerchief in her hands.

"I can't! I can't convict him by lying!"

"We aren't convicting him - a court does that," replied Sally Miller. "We'd just be providing some evidence so that the police would be compelled to consider another possibility. It would be the job of a jury to decide if he's guilty. The appeal hearing is coming up soon. It could be William's last chance. Unless there is new evidence, all the lawyer can do is to appeal for clemency. We've got to give the lawyer something to go at."

"You mean, feed him Gerald."

"I mean get the court to accept William may not be guilty – and if the police get serious – who knows what they might uncover. By the way, who is William's lawyer for the appeal, David Singleton?"

"No, Mark Schwartz has agreed to take the case. He's followed the case in the papers and discussed it with David Singleton. He called me and offered to represent William at the appeal hearing. I haven't told Gerald yet."

"Mark Schwartz - the top lawyer! He will be surprised." Sally Miller gave Susan another of her sly looks. "Let Gerald find out when you have your meeting. It'll add another twist." Sally Miller sensed Susan was avoiding a decision on her proposal.

"So," she said, "do you want me to explain what I think we should do to implicate Gerald, or do we just drop it?"

"I can't just drop it, not now that there may be a way of helping William. How do we do this?"

"It's very simple. We produce one of Gerald's shirts stained with blood – but it won't just be anyone's blood. It will be Angela's."

205

Susan was aghast. For an instant, she wondered if Sally Miller had been struck with senile dementia.

"How on earth can we get a sample of Angela's blood?" Sally Miller saw the look of anxious bewilderment on Susan's face.

"We can't. But Angela was type *AB negative*. It's a very rare blood type; only about one in 150 is this blood type. Gerald's shirt will have splatters of *AB negative* blood from a sample."

"A sample!" exclaimed Susan. "It's not something we can ask for over the counter!" She was feeling distinctly unhappy at the way this was going. Mrs. Miller's plan seemed naively simple, and impossible to carry out.

"I have a possible source," replied Sally Miller, playing her trump card. "But before I go any further, I want to know if you are willing to do this? It will involve telling another person and we will need their cooperation. But I'm not prepared to go any further if you don't think it's the right thing to do."

"Right thing? I used to know what the right thing was. I had a conscience, a little voice that told me. But it's been disturbingly silent on all this. I prayed for something to happen that would point to Gerald – I know he did it, murdered Angela. My conscience was clear. But this; taking direct action to implicate Gerald – it's as if a magnetic storm has engulfed my moral compass."

"Are you concerned about your conscience to the extent that it prevents you from taking any action? Can any of us afford to be so principled? For me, it's a decision about good and evil. Gerald may or may not have intended to murder Angela. It might have been a crime of passion, it might have been a fight over something else, blackmail, who knows - but in the end, he shot and killed her. The real evil is that he's willing to let William be executed for a crime he knows William didn't commit. The voice in my head tells me to get the bastard. It's clearly not my conscience, but then I'm not worried about moral principles, otherwise I wouldn't be making this suggestion. It's simple for me. William mustn't be allowed to die for the sins of his father; and you have a doting, loving son."

Susan bit hard into her bottom lip. She swiped her tongue at the trickle of blood that began to seep between her teeth. Her eyes were red and angry. She was angry with herself for being so weak. Sally Miller was right. Her own innate principles and sense of morality were no longer appropriate, not for this situation. They had to force Gerald into the open, for William's sake. She straightened up and looked directly at Sally Miller.

"You are right," she said with the intensity that startled Sally Miller. "I want to do this – I want William out of that stinking jail."

"The person I referred to knows nothing of this, as yet," said Sally Miller.

"It's Inez Knight, isn't it?" said Susan. Sally Miller smiled.

"I think you know that Inez and I have been friends for many years. You probably also know that she works at the University."

"Yes, I knew that, but she's not someone I've come across. But then it's a huge place – several thousand staff."

*

Inez was the Senior Laboratory Manager in the Department of Medical Science with responsibility for the administration of their various laboratories, including those relating to haematology and the relatively new area of forensic biology. Nothing happened in these laboratories without her authorisation. She had been instrumental in getting the University to provide initial funding for these laboratories – an investment that had paid off handsomely. Funded commercial and research projects were a major part of the work of the Medical Sciences Department, and much of this resulted from the laboratories Inez managed. A growing part of their commercial work was in Forensic Biology.

Inez was a little apprehensive about meeting with Susan. She knew about the murders from what she had read in the papers and what Sally Miller had told her. And there was the gossip. It had become a talking point at the University. The perceived wisdom, emanating from those who professed to know something about him, was that William was an oddball who had an unhealthy fixation with Angela Fisher. The almost universal view was that Susan Buckley was to be pitied. She'd had to cope with a very difficult and diffident son as well as an arrogant and pretentious husband.

Inez only agreed to meet because of her long friendship with Sally Miller, someone whose judgement she trusted implicitly. They sat at the kitchen table while Sally Miller reviewed what had happened – the murder of Angela Fisher and the subsequent shooting of Jake Fisher, the confession by William, the court's verdict and the sentence William had been given. And then she carefully went through the evidence that pointed to Gerald.

"We know he did it," said Susan. "He's willing to let William be executed," she added. "He thinks he's got away with it."

"Why do you want me involved?" asked Inez, hoping it wasn't for the reason she suspected.

"We want to implicate Gerald," said Sally Miller, boldly. "We want some evidence that points to him

208

being at the scene. We want the police to consider him a suspect." Inez Knight gasped. This wasn't just about getting access to police evidence; this was far more serious.

"And you want me to give you some ideas on what evidence might convince the police?" she probed.

"Not exactly," replied Sally Miller. "Angela Fisher was blood type *AB negative*. We want a blood sample we can use on an item of Gerald's clothes."

"You want me to help you fabricate evidence!" exclaimed Inez. "There is no way I'd ever be involved in anything like that and if you'll take my advice, you'll forget this whole idea!"

Sally Miller was not deterred by her friend's reluctance to be involved. She had expected this would be her reaction.

"You think what we are proposing is wrong, don't you?"

"I know it's wrong," replied Inez. "It's not just that it's illegal and could get us all in serious trouble - it's immoral. Gerald may well be guilty, but you should let the process of law determine that."

"Oh, we will," replied Sally. "We just need something to kick-start the process." Susan felt like an impotent bystander listening to these two friends debating the ethics – the highly dubious ethics – of what they were proposing.

"Look," said Susan, "I don't want you two to fall out over this. Your friendship is too important. I think we should forget the idea. Maybe the Appeals Court will show some leniency."

"And perhaps they won't," said Sally Miller. "Inez, I know you think I should never have involved you in this, but there is no one else I could turn to." She paused and drummed her fingers gently on the table.

209

"You remember telling me that if there was anything you could do for me...well, this is it."

"You saved my life," Inez replied. "But that was a brave and courageous act – there was nothing shameful in what you did for me."

"Do you know what I did that day?"

"Of course I do. I may have been barely conscious, but I remember you bursting in and hitting him with a baseball bat," replied Inez.

"I hit him very hard two or three times. I cracked his kneecap, smashed his arm and gave him a blow to the head that left him concussed. I knew he was incapable of doing anything at that point."

"But that was the bravest thing anyone could have done," said Inez.

"But I didn't stop there," replied Sally. "I hit him over and over again. He was completely defenceless, but I wanted to do more. I wanted to hurt him – and I wanted to damage him, permanently." Susan and Inez sat transfixed by Sally's account of her assault on her friend's attacker. "He never walked again. He's been in a wheelchair ever since. I did it because of all the people he had attacked and because he could easily have killed you, Inez. But also going through my head was the thought that he might get off with some meaningless sentence that would have seen him back on the streets. I dispensed my own brand of justice. Was it wrong? Probably. But is society safer and better off? Definitely."

Inez sucked air through her teeth, fighting to stay in control of her emotions. "But we can't go around playing at being judge and jury. If you don't follow society's rules, then you have anarchy."

"Look, Inez, the bottom line here is that Gerald is a bastard. He's prepared to let his son be executed for a crime that he committed. This isn't a vendetta against

Gerald, it's a last-ditch attempt to get William off Death Row. And we can only do that by signalling Gerald's involvement."

Inez took a different tack. "We need to discuss just what's possible. I need you to understand something about the forensic procedures regarding blood samples. If it seems it might work, then I'll help you." Susan felt as though she'd been holding her breath for several minutes. She exhaled and felt her chest and stomach begin to relax. She glanced at Sally Miller, who looked as fierce and determined as ever.

"Thanks Inez," said Sally, reaching across the table to touch her arm.

"Don't thank me yet," replied Inez. "We'll do this in stages. First, I'll go through the forensics. If we are all still convinced, then I'll agree to help."

Chapter 19
Blood

They met the following evening at Sally Miller's house. It was getting too dangerous to be meeting at Susan's, with Gerald showing signs of paranoia at the frequent visits made by Sally Miller. Sally's house was a white, single storey wood-framed construction with a green shingle roof. The garage, which appeared disproportionately large, was set back along the side of the house. Three wooden steps led to the porch. The main door led off the porch into a wide hallway that had an array of jackets dangling from a circular hat and umbrella stand, and a grandfather clock standing against the wall like a sentry metering and guarding the passage of time.

Ron had removed the partition wall separating the living room and dining room, shortly after they took possession of the house. It had created a very large living area with a bay window overlooking the front lawn, and a large window at the opposite end of the room that overlooked their back yard.

Susan and Inez made themselves comfortable at the large oak dining table in the main room, while Sally Miller carried in a coffee pot and mugs from the kitchen. Inez Knight took the initiative.

"It's important you understand a thing or two about forensics." Sally and Susan sat, attentive and alert.

"Forensic Biology deals primarily with the discovery and identification of blood and body fluids on physical evidence," explained Inez. "It may deal just with blood, but it might also involve other body fluids – you know - semen, urine, saliva, faeces. All the good stuff!"

Susan leaned forward. "Sounds disgusting," she commented.

"Oh, there's nothing pleasant about it," acknowledged Inez, "but a clever lawyer can paint a vivid picture from forensic evidence."

Inez took a few moments to sip her coffee. This was very familiar ground to her. In addition to delivering lectures to medical students on just such procedures, she'd also provided advice to criminal lawyers and had conducted most of the relevant tests during her time at the University.

"Finding a bloodstain is easier than you might think," she said. "Traces of blood can be detected using a luminal spray. Any blood residue will fluoresce – glow – under ultra-violet light. I've known it to be effective even when someone has scrubbed at a blood stain." Inez was in full flow now. She loved the reverent silence that usually accompanied her descriptions of her work.

"When a stain is found at the scene of a crime, there is a simple test to determine if it's blood or some other bodily fluid. Determining which person the bloodstain belongs to involves an investigation of blood types. Tests are used to identify the three blood groups: *A*, *B* and *O*. It's the same test used to determine compatibility for blood donors and recipients." Inez paused. She could go into antigens and proteins, false negative and false positive results, and a host of technical detail, but decided to keep it as straight forward as she could.

"Angela was *Rhesus negative*. All the blood groups can be negative or positive. It involves a further test to determine the presence of a blood protein known as the Rhesus factor – it was first seen in Rhesus monkeys, hence the name."

"Oh!" said Susan. "I've always wondered."

"And now we know," added Sally, with a hint of sarcasm. "Is there any other important bit of information we need to know?" she asked.

"I'm sure there is. I've tried to give you the basics. Blood splatter tests have become quite important. Juries seem to like them."

"What does that involve?" asked Susan.

"It's not very scientific," replied Inez, dismissively. "There are so-called experts who claim they know what sort of blood splatter pattern is made by a knife wound, a gunshot, or a blow to the head. It's pretty subjective stuff – I don't think it's anything to worry about."

Sally shuffled in her chair. She could see why courtrooms would love this stuff – it was the theatrical equivalent of throwing water across the stage.

"Don't let's get too complacent," she suggested. "It's best we are aware of this approach ... even if it doesn't fit in with the hard scientific evidence."

Inez snorted. "No scientific rigour – it's not repeatable, you see."

"Okay, Inez," said Sally, smiling. "We didn't mean to knock you off your perch!"

Inez laughed. "I can feel myself coming back to earth."

"How would we get a sample of blood?" asked Susan. "Without it being detected, that is?"

"We keep some samples of all the blood groups in our Department of Serology," replied Inez. "We keep a record of the amount and the date it was stored. It's on a simple spreadsheet which I keep in the lab admin files. Blood stocks are replenished after a year in store.

And then there are the occasional spills and breakages, but they are fairly rare."

"What happens when a sample is due to be discarded?" asked Sally.

"It's treated as hazardous waste. All hazardous waste is collected by a company licensed to handle medical wastes. They treat hospital waste in exactly the same way. I believe it's all dumped into a container for treatment prior to disposal. Probably sterilised and chemically treated."

"So getting a sample that's due to be discarded is the obvious way," commented Susan.

"Yes," replied Inez. She hoped it was foolproof.

*

Inez sat at her desk and stared at the dark-red tube of blood standing on the work surface like an admonishing finger. She'd not really had time to reflect on what she had agreed to do; not until now. She felt weak and dizzy, now that the feeling of excitement at being involved was draining from her as if the blood in front of her was her blood.

Taking the phial of blood was easy. She'd simply gone through the records, identified a sample of *AB negative* that was due to be discarded, altered the record to show it had been disposed of – but instead of sending it down the chute marked 'Hazard Waste Only', she kept the sample which now sat on her desk. She could stop this insanity right now by lifting the thing and depositing it into the chute.

Her friend Sally had asked her to do too much. She'd asked her to commit a crime – to steal from the lab she had helped create. She'd developed the operational procedures, she'd written the training manual, she'd tried to instil the importance of their work to all the lab technicians, and now she had violated her own principles and the sanctity of the laboratory. And why was she doing this; why was she putting her job on the line? She knew why – because her friend Sally had put her life on the line. *Oh, Sally,* Inez thought, *this brave thing you're trying to do – save the life of your friend's son – I wish I was as convinced as you are that this is the right thing to do.*

The thought that she might be found out and lose her job was frightening – as was the knowledge that she would have to live with what she had done. But she owed so much to Sally; *and perhaps,* she thought, *I deserve to be tested in this way in order to repay Sally.* She sat for a long time, staring at the red sample – red for danger, perhaps?

*

Susan arranged to meet with Mark Schultz alone. She didn't want Gerald involved in these discussions. Gerald was fairly dismissive about the appeals process, anyway.

"It's pointless," he told Susan. "It will cost a fortune - especially with Mark Schultz - and for what? So you can satisfy your conscience?"

"My conscience!" exclaimed Susan. "I'll do whatever it takes to get William off Death Row. As for the money – exactly what price do you put on William?"

"How about bankruptcy?" replied Gerald, with an icy sarcasm. Susan didn't rise to his remark. This wasn't the time to get into a steaming row with Gerald. Instead, she turned away and headed for the relative sanctity of the kitchen, and calmed herself by going over in her mind what she wanted to discuss with Mark Schultz.

The office that Mark Schultz occupied was considerably bigger and grander than the one David Singleton used. It felt cavernous by comparison. It

216

struck Susan as being impersonal and lacking in character. There was none of the personal memorabilia that adorned the corners of David Singleton's office. The walls were plain, except for a rail that supported five framed certificates of Mark Schultz's qualifications. A huge conference table dominated one end of the room, and in front of a bay window, overlooking a small park, was a large modern desk with a matching ergonomically designed chair - it was all steel pulleys and levers, and had an uncompromising arched back support.

He beckoned her to sit on one of the modern chairs at the conference table. They were surprisingly comfortable. His secretary walked briskly into the room from an adjoining office carrying a tray with two cups of coffee, a small jug of milk, and a matching bowl of sugar. Susan caught the briefest nod from Mark Schultz and an equally brief flicker of acknowledgement from his secretary.

"Please – help yourself to milk and sugar," gestured Mark Schultz, as he took a seat at the conference table across from hers. The distance between them seemed like an enormous empty plain.

Mark Schultz was in his fifties. He was immaculately dressed in an expensive-looking dark pinstripe suit, that appeared to retain its pleated shape irrespective of how he moved. He flicked open the single button on his jacket to reveal a matching waistcoat that wrapped comfortably around his developing paunch. His shirt was startlingly white and his pale-blue silk tie was held slightly proud by a large gold tie-pin. His face was pink and shiny, as if it had been recently scrubbed with some expensive cream, and he had a smooth, large, alabaster forehead and thinning dark hair brushed back hard against the top of his head. There wasn't a hint of grey – just a slick of black. He looked imposing and a little scary. But his smile was something entirely different. He had a bright comforting smile that radiated an embracing warmth and eyes that softened to a glow, so stark in comparison to the piercing stare she had encountered on entering his office. He gave the impression that meeting her would be one of the highlights of his day. This highly personal charm made her feel very special indeed. Susan's first impression had been that of a stern and formidable lawyer. She now felt comfortable, at ease, and not in the least bit intimidated. But she was under no illusion that he could switch his persona as and when required.

"I've discussed this case with David Singleton at length..."

Susan didn't like the suggestion that he was just another client – it sounded very impersonal. She wanted to scream, *William! It's not just a collection of papers in a loose-leaf legal file – it's my son, William, we are discussing!*

"...and I don't want you to be under any misapprehension as to the difficulties your son faces." Susan nodded. "There are some procedural issues that I can draw to the attention of the appeals court, especially concerning his so-called confession to Angela Fisher's murder. I'll have one or two things to say about the way William's statement was taken. And I'll focus on the police investigation. They decided very early on that William was the guilty party. They weren't particularly thorough at the crime scene, and they made absolutely no attempt to consider any possibility other than William committing the murder." Susan nodded again. She felt strangely comforted by his analysis of the situation, despite his rather pessimistic assessment.

"Quite frankly," he said, suddenly looking very stern, "without some further evidence, something that might suggest that someone other than William murdered Angela Fisher, this is just going to be an exercise in damage control." Susan felt her heart race. Her mouth felt dry. This was the moment.

"I think I have something," she said.

Chapter 20
Evidence

Mark Schultz leaned forward and stared into her eyes, as if waiting to see who would blink first. "Tell me what you have," he said, in a stern, no-nonsense, tone of voice.

Susan reached round for her calico bag, the one she usually used to carry her library books. She lifted out the plastic bag from Coles' Store and offered it to Mark Schultz.

"What is it?" he asked, without making any attempt to take the bag. Susan pulled the bag back towards her, feeling slightly awkward.

"It's a shirt. It's got stains on it – I think they might be bloodstains." Susan's heart was banging hard. She suddenly felt guilty and for an instance thought about grabbing up her things and running out of the room. And then the inquisition began – just as Sally Miller had predicted it would.

"Where did you find this?" asked Mark Schultz.

"I didn't," replied Susan. "It was my housekeeper, Sally Miller. She was cleaning up in the spare room and found it at the back of the dresser. It was stuffed behind a suitcase."

"Who has access to the room?"

"Well, all of us. Me, Mrs. Miller - she's helped look after William since he was a baby - and Gerald, my husband." She tried to say Gerald's name as calmly and normally as she could, but her throat felt constricted and she felt sure her hesitation would be obvious. Mark Schultz appeared not to have noticed. He continued to circle round this piece of new evidence, prodding gently with his questions as if wanting to tease away the outer layers to expose anything that might be toxic; something dangerous.

"Who took the shirt out of the bag?" It was a simple question, but it threw Susan for a moment or two. She'd expected him to be concerned more with the contents of the bag rather than the details surrounding the assumed find.

"Mrs. Miller brought the bag to me. She wondered what it was. I saw that it looked like one of Gerald's shirts. When I took it out – that's when we saw the stains."

"We?" asked Mark Schultz.

"Mrs. Miller was standing next to me. She thought the stains looked like blood – so did I."

"And you think it's one of Gerald's shirts?"

"Yes, it is. I recognised it as soon as I took it out of the bag. It's one of his blue Oxford shirts. I bought several for him about six months ago."

"You'd better let me have a look at it," said Mark Schultz. Susan slid the shirt out of the plastic bag and laid it out on the conference table so that the stains could be seen. Mark Schultz looked carefully at the evidence.

"I think you are right – these are bloodstains. The streaking and splatter patterns are a bit unusual – but that may be due to the shirt being stuffed into that bag." He pulled out a yellow legal pad from his desk drawer and proceeded to make notes. "I want to record what you've told me and I also want to make some notes about the shirt – the colour, the make and size, the location of the stains and its general condition." He reached into one of the other desk drawers and located a small camera. He proceeded to take several photographs of the shirt and close-up shots of the stains. "Did you tell Gerald about this – ask him for an explanation?"

"No," replied Susan. "I didn't want to alert him – I didn't want him to know I'd found the shirt and I certainly didn't want him to know I was bringing it here to show you."

"If this is Gerald's shirt - and let's suppose it is, just for now - is there any explanation as to how he might have got these bloodstains?"

"He told me he'd got it quite badly stained from a cut on his hand. He did have a bad scratch on his hand which he said he caught on a fence. I asked if I could get it cleaned but he said it was too badly stained and that he'd thrown it away."

"And now the shirt has turned up?" asked Mark Schultz. Was there a hint of scepticism in his voice? Susan felt a bit alarmed.

"He must have hidden it, intending to dispose of it later," replied Susan.

"Anything else – what about other items of clothing?" asked Mark Schultz.

"Oh, yes – he mentioned his jacket. He said it only had a couple of spots of blood so he took it to the cleaners. And his tie – he said he'd thrown that away as well."

"This all sounds entirely plausible," said Mark Schultz. "Don't you agree?"

"He bought a new shirt in Coles," said Susan, quickly. "Mrs. Miller bumped into him in the old mall and noticed he was wearing a yellow shirt."

"Mrs. Miller features a lot," replied Mark Schultz. "How do you know this ... how do you know he bought a shirt in Coles?"

"Mrs. Miller asked in the store. One of the assistants remembered serving him."

"Ah, Mrs. Miller again," commented Mark Schultz. "Nanny turned detective!" Susan blushed. "What else have you two sleuths uncovered?" He sounded very dismissive, as if she was just a distraught mother, clutching at straws.

"Mrs. Miller talked to a mother who regularly walked her pram in the park opposite the mall. She remembers seeing a man walking across the park, heading towards the mall around four pm. He must have come from the alleyway at the back of the Fisher's house – it leads onto the park." Susan glanced up at Mark Schultz. He sat scribbling on his yellow pad in tiny, neat writing, appearing almost uninterested in what she was telling him.

"And there was a high school kid riding a bike along the alleyway. He almost ran into a man wearing a dark jacket sometime around four." Mark Schultz continued writing on his pad for a few moments and then placed his black pen diagonally across his notepad. It looked to Susan like a thick line drawn across his notes.

"Anything else?" he asked, a question which suggested to Susan that he was far from convinced about Gerald's involvement.

"Little things," replied Susan. "Gerald rarely goes to the old mall, and I've never known him buy clothes there. I buy his clothes for him, sometimes on my own and sometimes dragging him along, usually under much protest. He apparently went to buy a shirt in the sale in Coles. The lady who served him said he grabbed the first shirt in his size and was in such a rush, he left without collecting his change – over ten dollars. That is so unlike Gerald. And then there was his lame excuse about going to a shop that sells crafts. Gerald has never been the faintest bit interested in such things."

"It could have been just that – an excuse. We all make excuses from time to time."

"Yes, but this was completely out of character." Susan paused, wondering if there was any point in going on. Mark Schultz seemed to think that everything that had happened was explainable.

"I found his shoes – his favourite pair." She thought it best to omit any further reference to Sally Miller. "They'd been scrubbed to remove stains. I think he might have been trying to remove bloodstains."

"But his hand was bleeding. Couldn't that be the explanation?"

"I suppose so," replied Susan. She felt all her arguments had been undermined. A rush of thoughts swirled into her mind. Had she made a terrible mistake? All she had were coincidences, coincidences that had led to the conclusion she'd convinced herself was the right one. Her assumptions now seemed weak. Was Gerald entirely innocent as Mark Schultz's questions seemed to imply? She'd involved both Mrs. Miller and Inez in a deliberate attempt to fabricate evidence she'd hoped would implicate Gerald, because she was convinced he was guilty. Or was it that she wanted to believe he was guilty?

"Is that it?" asked Mark Shultz. Susan took a deep breath and exhaled. It sounded like a resigned sigh. Susan's eagerness to meet with Mark Schultz and her assumption that he would view the 'evidence' she had brought as being compelling, even conclusive, had been shattered.

"Just one last thing. There was a cup of black coffee in the kitchen – partly finished, I think the report said." Mark Schultz opened the manila file in front of him and took out the police report. He leafed through until he found the reference to the cup of coffee.

"Here it is," he said. He read from the report. "*A cup containing some black coffee was found in the kitchen on the counter top. A thumb and finger print were found on the rim of the cup which matched those of William Martin.*"

"But William doesn't drink black coffee," protested Susan. "Gerald does," she added quickly. Mark Schultz looked up and tapped his pen on his notepad.

"Now that could be worth pursuing," he remarked.

"And Angela didn't drink black coffee," added Susan.

"I was going to ask that," remarked Mark Schultz. "But what also interests me is that the only prints they found of Williams were those of his thumb and finger on the rim. That suggests someone lifting the cup like this." He demonstrated what he meant by lifting his own coffee cup. It's not the way you'd hold a cup to drink from it." Susan allowed herself a quick smile.

"I don't want to give you any false hope," he added. "In fact, most of what you've told me borders on speculation, even fantasy – unless we can show that Gerald was in the house. And to do that we need to establish that Gerald is a suspect. I'll get this shirt tested. Let's see if the blood type is AB negative." Susan felt drained by their conversation. She'd all but given up hope of convincing Mark Schultz that Gerald might be a suspect. And now, it had suddenly fallen into place based on the one bit of information she'd almost forgotten about.

"The report states that there were lots of other fingerprints in the kitchen," continued Mark Schultz. "That's not unexpected. And the only ones they were interested in at the time of the investigation were William's. Now if the blood analysis comes up as *AB negative*, I will ask the police to consider Gerald as a possible suspect and compare his fingerprints with those found in the kitchen."

"Thank you," said Susan. "It's giving me hope..."

"That Gerald is guilty or that William is innocent?" asked Mark Schultz.

"Both, I think," replied Susan.

"There is one other major factor to be considered," commented Mark Schultz. "Motive - what motive would Gerald have for killing Angela Fisher?"

*

Mark Schultz was not one who normally dithered about any decision he had to make. He prided himself on having an instinct for what needed to be done. Just occasionally, this meant skirting on the edge of what might be regarded as ethical practice. He'd achieved notoriety for his handling of a manslaughter charge against a young actor, Martin Woods, who'd shot a drug dealer during a deal that had gone wrong.

He was guilty; Mark Schultz knew that. But Mark Schultz had found a way to get him off without adding a thing to the speeding fines that were the only items on the young man's record. He had torn shreds through the evidence presented by the prosecution. They had relied on the testimony of three gang members. Two of them had been accomplices of the man who'd been shot and killed, and the third was a rival gang member; one of a pair who'd been conducting the drug deal. He had turned into the path of one of the patrol cars and found himself hammered against the railings of a tenement building before he even had time to throw away his weapon. His accomplice had somehow managed to melt into the shadows of the lofty tenements, cackling and shrieking like a hyena. The others had been arrested, along with the defendant, in a police swoop immediately following the shootings. The hoods had

226

seen the actor's shiny, white corvette inching along the pavement as he'd approached the dealers on their patch. Martin Woods had a hand gun on his lap – just in case. As he'd lowered his driver's side window, his skin tingling with frightened nervousness, a gun had been fired from somewhere across the street, snapping the still, warm air with an ear-splitting retort that reverberated off the high walls of the tenement buildings. One of the dealers had gone down on his knees, clutching his arm. In an instant of hot blind panic, Martin Woods had fired his gun in the direction of the nearest hood, hitting him in the throat and splintering the base of his skull. He'd staggered, staring wide-eyed, and then slumped across the front of Martin Woods' car with a thump and had slowly slid down to the ground, smearing a pool of crimson blood, stark against the white metallic paintwork.

Mark Schultz had used the gang rivalry to good effect. They had to be physically restrained from confronting one another in the courtroom and were warned several times by the judge for shouting out threats at one another. Mark Schultz had to do very little to encourage them to demonstrate their bravado and absolute contempt for the law once they took the witness stand. He showed them to be completely unreliable, more concerned with their reputations than with the prosecution's attempt to use them as witnesses to the shooting. They'd revelled in the publicity that Mark Schultz deliberately accorded them, each trying to show themselves to be tougher, dirtier and uglier than their rivals. And they had given such different versions of the shooting which, under Mark Schultz's cross-examination, became so cavernous they might well have been describing different events.

In his summing up, Mark Schultz portrayed the gang members as a collective of violent thugs, each willing to engage in acts of extreme violence and commit murder to promote fear and establish a reputation for uncompromising thuggery that required even more gratuitous acts of violence just to maintain their status. He had berated the prosecution for giving the gang members immunity if they were prepared to testify. He had also suggested to the court that in future, any evidence from criminals - and especially gang members - who stood to benefit from giving testimony, should only be relied upon if it were corroborated by independent witnesses. The jury were entirely sympathetic with defendant and he was acquitted of any charge relating to the shooting. It was recorded as death by misadventure. And the suggestion made by Mark Schultz about the veracity of violent witnesses who were offered immunity from prosecution made it all the way to the Supreme Court.

He had a reputation for successfully defending seemingly cast-iron murder cases. But he was selective. The issue for him was not the guilt or innocence of the person he was representing - it was the evidence. Mark Schultz felt he could make a successful defence of a murder or manslaughter charge if there was a chink in the train of evidence that that he could expose. In the end, it always came down to instinct. Even if he felt there might be a way through a prosecution's argument, he needed an inner sense of conviction that he could develop a defence strategy that would work. And he had an excellent record. He'd only failed to get three acquittals in the fifteen cases he'd taken on.

He didn't yet have that instinct for this case. This wasn't unusual. It always took him a little time to get familiar with the prosecution's case, the evidence and the various reports from the police incident teams, the duty officer, the coroner, the medics and any expert witnesses who'd been deposed. Up until now, there hadn't been anything about the case that had caused him to be anything other than circumspect. He needed the 'high', the adrenalin rush that triggered his instincts, something that he then couldn't ignore, no matter how hard his logical processors objected. This new bit of evidence had spiked his instinct. Now he felt he could take the case.

Chapter 21
Further Evidence

Mark Shultz decided to pay a visit to the District Attorney, John Sweetman. He'd known John over ten years, ever since he was appointed assistant DA. They had both attended law school at the University of Minnesota but Mark had graduated about three years earlier. Although they weren't friends, their meetings were always cordial and professional and, in common with many alumni, they liked to follow the University's football team. It provided an easy way into their discussions.

"They were awful!" commented John Sweetman, nodding in the direction of the publicity photograph of the U of M footballers, the front row on one knee with one hand resting on their helmets, the others standing in ranks on elevated benches; all wearing their huge padded shoulders, making them look like something out of a 'Superman' comic.

"Yeah," replied Mark Schultz. "There was no way they were going to get two touchdowns in the final quarter – not against a team like *Notre Dame*." John Sweetman grunted in agreement.

"I guess you aren't here just to discuss the fortunes of the Wolverines?" Mark Schultz gave a low chuckle.

"Not if they keep playing like that! No, John - it's about the William Martin case."

"I heard you'd taken over from David Singleton," replied John Sweetman. "Not like you, though, to take on a hopeless case!"

"Yeah," replied Mark Schultz, resisting the temptation to respond. He gave a quick smile and straightened himself in the leather chair in John Sweetman's office, signalling it was time to get serious.

"I've got something I need checked out."

"To do with the Martin case?" asked John Sweetman.

"Could be. Let's just say I'd like to see if it has any bearing."

"Okay... what have you got?"

"It's a shirt belonging to Gerald Martin, William's father," Mark Schultz replied. "It's got some bloodstains."

"And you think they might be Angela Fisher's?"

"I'm not saying that. There may be a perfectly good explanation. He did cut his hand and it could well be his blood on the shirt. I just want a quick test to see what blood type it is. He's type *O*."

"And Angela Fisher is *AB negative*," said John Sweetman. "So you're not submitting this as evidence?"

"No," replied Mark Schultz. "At this stage it's just a bloodstained shirt belonging to a guy who cut his hand."

"But not any guy," replied the DA. "Okay, since it's you, Mark, I'll send it to the Police Forensics lab – ask them to do a test for blood type. Why didn't you get it tested yourself at one of the private labs – there are quite a few touting for business?"

"If the blood turns out to be *AB negative*, then this will become evidence and I don't want any suggestion of failing to follow procedures."

"Or have a lab accused of cross-contamination."

"Exactly," replied Mark Schultz.

*

Three days later, Mark Schultz received the results from the laboratory. They were given simply and clearly in a standardised table for reporting the test results. The top section gave a brief description of the item, the date it was received, a reference number and the name of the chief laboratory technician. The table underneath described the serology tests that had been conducted and an adjacent column gave the corresponding results. The first tests confirmed that the samples were stained with human blood, ruling out similar stains. The second set of serological tests was to establish the blood type. The results jumped out of the page, as if the typesetting was substantially larger than that used in the rest of the report.

Blood type: *AB negative*. Replicate tests gave a total of twelve results, each confirming the result – blood type *AB negative*.

Mark Schultz grabbed the phone and called the DA's office.

"John, it's Mark. I've just got the results."

"I know, I got a copy sent through earlier this morning," replied John Sweetman. "Blood type *AB*. I was just about to call you. We need to talk. Can you come over?"

"What, now?" asked Mark Schultz. He hadn't anticipated that John Sweetman would have been provided with a duplicate copy.

"Yes, now," replied John Sweetman. It wasn't everyday he got the opportunity to exercise his authority over a hot-shot lawyer like Mark Schultz.

"This changes things," he remarked, as Mark Schultz got himself positioned once again on the leather chair in the DA's office.

"Certainly does," said Mark Schultz. "We need to have his fingerprints checked against those found in Angela Fisher's house."

"Just what I was thinking," replied John Sweetman. "He's got a bit of explaining to do."

"I think it might be best if you just tell him it's routine – that you want to eliminate him from your enquiries. He won't believe you, but until you've checked his fingerprints, you don't really have any basis for arresting him." John Sweetman was a bit annoyed with himself for over-reacting.

"You're right, of course. I'll alert the Police Chief. Tell him what we need."

*

Detective Sparrow rapped on the door of the Dean of Education's PA, Lillian Gustafson and pushed it open. "We'd like a word with Professor Martin," he said, giving a nodding gesture towards his partner, Detective Murphy.

"Lovely to see you again Detective Sparrow, and you too Detective Murphy," she said, peering over Detective Sparrow's shoulder at the apparently disinterested Detective Murphy. It was if she was greeting old acquaintances. "He should be in his office. Anything I can do?"

"No, thanks," replied Detective Sparrow, tersely. "We know where his office is. Don't bother to call him."

"I wouldn't dream of it," replied Lillian Gustafson. "I'm sure he'll enjoy the surprise."

Gerald had allocated the morning to preparing some reports for Professor Steele. It was mundane stuff, the sort of thing that would have irked him in the past, but

233

now he was quite content to be doing something to occupy his time that was useful without being taxing. He was quite enjoying the routine. Being back at work had given him a lift. It gave a sense of normality to his life and it was good to get away from the house and from Susan. At first, it was obvious that his colleagues were avoiding him, as if he was afflicted by something unpleasant. After a few days, however, his colleagues lost their initial reticence and had become quite sympathetic. 'You mustn't blame yourself,' was the prevailing view.

"He'd tried his best. William had been a difficult kid – something of a loner," Gerald told them. "He blamed her," he confided to two of his associates who had offices on the same floor. "She'd been a bad influence."

The knock on his door was sharp and crisp. *It must be that witch, Lillian Gustafson,* was Gerald's immediate thought. His jaw dropped when he saw Detectives Sparrow and Murphy hovering in the door frame.

"Mind if we have a few minutes?" asked Detective Sparrow. Gerald couldn't muster a coherent reply and before he knew it Detective Sparrow was taking a seat while Detective Murphy closed the door. Gerald sat heavily on the chair behind his desk and waited for one of the detectives to speak. Detective Murphy remained standing near the door; Detective Sparrow sat upright and peered at Gerald with something approaching a smile on his face. Gerald felt that the pounding in his head was the loudest thing in the room. Much to Gerald's relief, Detective Sparrow eventually leant forward.

"Sorry to bother you, Professor Martin. Something has come up – and the DA's office is keen that we play this by the book and eliminate everyone from our enquiries. I guess he doesn't want any mistakes to be made with the appeal hearing just around the corner."

Gerald felt relieved that they hadn't just come to arrest him. But then why should they? The court case was over. There was just the appeal. Appeal – the word sounded in his head like a crescendo of warning bells. The appeal was just about getting a reduced sentence for William; nothing more. He knew that.

"We just need you to come down to the station to do the fingerprinting the DA's office is so het up about," continued Detective Sparrow.

"Fingerprints?" exclaimed Gerald.

"Sorry, didn't I say that? Yes - just routine, though."

"It would get the DA's office off our backs for a start," commented Detective Murphy, with a grin. Gerald tried to muster a reaction, but his facial muscles felt paralysed.

"When?" he asked, squeezing out the words.

"Well, now, if that's alright," replied Detective Sparrow. "It won't take long – we'll have you down and back to your warm office in no time. We can let Mrs. Gustafson know..."

"That won't be necessary," said Gerald, quickly. Detective Murphy held open the door for him and nodded in the direction of the side entrance. "We parked at the back of the building. We like to be discreet," he said.

Gerald was back in his office in less than thirty minutes. He felt dirty. His fingertips still had some staining from the ink, despite several attempts to wipe them clean. A station sergeant had carefully rolled the thumb on his left hand in an ink pad and then transferred the stain to a card that would carry his prints as a permanent record. He repeated this for each finger and then again for the thumb and fingers of his other hand. Gerald allowed his hands to be guided by the sergeant without offering any resistance. It was a ticklish sensation that reminded Gerald of a childish game. It had an intimacy that almost made Gerald smile. The sergeant then photographed the palms and backs of both hands as if it was routine, but Gerald had the unnerving thought that he was paying particular attention to the scratches on the back of his hand.

Every time he touched a piece of paper it left a faint but visible print of his fingers with the characteristic shapes that were the markers for everywhere he had been – everything he had touched. He rushed down the corridor and into the Men's washroom. He pumped liquid soap from the wall-mounted dispenser onto a small scrubbing brush, and attacked the ends of his fingers until they were pink and shiny. He could feel them twitching as he dried them on the towel. He felt knotted and tense. His breaths came in gasps that sucked against his teeth. For a brief moment he had an urge to flee – to jump in his car and just drive. He shook his head, caught a glimpse of the frightened man in the mirror, and returned to his office.

He hadn't got a lawyer. He had never needed one, until now. He grabbed the 'phone book, scanned the yellow pages, and called the firm with the largest ad.

*

John Sweetman called Mark Schultz.

"We've got Gerald Martin's fingerprints and checked them against some of those found in Angela Fisher's kitchen."

"And?" said Mark Schultz.

"He was there," replied John Sweetman. "His fingerprints were all over the place." He heard Mark Schultz exhale, almost like a low whistle.

"Are you going to arrest him?"

"We are," replied John Sweetman. "He'll be held on a suspicion of murder. A couple of detectives have just been despatched to pick him up."

"It'll be interesting to hear what he has to say," commented Mark Schultz.

"It certainly will," replied John Sweetman.

*

Gerald had managed to secure the services of a lawyer within minutes of returning from the washrooms. He felt a bit better now that his fingers were scrubbed and clean. Leo Green was a partner in the law firm of Bateman, Green, and Samuel. He was just walking in from lunch with one of the junior lawyers, Frank Wiseman, when the receptionist picked up the phone.

"It's a Gerald Martin," she said, holding her hand over the end of the receiver. "He's looking for some advice."

"Gerald Martin – isn't that the father of the kid found guilty of a double homicide?" asked Frank Wiseman.

"It certainly sounds like it," replied Leo Green. "Put him through to my office," he said as he headed through the glass doors leading to the main corridor. He picked up the receiver.

"This is Leo Green. I believe I'm talking to Gerald Martin?"

"Yes," replied Gerald.

"And is this in connection with the William Martin case – your son?"

"That's correct," replied Gerald. "But it's not William – it's me I'm calling about."

"Well, I did hear Mark Schultz was handling the appeal."

"I think I'm in trouble," said Gerald. "The police have just taken my fingerprints."

"I take it you haven't been charged with anything?"

"No," replied Gerald,

"And could it be anything to do with the murder cases your son was convicted of?" persisted Leo Green.

"I think it might be," said Gerald.

"I take it you would like me to represent you?"

"Yes," replied Gerald, nodding his head as he spoke. Leo Green didn't pause.

"You'd better get down here as soon as possible – in about thirty minutes, is that okay?"

"Yes," replied Gerald. "I know where your offices are."

"Good," said Leo Green. "You had better take this number down – it's my cell phone. Any trouble, just give me a call. And I like my clients to call me Leo. I think it makes for a more intimate relationship."

Gerald was just on the point of leaving when there was a light tap on his door. Before he could react, Detective Sparrow led Detective Murphy into his office. Gerald knew instantly what they were going to do.

"Gerald Martin, I have a warrant for your arrest on a charge of suspicion of murder. Read him his rights," he said to his partner, as he reached out to Gerald with a pair of handcuffs. Gerald stood quietly, not saying a word. His legs felt weak and, with his hands clasped in front of him, he felt giddy and unbalanced. The two detectives steadied him as they escorted him towards their car.

Gerald called Leo Green from the interview room. The phone was answered after a couple of rings.

"Leo – it's Gerald Martin. I've been arrested." The room acoustics gave his voice a shrill tone.

"What's the charge?" asked Leo Green, bluntly.

"Suspicion of murder - murder of Angela Fisher," replied Gerald.

238

"Don't say a word," replied Leo Green. "I'll be there in fifteen minutes."

When Leo Green arrived, Gerald was still in the interview room, nursing a cold cup of black coffee in a Styrofoam cup. Gerald had barely touched the drink. It had a thin brown scum that had stained the inside of the cup like a tidemark of dirty water.

"I've just arranged a meeting with the DA's office for tomorrow morning. They obviously feel they have strong grounds for making the arrest and I will need to discuss these with you tomorrow."

"What about bail?" asked Gerald.

"I'll try and get a date for a bail hearing. If the DA's office thinks there might be a risk of your going on the run, they won't grant bail. It's essential that you are completely honest with me. Remember, I'm not here to judge you, convict you or give evidence against you. My job is to get a verdict of 'innocent' if at all possible – or to get a lenient sentence, if you are found guilty." Gerald shuddered at the thought.

Leo Green pushed himself out of the uncomfortable metal chair in the interview room, and made for the exit door. He turned back towards Gerald, who remained seated and grim-faced, staring at his hands resting on the table in front of him. "I'll see you in the morning, about ten."

*

It was about ten-thirty before Leo Green arrived the following morning. Gerald had assumed he would arrive exactly on time, and kept looking at his watch every few minutes. He was relieved when the guard swung open the door and announced that Mr. Green was waiting for him in the interview room.

"Sorry I'm late," said Leo Green. "The meeting with the DA took longer than I had expected." Gerald sat at the table, opposite Leo Green. "I've been through the

239

grounds for your arrest with the DA. I have to tell you – they have some strong evidence."

"Just what, exactly?" asked Gerald. He didn't feel as afraid as he had done the previous afternoon when he'd been arrested. He'd had all night to think about it. Had someone seen him enter the house – or leave the house? Perhaps the sales lady had been suspicious when he'd bought that shirt in Coles? It must be something, something like that. How else could he be linked to Angela's murder? But the fingerprints – that's what really scared him. Was it just routine? And then his arrest. No, that was too much of a coincidence. His prints would be all over the house. They knew he was there.

"They have a shirt of yours; it's got blood on it. It's the same type as Angela Fisher's."

"But that's not possible!" replied Gerald. "It just isn't possible!" he repeated, staring wild-eyed at Leo Green.

"And then there are your fingerprints," added Leo Green, ignoring Gerald's protestation. "They've been found in Angela Fisher's house – in the kitchen in particular." Gerald let out a resigned sigh. Leo Green sat back and waited for Gerald to compose himself.

"I was there," he said, eventually. "But I didn't kill her. I didn't kill Angela Fisher. I swear to God I didn't kill her."

"Look," said Leo Green, "as I told you, I'm not here to judge you or pass sentence. I'm here to defend you – and I can only do that if you tell me the truth."

"I didn't kill her," repeated Gerald.

"But you were there?" Gerald glanced nervously around the room as if looking for hidden microphones.

"Yes – I was there. I went to have it out with her ... to tell her not to play William along."

"What do you mean – play William along?" asked Leo Green.

"He had become infatuated with her. He blushed scarlet every time her name was mentioned. And he was spending more and more time alone with her. She always arranged William's lessons when Jake Fisher was on duty."

"Did you think there was something going on between them?" asked Leo Green.

"I know there was," replied Gerald.

"You knew?" asked Leo Green, raising an eyebrow. Gerald realised he'd gone too far.

"Well, not exactly, but I was a convinced as any father could be that she was leading him on. If they weren't having sex, they were getting damn close," replied Gerald.

"So, you were worried that she was encouraging William to have a sexual relationship with her."

"Yes," replied Gerald, "that's exactly what concerned me. She was his teacher - not a sex therapist!" Leo Green frowned at Gerald's remark, and continued.

"Did you discuss this with William, or with your wife, Susan?"

"I didn't talk to William, but I did mention it to Susan. I told her I thought William was obsessed with Angela, and that it might lead to trouble."

"And so you went round to see her. What happened?" asked Leo Green.

"I went shortly after three. I'd planned to go to the mall to get a shirt and thought I might as well drop in to talk to Angela on the way. She asked me to come in, and offered me a cup of coffee. I told her I just wanted to talk to her because I was a bit concerned that William was becoming infatuated with her."

"And how did she react?" asked Leo Green.

241

"She was a bit upset. She said she had never intended to give William that impression. I reminded her of the duet piece that I knew William had been playing with her. Then she got annoyed and said I should leave. I said maybe it would be best if I came back to see her with Susan. She seemed okay with that suggestion. That's when I left."

"So, when you last saw Angela she was perfectly fit and healthy?"

"Yes," replied Gerald.

"And then what?" asked Leo Green. "Where did you go when you left Angela Fisher's house?"

"I went on to the mall. I left through the kitchen door at the back of the house."

"But why not leave through the front door?" asked Leo Green.

"The back door leads to a lane and then the park across from the mall. Angela told me it was the quickest way," replied Gerald.

"So, what you want a court to believe, Gerald, is that you visited Angela to talk to her about what you thought was becoming an unhealthy, and possibly sexual, relationship with William. You had coffee in her kitchen, left through the back door and went to the shopping mall."

"Yes," replied Gerald.

"And that the murder must have taken place after you left?"

"Guess so," replied Gerald. He felt pleased with the way this was going.

"Tell me what you did at the shopping mall."

"Not much to tell, really. I bought a shirt in Coles – they had a sale on. I bumped into Mrs. Miller as I was coming out of the men's room. I had a couple of words with her and then I popped into the pharmacy to get some dressing for some scratches on my hand."

242

"How did you get those?" asked Leo Green.

"I caught my hand on the fence as I was leaving Angela's."

"What then?"

"I walked back to get my car and headed back to the office," replied Gerald.

Leo Green was turning pages in his file as Gerald answered his questions. He'd been up until two in the morning reading through the police reports and the transcripts from William's trial.

"Mrs. Miller; she's been involved with helping with the house, looking after William, that sort of thing?"

"That's right," replied Gerald. "She's been around since William was a baby."

"She said that you told her you were going to a craft shop – The Model Store."

"I just wanted to get away. She tends to go on a bit."

"She claims you were wearing a yellow shirt – the one you'd just bought in Coles. Your wife, Susan made the same comment in her deposition. She said you left in the morning wearing your blue Oxford shirt and when she next saw you, you were wearing the one you bought in Coles. Is that right?" Gerald shifted nervously in his seat.

"I got changed in the men's room. I'd got some blood on my shirt from the scratch on my hand so I just decided to change – spur of the moment."

"What happened to the blue Oxford?" asked Leo Green.

"I put it the Coles bag and took it home," replied Gerald. "I must have thrown it in the wash basket."

"Anything else?" asked Leo Green.

"No, I don't think so," replied Gerald. "I went back to the office – that's when the two detectives came to tell me William had been arrested." Leo Green opened his briefcase and collected up his papers.

243

"I didn't do it," he said. "That shirt with bloodstains – it can't possibly be Angela Fisher's blood. I know it can't." He looked pleadingly at Leo Green as he turned to leave.

"I'll be back tomorrow – It will be in the late afternoon."

"Okay," replied Gerald.

*

Mark Schultz called the DA's office. He'd been pondering over the scratches on Gerald's hand. If he was guilty of murdering Angela Fisher, then it was likely that he had lied about how he got the scratches. Maybe, just maybe, Angela had scratched him.

"John, it's Mark. There's an angle on Gerald Martin you might want to consider. Those scratches on his hand ..."

"I'm just ahead of you on that one, Mark. You think they could have been made by Angela Fisher - am I right?"

"Yeah," replied Mark Schultz, impressed by John Sweetman's scrutiny. "It's worth a shot."

"We had the forensics boys take a detailed look at her hands. They took some scrapings from under her fingernails."

"And?"

"Nothing back yet," replied John Sweetman.

Chapter 22
The Truth

Two days later, Mark Schultz got the call from John Sweetman he had been waiting for.

"As we suspected, Mark, they found blood and skin under her nails. And as far as they can tell, it's not her blood."

"As far as they can tell?" repeated Mark Schultz. "What does that mean?"

"The test samples were smaller than they would have liked, and they'd degraded quite a bit. The blood type is type O, which is the same as Gerald Martin's – but the evidence will be ruled as inadmissible because of the sample size. The good bit of information is that lab was able to state, based on the accumulation of blood and skin under her fingernails, that she had scratched someone shortly before she was killed."

"What about the scratches on Gerald Martin's hands?" asked Mark Schultz.

"I was coming to that," replied John Sweetman. "Forensics had a close look at the photos we provided. The scratches on his hand are consistent with those made by fingernails. There are two deep scratches that were probably made by the first and second finger, and a more superficial scratch that would have been made by the third finger."

"What's your next move?" asked Mark Schultz.

"We've charged him with the murder of Angela Fisher," replied John Sweetman. "His lawyer is with him now."

*

Leo Green looked at his client. He was a frightened man. He squirmed nervously in his seat as Leo Green approached.

"I didn't do it, Leo, I didn't kill her. This is a set-up ..." Leo held up his hand and stopped him in mid-sentence.

"They have new evidence, Gerald."

"What, more stuff that's nothing to do with me?" sneered Gerald.

"It's very much to do with you," replied Leo Green. "It's about those scratches on your hand." Gerald instinctively pulled his hand back and covered the scars with the palm of his other hand. "You didn't get those from a wire fence, did you?"

Gerald sat for almost a minute, slowly rubbing the back of his scarred hand. His mind was racing, searching for a plausible answer.

"They found blood and skin under her nails," said Leo Green, breaking the silence. Gerald looked tired, as if worn down by the sheer weight of evidence that was accumulating against him.

"She scratched me," said Gerald in a resigned tone. "It was when she got mad and told me to leave. I thought she was going to hit me, so I grabbed her wrist – I just wanted to calm her down. That's when she gouged the back of my hand. She reached for me with her other hand and dug her fingernails into me." He held up his hand, as if displaying the evidence.

"What happened next?" asked Leo, sounding sharp and annoyed with his client.

"I let go of her wrist. I think she was a bit shocked by what she'd done. I told her she was mad – and then I

246

left through the kitchen door. I wanted to get away from her as quickly as I could." Leo looked intently at Gerald.

"As your lawyer, Gerald, I have to advise you that it doesn't look good." Leo Green paused, expecting some reaction from his client. He then continued. "I think you should consider a plea bargain." Gerald suddenly looked alert and wide-eyed.

"No way!" he said. "I'm innocent. I didn't kill Angela Fisher!"

*

The trial didn't go at all well. It wasn't just the evidence. Once the jury had started to accept the prosecution's verdict, which was compelling enough, they became incensed with the idea that a father could commit murder and then allow his son to be charged and found guilty - and end up on Death Row! In the jury room, they began to talk of little else other than their contempt for Gerald, and openly expressed sympathy both for William and for Susan. The jury foreman made little attempt to get the jurors to refrain from expressing their disdain for Gerald. The more they discussed the case, the more entrenched they became in their opinion that Gerald was guilty. Leo Green was as convinced as anyone else that Gerald had murdered Angela, but he was the consummate professional and prided himself on doing the very best for his clients, no matter what the circumstances and no matter what personal opinions he held.

The prosecution focussed on the hard evidence: the blood found on his shirt, which was the same as Angela's, type *AB negative*; his fingerprints, which were found throughout the kitchen, on the coffee cup, and on the front and rear doors; and the scratches on the back of his hand, as well as the samples of blood and skin found under Angela's fingernails. They referred several times to the way his story had changed from initially denying having anything at all to do with Angela, to then admitting he'd been to see her. At first, he said he'd injured his hand on a fence, and then he admitted Angela had scratched him following an argument in her kitchen.

Then there was the circumstantial evidence. The timing of Gerald's visit to Angela's house and his unusual behaviour at the shopping mall. Why was he in such a hurry to buy a shirt? Why did he change into the shirt at the mall, and why did he make an excuse to visit the craft shop, despite his admission on the stand that he'd absolutely no prior interest in any of the products they sold?

Leo Green focussed on two issues – the lack of any established motive, and the failure of the police to provide any direct evidence linking Gerald with the murder weapon. Leo reiterated the story Gerald had given him. That he'd gone to Angela's house to confront her about her relationship with William. They'd argued, she'd tried to hit him, and in restraining her she'd scratched his hand.

"Why hadn't he told all this earlier to the police?" said Leo Green, posing a rhetorical question to the jury. "Because he was frightened he would implicate himself," he told them. "And as despicable as it may seem to the members of the jury, he didn't think there was anything to be gained by admitting he had seen Angela Fisher on the day of her murder since it was obvious, at least to the defendant, that his son, William Martin had committed the crime."

It seemed to Leo Green that Gerald got nearer and nearer to telling the full story about exactly what happened, the more the trial progressed. During recesses from the courtroom, Gerald kept repeating his claim that he hadn't killed Angela Fisher, and now added that there was something wrong with the evidence regarding Angela Fisher's blood on his shirt. "It couldn't possibly be hers," he said, on several occasions. But when Leo Green asked him to elaborate, he simply refused. Gerald was caught. He knew that the shirt he had been wearing – the one contaminated with Angela's blood – was in a sack at the bottom of a river. But to reveal that would be to admit his guilt. His only option, he decided, was to let the court decide. Surely they couldn't convict him on what was largely circumstantial evidence?

He smiled to himself. Leo Green had been good – very good. The jury were obviously listening carefully when Leo Green had focussed on the lack of any plausible motive, and the incontrovertible fact that there was no direct evidence linking him with the murder weapon.

The jury deliberated for less than two hours. Gerald watched them as they filed in to take their seats. They looked grim-faced. Most avoided looking in his direction. Gerald had the bizarre thought that he should wave – to let them know where he was. The judge waited patiently for them to get seated.

"Have you reached a verdict?" he asked, directing his question to the foreman of the jury.

"We have," he replied. "We find the defendant guilty of the manslaughter of Angela Fisher." There were no groans of alarm, no protestations, just nods of agreement from the public gallery.

"And that's the opinion of all the jury members?" asked the judge.

"Yes, it is," replied the foreman of the jury, simply and clearly.

*

Neither Susan, nor Sally Miller, had gone to the trial. The thought of watching Gerald suffering through the trial was more than Susan could bear, even though she knew that Gerald had to be found guilty if William's appeal was to have any chance of success. She felt she had stabbed him in the back. And the fabrication of evidence – did the end justify the means? *It had to*, she told herself, over and over again. She knew that this act would haunt her for the rest of her life.

Mark Schultz called Susan as soon as he'd learned of the verdict. Susan had been waiting for his call for most of the day. She couldn't do anything. It was impossible to take her mind off what might be happening in the courtroom. It was late in the afternoon, and Susan was jolted by the ringing of the 'phone, as if it had given her a sharp electrical shock.

"Susan, good news – Gerald's been found guilty, a verdict of manslaughter." Susan wasn't sure if it was good news or not. It was all she had wanted ever since William had been found guilty – to have someone else convicted for Angela's murder. Gerald did it; she was convinced of that. But her role in establishing his guilt engulfed her with shame. And then she thought of Gerald – letting William be convicted for his crime! It was so disgusting, so evil.

He's not my husband, he's not William's father – he's a man who committed murder, she told herself. *Someone I no longer know, or want to know.*

"What will happen – to Gerald, I mean?" she asked.

"He'll be imprisoned for a long time – probably ten to fifteen years. He'll have the right of appeal, of course, but I don't imagine that will change things any. His lawyer may well advise him simply to accept his sentence." Susan felt relieved – and slightly disappointed at the same time.

"Ten years – that's not very long," she commented.

"It will seem like an eternity to Gerald, believe me," he replied. This made Susan even more depressed. What she wanted above anything else was to get William off Death Row. If Gerald had simply disappeared, never to be seen again, she would have been perfectly happy. To have him suffer at her doing made her feel as though she'd committed the most heinous of crimes.

*

Leo Green visited Gerald in the county jail a couple of days after the trial had ended. He'd found Gerald to be a difficult client and he was in no rush to go and see him. He had to discuss a possible appeal on Gerald's behalf, but he was hoping that Gerald would just accept the verdict that he'd been given and waive his right to appeal.

Gerald seemed pleased to see Leo Green. Three long nights and two slow monotonous days had given Gerald lots of time to think. He gone over the trial and revisited the events preceding his arrest many times during his short incarceration. He was quite excited about meeting with Leo Green. He wanted to tell him again that he was innocent, that he did not murder Angela Fisher. And the shirt – his shirt stained with her blood? Only one was the genuine article – and that was in the river. When he lay on his narrow hard bed in his cell, drifting in and out of sleep, his mind was filled with images of two Oxford shirts. One was clean and ironed and floating above the other, which was rumpled and stained with blood. They suddenly became entangled, as if the dirty shirt had reached up to grab the clean one. And then they hung in the air, both looking wrinkled, and both splattered with bloodstains.

Gerald no longer suspected - he was convinced - that someone had planted the stains on his shirt. It had depressed him at first, the thought that someone would deliberately set out to implicate him in Angela's death. But now, now he'd had time to dwell on this one crucial piece of evidence, he realised that this false evidence was his one hope.

He sat in the visiting room, impatiently waiting for Leo Green to arrive. Leo was pleased that Gerald had dropped the sullen, pouting, look he had towards the end of the trial. Gerald greeted him as if they were about to stroll down to grab a coffee.

"Hello, Leo. Take a seat," he gushed.

"Glad to see this place is agreeing with you," replied Leo Green. Gerald ignored his remark.

"You've got to start working on my appeal."

"Your appeal?" said Leo Green, sounding unenthusiastic. "We need good reasons for making an appeal and quite frankly Gerald, I don't think you have any likelihood of being successful. The evidence is just stacked against you."

"Look Leo, I've been thinking through this for the last two days. What would happen if it was shown that evidence had been fabricated?"

"What the hell are you saying, Gerald?" snapped Leo Green. "This isn't a game. You've given so many versions of what you did or didn't do that nobody is going to believe a last-minute accusation by you that evidence was tampered with."

"I'm not suggesting that we accuse the police of tampering with the evidence."

"I'm relieved to hear that," replied Leo Green. There was a pause before Gerald tried again.

"Please answer me, Leo. What would happen if it can be shown that evidence was fabricated?" Leo Green couldn't be sure whether this was a game of some sort or if Gerald was becoming delusional - or maybe he had something to reveal?

"I'll assume for the moment that it's a hypothetical question."

"If you like." replied Gerald.

"If evidence is contaminated, or cannot be relied upon for some reason, or if a witness can be shown to have misled the jury, or lied under oath - then it would make any claims made as a result of that evidence totally invalid. If someone has committed perjury in order to secure a conviction, then two things would happen. The accused would be freed based on a mistrial, and the person committing perjury would be charged with that offence. A similar course of events would apply to the fabrication of evidence. The evidence would be inadmissible, a mistrial would be declared, and the accused would be free to go."

"Thanks," replied Gerald. "That's what I hoped you would tell me. I presume anyone convicted of fabricating evidence would be charged with a felony?"

"It's a serious offence," replied Leo Green. "If convicted, they could face up to five years, maybe more." Leo Green was starting to feel uncomfortable. "Just where are you going with this?" he asked. "Is there something you want to tell me – something that could help your case?"

"The shirt found by Susan and Mrs. Miller had Angela's blood on it, and that's what kick-started the whole investigation that led to my conviction."

"I guess that's right," replied Leo Green. "That's what led to your arrest on suspicion of murder, then the fingerprint evidence and the various pieces of circumstantial evidence. That's what got you convicted, and in my view, the jury had little option but to find you guilty." He wanted to get Gerald to accept that he had been convicted of a crime he committed. He'd seen it all before. Convicted murders clutching at straws, hoping for something – sympathy, understanding, even compassion.

"I want that shirt examined again," said Gerald.

"But why?" replied Leo. "It's got Angela's blood on it; the forensics lab has provided incontrovertible evidence."

"I've been thinking about that ... the blood evidence. It's the same blood type – but that doesn't mean it's her blood."

"But she's a rare blood group – *AB negative*. You are type *O*, so it has to be her blood."

"But it's not an absolutely positive confirmation that it's Angela's blood. I want further examination. I want you to find out if it is Angela's blood and not just her blood type. There's a new test..."

"A DNA test, you mean?" replied Leo Green.

"Yes," replied Gerald. "It's starting to be used in England."

"I'm aware of that," replied Leo Green. "But it's not been accepted by the courts here as yet. Not in Ohio anyway. I read up on recent cases in preparing for your appeal. Blood-typing is still the standard. The first appellate court in the US to admit DNA evidence was just last year, *Andrews vs Florida, 1988*. And besides, the only labs equipped to DNA tests are those run by the FBI and they only started accepting a few cases from state forensic labs in January this year."

"This is important Leo. It's my life, for fuck's sake! I don't want to be locked away in a stinking prison – I'll die in there. This evidence has been fabricated, I know it has. It must have been. This is my last chance, Leo. I need that test."

"You are telling me that the blood was planted on your shirt."

"That's exactly what I'm saying," replied Gerald.

Leo Green didn't like this one bit. Any suggestion of tampering with evidence was always met with a huge degree of scepticism by the police and the District Attorney's Office, especially when someone had already been convicted. This case was already very unusual. Leo Green had been a practicing lawyer for over twenty-five years, but he'd never encountered a situation where both father and son had been tried and convicted for the same murder. One of them committed the murder, and his gut instinct told him it was Gerald. But he was employed to defend his client and, if what Gerald was suggesting was correct, then it was highly likely that the case would be dismissed. William's lawyers would be able to make a stronger appeal if Gerald's conviction was upheld. If Gerald's case was dismissed, William's lawyers might have considerable difficulty at their appeal hearing.

Leo spent a difficult morning with the DA, John Sweetman, trying to convince him there was need for a DNA test on the bloodstains on Gerald's shirt.

"We need to know, John. We've all assumed it was Angela's blood. What if it isn't? What if it's someone else's blood of the same type?"

"But there's no other possible suspect, Leo."

"My client is adamant that the blood on his shirt isn't Angela's."

"So, what are you suggesting – that we fabricated this evidence to get a conviction?"

"Of course not," replied Leo, although both he and John Sweetman knew that this sort of thing wasn't unknown. "But if we don't check it out now - and if I know my client - he'll make the loudest noise he possibly can. If the press pick it up, they're going to make all sorts of unpleasant assumptions and accusations."

"But we've never used DNA evidence, not in Ohio," said Sweetman. "This case is exceptional as it stands without now introducing DNA evidence."

"I know that," replied Leo Green. "But it's been admitted in Florida and most states have now agreed to allow DNA evidence, including Ohio. This will settle it, John. He could be telling the truth."

Leo Green paused to allow John Sweetman to absorb what was being asked. John Sweetman knew that to refuse to have the shirt tested could backfire. He'd received several documents over the last month, advising on the implications of the decision to allow DNA evidence. *Leo's right,* he told himself. *The last thing I need is bad press implying some sort of cover up. And anyway, Gerald Martin is guilty. This will just confirm it.* He looked up at Leo Green who was staring out of the window, waiting for him to speak.

"Okay, okay," said John Sweetman. "I'll instruct forensics to get the shirt and samples of Angela's blood taken from the crime scene sent off to the FBI lab for DNA testing. That bastard's guilty, Leo. I know he is. If this is what it will take to shut him up, we'll get it done."

"Thanks, John," replied Leo Green.

Chapter 23
Analysis

John Sweetman had his worst fears confirmed – the DNA results showed that the bloodstains on Gerald Martin's shirt were not those of Angela Fisher. He immediately called Leo Green.

"Leo, I don't know how you knew this, but you are right - the blood samples don't match. The blood on the shirt that we used as evidence is not Angela Fisher's."

"I didn't know," replied Leo Green. "But Gerald Martin was adamant that the stains weren't his. He's equally adamant that he didn't murder Angela Fisher."

"If he didn't do it, then that potentially leaves his son on Death Row," said John Sweetman. "If it wasn't Gerald Martin, then I guess the conviction of young William Martin will be upheld."

"Mark Schultz won't be too happy to hear the news," commented Leo Green.

"And you don't have to tell me what your next move is going to be," said John Sweetman.

"I don't – but I will," replied Leo Green. "Based on this new evidence, I'll be requesting an immediate dismissal of the charges against my client."

John Sweetman's next call was to Mark Schultz. There were times when he hated his job.

"It's the Gerald Martin case, Mark. There's a problem – a serious problem."

"Why? What's happened?"

"The bloodstains on the shirt you submitted as evidence turned out not to belong to Angela Fisher."

"What?" exploded Mark Schultz. "That's not possible – it can't be."

"We had the FBI lab run a DNA check. The DNA of the bloodstains on the shirt don't match the blood samples we took from Angela Fisher's body."

"DNA test? Who ran a DNA test – and who authorised it, anyway?"

"I did. Leo Green wanted the tests done. I didn't have much choice. As you will probably know, the state has recently agreed to allow DNA evidence, and Leo Green was going to make a lot of noise if I didn't get the tests done."

Mark Schultz had read about the likely introduction of DNA evidence, but the last thing he'd expected was for it to be used in this case. That case in Florida had broken new ground - he'd said as much to David Singleton and the rest of the firm's attorneys only the other day.

Mark Schultz let out a low groan. "Fuck Leo Green. This is the worst news. I guess he's going to request an immediate dismissal of the charges?"

"As we speak. He's hoping to get Gerald Martin released by tomorrow. He's calling this a grave miscarriage of justice. There's going to be hell to pay. Just wait until the press get hold of this."

"Not just the press - the mayor's office, the chief of police, the court judge – I can hardly wait!"

"And then there's your reputation," added John Sweetman, acidly. He felt Mark Schultz had got him into this mess.

"That was uncalled for," replied Mark Schultz.

258

John Sweetman mumbled an apology. "It looks like Gerald Martin may have been telling the truth. Maybe it happened as he described," he said.

"And that leaves William Martin as the only one who could have committed the murder."

"Not only that," replied John Sweetman, "there's the issue of fabrication of evidence. Susan Fisher has got a lot of questions to answer."

"Are you going to have her arrested?" asked Mark Schultz.

"Not yet," replied John Sweetman. "I'll let you talk to her first."

*

Susan had called Sally Miller as soon as she'd heard the verdict. She was still racked with guilt at the thought of what they had done, but now it was all over. Gerald had been convicted. They both knew what this meant – William's conviction for the murder of Angela Fisher would be dismissed. He would escape the death sentence.

"I heard," said Sally Miller. "He's been convicted. It's the best possible news, and the best possible outcome for William," she added, as if feeling the need to remind Susan why they had deliberately put suspicion on Gerald.

Susan had begun to think about what might happen next. William's conviction for the murder of Angela Fisher would be dismissed. Maybe the appeals court would be lenient and recognise that William had shot Jake Fisher under duress? They might accept that William had not intended to shoot Jake Fisher, and maybe his charge would be reduced to manslaughter? Perhaps he might get a suspended sentence? Susan couldn't stop herself. It was a roller-coaster of optimism and emotion that, for the first time since

William's conviction, gave her some confidence that William's appeal would be upheld.

"I haven't heard from Mark Schultz," Susan told Sally Miller. "I thought he would have called me before now." A sudden thought that something might have gone wrong nagged at her optimism. "You don't think there's a problem?"

"Not in the slightest," replied Sally Miller. "Gerald's been convicted of the murder of Angela Fisher. He'll have the right to an appeal, of course – that's if he's got any basis for an appeal. He hasn't. This is all over, Susan, believe me."

"Thanks, Sally," replied Susan. "I've been living with this nightmare for so long I get paranoid when..."

"When things don't quite go as quickly as you'd like."

"I guess so," replied Susan.

"Be patient. There'll be things for Mark Schultz to take care of. He'll call soon."

Susan jumped when the phone rang. It was late in the afternoon and she had been hovering around the phone all day, unable to eat. She felt dizzy and weak but she didn't want to eat, not yet. *He'll call soon,* she kept reminding herself.

She was in the kitchen and had just poured herself a third cup of coffee. She ran to the phone, almost sending it flying as she grabbed the receiver.

"Susan, it's Mark Schultz." He sounded serious – not quite what she had expected.

"I've been in a meeting most of the day with Gerald's lawyer, Leo Green, the district attorney, and a circuit court judge."

"Is it to do with Gerald's case?" asked Susan, nervously.

"Leo Green has filed a motion for the immediate dismissal of the case. The judge has agreed. Gerald will be released on bail tomorrow and will be a free man once the dismissal has been confirmed – and it *will* be confirmed."

"But why?" asked Susan, her voice shaking.

"They have proof that some key evidence was fabricated." The receiver slipped from Susan's hand, clattering onto the phone stand. It dangled down by its cord, almost touching the carpet. Susan sank to her knees and slowly grasped the receiver. She could hear Mark Schultz's voice, sounding tinny and distant as he called into the telephone.

"Susan, Susan – are you alright?"

"Sorry – yes, just a bit dizzy that's all. I'm alright now. I haven't eaten – I'll get a banana, or something." It sounded to Susan like a pathetic appeal for sympathy. Mark Schultz's voice didn't, however convey any sympathy.

"Grab something quickly if you must. I need you in my office straight away."

Susan tried to stay calm as she drove across town to Mark Schultz's office. She felt a little better. She'd eaten a banana and gulped down a large glass of milk before heading off. What frightened her most was the thought that William's appeal would be jeopardised. She was ushered into Mark Schultz's office as soon as she arrived. The receptionist had instructions to bring her straight in.

Mark Schultz beckoned her to take a seat. He looked cross and agitated.

"You have done something very stupid," he said, staring directly at her. "That shirt you brought to my office, the one you said had been found in your house splattered with blood – it was blood alright, the right blood type, but it wasn't Angela's blood, was it?"

Susan's head sank. It was what she had dreaded. She felt powerless, unable to utter even an expression of remorse. There was nothing she could say that could be defended. All she could do was sit and listen to Mark Schultz.

"I'm mad at myself for not being more sceptical about what you had supposedly found. I assumed you were being completely honest with me. I never suspected you would be this devious. And you would have got away with it, if Gerald hadn't convinced his lawyer to get DNA tests." Susan tried to mutter something, but the words weren't words at all, just sounds gurgled up from her aching throat. Mark Schultz glanced up at her as if daring her to interrupt him.

"I guess I wanted to believe you. That's the biggest error a lawyer can make – trusting his client. I usually work with minor celebrities who think they can get away with anything. They come to me because they are guilty and my job is to get them off. I never accept their accounts – not completely. In your case, I believed you entirely. I allowed myself to be hoodwinked by you and whoever your accomplices were."

"Accomplices?" said Susan.

"Don't tell me you did this all on your own. I just won't believe you. I have no doubt that Sally Miller was involved, somehow, and you needed access to a source of blood. Not just any common or garden blood type. It had to be *AB negative*. Someone else was involved, someone working in a lab, probably in forensics. You know what sickens me about this?" he asked, rhetorically. "You've jeopardised any chance your son William might have had for an appeal; you've put suspicion on the police department that they might have fabricated the evidence to get a verdict; you've succeeded in getting Gerald's conviction dismissed, which could leave William on Death Row; and you've damaged my reputation."

Susan could only think of the consequences for William. She looked at Mark Schultz, determined not to break down and weep. She steeled herself and glared back at him.

"I did what I thought was necessary to expose Gerald – and get William off Death Row. I'm not ashamed of what I've done. No one was going to believe me that Gerald was guilty. I did what I had to. I had to get the police investigation to focus on Gerald. And now everyone knows he did it. He was found guilty. If I hadn't done this, William would be on Death Row and I would have had to live with not having done anything to help him. I know William is innocent – just as I know Gerald is guilty. If the consequence is that I go to prison, then that's the price I will have to pay for trying to prove my son didn't murder Angela Fisher. William might remain on Death Row, in which case all this might be pretty futile. It was a risk I had to take. And as for your precious reputation ..."

Mark Schultz held up his hand. For a moment Susan thought he was going to have her arrested. Then she realised he was looking at her differently. The angry look had gone. His face creased into something close to a smile.

"You are a tough cookie," he said. "I wish I had your guts." Susan wasn't sure how to respond. She sat with her back upright and her jaw firmly set, accentuating her pointed chin. "You are in a lot of trouble. I was going to tell you that I wouldn't be representing you or William anymore – something to do with my professional pride. But I've changed my mind. I'm going to do what I can to help you and William."

"Thank you," she managed.

"There are conditions. I need to know everything. Who was involved, whose idea it was, exactly how it was done. I can probably guess at most of your answers, but I want to hear it from you."

"It was my idea," replied Susan.

"We'll come back to that," he told her, his face again looking stern and challenging. "Let's start with the obvious question. Who else was involved?" Susan sat for several moments, her eyes fixed at some spot high on the wall. "I'm not sure I can ..."

"If I'm going to help you, you've got to tell me everything – including who was involved. This is a confidential discussion between you, my client, and me, your attorney. I can't promise their names won't come out in the course of the police investigation, but they won't hear it from me." Susan gave a resigned sigh.

"Sally... Mrs. Miller. She helped me with my plan – she helped me stay strong."

"I'd assumed she was involved," replied Mark Schultz. "She allegedly found the shirt. Was that her idea?"

"This was all my idea – the entire plan," replied Susan, in as strong a voice as she could muster.

"And what about the blood sample. I presume that neither you nor Sally Miller had direct access to a sample of blood, and least of all a sample as rare as type AB negative?" Susan paused again, looking up at the same imagined spot on the opposite wall.

"It was a friend of Sally Miller's - Inez Knight. She's a neighbour of Sally's."

"And she just agreed to be involved?" asked Mark Schultz.

"Not at first. She was very reluctant. Sally saved Inez's life many years ago. Inez was attacked in her home by a thug who almost killed her. Sally heard her screams and beat him off with a baseball bat. She left him a cripple."

264

"It sounds as if Sally Miller likes to impose her own brand of justice. And as for Inez Knight, she didn't have much option, did she?" Susan didn't rise to the bait.

"Sally has a very loyal friend, that's all," commented Susan. "Inez works in the Serology lab at the University," she said. "She got the blood sample for us. She also told us how best to apply the blood, to make the stains appear as genuine as possible. But that's all – Sally and I did the rest."

"You make it sound as if she'd taken a roll of adhesive tape," said Mark Schultz. "This was conspiracy to commit a crime. Inez Knight is just as involved in this as you and Sally Miller. There are no innocent parties here."

"So, what happens now?" asked Susan. "Do I go home and wait for the police to come and arrest me?"

"You've got two hours to meet with Sally Miller and Inez Knight. You need to tell them what's happened. And don't pull any punches. They need to know just how much trouble you are all in. Then I want you back in my office by four pm. I'll take you down to the DA's office where you'll be formally charged. In the meantime, I'll try and fix bail."

*

As soon as she'd been released on bail, Inez Knight wrote a letter of resignation to the Dean of the School of Medical Sciences. She outlined what she had done – taken a sample of blood in the full knowledge that it would be used to fabricate evidence. She briefly explained that it involved Gerald Martin's conviction for murder. She also warned of the police investigation into lab procedures that would inevitably follow.

The Dean was shocked. Inez Knight was a highly valued member of staff. He read her letter several times to make sure he understood the implications of what

265

she had done. He wrote back, accepting her resignation with immediate effect; he knew he had no alternative. The University President insisted on a full internal enquiry and also insisted that Inez be required to give evidence. Her long association with the University was over. She would never again work in a professional capacity. Susan, Sally Miller, and Inez Knight were formally charged with perverting the course of justice. Mark Schultz warned them that they were facing jail. They had to be prepared for up to five years imprisonment. Susan moved in with Sally Miller. She couldn't face seeing Gerald, let alone living with him in the same house.

Mark Schultz did his best, but the evidence against Susan, Sally Miller and Inez Knight was overwhelming. They all pleaded guilty to the charge of fabricating evidence. There was little they could say to justify their actions. Mark Schultz emphasised the considerable stress that Susan had faced with the prosecution of her son for a double homicide, his subsequent conviction, and the sentence which resulted in him being on Death Row. He explained the circumstantial evidence that convinced them that Susan's husband, Gerald Martin was the person who was responsible for Angela Fisher's death.

"And no matter how irrational this may seem," he told the jury, "it was an act drawn out of a love for her son, William."

He explained that Susan persuaded her friends Sally Miller and Inez Knight to assist her in this scheme, and that Susan wished more than anything else that she hadn't drawn her friends into the deceit they perpetrated.

Mark Schultz knew that the case was hopelessly lost. All he could do was to give the judge and the jury a sense of the emotional turmoil Susan was under and her desire, as a mother, to rescue her son from Death Row.

"Imagine how you would feel, imagine how you might act if you were faced with similar circumstances," he said to the jury in his summing up.

The verdict was more lenient than Mark Schultz had dared hope for. Sally Miller and Inez Knight were seen as being misguided in their attempts to help their friend. They were each given suspended sentences. Susan received the harshest penalty. She was given a two year jail sentence.

"We'll lodge an appeal," Mark Schultz told Susan. She, however, seemed more concerned with the sentences her two friends had received and the damage done to their lives.

"I created this mess," Susan told him, stoically. "I've allowed my friends to become embroiled in this. If it wasn't for me, none of this would have happened. I deserve what's coming – I'm just relieved that Sally and Inez aren't going to jail."

"But they made a choice," replied Mark Schultz. "They could have simply said no."

"It's me who should have stopped it. We were so convinced it was the only option we had to get the focus on to Gerald."

"All you've succeeded in doing is destroying their reputations. From what I hear, Inez Knight has resigned. She'll never work in a professional capacity ever again."

"I know," said Susan. Her voice quivered with the pain and anguish she was feeling. She lifted her head and looked directly at Mark Schultz. "That's why I don't want any appeal. I've caused enough hurt. I don't want this to be dragged back through the court in some pointless exercise. I can't see what it will achieve."

Chapter 24
The Find

Ray Hart and Jim Stokes had been pals since primary school. They were now both fifteen years old. Jim was the older by approximately three months, but Ray was the leader; the one who always wanted to do something a bit more adventurous than his more cautious friend. Ray had an urge to look for ever-more challenging escapades, which, for Jim, were increasingly worrying and potentially dangerous.

It was late October and the unusually mild spell of weather had resulted in a series of torrential downpours, often accompanied by near-gale-force winds blowing moist air from the south. The swollen rivers were a boiling brew of muddy water pushed into a rage of tiny eddies and swirling vortexes by rocks and boulders that dared to impede their gushing path. The rain had eased when Ray and Jim slid down the bank and jammed their feet against the large concrete pier, just above the water line. The noise of the river was deafening, so different from the quiet rippling amble that the river normally took. The wind whipped at the river, creating waves that lashed against the piers, spraying Ray and Jim as they crouched down under the bridge. Don shouted to be heard, even though Jim was standing less than an arm's length away.

"Let's climb up," he said, motioning to the steel structure that supported the bridge. Jim slowly looked up at the graceful arc of heavy metal frames rising from the piers like interlocking fingers, the road seemingly balanced on their extremities. He started to shout back, but Ray had already pulled himself on top of the pier and was motioning for his friend to join him. Jim shook his head, but Ray kept waving at him, beckoning him to follow.

Jim reluctantly hauled himself up and clung to the cold steel, trying hard not to expose his fear. He managed a weak smile in response to Ray's broad grin. They climbed up and along the first section. The steel beams had been fabricated with a series of oval-shaped holes in the flanges which helped their climb and gave Jim some confidence that he wouldn't slip. They were now about ten feet above the river and a similar distance in from the pier. It was much quieter under the bridge and the girders weren't dripping with river water.

Ray swung by his arms, letting his legs dangle in one of his typical acts of bravado. He suddenly looked frightened. His arms had weakened and he couldn't pull himself back onto the piece of girder that he had swung from. His eyes said it all. Jim knew if he didn't do something quickly, Ray would plummet into the raging torrent. He climbed out towards his friend and tried to grab him, but he was just out of reach. He had an idea.

"Swing your legs - I'll try and grab you," he shouted, losing all sense of fear in his urgency to rescue Ray. He reached with one arm as Ray kicked his leg and swung, pendulum-like, first towards the bridge, then back out over the river and then, with a wider arc, back towards Jim's outstretched hand. Jim grabbed at Ray's jacket. His fingers latched onto the heavy denim as Ray's momentum swung him further towards the bridge than Jim had expected, almost knocking him off the girder. Ray grabbed at both Jim and one of the upright stanchions and held on, hugging Jim and himself against the steel frames. Jim could feel his heart pounding with the excitement at what had happened.

"Thanks," said Ray, grinning nervously. "That was close. I thought I was a goner."

Jim was too exhilarated to be frightened. He was just glad he'd had the courage to act quickly and save his friend. He felt confident and emboldened. He let out a whoop which was just loud enough to fight the wind whistling through the girders. Ray was still feeling a bit shaken by his brush with what would have been a fall to his death; drowned in the unforgiving flood waters.

"Let's head back," he said. "Maybe this wasn't such a good idea."

Jim was enjoying his new-found courage. He looked down at the river and felt a sense of vertigo as the waves of water acting against the stability of the steel structure gave the feeling that the bridge itself was moving. He felt detached, almost euphoric, dangling in this swaying, moving world not knowing, for the moment, what was moving – him, the stream, the bridge, the river bank. They all seemed to be completely unconnected. He shook his head, and grinned at Ray.

"Okay, I'll follow you down." Jim took a last look at the bridge, his bridge, before turning to follow Ray. And then he saw it - a sack nestled on a joint between three of the steel girders. He kicked at Ray's shoulder with his foot and pointed towards the location of the sack. Ray didn't see it at first, not until he climbed back to where Jim was.

"Leave it," said Ray. "It's probably a cat someone was trying to drown."

"What if it's still alive?" replied Jim, shouting to be heard. "We can't just leave it there." Jim had two cats

270

of his own. He'd got them as kittens and they were as much a part of his family as his younger sister and older brother. Ray shrugged his shoulders.

"Probably dead now, anyway," he said. Jim had already decided. He started to climb towards the sack. It was about fifteen feet further towards the centre of the bridge and considerably higher than where they were. Ray shouted after him.

"You're mad, Jim. It's not worth it!" But he could see that his pal was intent on reaching the sack. Ray couldn't help but admire his friend. Jim was the one who always looked scared whenever they did something a bit dangerous. He nudged himself carefully along one of the girders to get a bit closer to Jim.

"Got it!" shouted Jim, lifting up the sack. "There's something in it, alright." He inched back carefully towards Ray.

"Toss it in the river," said Ray. "You're sure to slip trying to get it down." Jim ignored him and clung tightly to the end of the sack. There was a brick or a rock in the sack, he was sure. He could feel its sharp edges rubbing against his leg.

"I think it's a cat," he told Ray, when he got closer to him. "There's a rock in there to weight it down."

They reached the concrete pier and jumped down onto the river bank.

"It'll smell something awful," said Ray, as Jim began to undo the tight wrapping of cord that sealed the top of the bag. Jim carefully opened the neck of the sack and tried to see what was inside.

"Just some old clothes, I think" he said and began to reach inside.

"Careful," said Ray. "Could be anything – snake, lizards."

271

"There's nothing moving, can't be anything alive," he replied. He could feel the rock in the bottom of the sack and what felt like something thin and silky. He instinctively jerked his hand out of the bag.

"What is it?" asked Ray.

"Don't know," replied Jim. He started pulling out the larger piece of cloth. "It's a shirt," he said. He pushed it back in the sack and grabbed the silky item. "Huh, just a tie," he said.

"Got a lot of ketchup on it," remarked Ray.

"So's the shirt," said Jim, pulling it back out of the sack.

"Wait a minute," exclaimed Jim. "That doesn't look much like ketchup - it's too dark. I think it might be blood!"

"Looks like blood," Ray remarked.

"I'm taking this home – I'll let my dad have a look."

"Okay," said Ray. "See what he thinks. You'll have to tell him where you found it – he won't be too pleased at us scaling the bridge with the river like it is." Jim grinned. For once, he thought his dad might be just a bit proud at this particular adventure. He often boasted to his son about what he'd done when he was a kid, as if challenging Jim to show he had 'what it takes'.

*

"Shouldn't have done it, Jim. That's a dangerous structure. I tried it once when I was about your age – scared myself to death. And in this weather! One slip and you'd ..."

"But I didn't, Dad. I'm okay."

"And this is the sack you found?" asked Jim's dad, pointing to the small sack lying at Jim's feet.

"Yeah, there's a shirt and a tie in there. They've got lots of dark-red stains. Think it might be blood." Jim's dad untied the top cord, reached in to the sack and carefully pulled out the blue Oxford shirt and the silk tie.

"Think you're right, Jim. It certainly looks like blood, and lots of it. Tell me where exactly you found the sack?" Jim gave as precise an answer as he could. Jim's dad was impressed. "That was quite a climb – and you got it, you climbed up?"

"Yeah – thought it might be a kitten, or something."

"You did well son, but don't go climbing that bridge again – you hear?"

"Okay, Dad." It wasn't much of a reprimand, more of a back-handed compliment.

"We'll take this to the police station. Might be nothing. They'll probably want you to explain where you found it."

The duty sergeant happened to be Brian Witney. He'd been at the desk the day Angela Fisher was murdered. He knew Barry Stokes, Jim's dad. Brian was still a member of the same Elks Club Barry attended, although he hadn't been there for nearly two years.

"Hi, Brian – been a long time."

"Hello, Barry. What brings you here?" Barry Stokes placed the sack on the counter.

"This is my boy, Jim." He placed his hand on Jim's shoulder. Brian Witney nodded.

"He found this sack stuck up in the girders under that old metal bridge, the one on Elmer's Road."

"Across Raven's Creek. Yes, I know it," replied Brian Witney. "Took a bit of a risk climbing that," he said, looking directly at Jim. "That creek is carrying more water than I've ever seen."

"Yeah, anyway," continued Barry Stokes, "like I was saying, he found this sack jammed between a couple of girders. Thought it might be a cat someone had tried to drown."

"Happens," commented Brian Witney. "Have you opened it?" he asked.

"That's why we're here," replied Barry Stokes. "There's a shirt and tie covered in what looks like blood. Got a brick in, too. Looks like someone was trying to get rid."

Brian Witney opened the sack as wide as he could and removed the contents, laying them carefully on the counter – a blue button-down Oxford shirt, which looked fairly new, and heavily stained with what certainly looked like blood. And a silk tie with similar stains. He grabbed some evidence bags and placed the four items; the shirt, the tie, the sack and the brick in separate bags.

"I'll need to take statements from both of you. When and where you found the sack, Jim – and what you did, Barry, when Jim showed it to you."

"I came here," protested Barry.

"I know you did," replied Brian Witney. "But we've got to have it written down and a signed statement. You did the right thing, Jim, taking this to your dad. Just don't go climbing any more bridges," he added. He led them through to the interview room and called over to one of the other police officers to take their statements.

As soon as Brian Witney had got things organised at his end, he called the DA's Office.

"It's Brian Witney, police desk. I need to speak to the DA. It's important."

Brian Whitney and John Sweetman had known each other professionally for a number of years. John had a great deal of respect for Sergeant Witney and knew he wouldn't be calling his office unless it genuinely was something that wouldn't wait - something urgent. The Mayor's Office called, just as he was about to return the call to Brian Witney. It was twenty minutes later before he had a chance to 'phone.

274

"Got your message, Brian - something urgent?" Brian was a bit miffed that John Sweetman hadn't called back straight away. There was a slight pause which John Sweetman detected. "Sorry I couldn't get back to you quicker. The Mayor's Office called." Brian Witney felt a bit foolish.

"That's okay, John. You aren't going to believe this – a kid's just walked in here with a sack containing a blue Oxford shirt and a tie, both badly stained with what looks like blood. Found it jammed in some girders on that bridge over Raven's Creek."

"What!" exclaimed John Sweetman "Are you saying that another blue Oxford shirt has turned up?"

"Yeah, and lots of splatters and smears. Looks like blood. And a tie – it's also stained. They were in a sack that had been weighted down with a brick. Looks like someone pitched it over the side, just at the wrong spot."

"What do you mean?" asked John Sweetman.

"I know that bridge well – it's popular with teenagers in the summer. Always a few drug pushers doing some mingling. That bridge is in three sections set at angles for the bend in the road. I reckon whoever dropped it either didn't realise, or dropped it in a hurry and it caught just on the angle, where the girders stick out. From the kid's description of where he found it, I'd say that's what happened."

"Have you got a statement from the kid?" asked John Sweetman.

"And from his dad," replied Brian Witney. "This kid was climbing the bridge with a pal. He spotted the bag – thought it might be a cat – got it down, saw it contained a shirt and tie with what he thought were bloodstains. He took it home, showed his dad and the two of them came in about forty minutes ago."

"What about the pal?"

"We're on to that. We should have a statement from him very soon. One of our officers is going to take Jim over to his pal's place after he's given his statement."

"What about the items he brought in?"

"Each item is in a separate evidence bag," replied Brian Witney. "The shirt, tie, sack and the brick. Dated, signed by me, and witnessed by one of the other officers."

"Good job, Brian," said John Sweetman. "Get them sent over to the FBI lab. We need DNA tests."

"First time we've done that – asked for DNA tests," replied Sergeant Witney.

"I know, Brian. But this is no ordinary case. I want to know if the stains are blood and if so, is it Angela Fisher's blood? Oh, and the shirt. Get them to check if it's similar to the shirt brought in by Gerald Martin's wife, Susan Buckley."

"What about the tie?"

"Same thing, blood tests – and see if Susan Buckley and Sally Miller recognise it. Ask the secretary at his work, the Dean's PA, if she remembers him wearing the tie. This has to be top priority, Brian."

"Understood," replied Brian Witney. "I'll get on to it straight away."

Chapter 25
Another Twist

John Sweetman opened the envelope from the FBI Lab. It was the blood DNA results from the shirt and tie the kids found under the bridge. The report was on a standard template, similar to the one used by the state crime lab. John Sweetman knew just where to look. The 'Summary Statement of Findings' gave him the information he required.

i) The stains found on the shirt and tie are human blood, type AB negative.

ii) DNA of blood samples found on the shirt and the tie are an identical match with the DNA of blood samples taken from Angela Fisher.

Conclusion: The bloodstains on the shirt and tie are from Angela Fisher.

iii) Some spots of blood were found on the left cuff of the shirt. These are type O. *Conclusion: These bloodstains are not from Angela Fisher.*

John Sweetman glanced quickly through the rest of the report. It provided details of the procedures used, and no other conclusions of any relevance. But he knew immediately what this meant. This was the shirt the murderer had worn when Angela Fisher was killed – and that person, he presumed, was Gerald Martin. He hoped the drops of blood found on the cuff would provide the confirmation needed. He called Detective Sparrow and told him about this new development.

"I need you to pick up Gerald Martin – we need to get a saliva sample to send to the FBI lab for DNA testing," he said. "Tell him it's about destroying evidence – no charge, just helping us with enquiries. Drop a hint about a warrant for his arrest if needed. If he'd help now, it would avoid any embarrassment."

"Okay," replied Detective Sparrow. "I know the procedure," he added, referring to the course on obtaining samples for DNA evidence he had attended. John Sweetman misunderstood him.

"Just be careful," he said. "I don't want any accusations of false procedures." Detective Sparrow wasn't pleased at having the DA tell him how to do his job.

"I know what to do, District Attorney." John Sweetman wished he'd kept his mouth shut. A detective with a bad attitude was no help.

"Sorry," he said. "This has been a difficult case."

*

Gerald was completely taken aback when the Dean's PA, Lillian Gustafson, poked her head around his office door and announced detectives Sparrow and Murphy were here to see him.

"Please go in," she said, pushing the door wide open. Gerald had a sense of *déjà vu*, and it wasn't one he was enjoying. The two detectives seemed bigger and burlier than Gerald had remembered. They moved towards Gerald, looking relaxed, almost pleasant. But Gerald knew this wasn't a social call.

"Hello, Professor Martin," said Detective Sparrow. "Thanks for seeing us." Gerald wasn't aware that he'd been given an option. "We need to rule you out of any connection with what appears to be an attempt to destroy evidence in the Fisher case."

Gerald felt on edge. He couldn't believe what was happening. The murder trial was over – wasn't it?

278

Evidence – what evidence? Had he been foolish not to get rid of the shoes he'd been wearing? What about the jacket he put in for cleaning? At least he'd got rid of his shirt and tie, he told himself. He tried to remain calm.

"You're not here to make an arrest?" He hoped it sounded as if he was making light of their visit. He tried to force a hesitant laugh.

"No, just to get your help. In our work, it's all about eliminating possibilities. Of course, if you want us to do this formally..."

"No - that won't be necessary. What is it you are asking me to do?"

"We just need a sample of saliva, so we can get this thing put to bed." Detective Sparrow sounded as if he was asking Gerald to do nothing more than share a chocolate bar. "I can do it here and now," he said, reaching into a bag. "Just need to get a sample on this spatula."

"I suppose it's okay," said Gerald. Detective Sparrow had pulled on a latex glove and reached forward with the swab.

"Just a quick wipe from your tongue...that's it. Thanks, Dr. Martin." Detective Sparrow carefully placed the spatula in a small plastic pouch and sealed it with a swipe of his thumb and forefinger.

When the two detectives had left, Gerald sat pondering over what this might be all about. He wished he hadn't given the sample of saliva – but they'd only have come back with a warrant of some kind, he told himself. And anyway, the trial was over. He called Leo Green.

"They did what?" exclaimed Leo Green. "And you volunteered to let them take a sample?"

"I guess I did." Gerald felt like a confused idiot.

"Did they threaten you in any way?" asked Leo Green.

"No," replied Gerald. "They just said it could be done now – in my office – or more formally."

"An implication you might be arrested," suggested Leo Green.

"I wasn't keen on that," replied Gerald.

"Look," said Leo Green, sounding cross, "if they contact you again you call me first! I can't protect you from yourself, but I can give you the right advice – that's my job." The phone clicked, leaving Gerald holding the receiver to his ear as if he was still having a conversation. He had a growing feeling that something was wrong.

Leo Green tried to get hold of the district attorney as soon as he'd finished his call with Gerald. His PA said he was busy at the moment – she'd leave a message. About thirty minutes later, after John Sweetman had a conversation with Detective Sparrow, he called Leo Green.

"What's this about – getting my client to give a sample of saliva?" Leo Green demanded.

"He volunteered," replied John Sweetman. "We just needed a sample of his DNA," he replied, obtusely. "Just want to complete the file."

"Volunteered! You may think asking someone for a sample of saliva is the same thing as asking someone for their autograph – but I don't! Just remember, my client has been found innocent of the murder of Angela Fisher." He hung up before John Sweetman could add anything further. He was glad Leo Green hadn't pressed him for a fuller explanation.

*

The FBI lab report was faxed through to his office a couple of days later. John Sweetman arranged the copies in front of him, clipped them together and turned to the relevant section. It confirmed what he'd hoped.

The DNA of the blood droplets found on the left cuff of the shirt match the DNA obtained from the saliva taken from Gerald Martin.

Conclusion: In addition to the bloodstains identified as belonging to Angela Fisher, there are droplets of blood on the cuff of the same shirt which belong to Gerald Martin.

John Sweetman called Detective Sparrow. "I want you and your pal, Murphy to go and arrest Gerald Martin."

"But this will be the third time he's had a visit from us. He'll be making a case for harassment if this goes on."

"I'm well aware of that," replied John Sweetman, in a tone suggesting a degree of exasperation. "The charge is attempting to destroy evidence."

"The Fisher case?"

"You guessed it," remarked John Sweetman. He called Leo Green a little later to let him know his client was being arrested. He felt he owed him that much. Then he called Mark Schultz.

"We've got some new evidence, Mark. Some kids found a shirt with bloodstains. We've had the FBI lab run DNA tests – the bloodstains came from Angela Fisher."

"That's incredible!" exclaimed Mark Schultz. "Do we know who the shirt belonged to?"

"We certainly do – it's Gerald Martin's. In addition to the bloodstains from Angela Fisher, there were a few droplets on one cuff that weren't hers. We matched the DNA with Gerald Martin's."

"Wow!" exclaimed Mark Schultz. "So, the girls were right all along."

"The girls?"

"His wife, Susan Martin and her friends, Sally Miller and Inez Knight."

"Well, right in their assumptions – not in their methods," replied John Sweetman.

"Point taken. What are you planning to do?"

"We're arresting Gerald Martin on a charge of destroying evidence that might incriminate him."

"Is that it?" asked Mark Schultz.

"No – we're going to charge him with the murder of Angela Fisher," said John Sweetman, in a slow methodical tone. "It's risky," he added.

"You're in very difficult legal territory," commented Mark Schultz.

"I know that," replied John Sweetman. "I just want the bastard to face the charge. We have the proof – he murdered Angela Fisher."

*

Leo Green was incandescent with rage. "You are going to do what!"

"Charge Gerald Martin with the murder of Angela Fisher," replied John Sweetman.

"But you haven't a prayer. It'll be thrown out of court – I'll make sure of that. And if this continues, I'll be filing for harassment on behalf of my client."

"You do that," replied John Sweetman. "You do just that. The publicity will do more for the innocent parties in this case than any court of law ever could."

"So that's what it's about," said Leo Green, angrily. "You want to convict my client through the media rather than through the court."

"We have the evidence that he committed the crime. If the court won't find him guilty, then at least we'll ensure the court of public opinion will," replied John Sweetman.

"The only evidence you have is circumstantial," said Leo Green, forcefully. "You can't prove he shot Angela Fisher. The best you can do is prove he was there."

"And you think that isn't enough?"

"That's not for me, or you to decide," replied Leo Green. "It's up to a court of law to make that decision – as you know perfectly well."

"What I do know is that his son has been wrongly convicted and that three misguided women had come to the same conclusion," replied John Sweetman, his voice rising in anger and frustration. "If this is what it takes to get that kid off Death Row, then it's a decision I can live with. Difficulty for you is that you've got to go on representing a guilty man."

Leo Green moved into action straight away. John Sweetman didn't deserve to be a DA, he told himself. He'd let his emotions get in the way of proper legal processes. He smiled to himself. This young DA was going to be made to look foolish, and he'd enjoy every minute of this charade. As for Gerald Martin – he was just a client, and like all clients, they deserved the best legal protection he could give. And in this case, the publicity the DA was intent in obtaining would only enhance his own reputation as a competent and skilled attorney. He moved for an immediate hearing with the circuit court judge. The hearing was scheduled for two days' time.

*

"Look, Gerald, I'm as annoyed at this as anyone. It's a complete distortion of due legal process. The hearing is set for the day after tomorrow. I'll get you out of here – that's a promise!"

Gerald slowly nodded his head. He looked bewildered and forlorn. Gerald felt he was starting to hallucinate. He kept imagining a long corridor with series of loud metal doors. Every time he pushed one open it slammed behind him, revealing yet another long corridor with a black metal door at the end.

"You've got to get me out of here - it's driving me mad! I didn't kill her," he suddenly added. "This just isn't fair."

"Gerald," said Leo Green. "Gerald – please listen. I'll get you out. But I'd like to know why you didn't tell me about the shirt they found. Do you want to tell me?" Gerald shook his head.

"I didn't kill her," he repeated. "You believe me, don't you?"

"I don't have to believe you, Gerald," replied Leo Green. "My job is to make sure you are protected by the law."

"You think I killed her, as well." Leo Green ignored his client's comments. "You're all bastards," muttered Gerald, as Leo Green gathered up his papers.

*

The nationals had caught the headline in the local newspaper.

'The Father – Not the Son!'

The opening paragraphs were similar.

In yet another dramatic twist in the fatal shooting of Angela Fisher, Gerald Martin has been charged with her murder. Gerald Martin is the father of William Martin, who is currently on Death Row for the double homicide of Angela Fisher, his music teacher, and her husband, Police Officer Jake Fisher.

Mark Shultz, William Martin's attorney, was quoted as saying that this proves his client is innocent.

Leo Green screamed down the 'phone at John Sweetman. "You realise this compromises my client's right to a fair trial! No judge in the State will allow your charges to go ahead. You've completely fucked up. My client will be walking out of the hearing a free man! You fed this to the press – and now they'll roast you alive. I'd say you'll be looking for another job pretty soon, Mr. DA." John Sweetman waited until he could hear Leo Green's breathing get slower.

"Cut the bullshit, Leo. You and I know the judge will have no option other than to dismiss the charges against Gerald Martin, despite the new evidence. The law of double jeopardy applies. He's already been tried and acquitted. He can't be tried again for the same crime." John Sweetman could hear Leo Green laughing down the 'phone.

"So, it's just as I suspected. You just want publicity implicating Gerald Martin so that his son will get a favourable outcome at his appeal."

"I just want justice," replied John Sweetman, calmly. "Isn't that what you want, Leo?"

*

John Sweetman took a deep breath, and addressed the judge.

"We have new evidence which establishes, incontrovertibly, that Gerald Martin was in the kitchen when Angela Fisher was killed. We now have his shirt and it's covered in her blood, as well as having some spots of his own blood."

"Yes, I've read your report," commented the judge. He looked sternly at John Sweetman.

"District Attorney, you must have realised that I have no option other than to have the charges against Gerald Martin dismissed. In this country, the law of double jeopardy still applies. No one can be tried twice for the same crime, as you well know. It's a fundamental part of our Constitution, for God's sake!" John Sweetman sat in silence. He knew this was coming.

"Perhaps he needs a refresher course," sniggered Leo Green. "Quite frankly, I have to question his standing as a district attorney!"

"That's quite enough," barked the judge. "This hearing is not the place to settle professional rivalries. I'd be grateful if you, District Attorney, would provide some rationale for your decision to charge Gerald Martin with murder – given that he's already been acquitted of this crime."

"With respect, judge, the charge of manslaughter was dismissed on appeal..."

"Because of fabricated evidence," interjected Leo Green. John Sweetman twisted in his chair so that he was looking directly at the judge.

"As you know, judge, an exception to the law of double jeopardy can apply if there had been a mistrial ruling. It is then possible for an accused to face a retrial. In this case, Gerald Martin was originally found guilty of the manslaughter of Angela Fisher. Had the court known that the key evidence was fabricated, it is highly likely the judge would have ruled a mistrial."

"That didn't come to light until later," exclaimed Leo Green. "That's why the appeal was successful," he added. The judge nodded in agreement with Leo Green, and turned to John Sweetman.

"I'm well aware on the nuances of the law, Mr. Sweetman, and I'll let you continue," said the judge, "but only because I'm intrigued to hear what you're going to say next!" He paused, and looked at John Sweetman over his half-frame reading glasses. "But please tread very carefully."

Leo Green gave an audible snigger. John Sweetman knew he was on very weak ground. He wished he hadn't got himself into this mess. He now had no option but to continue.

"I'm suggesting the appeals court should have declared the original decision to be invalid and have ruled a mistrial. The subsequent discovery of the new evidence - Gerald Martin's shirt stained with Angela

Fisher's blood - would then have made his arrest for the murder of Angela Fisher perfectly legitimate."

"You're asking me to accept that the appeals court should not have just dismissed the case, but should instead have ruled that Gerald Martin's conviction couldn't be upheld and that a mistrial should have been declared - because it was then known the key evidence was fabricated?"

"Yes, Judge," replied John Sweetman.

"And of course, a mistrial doesn't offer protection under double jeopardy when new evidence comes to light," continued the judge.

"Exactly," replied John Sweetman.

Leo green was itching to say something, but the judge held up his hand.

"Nice try, Mr. Sweetman. Nice try. But in my opinion, there is no basis for considering that the outcome of the appeal of Gerald Martin's conviction should have been to rule mistrial and not an acquittal. The appeals court was made aware of the fabricated evidence and, in my view, took the correct action. This may not help your case, Mr. Sweetman, given that new evidence has been found that appears to implicate Gerald Martin. However, due legal process must be followed. The appeals court has made its decision. What you are proposing appears to me to be trying to bend the rules simply to get a retrial. I repeat, there is no basis for supporting your suggestion that a mistrial should have been the outcome. You have the option, of course, of taking this further by an appeal to the Supreme Court – but given the irregularities in this case, it's not something I'd recommend. On that basis, I find that the law of double jeopardy applies, and Gerald Martin is a free man."

He began signing the necessary paperwork, and then looked up and addressed John Sweetman.

"Mr. Sweetman; if I thought that the purpose of this charade was to bring Gerald Martin's murder charge to the public's attention, I would take a very dim view indeed."

Chapter 26
Louis Allain

William was concerned to learn that the visitor waiting to see him was not his mother. The man sitting at the table in the visiting room looked completely out of place in his expensive dark suit, gleaming white shirt and shiny tie. William, looking thin in his oversized orange boiler suit, shuffled over, led by a prison guard who clasped the manacle attached at William's wrist to an anchor point on the metal frame of the table. William slid gently onto his chair, keeping his head bent down and his eyes trained on his fingertips gripping the edge of the bench top.

"William, I'm Mark Schultz. Your mother told you I'd be representing you at your appeal hearing."

"Where is she - where's Ma?" asked William, lifting his head for the first time since entering the room. His face looked pale; the pallor of white emulsion in the unflattering neon light.

"She can't come – not for a while."

"Why? Why? Is she alright?" His voice rose in agitation, causing the prison guard to look disapprovingly in his direction.

"She's okay, William. There have been some developments that you need to know about. Your mother gave me a letter for you. It explains a lot about what has happened," said Mark Schultz.

He slid an envelope across the table to William. It had been opened and the sticky flap had been removed by one of the prison officers. William clamped it to the table with his forefinger as if protecting it from a sudden gust of wind. He made no attempt to open it.

"You read it?" asked William, his eyes fixed on the envelope. Mark Schultz nodded.

"What does it say?"

"Your father was arrested for the murder of Angela Fisher," he replied, cautiously.

"Dad!" exclaimed William. His eyes suddenly flashed and he gripped Susan's letter in his fist. "He did it – he murdered Angela?" It was a reaction more of anger than surprise, as if he suspected somehow that this might be a possibility.

"At his trial he was acquitted – found not guilty," replied Mark Schultz. "The evidence against him had been fabricated – made up."

"Made up – who by?"

"It was your mother, with Mrs. Miller and a friend of hers, Inez Knight."

"Mum ... Mrs. Miller ... they fabricated the evidence against Dad? Why?"

"They were sure he killed Angela, and they wanted to get him convicted. Your mother wanted to have your conviction for Angela's murder quashed. She wants you off Death Row."

"But is Dad the scapegoat – was Ma trying to stitch him up just so I would get off Death Row?"

"Look William, this must be very upsetting – but I think your mother had strong reasons for suspecting your father committed the crime. But she shouldn't have tried to fabricate the evidence. After the trial, after your father was found not guilty, new evidence was found which suggests your father did kill Angela Fisher."

"So he did do it?"

"It certainly looks that way," replied Mark Schultz, feeling distinctly uncomfortable at having to be so categorical. "Of course, there hasn't been a trial. He hasn't been found guilty in a court of law."

"And will there be a trial; will he be arrested?" asked William.

"He was arrested and charged with the murder. But he's been released on a principle of law – that he can't be tried twice for her murder."

"Even though he's guilty? That doesn't make any sense."

"Seems that way, at times," replied Mark Schultz. "But it's a part of our Constitution. You get one shot at proving someone guilty – even if new evidence says that the person committed the crime. Your mother didn't know, of course, that new evidence would be found. It's a cruel twist that the very evidence your mother and Sally Miller fabricated was found later to be true. But your father is a free man."

"And Ma is in jail - the bastard!" said William, through clenched teeth. "He's free, then? He'll never be tried for her murder?"

"No, he won't," replied Mark Schultz. "As far as the law is concerned, he was acquitted of the crime and cannot be tried again."

"What about Ma? What's going to happen to her?"

"She was found guilty of fabricating evidence." William's jaw dropped. His body sagged as if the very foundations of his existence had been jerked from under him. He looked confused and bewildered, unable, or unwilling, to comprehend what was happening to the safe world he once knew. He swayed in his chair. His eyes looked glazed and distant and, for a moment, Mark Schultz thought he was going to pass out. He signalled over to one of the guards.

"William needs some water," he said, extending an arm to William's shoulder. The guard ignored the rule violation that prohibited physical contact and quickly got a plastic beaker filled with water from the sink in the corner of the room. Mark Schultz held the beaker for William while the guard hovered over them.

William's hands shook violently as he clasped them round those of Mark Schultz, and attempted to tilt the cup. Water spilled down William's chin and out of the corners of his mouth. He spluttered and coughed. Tears slid down his cheeks. William wiped the back of his arm across his face, determined to hide his tears in the splashes of water from the plastic beaker. He let out a loud and prolonged wail. It was deep-bellied; a sound that had been building. The entire room went silent. No one moved, not even the guards. Then one of the inmates at a nearby table stretched over towards William.

"You alright, kid?" William gritted his teeth, and nodded.

"Yeah – thanks," replied William in a hoarse, almost inaudible, voice. It was the signal for the room to return to its normal level of hushed and whispered exchanges. Mark Schultz leaned forwards towards William.

"Who's that?" he asked, giving the slightest of nods in the direction of the large, muscular, tattooed prisoner. William paused momentarily as if concerned he might be revealing something only he should be privy to.

"That's Louis Allain. He's in the next cell."

*

Louis was on Death Row, having been convicted of a series of murders in New Orleans. He was Cajun and spoke English with a heavy accent littered with both French and English expletives. He'd been in and out of trouble since he was sixteen years old. His father would react in the same way he always did – cursing loudly at his son before running him down and then beating him with a thick switch until the shirt on Louis' back was slashed into ragged strips, and blood wept from the lacerations on Louis' back. His mother was powerless to intervene. She'd felt the back of his hand and sometimes a sharp blow from the switch of wood on many occasions.

Pete LePatourel was related to Louis' mother. They were cousins, although some said they had the same father. Pete usually showed up a couple of days later - after he'd heard that Louis' father had once again beaten his son, and taken himself off to a shack somewhere in the swamps where he could hole up for a couple of weeks or so and drink himself into oblivion.

Louis knew the sound of Pete's old pickup truck. It spluttered and coughed as if announcing its arrival and apologising for any disturbance it may have caused. The truck reminded Louis of an old horse - slowly sashaying towards the house with its steel sides swaying on the truck's soft springs. Pete would slowly step down in his brown cowboy boots, faded blue jeans and a check shirt unbuttoned nearly to his waist. He wore an old black baseball cap with an arched fraying peak. A packet of *Marlboroughs* in his shirt pocket completed the look.

Pete was about fifteen years older than Louis. He was tall and slim with wide shoulders, long muscled arms and hands like shovels. They were prizefighters' hands, and Pete had won more than his share in the illegal rings that dotted the area. He had a shock of black wavy hair and an olive complexion that glistened as if it had been rubbed with light oil.

Louis liked Pete. It made him feel good every time Pete turned up, despite his cut and bruised body. Pete pretended he'd dropped in to find out how Louis was. "I just heard ... Shit kid, he really gave it to you this time." In truth, he came round to see Louis' mother. Louis didn't mind. Pete was good to her; he made her smile and got her to play the piano, stomping his boots on the wooden floor with the beat, and throwing his arms round her after each piece. He told them stories about his most recent fights, and boasted about the money he'd made from side bets.

"You'll spoil that nice face of yours," Louis' mother often said, stroking his cheek after one of their longer embraces. Pete never asked what had happened to Louis. He saw no point, and besides, every time Louis' father took off it gave him an excuse for coming round. He taught Louis how to fight and how to defend himself.

"You're getting good, kid. Won't be long before you beat the crap out of him."

Louis' mother wasn't so sure, but she was grateful for what Pete did – it seemed to give Louis back his confidence. Beer and smokes were shared as if Louis was an adult. His tired body and would eventually succumb to the alcohol. Pete would help Louis to his bedroom, his strong arms supporting him as Louis stumbled towards his bed. Louis never minded that Pete and his mother slept together. He often liked to listen in the early hours as the bed next door creaked, and his mother groaned in that different way that signalled pleasure.

When Louis got a bit bigger and stronger, arguments with his father became 'last man standing' bare-fisted fights. Louis won only once. He beat his father to a pulp, almost killing him. He only stopped because he heard his mother's screams. It was the last fight they had. From then on, Louis' father simply ignored his son, no matter what trouble he had caused.

294

His mother persuaded Louis it was time to move on. "Your father won't hurt me now," she told him. "Not now you've given him a beating."

Louis moved out, and within a couple of months had decided to marry a distant cousin. He was twenty-two and she was sixteen. In many ways, Louis was a carbon copy of his father, and like his father, Louis' violent ways were never far from the surface, despite frequent promises he made to reform. In the early years, his disputes were with other 'family' members; distant cousins, and others who'd married into his close-knit circle of kin. And then there were disputes with other 'families' over territory, women, drugs and family honour, although if truth be told, it took very little for Louis to see the need to seek out and 'punish' someone who'd been foolish enough to cross him.

He was now a mean man with a mean reputation. Eventually, after the marriage ended and his violence became even more aggressive and extreme, he was turned in by family members and jailed for attempted murder. After his release, he never again returned to his southern Louisiana home - much to the relief of others living in his territory - and instead teamed up with an equally dangerous murderer he'd met in prison. They became enforcers for bosses running drugs and prostitution in the city of New Orleans. He was a regular in the French Quarter, sauntering under the ornate wrought-iron balconies and collecting from the brothels, lap dancing clubs and transvestite bars that were part of his boss' empire. The restaurants and jazz bars were off-limits. They preserved the reputation of the French Quarter, generating tourists, many of whom would find their way to one of the more risqué establishments he patrolled.

Louis became an embarrassment to the drug lords - too violent, too easily recognised. He was advised to move away. He ended up in Ohio where he teamed up with Pete Le Patourel. Like Louis, Pete had needed to get away from his violent past. He'd given up being an enforcer. He was getting too old, and besides, he wanted to move carefully and be selective. He'd seen too many of the violent men end up dead, disappeared or imprisoned.

He had his connections with a few of the crime bosses in the City and was sometimes called upon to organise hits on their behalf. But it was a discreet business. His clients required complete anonymity and he had to be careful to employ people he could rely on, hard men able to exercise just the right level of intimidation to get what was required. It wasn't an easy game. Thugs were notoriously difficult to control, and most lacked the sophistication and finesse required at the levels he operated. He had hopes for Louis. He wanted to groom Louis to be the type of hard man he required. But Louis' temper and his need to be seen as one of the most feared hoods around meant he would never be capable of reaching Pete's expectations. On only his third 'job' he knifed and killed two men, one of whom was an undercover narcotics officer. His record from his time in New Orleans did nothing to help his conviction. Nor did his absolute refusal to plea bargain and provide any information about those he was working for. For that, at least, his uncle was both grateful and proud.

*

On the recommendation of the district attorney, Louis received the death sentence. That was three years ago, and he was slowly inching his way towards the death cell; the last cell before being escorted to the execution chamber where he would receive a cocktail of lethal injections. He'd calmed down in that period, and claimed to have found comfort in his religion.

296

A Catholic priest visited once a month; Louis was making preparations for what he knew was coming. He refused to wash or shower for several days after each of the priest's monthly visits. It was if he wanted the holy water, with which he was liberally sprayed after taking the sacrament, to be slowly infused into his skin. After a week or so of sweating in his hot cell he smelled as rank as any back-water creek in the bayou. In Louis' mind, this was an essential part of the process of ridding himself of the evil within.

The head warden was a bit concerned at putting William in the next cell, but Louis had become a different character. He was now quiet and often introspective, compared to some of the other inmates. He'd taken to reading. He was painfully slow and often wrote out lists of words he wasn't sure he understood. But he was a dogged scholar and, as a consequence, he'd gradually improved.

His uncle, Pete LePatourel, had been very supportive. He felt guilty that he hadn't nursed Louis along a bit more before giving him contracts. The first two had gone reasonably well and Louis had quickly persuaded a couple of City officials to ensure a planning application went ahead. But it all went wrong when a narcotics agent wouldn't cooperate. When he called Louis 'a fucking French fag', Louis just lost it, smashing a fist into the agent's face - and when he saw him reaching for a gun in a small holster tucked behind his jacket, Louis lunged at him with a knife, striking him under his ribs like an upper cut. And as the agent collapsed to the floor, he chased down a man trying to escape the scene. Louis grabbed him as he struggled with a door handle that didn't want to turn, and plunged his knife into the man's neck.

*

297

Louis took no notice of the clanging of the cell door next to his when William was first incarcerated. He saw him the next day when they were evicted from their cells to a small exercise yard. It was an obligatory period of release from the confines of their cells for two hours each day. It gave the prison officers time to go through each of their cells, checking for drugs that might have been smuggled in or knives stolen from the kitchen, or the workshops, and passed on by other inmates. Lifers rarely attacked one another. There was a sort of mutual respect for what was left of their lives, but suicide attempts did occur - and when they were successful, there were significant political repercussions.

Louis did a double take when he saw William in the exercise yard. He looked like a fourteen-year-old, and the runt of the litter at that. It tugged at his newly found compassion to see someone so young, so vulnerable, on the same death march as himself. He saw it as his duty to protect William and make sure that the other prisoners and the prison guards didn't try to intimidate him. Louis' reputation had gone from instilling outright fear of the man who would kill with the slightest of provocation, to respect for his reformation. He'd become the self-appointed spokesman of the lifers on Death Row and had taken to providing the prison officers with lists of requests and requirements. They were usually acceded to. The thought of Louis Allain returning to his violent past was enough incentive for the warden to give his requests every consideration.

Louis began talking to William when they were in the exercise yard. At first, William had been so scared by this big ugly prisoner that he shuddered every time Louis came near him. But he soon realised that Louis had no intention of hurting him. Quite the contrary.

"You come to me if there's any trouble," he told William.

"Any trouble?" he'd ask. "Other prisoners, guards?" There was none, of course; not with Louis treating him like a kid brother.

"I heard you killed a cop," Louis said on one of their strolls around the exercise yard. There was nothing judgemental in his voice - no hint of condemnation and no suggestion of admiration - just a simple statement which didn't require an answer, not if William didn't want to talk about it.

"I didn't mean to," replied William. "It was an accident. I just wanted him to leave me alone." William's steps became slower as if this reminder had sapped some energy from his legs. Louis didn't even break stride.

"Keep up, kid. Didn't mean to upset you." Louis smiled to himself. It was what Pete LePatourel used to call him when he came to their house.

"No ... it's just it doesn't seem real, not in the daytime. It's as if I'm a spectator - as if it wasn't me. At night, it's always in my head. His big face with blood and brains dripping down, and Angela – dead on the kitchen floor." He shuddered. Louis clamped a big hand on his shoulder.

"Angela? Tell me about her, kid. Who was she?"

"Angela Fisher," replied William. "She was my music teacher." He paused for a second. "Jake Fisher, the cop; he was married to Angela." William turned his head away and buried his forehead in the crook of his arm. He bit his lip, hard. He didn't want to break down. Not in front of Louis, not in front of the guards, and not in front of the other prisoners. Louis kept walking. If anything, his stride got longer and his pace quickened.

"Keep with me, kid," he said, keeping his eyes fixed on some point straight ahead. "Walk fast – you'll start to feel a bit better." William stretched out, almost having to break into a run to keep up with the big-striding Louis. He had to concentrate to keep moving quickly. He felt better almost straight away.

"Let's talk," said Louise, easing up a fraction. "This cop, Jake Fisher ... you kill him?"

"I shot him," replied William. "I didn't mean to – It was an accident. The gun went off. Next thing I knew he was leaning over the door, staring at me. His head was half blown off." William stumbled. Louis caught him by the collar of his boiler suit and hauled him to his feet.

"You 'aint much of a killer, kid. Believe me, I know. Okay, this Angela Fisher, the cop's wife. What happened?"

"I drove to her house for my music lesson. It was always at her house, when Jake Fisher, was on duty. I rang the bell, but there was no answer. The door wasn't locked so I went in, calling her name. It felt strange – she'd always been at the window or the door, waiting for me to come. I kept calling her name. I was sure something was wrong – it just felt weird. Then I found her in the kitchen. She'd been shot. She...she was alive. I held her head. She tried to speak, but it sounded as if she was choking. I think her mouth was filled with blood. Her eyes looked wild – terrified. I hugged her tight. She gasped, and I thought I must have held her too tight. But then I saw her eyes. They were wide-open and still. Not a flicker. I knew she was dead." William paused, and almost came to a standstill. Louis gave him a gentle nudge.

"Keep going, kid, you're doing fine." William wasn't sure if he was referring his story or his walking. Probably both, he figured. He found his pace and picked up on his account of what had happened.

"I panicked. I was all confused. I suddenly couldn't remember a thing – why I was there, what had happened. There was a gun on the floor. I must have picked it up. I wanted to get help. I ran through to the front room, and next thing, I heard a car. I looked out of the window and saw Jake Fisher pulling up across the road. I was scared. I jumped in my car and took off. Cop cars were chasing me – I'd never driven so fast. Then I crashed. My car was leaning over against the passenger door – it had opened in the crash. I rolled out, and crouched behind the door. Next thing, the car chasing me screeched to a stop on the other side of the road. I could see two cops getting out. They had guns pointing towards me. Then I realised I had the gun in my hand. I must have grabbed it when I rolled out of my car. One of them kept talking, telling me to stay calm. He told me to throw out the gun. Before I could do anything, another cop car came speeding up – really fast. I thought he was going to crash into the others. He must have stopped in time. I didn't look. All I could hear was his tyres screeching. It was Jake Fisher. He started walking towards me. He was shouting; said he was going to kill me. The other cops were telling him to get back. I heard one say something like 'they had it under control'. Jake Fisher just kept coming – I could hear his footsteps on the road. I wanted to die. I wanted to kill myself. I rolled over onto my back with the gun, and the next thing, it went off. I'd hit Jake Fisher in the head. I didn't know that until he crashed onto the door. I peed myself and started shaking. Then they grabbed me – the other two cops."

Louis didn't say anything at first. He kept walking, but slower now, as if the need to walk so quickly had passed. They'd walked the length of the exercise yard before he broke the silence.

"You okay?" he asked.

"Yeah," replied William. "That's the first time I've been able to talk about it. Funny thing is, I could remember every detail. Before, it had been like looking though a fog."

"What about Angela - you do it - you kill this Angela Fisher?"

"No! She was everything to me."

"You in love with her?"

"I suppose I was. I couldn't wait to see her. She was a brilliant teacher." They walked more slowly now. The difficult part of the exorcism had passed.

"What do ya play?" asked Louis, his voice suggesting that this was just as important to him as information on the killing of Angela and Jake Fisher.

"Oh, piano," replied William.

"Piano. My mother played piano – jazz, honky-tonk. You ever play that?"

"Sometimes," replied William. Louis smiled.

"I like jazz," he said. And in almost his next breath, he returned to the murder of Angela Fisher.

"You know who killed her?"

"Yes, I think so," William replied.

"Think so?"

"I know so," said William, emphatically. "I found out day before yesterday."

"That when you got all upset at visiting time? You let out a bit of noise there."

"Yeah," replied William. "That was the lawyer. He told me what had been happening. Ma wrote me a long letter, explaining things. She's in big trouble. She's been convicted – she's in prison."

"In prison – what for? What's she done?" asked Louis, his low, deep voice expressing genuine concern.

William felt comfortable with this big man at his side. It was like having Mrs. Miller talk to him; treating him in a way that made him feel an equal, never inferior. Few people would ever have known Louis Allain as anything other than a dangerous, violent, murderer. William didn't view Louis in those terms. William's judgement of others was based on how someone treated him and how comfortable he felt in their presence. It was an unconscious evaluation, too honest and simplistic for most relationships. Louis had the same instincts when it came to friendships, not that he'd had many in the course of his life. And because the majority of people he encountered were put off by his reputation and his latent physical menace, he invariably acted in a surly and aggressive manner. It was his form of self-protection, his default reaction to the same simple and instinctive evaluations of people and their motives that William made. It had been a very long time since Louis had felt so completely at ease with someone else. William was a friend; he knew that within a few minutes of talking to this thin scrawny kid. William was someone just like Louis.

The guard's whistle sent a shrill whining pitch across the exercise yard. Their two hours of 'exercise' - their two hours of chat and conversation - had come to an end. Louis could see the look of disappointment on William's face.

"We'll talk some more tomorrow. Think you can make it?" he said, with a grin. It was one of the few occasions that Louis had managed a smile in recent years. It made him feel light-headed. It was an experience he'd almost forgotten.

Louis gave William a playful nudge as they walked out into the exercise yard the following day. "C'mon kid, we've got some talking to do."

William responded with a quick grin. He stayed close to Louis as they were led out in single file. It was getting cooler now, even in the late-morning sun, and they were each given jackets to wear as they paraded out. William's jacket was, inevitably, several sizes too big, but it served its purpose. His arms hung straight down and his hands extended easily into the deep coat pockets as he stepped out into the cool morning air.

"It's good to be out," said Louis. William wasn't sure if Louis was making a joke, or simply stating the obvious.

"Sure is," replied William.

"Okay, kid, you were telling me about your Ma. She's in prison - right?"

"Yeah," replied William. "She got some evidence made up to try and get someone convicted for Angela's murder." Louis shrugged as if he'd heard of this sort of thing many times in the past.

"She must have had good reason," he said.

"Yeah," replied William. "She was sure she knew who'd done it." Louis paused and waited.

"You gonna tell me who that was?" asked Louis. It was as much a demand as a question. Louis realised William was struggling with this. They walked in silence for a while, with William slowing at almost every step.

"It was my Dad," he suddenly said. William had an urge to scream obscenities at the top of his lungs. He gasped at the air as if trying to force back the words that seemed determined to escape and destroy the quiet of the exercise yard. One of Louis' big hands gripped his arm.

"The fuck it was!" he said in his slow deep voice. "Hell kid, that's tough." For the next few moments, nothing was said. They just kept walking, side by side, with Louis gripping William's upper arm.

"Ma and Mrs. Miller - she's Ma's friend – they knew Dad had done it, but they couldn't prove it. So they got one of his shirts and splashed it with blood the same as Angela's. But then the police did more analysis and found the blood wasn't Angela's, and that Ma and Mrs. Miller had made up the evidence. Dad was released and Ma was arrested, along with Mrs. Miller and another friend who'd helped. That's how Ma ended up going to jail."

"No wonder you were upset, kid," said Louis.

"There's more," said William, as they started to walk again. "After this had happened, some kids found a shirt under a bridge. It was Dad's. It had blood from Angela, as well as some blood from a cut he had. That's why Ma and Mrs. Miller had the evidence made up. They knew what had happened, but they couldn't find the shirt Dad had been wearing."

"He'd thrown it away," commented Louis.

"Yeah," said William.

"So they all know he did it - the cops, the DA's office, your Ma – everybody," said Louis, his voice suddenly upbeat.

"Yeah," replied William. "Dad got arrested again."

"He's been found guilty – right?" said Louis, his voice sounding even more upbeat.

"No," replied William. "That's what really stinks – he got off, because of the law." Louis relaxed his grip and let his hand drop from William's arm.

"How come?" asked Louis, disbelievingly.

"He can't be tried twice for the same crime," said William.

"Oh, yeah," replied Louis, remembering something he'd previously heard. "Even if everyone knows he did it?" William nodded.

"He's a free man now," he added.

"For what it's worth kid, no one's free – not after they've murdered someone," said Louis. "And your Ma's in jail for trying to prove what she knew," he added, rhetorically. "It ain't right."

"I know," said William. "The only good thing, I suppose, is that my lawyer thinks I'll now get a reduced sentence – and maybe Ma will, as well."

"That's what should happen," Louis commented. "What about your dad?" he asked.

"Fuck him!" replied William. "He's not my Dad anymore. He never was a dad ... not really. Ma and Mrs. Miller - they brought me up. Not him. If I could murder anyone, it would be him. He's killed Angela, he's ruined Ma's life - and Mrs. Miller's - and he's put me in prison. He's the one who should be here, on Death Row." They fell silent for few moments, as they continued to shuffle round the yard.

"Along with all the other murdering bastards," said Louis in a quiet, almost inaudible voice. William wasn't sure he heard what Louis had said.

"What's that, Louis?"

"Oh, nothing, kid."

Chapter 27
Appeal

Mark Schultz prepared for the appeal hearing as diligently as he had done for any of his cases involving high-profile celebrities. There was a lot of public interest, something he'd encouraged through his contacts with the media. The role William's father had played had been almost a daily item in the newspapers, since the details of his acquittal on grounds of double jeopardy had been released. Mark Schultz relished the publicity and was a master at using it to his benefit, especially when he knew it would help get a successful outcome – it was a case that had aroused fervent public interest.

The more difficult of the two appeals was Susan's. He'd persuaded her that she must allow him to lodge an appeal, now that the new evidence had come to light. She'd been very reluctant, but Mark Schultz convinced her that it was the only way she had of helping restore the reputation and dignity of her two friends, and it might help William, especially if her sentence was reduced. He knew there was no legal argument for appealing her case. She had been found guilty of fabricating evidence and there was nothing he could do to overturn the verdict. His only possible recourse was to appeal the sentence 'due to mitigating circumstances'. And he would attempt to establish mitigating circumstances based on the success he hoped to achieve on William's behalf. The basis for William's appeal was that the new evidence had not been available at William's trial – the so called 'collateral appeal'.

The Appellate Court listened intently to Mark Schultz's opening brief. He argued that while there had been no conviction of Gerald Martin, because of the double jeopardy law, there was nevertheless, sufficient evidence to have Gerald charged with the murder of Angela Fisher. There was, he argued, a sufficient body of new evidence to question the original verdict that William was guilty of Angela's murder. The Appellate Court agreed and concluded that the only murder William could be found guilty of, beyond any reasonable doubt, was that of Jake Fisher. They also accepted, but not unanimously, the argument made by Mark Schultz that it was highly likely that William had not wilfully shot Jake Fisher. The original trial judge was asked to reconsider the sentence imposed, with the strong recommendation that William's sentence be reduced to one of manslaughter.

The trial judge was only too willing to agree with the Appellate Court's recommendation. He had been hounded by the press ever since the death sentence had been imposed, and the recent developments following Gerald's arrest and the failure of the case because of the double jeopardy law had only served to intensify the ground swell of public opinion questioning his original sentence. The judge prided himself on always steering the court to a sentence appropriate to the crime with which a defendant had been found guilty. His consolation was that the new evidence provided a legitimate basis for reconsideration of the sentence he had originally imposed.

He felt a great sense of relief when he had finally signed the legal documentation confirming William's change in sentence, from capital punishment to manslaughter. He imposed a sentence of five years with the recommendation of parole, and early release after two years. He was cheered out of the courthouse and it gave him a sense of enormous pride to read the reports in the newspapers over the following days praising him for his humane and compassionate decision. He was also grateful to Mark Schultz for so successfully making the case to the Appellate Court based on the often difficult 'collateral appeal'. He didn't tell him as such, but it was clear from the looks they shared that the judge felt he owed a great deal to Mark Schultz and his legal skills.

Mark Schultz was quick to capitalise. His appeal on Susan's behalf was directly to the same judge, who had also presided over Susan's trial in federal court. The judge was under no illusion as to what Mark Schultz wanted. This was payback time. He decided to take the brave and dangerous step of allowing Susan's sentence to stand, but that it would be suspended on the explicit understanding that she would not be able to serve on a jury or give evidence in court for a period of five years. It was potentially dangerous because the prosecuting attorney could appeal his decision to the Supreme Court. There was also the risk of the media and the court of public opinion railing against his decision. But the press and the public were just as complimentary about this decision as they were for that given for William's appeal. *'A Victory for Common Sense'* was how the press typically announced the results of the two appeals. In the mind of the public, the two were inextricably linked.

William was given the news by Mark Schultz. The head warden had offered to meet with William – "Save you a trip," he said. It was something he usually did, something he regarded almost a perk of the job. But Mark Schultz was adamant.

"It was too sensitive a matter," he told him. In truth, he didn't trust the head warden not to make a mess of it. And besides, it was his client and it wasn't everyday he had the opportunity to convey good news to someone on Death Row. He suspected, as well, that William would be just as concerned with his mother's situation. It was the first question William asked.

"What's going to happen to Ma, Mr. Schultz?" Mark Schultz saw the look of hopeful anticipation in William's face. It reminded him of a puppy waiting to be stroked.

"Good news, William. She's going to be released. She's been given a suspended sentence. It means she won't have to spend any more time in jail."

Tears streamed down William's face. The two prison guards in the interview room turned away, trying to make themselves as inconspicuous as possible.

"When - when will she be released?"

"Tomorrow morning, just as soon as the paperwork is completed." William smiled.

"Thanks Mr. Schultz," he said and smiled again, wiping the tears from his face with his forearm. Mark Schultz reached in his pocket, and gave him his handkerchief. It was still folded, and looked as if it had been just purchased.

"There's more," said Mark Schultz. "Your sentence has been changed to manslaughter. You will no longer be on Death Row." William looked disinterested, as if he'd heard all the news he wanted to hear. Mark Schultz paused for a few moments, hoping William was aware of what he was saying. "You'll be moved from Death Row. The charge against you for the murder of Angela Fisher has been dropped."

310

William suddenly looked up. This was more than he could have hoped for.

"Really?" he said in an excited voice.

"Yes," replied Mark Schultz.

*

Gerald was pleased when he heard that William's sentence had been commuted from a capital crime to manslaughter. It made him feel better, just for a brief moment.

"Thank God," he said out loud. He knew he should be wracked with guilt at what had happened but, in the end, he was more concerned with his own life than he really was with William's - or Susan's, for that matter. He had tried over and over to explain to himself how this had all come about, looking for some loophole that justified his actions. There were things that kept repeating in his perverse analysis of the preceding events. The most important to Gerald was that he hadn't intended to kill Angela Fisher. *It was an accident* he told himself, again and again. If only she'd gone along with it. A bit of fun, that's all he wanted. No one would have got hurt, no one would have known.

The more he dwelt on this, the more annoyed he became - not at himself, but at her stupidity! Then there was the importance of his life compared with William's or Susan's. Okay, he hadn't done as well as Susan – God knows who she was screwing to get on so quickly – but *he* was the intellectual. He didn't deserve to go to jail, and he certainly didn't deserve to be on Death Row. The very thought made him shudder. He had so much to give, so much intellectual capacity to devote to his subject and to the University. He couldn't let that asset to be lost. For the benefit of all of them all, he had to be the one to continue. In time they'd all recognise just how right he was.

This sorry episode had at least done one important thing; it had made him realise that he'd failed to demonstrate just how intellectually clever he was. It was a wake-up call to get on with his career. His legacy would be in terms of what he achieved as an academic, not what he left as genetic seed. As for William, he could now feel completely at ease at what had transpired. He was in jail for manslaughter, for a crime he had committed. William had to pay the penalty for his crime, and it made him feel good that justice had been served. However, he was appalled at the decision to give Susan a suspended sentence. She nearly got him convicted of murder – the bitch! She had fabricated evidence, along with Sally Miller and that friend of hers, Inez Knight. They should all be in prison, the three of them! This was a grave miscarriage of justice. He'd tried calling his lawyer but he was never available to take his call, and he hadn't called back. *He had his money, of course,* thought Gerald.

He couldn't stay in Ohio, he knew that. Dean Roberts had written 'suggesting' he should resign. Why? He hadn't been convicted of anything. If anyone should be resigning, it should be Susan. But everyone seemed to be against him: the press, with their slanderous articles virtually accusing him of murdering Angela Fisher, the neighbours, who deliberately looked the other way whenever they saw him, and his colleagues, who shunned him as if he had some hideous infectious disease. Even people he'd never met before pointed him out and muttered to others until heads turned to stare at him as if he was a freak. And the cops; they looked at him as if they were itching to have an excuse for beating him to a pulp. He'd walked into a store yesterday and there were two cops sipping coffee at the deli counter. They had both put down their plastic cups and turned to stare at him, in a most unpleasant and threatening way. They'd unclipped their holsters and had taken out their police batons. One rubbed his hand along the length of the stick and the other repeatedly slapped his into the palm of his hand, neither of them taking their eyes off Gerald. He felt trapped by their crude, angry, stares. He plucked up the courage to move, and then quickly walked out of the store.

*

Gerald received a letter delivered by special courier. It was from Susan and contained a short list of her demands.

Gerald. Firstly I want to make it clear that I never want to see you again. I doubt this will come as a surprise. I know there is no point in my telling you what a despicable self-centred reptile you are. But you have to live with the fact that you allowed William to take the blame for the murder of Angela Fisher and, had it not been for a very good lawyer, he would have been facing death by lethal injection. I hope an image of William strapped onto a bed in the execution chamber while they pump him full of drugs to snuff out his life stays with you and haunts you for the rest of yours.

I will be staying with Sally Miller. However I do need access to the house to collect my things. I want you to move out of the house in eight weeks time and in the mean time, the house is to be put on the market. Once you are out, I will come back to collect my things and get it ready for sale. You are not to come back to the house once you have moved out. These are my demands:

1.   You move out of the house in eight weeks time.

2.   You sign the documents to put the house up for sale.

3.   I want an uncontested divorce and I have instructed my lawyer to start proceedings straight away.

4.   You are not to make contact with William ever again.

You will have your lawyer contact Mark Schultz's office confirming your agreement by the end of the week. If you fail to do this, I have instructed my lawyer to start a civil case against you for your role in perpetrating a miscarriage of justice.

Gerald couldn't help but smile to himself. This was vintage Susan – organised and efficient. He'd have expected nothing less. He'd known something like this was coming, and at least he now knew where he stood. He certainly didn't want to end up in court again, even if the civil action was merely a threat. In a way, he was pleased to get the note from Susan. It was a catalyst of sorts. It would spur him on to get himself organised and plan his future. There was nothing here for him, he knew that. In his head he'd been planning to go back to England. Someone with his qualifications would have no difficulty in getting a suitable academic post, he reasoned. The last thing Gerald wanted was to land back in court revisiting the same issues.

*

Louis and William had a chance for one last chat in the courtyard, before William was transferred.

"That's great news, kid," said Louis. "It's the right thing. You don't belong here. You've a life in front of you now." He was silent for a couple of moments.

"Tell me about your Ma," he finally said. "What's happened to her?"

"That's the thing," replied William. "She won her appeal. She got a suspended sentence. She's going..." William stopped himself. He nearly said *home*. "She's staying with Mrs. Miller. She's gonna get Dad out of her life - our lives - and sell the house. Then get a new place. She wants me to help her choose it. She'll bring in photos to let me look at." William was almost breathless in his enthusiasm.

"Sounds great, kid," said Louis. There was a long pause.

"Louis," said William, eventually. "Thanks for everything. I don't think I would have got through this if it hadn't been ..." Louis didn't let him finish.

"Don't have to thank me kid. Just pleased to help a little runt like you. Besides, it did me good, talking to you, hearing about your Ma and all. And I'd love to have heard you play the piano – jazz though, just like my own Ma."

"Maybe you'll get to meet her," said William, excitedly. "I bet she'd come and visit." Louis smiled and placed one of his big hands on Williams shoulder.

"I'd have liked that, kid. But it's too late for me. My last appeal was turned down." Nothing was said for a while as if a silence had been created by a huge intake of breath that had sucked in the air around them.

"When is it?" William asked.

"Two weeks. Two weeks today," replied Louis. There was no self-pity, just a hint of resignation in his voice.

"That's soon," replied William, his eyes misting with tears. Louis didn't reply. He couldn't speak. The constriction he felt in his throat produced an ache he hadn't experienced in years; not since he was a boy.

Chapter 28
The Recital

William asked to meet with the head warden. He presumed it was to discuss William's transfer from Death Row, and quickly scheduled a time in his diary. He wanted to make sure William was well-treated. He was a nice kid and the enormous publicity his case had generated meant it was important that he be totally supportive.

"Come in, William. Take a seat. Like a drink. Tea, coffee?"

"No thanks," replied William. He didn't particularly like the idea of a cosy chat with the head warden.

"I guess you want to talk about your transfer?" William gave him a blank look as if he'd said something out of place. He was obviously preoccupied with something, but it wasn't his transfer.

"It's about Louis," he said, in a quiet voice.

"You know that he's going to be executed the week after next?"

"Yes," replied William. "That's what I wanted to see you about." The head warden wasn't sure where this was going. It wasn't his policy to discuss the fate of prisoners with other inmates; in fact he had made it an explicit rule banning prison officers from having any discussions of this nature.

"I'm afraid it's out of my hands. There is nothing I can do to stop the execution going ahead. I'm sorry, William."

"I know that," William replied. "I haven't come to plead for his life." The warden felt relieved. He wanted to end this discussion as quickly as possible. William jumped in before he had time to react.

"I want to play the piano for him," he said simply. The head warden was taken aback.

"You want to do what?" he asked with a look of incredulity.

"Play the piano for him," replied William. "He's been like a father ..." William paused, "better that any father I know. I want to do something for him before it's his time." William paused again as if checking some imaginary list of things he needed to say. "He likes jazz," he suddenly added. The head warden looked at William's eager face. Gone for the moment was the vacant, aimless look that he'd seen when William had been admitted.

He pretended to read through William's file. He needed time to think. He knew about William's musical gifts; he'd been told about his prodigious talent. He knew about the very close bond that had developed between these two prisoners with such different backgrounds. He knew it was within his power to facilitate William's request.

"I'll give it some thought," he told William. "I'll let you know by the end of the day."

Later that morning, the head warden received a call from the Governor's Office of the State of Ohio. William had written to the Governor appealing for him to use his influence to let him play for Louis. Someone had slipped up on the vetting procedure they used for all mail sent out by Death Row prisoners. He felt trapped. He would have no option. "Damn, damn,

damn!" he said out loud. "Fucking Governor," he added, under his breath.

The Governor had turned down all the pleas for a stay of execution. This man had a notoriously violent record and there was no doubt in the Governor's mind that he deserved to be executed. However, he hated being the final arbiter on appeals from inmates on Death Row. But he also knew if he didn't take a hard line, his job as Governor would be very short lived. This request couldn't hurt, could it? It would be an act that those who advocated the death penalty could hardly oppose and it might be seen by those who wanted the death penalty abolished as a humane gesture. He smiled to himself. It was as if the execution was now a secondary event; something of little consequence compared to the act of agreeing to this request.

*

The room normally used for monthly meetings with other head wardens and senior police captains was prepared for William's piano performance. It was long and narrow, and had two large windows with drapes that hung to the parquet floor.

There were concerns. The table wasn't bolted to the floor. The chairs didn't have restraining chains, the windows didn't have reinforced glass, and the dangling electric lights in the middle of the room could be reached and grabbed by a big man like Louis Allain. Worst of all, the room was in a relatively insecure part of the prison. This was a risk and it could all go horribly wrong. It was easy for the Governor. He could tell all his pals that he had what it takes to be strong and compassionate at the same time.

Concerns had been expressed by a number of the senior prison officers, but the head warden had no option but to insist it go ahead. "If anything goes wrong," he told them, "if Louis Allain attempts anything that puts either himself or the prison staff at risk, you immediately take any action that's necessary. Batons, truncheons, stun guns - the lot. Is that understood?" They all nodded, relieved to a man that the head warden had taken a hard-nosed approach to dealing with any emergencies.

"What about the kid?" asked one of the officers.

"Same applies to him," replied the head warden, hoping the problem would be purely hypothetical.

William waited restlessly throughout the afternoon. He desperately wanted to know if the head warden was going to let him play for Louis. He hoped his letter to the State Governor had helped, but now he wasn't sure if it had been the right thing to do. It had seemed such a brilliant idea at the time, and he'd rushed off his letter almost immediately. *It probably didn't get sent,* he thought. And now he hoped it hadn't. He worried that the head warden would be so annoyed that he'd refuse his request, no matter what. As the day progressed, he became disheartened. He'd quite decided that the idea had been turned down.

When a sealed envelope from the head warden was passed to him by a severe-looking prison officer, he didn't want to open it, not at first. Somehow, not opening the letter meant the answer hadn't yet been given. William slid his finger under the flap and took out the notepaper. It was folded in half. He flipped it open and blinked. The message was brief and direct. It simply said:

Your request has been approved. The piano recital will be held next Friday afternoon from two-thirty pm until three pm. You will be escorted to the room at one-thirty pm to give you some time to practise before your recital starts.

William sat staring at the note as he held it delicately in his hands, as if it was a precious piece of parchment. He carefully stuck it to the wall with a piece of chewing gum. Then he started to think about what he was going to play. Thirty minutes. That wasn't long, it didn't sound very long – but to play without a break for that length of time wasn't going to be easy. He needed to know exactly what he was going to play. He needed to have a repertoire that was just right, and he needed to practise!

William asked if he could visit the music section in the prison library. The request went all the way to the head warden. No prison officer would sanction the movement of a Death Row inmate to a less secure section of the prison without permission, irrespective of a successful appeal and imminent transfer.

"What now?" said the head warden when he heard William had made another request. "The sooner we get that kid transferred, the better!"

"He wants to visit the music section in the library; something to do with this piano performance," said the deputy warden. "Shouldn't be a problem," he added. "The kid's no trouble, never has been. And what with his transfer next week..."

"Okay, okay," replied the head warden. "Just make sure he's under escort at all times. And do it quietly. He's still technically a prisoner on Death Row, and I don't want any of the others getting ideas."

William was surprised at the number of recordings held in the prison library. Most were on tapes, although there were also rows of vinyl records stored vertically in their sleeves and dust jackets. There was an older model stereo system with an amplifier, tape player, and record deck in a vertical stack flanked by two large black speakers. A set of earphones were plugged into the amplifier and hung down, almost touching the floor.

There was also a small tape player, with a neater and smaller set of headphones coiled on top of a rack of tapes.

William spent some time just browsing through the collection. It was like being reacquainted with something precious and personal. His fingers traced the edges of the vinyl records, pausing occasionally to slip out a record and linger over the titles. The entire collection was organised into sections for each type of music and the vinyl records and tapes were grouped, each arranged alphabetically.

And then he found the jazz section. He slowly scanned the collection of tapes and pulled out the ones he wanted to listen to; Count Basie, Duke Ellington, Oscar Peterson, Henry Butler and Fats Waller. Then he turned his attention to the older recordings stored on tape and selected Herbie Hancock, Art Tatum and Bill Evans. The vinyl records had many of the same artists, but he also found old recordings of Jelly-Roll Morton, Scott Joplin, Bill Evans and Tommy Flanagan. He decided to add them to his collection, more out of curiosity than anything else. He wanted to hear how they played in the early days when Dixieland jazz was first becoming popular.

William listened intently to the tapes and records he had selected. He wanted an eclectic mix that covered the type of jazz Louis was likely to have heard in those early days when his mother had banged out tunes in what he imagined was a honky-tonk style. He eventually chose his first piece, *Slow Blues*. It was a classic piece often played by Count Basie and Oscar Peterson. Next would be another Count Basie favourite, *Basie Boogie.* This was a thumping, fast moving piece in the style of Jerry Lee Lewis' *Great Balls a' Fire.* And then to a Fats Domino classic, *Blueberry Hill,* followed by a Henry Butler's *Basin Street Blues.*

William reckoned he would have used about 16 to 18 minutes of his allotted time. He decided to add a classical piece; something he had played for Angela. He chose Rachmaninov's *Rhapsody on a Theme.* It was the piece he had learnt to play with Angela sitting next to him on the piano stool, and he wanted to share with Louis something special – something that was a part of Angela. Then it would be swing in *Ain't Misbehavin'* followed by *St. Louis Blues* and *Sweet Lorraine.* The final piece would be *Hymn to Freedom*, a jazz and gospel piece that William thought would be a fitting end to his performance.

Now that he had selected the pieces he wanted, he sat and listened to each of them over and over again, letting each note, each change of rhythm and every bit of improvisation fix in his brain, like a master copy. He could feel the intensity of the notes, the drifting scales, the swirling arpeggios and the underlying rhythms that made up each piece. He stayed in the library for several hours, only lifting the head phones to change the music, and occasionally breaking off for a few moments to sip from a beaker of water. The prison officer in charge of the library was amazed. He'd never seen anyone devote such undivided attention to a task.

When he was eventually ordered to return to his cell, William found his evening meal on a plastic tray on his bed. It was cold and unappetising, but William was ravenous and quickly devoured every morsel. That evening, he decided to make a mock keyboard. He emptied one of the shelves above his bed and lifted off the wooden board. It was almost as long as a keyboard. He then took a pencil and his plastic ruler, and slowly and carefully marked out every black and white note on the shelving. The spacing had to be exact, and he went to great lengths to ensure that every key was the correct size and positioned accurately. It took over three hours before William was satisfied that he had created a reasonably accurate full-sized model of a key board. And then, without taking a break, he placed the board on his bed, pulled up his chair, and began to rehearse.

*

A small upright piano had been moved from the recreational wing into the meeting room. The oblong conference table was moved to one end of the room, and the piano stood at the opposite end, angled so that the piano keys were clearly visible. Five chairs were arranged in a semi-circle in the middle of the room, facing the piano. The centre chair was for Louis. The two chairs on either side of Louis' would be occupied by prison guards. They were to be unarmed. The last thing the head warden wanted was for Louis to grab a weapon from one of the guards. However, two armed officers would be stationed at the door into the room, and a third armed officer would stand guard outside. Guards would also be in positions at both ends of the corridor leading to the meeting room. If anything did go wrong, the head warden wanted to ensure that every precaution had been taken. He would sit at the back of the room and hope that nothing would go wrong.

William was escorted from his cell to the meeting room at about one-fifteen pm, a little earlier than he'd expected. He had spent most of the morning rehearsing the pieces on his makeshift keyboard, even refusing to go out to the exercise yard. The prison officers didn't push it; they knew about the piano recital. Louis felt at a loss without his pal and spent his time in the yard pacing slowly round, stopping occasionally to kick some dirt. A couple of the officers got a little worried. He looked more and more bad-tempered. They were relieved when it was time for him to return to his cell.

The meeting room looked out of place with its polished wooden floor, thick drapes, and ornate light fixture hanging from the centre of the ceiling. It was a far cry from the drab prison cells and the sterile corridors with their glaring fluorescent lights and painted concrete floors. William's eyes focussed in an instant on the upright piano at the end of the room. Ignoring the prison officers who had escorted him from his cell, he strode over to the piano, lifted the lid, adjusted the stool and began to finger the keys, playing a series of scales, testing its tone and quality. The two prison officers took seats on two of the chairs placed along the wall closest to the piano, where they could see the keyboard. It didn't matter to William that the piano badly needed tuning, or that some of the keys were stained where cigarettes had been left to burn, or that some were a little stiffer than the others. They all worked and both pedals functioned as intended. The room's acoustics were excellent. The high ceiling, the long narrow shape, the plane walls and the simple furniture enabled the sound to fill the room, and the drapes had the effect of dampening any excessive reverberation.

William started rehearsing his scales in the way Angela had taught him. He varied the pace, the intensity and the rhythm. As his fingers resumed their deft familiarity with the piano keys, he felt a freedom that only his music could bring. This room was the venue for his performance, he was the pianist, and very soon he would be playing for an audience. He was no longer a prisoner; he was in the world he loved best, playing his music and escaping the bits of life that he found difficult to deal with. Just at that moment, William felt that he could be in no better place.

William stopped abruptly when he heard the door open and loud voices spilling in from the corridor. He looked up and saw a bemused-looking Louis being led by two prison guards who were nervously shepherding him into the room. They had struggled to persuade Louis to leave the familiarity of his cell. He thought he was being punished for something he had done – he couldn't think what.

As soon as he saw William seated at the piano, he stood and gaped. Without being asked, he walked over to the chair in the centre of the room, taking the two guards by surprise. He ignored them as they quickly moved into position. Louis lowered his massive frame onto the chair. It creaked as if it had never encountered someone of his bulk.

"Is this for me?" he asked. William smiled.

"It's for you, Louis."

Without another word being said, William launched into his first piece, *Slow Blues.* Louis' face relaxed into a soft smile and his right foot began to tap with the beat. His body swayed slightly as the familiar sounds welcomed him to a place and time far removed from his cell on Death Row.

William barely paused as he began to play his second piece, *Basie Boogie.* The head warden watched nervously. The loud raucous beat of the base sounds began to ripple, with notes spilling from the higher registers, and Louis slapped his big hands against his thighs in rhythm to the music. The warden hoped the big man wouldn't suddenly jump to his feet in appreciation as he pounded ever more aggressively against his knees.

Blue Berry Hill. The head warden was delighted. This was one of his favourite pieces. Any concerns he had about Louis' behaviour disappeared as he allowed himself to become absorbed by the stunning version that William had created. He glanced around the room. Everyone - Louis, the other officers, and the guards - were softly, almost silently and surreptitiously, singing the words they could remember, as if it was something illicit, something they shouldn't be doing.

William played a few chords by way of an introduction to the next piece, *Basin Street Blues*. Louis smiled; it brought back memories of an almost-forgotten innocent time. It was one of his mother's favourites. She played it in the late summer evenings when the windows were opened wide and the first cool whiffs of the night air flicked at the net curtains, and the sounds from the high-pitched cicadas and the deep-throated bull frogs competed in the background - a perfect setting for her lazy, languid style of playing. Louis felt his eyes becoming moist and his throat felt constricted and sore. It had been a long time since he'd felt this kind of emotion.

William paused for several moments, before going onto the next piece. The head warden wondered if that was it; but then William lifted his arms and held his hands and his fingers perfectly still above the keys, as if signalling there was something special about the next piece. Louis sensed this was going to be something very personal, something very different. The room was quieter than it had been at any time during William's performance. There was a sense of expectancy, as if they were being allowed the privilege of sharing in a piece of music that had a deep and profound meaning for William. And then he began to play – *Rachmaninov's Rhapsody on a Theme.*

There was something sensual in the sounds he elicited from the piano; something emotional in the way he stroked the first delicate opening chords and then feathered the keys, before plunging into a rich staccato of sound that pealed through the room and caused spines to tingle and hairs to stand on the necks of men who had little knowledge or appreciation of the piece William was playing. But Louis knew. Louis knew why this was special. He knew this was for Angela. William finished on the last delicate notes and slowly lifted his arms, letting his hand hover above the keys in the same way that he'd done when he opened the piece. It left a silence that no one wanted to fill. The men in that room held their breath, not wanting to break the reverence of the atmosphere that had been created. It was only when William lowered his hands that there were audible sounds of stale air being exhaled from bursting lungs. They all felt they had experienced something they were never likely to experience again.

William slipped into the easy chords of *Ain't Misbehavin'*. It was as if he'd provided something sweet and comforting to reward them for their part in the solemnity of the previous piece. The audience relaxed; this was nice, easy and familiar. And when William slipped into a medley of *St. Louis Blues* and then *Sweet Lorraine* without a hint of a break, it continued the same warm feeling. The head warden looked round the room. The prison officers, to a man, were transfixed by William's playing. And as for Louis; they seemed to have forgotten he was also in the room. Not that this was any cause for concern. Louis hadn't taken his eyes off William since he entered the room.

The head warden glanced at his watch. William had exceeded the time he was allotted by several minutes. He was about to stand up to signal an end to the presentation, just as William was finishing the last chords of *Sweet Lorraine*. He hesitated for a moment and before he could react, William turned towards the audience and spoke directly to Louis.

"This is my last piece Louis. This one is from me to you." William played a few improvised chords which signalled the style and the beat of his final piece. It sounded like gospel music. Louis knew it as soon as

William moved into the opening bars. It was a piece he'd heard many times when his mother had taken him to Sunday Service, before his cousins told him that when you were ten, you didn't have to go to church, not unless you'd done something really bad. It wasn't a church as such; it was a place where religions, creeds, beliefs and superstitions had been blended to cater for the mix that was back-woods Louisiana, back-water bayou, and even urban New Orleans. It was *Hymn to Freedom.*

I've heard this somewhere, thought the head warden. When the slow strident tempo of the opening bars and the sudden improvised high trills gave way to the chords that almost sang the words, he recognised the Civil Rights gospel song. He felt distinctly uncomfortable. And then Louis began to sing the chorus line:

"That's when we'll be free ..."

The Head Warden felt his pulse race. The guards and prison officers had all turned to stare at Louis, not knowing if they should intervene. Louis appeared not to notice. He lifted his head and prepared to sing the chorus line of the last verse.

"That's when we'll be free."

Louis held the last note for as long as he could while William improvised, willing him to keep going for as long as possible. When the last of the sound had filtered throughout the room, Louis stood up, tears streaming down his face, and before anyone could react, he had taken two giant strides towards William. He practically lifted William out of his chair and wrapped his long arms around William's slender frame, hugging him with an affection that few in that room had ever witnessed. Everyone in the room was now standing, watching a shared intimacy as the two prisoners, the boy and the man, held each other in an embrace that

328

neither wanted to break. Louis eventually relaxed his arms, pushed William gently back and placed his hands on William's shoulders.

"Thank you son," he said out loud. "Thank you." He then turned and walked back towards the prison guard escorts. They were slightly taken aback.

"I'd like to go now," he said, giving a quick curt nod in the head warden's direction.

Chapter 29
Execution

William watched Louis being led out of the room by his entourage of prison guards. He felt breathless and giddy, as if Louis had taken any breathable air with him as he left through the door. It was the last time he would ever see Louis Allain. The head warden remained seated, wanting to give William time to compose himself. William turned towards him:

"Thank you, sir," he said, still struggling to hold himself together. The head warden nodded, pondering on what had happened.

"That was wonderful playing, William – and that was a wonderful thing you did. You should be very proud of yourself."

"I am, sir," replied William, his voice suggesting surprise that anyone should think otherwise. The head warden led William back to his office where another prison officer was waiting.

"Your paperwork came through earlier today. You have been transferred to the minimum security section. Prison Officer Reynolds will take you there." It suddenly struck William that he wouldn't see Louis again. He thought about trying to say something, but he sensed that it wouldn't do any good.

"It's for the best," said the head warden, heading off any attempt by William to lodge an objection.

*

Pete Le Patourel paid Louis a final visit. They were allowed to meet in a small room specifically reserved for Death Row inmates to see relatives for the last time prior to their execution. There was nothing sad in Louis' voice or his demeanour. Quite the opposite; he seemed resigned to his fate, almost glad to be leaving the world where he had done so much damage, created so much havoc.

"Maybe I'll be with Ma again?"

"Maybe," replied Pete. And then Louis told Pete about the piano concert William had given.

"He did it just for me, Pete. He's just a kid, but he's special, ya know?" Pete wasn't sure he did know. "Did it all by himself," continued Louis. "He got the warden to arrange it – imagine, the warden agreeing to a thing like this. Nobody had ever heard of anything like it. And could he play, Pete. It was beautiful – just like Ma, only better."

Pete hadn't seen Louis excited like this - not since he was a dirty, cheeky, little kid chasing round the place and seeing every stagnant pool, every broken piece of fence, every giant bull frog as something to splash in, kick at, or chase. And then he told Pete all about William. About William finding Angela Fisher dying, about the shooting of her husband – the police officer, about William's father letting William take the blame for Angela Fisher's death, about how William's mother had attempted to get Gerald charged with Angela's murder and how it had backfired. And about the evidence that was found proving his father was guilty, but that he got off because he'd already been tried and freed. It flowed out of Louis in a way Pete would never have believed was possible. He didn't say

331

a word. He just sat and listened. Louis finally sat back, looking emotionally drained. There was a long silence.

"That's some story," Pete finally said.

"Will you come, Pete; will you be there at the end?" Pete didn't like the idea of sitting and watching Louis stretched out and strapped down while they injected him with the drugs that would end his life, but there was a child-like pleading in Louis' eyes. Pete sighed.

"If you really want me to, I guess I can."

"I do, Pete. You're the only one left who'd come. It'd be a comfort."

"Okay," replied Pete, his voice heavy with a reluctance he wished he could suppress.

"Oh," said Louis in a hushed, serious tone. "There's one more thing ... and only you can do it."

*

Pete LePatourel was escorted to the wing that housed the execution chamber by two solemn looking prison officers. One of them held open the door into the viewing gallery. It was small, with three rows of tiered seats with ten chairs on each row. They were well-spaced, with almost a chair's width between them. Pete glanced around before taking his seat. At the far end of the second row was a guy with a notebook; a reporter, Pete figured. A few seats along was a priest fidgeting nervously and clutching a set of rosary beads. In front of them, on the first row, were two elderly women, both in their seventies, Pete thought. He concluded they must be relatives of two of the men Louis had killed.

Pete slipped into a seat on the second row, just in front of the entrance door. There was a glass window in front of the tiered seats that went from the ceiling almost to the floor and along the length of the seating area. Everyone would have a good view. A curtain was pulled across the window, and the execution chamber appeared to be in darkness. Pete glanced at his watch. It was three twenty-five. In five minutes' time, the execution would commence.

The lights in the viewing gallery were dimmed as the curtain began to slowly retract and the neon tubes in the execution chamber flickered into their uncompromising brilliance. The head warden was standing on the far side of the chamber. Next to him was a doctor with a stethoscope dangling around his neck. The head warden glanced out at the viewing gallery, and then signalled for proceedings to commence.

Louis was wheeled in strapped to a gurney, similar to those used to wheel a coffin into church. Both of Louis' arms were fastened to boards that projected from either side of the gurney. Pete could see the two shunts sticking out from Louis' forearms. They had each been inserted into a vein on each arm, and taped in place. Louis looked frightened. He'd just pissed himself, and sweat was dripping down his face. He was staring at the ceiling and breathing deeply, trying to compose himself.

The head warden looked round and then stared out into the viewing gallery and caught sight of the priest still fingering his rosary beads. He glowered in the priest's direction and within a few seconds, a deputy entered through a side door and grabbed the priest's arm, pulling him towards the door. Pete could see the priest mouthing an apology to the head warden. He went over to the gurney and laid the rosary beads on Louis' chest. He then stood close to Louis and said what looked like a prayer. Pete saw Louis mouth 'amen' as the priest blessed himself, and backed away.

Two medical staff in white coats approached the gurney and attached catheters to the shunts in Louis' arms. The catheters were connected to two bags of saline solution hanging from stands on either side of the gurney. They then opened the valve at the bottom of each bag, allowing the solution to flush the lines. The head warden approached the gurney and asked Louis if he had any last thing he wanted to say. Louis raised his head slightly as a microphone was lowered from the ceiling so that it dangled just above him. He looked round, scanning the faces in the viewing gallery until he found Pete. He gave a quick smile.

"Thanks, Pete," he said, his amplified voice crackling through the speakers. "You promise, Pete?" He looked anxiously in Pete's direction. "You promise?" he repeated, sounding agitated. Pete took the cue.

"I promise," he mouthed.

"Thanks, Pete," Louis said again and set his head back down on the gurney. The microphone rose into the ceiling and the two medics approached. They quickly disconnected the catheters from the bags of saline solution and attached the ends to syringes. They glanced at the head warden, who gave a quick and deliberate nod. Louis looked again at Pete as the injection of sodium thiopental entered his veins. It took less than a minute for the strong barbiturate to cause Louis to lose consciousness.

Pete let out a sigh of relief when he saw Louis' eyes close and his chest heave as his breathing began to slow to a normal rhythm. He looked peaceful in his drug-induced coma. The doctor stepped forward, checked Louis' pulse, and then nodded to the two medics. It was as if they were checking to see he was healthy enough to continue with the lethal part of the process. The saline bags were reattached as the syringes were prepared. A few moments later, the catheters were again plugged into the syringes, and a strong muscle relaxant was injected. Its paralysing effect on the diaphragm muscles halted Louis' breathing. He seemed to struggle as his face turned blue from asphyxiation. The priest blessed himself. There was an audible gasp from one of the two old ladies on the front row, and the reporter scratched furiously into his notebook. Pete wondered if he should leave, but it wasn't quite over. The two medics returned to the task and proceeded to connect another syringe to each of the catheters. They worked quickly and began the injection of potassium chloride. Louis' body gave a final jolt, straining the leather straps as the fatal injection induced a cardiac arrest.

There wasn't a sound in the viewing gallery, not even the scratching of the reporter's pencil. The stillness in the viewing room might have been out of respect for Louis, or out of horror at what they had witnessed. The head warden motioned to the doctor. He stepped forward again, placed his stethoscope on Louis' chest, and then turned and nodded to the head warden. Pete le Patourel realised it was over when the curtains began to close and the lights in the viewing room were brightened. A young prison officer stepped through from the side door. He looked as white as a sheet.

"It's all over now," he announced, as if clearing a theatre at the end of a show. Pete slowly lifted himself from his seat. He felt drained. His legs were wobbly and he stumbled into a couple of the seats. The reporter was fumbling with his notebook and looked equally queasy. The two old women hadn't moved. One of them had her head in her hands. She was sobbing.

*

Gerald had become virtually nocturnal. It was invariably midday before he rose to slowly open the blinds, reluctant to admit another day into his life. In the evenings, he kept the lights on and adopted an erratic routine of searching for jobs back in England,

335

watching TV, munching on comfort food, drinking whiskey and catching some sleep on the couch. His only other activity was to leave the house in the early evening, just as the dark was beginning to smother the daylight, and drive to the store to collect newspapers and provisions for the evening. Pete Le Patourel waited for Gerald to leave the house. Getting in would be easy. It was an old wooden three-storey with a front porch and a short driveway leading to a dilapidated shed, that at one time had served as a garage. The shed had wooden hinged doors at the front and a rear door that was wedged half-open and hung pathetically from its twisted frame, like a drooping eyelid. The door handle and door catch had been removed long ago. Pete took a look inside. It was virtually full of various household items; a bed and mattress, two large wardrobes, a bicycle, a kitchen table, several chairs and a few paint cans. It had been several years since it was used as a garage. The rear of the house had a small garden, mostly lawn, with a high wooden fence along the back. There were three steps leading to the back door, which opened directly into the kitchen. The house had old fashioned sash windows with large wooden frames. There was a burglar alarm, but it wasn't a very sophisticated type. Le Patourel smiled.

"Couldn't be simpler," he whispered to himself.

He waited in the old garage until he heard Gerald start up his car and drive off. He hoped Gerald was going on his usual trip to the store, which normally took about 45 minutes. Getting in was even easier that he'd hoped. One of the sash windows at the rear of the house had a very loose-fitting frame. Pete Le Patourel slipped a thin blade between the window frames, and pushed open the brass window latch. He lifted the window and peered in. There was a motion detector in the corner of the room, but he reckoned Gerald wouldn't have bothered to set the alarm, not just to drive down to the store. He was right. Once inside, he went quickly from room to room, making sure he knew where each door led. It quickly became obvious that Gerald was spending most of his time in the lounge. The couch had pillows and a duvet thrown in a heap at one end and two of the chairs were heaped with Gerald's clothes. Le Patourel helped himself to a whiskey, checked his gun, cleared the clothes from both of the easy chairs, stretched his legs and waited.

The lights from the Oldsmobile swept across the room as Gerald pulled into the driveway. Pete didn't move. He sat quietly in the chair and listened. He heard the car door slam, and then Gerald's footsteps on the porch. The key scratched in the lock, the latch clicked, and Gerald stepped into the hallway. He heard the rustle of plastic shopping bags as Gerald lifted them in from the porch. The door slammed shut and then he heard Gerald sliding the dead bolt and the door chain into place. Le Patourel spoke just as Gerald stepped through into the lounge.

"Hello, Gerald." The bags slipped from Gerald's hands. A whiskey bottle clunked onto the floor.

"What the hell ...?" Le Patourel flicked on a standard lamp next to his chair. Gerald stood, transfixed.

"Get out of my house," he said in a broken, barely audible voice. He felt weak and disoriented. "You want money? I've got a few hundred dollars ..." Le Patourel waved his gun in Gerald's direction. Gerald felt terrified. His body refused to act. All he could see was a gun in the man's hand pointed at his head. He felt paralysed and speechless. He forced himself to speak.

"What do you want?" he finally uttered.

"Take a seat," replied Pete Le Patourel, motioning towards the other easy chair. Gerald was grateful for the opportunity to sit down. He felt as though his legs might not support him much longer.

"Louis sent me," said Le Patourel, staring intently at Gerald.

"Louis? I don't know anyone called Louis," replied Gerald.

"He knows all about you, Gerald. That's why I'm here."

Gerald didn't like this one little bit. He felt more scared than he'd ever done in his life. His body didn't want to behave. He fought the urge to wet himself, and squirmed in his seat.

"Go ahead," said Le Patourel. "Have a good piss." Gerald tried to move. "Don't get up," he said, "you can piss yourself right there." Gerald felt the wet warmth trickle down his leg almost before Pete Le Patourel had spoken.

"Louis didn't like what you did to your son, William. Letting him take the rap for the murder you committed." Gerald's jaw dropped. He wanted to shout, to scream, but his throat felt big and swollen. He couldn't muster a sound.

"There's no excuse for that is there Gerald?" continued Le Patourel. "I mean, your own son. You were going to let him die, weren't you?"

Gerald couldn't think of anything to say. He hadn't any defence to offer, none that would make any difference. There was a silence, as if Gerald was expected to at least say something.

"What do you want me to do?" Gerald finally asked.

"Do?" exclaimed Pete Le Patourel, sounding particularly annoyed. "There's nothing you can do ... not now." Gerald began to shake. He felt bitterly cold. Pete LePatourel continued, telling Gerald what needed to be said, for Louis' sake.

"Louis said he was a special kid – never met anyone like him. I've known Louis since he was born. He had it rough and he turned out mean – real mean. He was on Death Row, the cell next to William." He paused for a moment and glared at Gerald. "He's dead now, executed in the state pen just last week." Gerald flinched at the thought.

"William was a good friend to Louis – maybe the only friend. He could talk to William. They talked a lot. I think it drained some of the poison out of him. We had a long talk, Louis and me, just before he was executed. William did something very special. He arranged a piano recital, just for Louis. Imagine, a kid convincing the warden to let him play the piano for a murderer like Louis. He played jazz – just like Louis's Ma used to when he was a kid. Louis was crying when he told me about it. I've never seen him cry, not even after his da had given him a beating – and they were some beatings. Tears were rolling down his face. But he was smiling. Smiling, laughing and crying all at the same time."

Pete Le Patourel pushed his face into Gerald's, staring his frightened eyes. "Louis' da was a piece of shit, just like you. I should have killed him years ago." He slowly stood up. "Might have given Louis a chance."

He began screwing the silencer to the end of his gun. Gerald felt exhausted. He didn't even have the energy to beg for his life. He slipped out of the chair and onto the floor, his legs splayed out in front of him. He sank his head into his hands and began to weep; huge gulping sobs, and then loud groaning howls.

"Shut the fuck up," said Le Patourel, raising the gun.

*

The very next day, William received a card that Pete Le Patourel had posted. It was from Louis.

Hi William,

I'll be dead by the time you get this. I deserve what's coming so don't feel sorry for me.

You made my last days very special. You are a great kid and I want you to have a happy life from now on.

I got things sorted for you and your Ma. Hope you tell her about you and me someday. You can get on with your life now.

Louis.

William smiled. He was pretty sure he knew what Louis was referring to.

Susan was staggered by the news of Gerald's death. She didn't know how to react. She felt guilty at feeling so overwhelmingly relieved that he was out of her life and, perhaps more importantly, out of William's.

The next day she received a card from William. There were very few words, but to Susan, it said everything. It simply read:

Ma,

There's just us now.

Your loving son,

William .

Lightning Source UK Ltd.
Milton Keynes UK
UKOW041346140513

210650UK00001B/1/P